This special signed edition is limited to
1250 numbered copies and 26 lettered copies.

This is copy 437.

SEX AND VIOLENCE IN HOLLYWOOD

SEX AND VIOLENCE IN HOLLYWOOD

RAY GARTON

SUBTERRANEAN PRESS | 2001

FIRST EDITION
October 2001

ISBN
1-931081-44-1

Subterranean Press
P.O. Box 190106
Burton, MI 48519

email:
subpress@earthlink.net

website:
www.subterraneanpress.com

Dedication

For
Dawn,
my love.

Acknowledgments

It seems I get a lot of help from a lot of the same people every time I write a book, while at the same time meeting some new ones on the way. The following have contributed, in one way or another, to the completion of this novel: Scott Sandin, Derek Sandin, Jane Naccarato, Ricia Mainhardt, A.J. Janschewitz, my wonderful parents, Ray and Pat Garton, my wonderful in-laws, Bill and Suzy Millhouse, Bill and Shelly Blair, Pamela Briggs, Gina Mitchell, Kelly Laymon, Rain Graves, and my friends in the Horrornet Cabal — you know who you are — Sheila Winston (don't deny it, Sheila, you helped!). A very helpful attorney I met through Allexperts.com provided me with a lot of useful information — and then I lost his name in a recent move. You know who you are, too — thank you! Thanks also to my agent Richard Curtis — the prodigal client has returned! And of course, thank you, Dawn, for everything.

1

<u>SEX</u>

"Dahling, how does one get laid in this dreadful place?"
<u>Tallulah Bankhead</u>
to Irving Thalberg during her first visit to Hollywood in 1931

✝

"My dear, you're sitting on it."
<u>Alfred Hitchcock</u>
to actress Mary Anderson when she asked about her "best side"

✝

"There's a broad with a future behind her."
<u>Constance Bennett</u>
commenting on a starlet in the 1930s

✝

"I'll never forget the night I brought my Oscar home and
Tony took one look at it and I knew my marriage was over."
<u>Shelly Winters</u>
on husband Anthony Franciosa's reaction to her first Oscar for
The Diary of Anne Frank

The hot Los Angeles sun came through the open window over the bed and fell on Adam Julian's sweat-slicked back as he pistoned in and out of Gwen Cardell. His loud breathing grew more rapid, punctuated by abrupt, dry grunts and gasps. He propped himself up on his hands, elbows locked, as he pounded into her faster and faster.

"No, no," she said. "Slow down, baby, slow—"

She stopped speaking and gently pushed him off. He was so lost in his pleasure, it took him a moment to realize what she was doing.

"I'm sorry, what did I—"

"Nothing, you didn't do a thing," she whispered. She put a hand on the side of his head, pulled him down and kissed him on the mouth. "Just roll over. On your back."

Adam's shaggy, dark brown hair flopped around his face in sweaty strands as he rolled onto his back beside her.

Gwen rose to her knees and tossed her long, honey-gold hair over her shoulders. Looked down at him, licked her smiling lips. Bent forward and her hair fell down in a curtain on each side of her face. Lips smacked wetly as she kissed his flat belly, which rose and fell with his chest as he continued to pant. She spoke between kisses.

"I'd forgotten…what boys…your age…are like. So quick…so eager to come."

It irritated Adam to be referred to as a "boy," especially in the condescending way Gwen had said it. Normally, he would not let it pass without a sharp retort. But he had no time to think about it. At the moment, his penis was throbbing in time with his heartbeat. So hard it hurt. Behind it, inside him, a thick, wet ache pressed for release.

She wrapped a hand around his erection and he lifted his head as she threw a leg over and slid down him slowly. "You want me to come, too, don't you?" she asked, breathing her words as she moved slowly on top of him. "I let it go the first time, but—" She stopped to smile and close her eyes, moan, "—but it's something you need to work on, Adam, and—ah, *ah*—there's no time luh-like the present. Right?"

He let his head fall back again, feeling far too good to be irritated by anything she said. Almost too good to hear anything she said. She ground on him hard, and when Adam lifted his head again, just for a moment, he saw her hand between her spread thighs. Two fingers moved between fleshy folds with staccato quickness.

Both of them panted like exhausted dogs and Gwen released a throaty, breathy laugh as the evenly-tanned flesh on her body began to quiver. When she came, loud "*ah*" sounds burst explosively from her, mixed with Adam's cries as he clutched her thighs and writhed beneath her, thrust his hips upward desperately.

They held their positions for about thirty seconds afterward, silent except for the sounds of their breathing. Then Gwen lay forward and stretched her legs out behind her until her body was draped over Adam's. Brushed her lips over his, licked his eyelashes, stroked his hair. Rolled off him and snuggled beneath his right arm.

The enormous bedroom smelled of Gwen's perfume—probably something obscenely expensive and French, with a name Adam could not pronounce—and the joint they had shared before having sex. The vague sounds of birds singing and a distant dog barking came through the window over the bed. Sunlight spilled through all the windows and fell on the cream and royal-blue decor.

"You're delicious," Gwen said, stroking his thigh. "You know that? Delicious."

"Thank you," he said. "But, I'm, you know…just a boy."

Gwen laughed as she dropped her left hand and squeezed his limp penis and testicles. "You're so sensitive. You need to toughen that skin, lover. The world is full of people like me. Some a lot worse. But not too many. You've gotta be ready for us."

"My skin's tough enough," he said quietly. "I just don't like to be condescended to. Especially when I'm fucking."

She rolled toward him, put an arm across his chest, and smiled, her nose a couple inches from his. "Look, you have to understand that to me, to anyone my age, you *are* a boy. You're…what? Twenty-two, twenty-three?" Adam said nothing. "And when you're forty, like me, you'll look back on this moment and you'll smile and think to yourself, yep, she was right."

Gwen rolled away from him onto her right elbow and opened a small cupboard door on her side of the headboard. Removed a softpack of Marlboro Lights 100's, an ashtray, and a lighter. Lit up and took a long drag on the cigarette. Tapped it over the ashtray beside her on the bed.

"Okay," Adam said, sitting up beside her. "So if I'm such a boy, why are you attracted to me at all?"

Her eyelids lowered slightly as she turned to him with a naughty smile. "Oh, you'll understand that, too." Turned her whole body toward him, moved her eyes over his body. Stroked his chest with her right hand, cigarette held between two fingers. "So smooth and silky. So fresh and untouched. I have a different perspective, that's all. My perspective is that you're beautiful and new and unused. And delicious."

"Hey, I never said anything about untouched or unused."

Gwen laughed.

"Then what are you?" Adam asked.

Another instant of eye contact—a little chilly this time—then she dropped back down beside him, laughing. "I'm a veteran, that's all."

"You mean, you're not new? You *are* used?"

She was silent for a moment. "Are you trying to piss me off, Adam?"

"No," he lied. He passed his eyes the length of her long, beautiful body, then back again.

Gwen's skin was darkly, evenly tanned, but somehow milky, too. The color of Malt-O-Meal with a little brown sugar stirred in, he decided—but much sexier. There was a smooth, intoxicating curve to her belly, which Adam delighted in nibbling. There were the inevitable stretch marks from bearing a child—she said she had a daughter from a previous marriage who lived with her dad — but they were negligible. Not much was real in Los Angeles, but Gwen's body was. All but the breasts.

He reached over with his left hand and gently stroked one. Brushed fingertips over the erect mocha nipple. "You have beautiful breasts," he whispered.

"Thank you," she whispered, blowing smoke through a smile.

"I bet they were beautiful before the augmentation, too."

There was a long silence. She took another puff on her cigarette.

Adam had been surprised to find that Gwen had breast implants. He had felt them the first time they had sex, the day before yesterday. The day after his birthday. Most breasts with implants did not move properly, stood erect when the body reclined. They lacked the smooth, flowing fleshiness of natural breasts. Saline implants were an improvement over silicone, but they were still implants, still unnatural. He found those unmoving mounds of taught flesh disgusting. But Gwen's were not like that. He had become quite good at identifying "reloads," as he and Carter called them, but Gwen had fooled him. Until he touched them.

"Okay…you *are* just trying to piss me off now."

"No, I mean it, they're beautiful." He was quite sincere. "I was shocked when I realized you had re — um, implants. They're…well, it's an almost perfect job."

"What do you mean, almost perfect?"

"Well, it's a job, that's what I mean. It's a job, so it's not perfect. That's why I said I bet they were beautiful before the augmentation. I bet they were perfect."

She sat up then, crossing her legs Indian-style. Looked at him with a suspicion that was almost angry. "What the hell are you trying to say?"

"Nothing, really."

"You mean, there's no point to this rambling?"

Adam shrugged with one shoulder and sat up with her. "Well, only that you probably didn't need them in the first place. You're beautiful. Your body is beautiful. You just did that for other people, I guess. Like everybody else in this town. In show business. But you didn't need it. That's all I'm saying."

Gwen smiled a little too suddenly, as if relieved. Pulled him toward her and kissed him deeply. Lips and tongue worked their way down to his shoulder. "You're such a sweetheart," she said, words garbled. "Saying that…and talking. You know, most men don't like to talk after sex…but you do. You're going to make a lot of women…very happy…I'm sure."

Adam said, "Mmmm," and smiled as she took his nipple between her teeth, sucked on it. He felt himself growing hard again.

"Just remember," she said. "Always ladies first in bed. And maybe you should start…working out."

"Working out?" he muttered, frowning.

She sat up and kissed his face gently, again and again. "You're a little scrawny, hon. That's all."

He chuckled as he leaned his head back and shook it slowly. She never stopped. Maybe she simply could not help herself. "You wanna do it again?" he asked, his voice hoarse.

"Mmmaybe…you?"

"I have to go to the bathroom."

"Okay," she said, pulling away. "Go. But don't be long."

He started to get out of bed.

Gwen smiled. "Can I come in and hold it for you?"

His eyes widened. "What?"

"Your cock. While you pee. Can I hold it for you?"

Adam slipped off the edge of the enormous bed, landed on the raised dais on which it was centered. Gwen was about to take another pull on her Marlboro, but laughed instead.

He peered over the edge of the bed, got to his feet. "You want to, um…hold my dick while I…"

"Why not?" she said with a shrug. "I've never done it before. I think it would be fun. And very sexy."

Adam was surprised to find that the idea excited him. He reached out with his right hand and said, "Cigarette." She handed it to him and he took a long, deep drag, let the smoke out slowly. "Okay, I can't guarantee I'll be able to go if you're holding my dick, but I'm willing—"

He swallowed his words and Gwen's smile fell away when they heard a sound through the open window over the bed. A familiar sound. The purring engine of a mint-condition 1958 Ferrari 250 Testarossa.

A surge of panic in his chest and stomach made Adam take a deep breath. But he let none of it show. Just raised his eyebrows a little when he said, "I guess I'll have to take a piss somewhere else. Your husband is home." His quiet, calm voice did not give away his thundering heart, or the fear that suddenly clutched his throat.

Gwen crawled toward him and got off the bed, stood in front of him. "Yes, I guess he is," she said, grinning as she slid an arm around him and plucked the cigarette from his fingers.

Outside, beneath the second-story window, the Ferrari's engine was killed.

"You know, if he smells that cigarette, he's going to know you've had sex with someone," Adam said.

"Why do you say that?"

The Ferrari's door opened, and a moment later, slammed shut.

"Because that's the only time I've ever seen you smoke cigarettes."

"Such an observant boy."

He took the cigarette from her hand. "There's that boy shit again." Took a quick puff.

Outside, footsteps sounded on concrete below.

Adam's already full bladder seemed to shrink.

"Do your parents know you smoke?" she asked. Her shoulders bobbed with silent, secret laughter.

Adam nodded and smiled, handed the cigarette back. Tried to stir up some saliva in his suddenly dry mouth. "Yeah. Very funny. I'll see you around."

He quickly gathered up his clothes and hurried out of the bedroom.

✝

In his bedroom, Adam slipped *Evil Dead 2: Dead by Dawn* into the DVD player and flopped onto his bed to watch.

He could not believe he was fucking his dad's new wife.

Maybe it's because I hate him, he thought. Then: *No, not maybe.*

He liked Gwen, and would even if they were not having sex. But they were, and it was incredible, and he liked her even more for it. She had a cool Grace Kelly beauty, but there was something more beneath it, something Adam had only glimpsed when she let her guard down. Gwen gave the impression of someone who knew a secret that no one else in the world knew, and of someone who would always keep it to herself.

The fact that his dad was married to her did not concern him at all. Adam could not muster a particle of guilt for his relationship with Gwen, and he had tried. Because he hated his dad so much. For killing his mother.

TWO

Adam took a seat at the dinner table as Mrs. Yu served the meal.

"Ah, you come eat, Missa Adam!" Mrs. Yu said excitedly, grinning. "Dat nice, dat nice. I get you prate." She hurried out of the dining room.

Gwen smiled at him and his dad turned to him slowly.

"Decided to eat with us for a change?" Michael Julian asked.

Adam shrugged. "I was hungry for a change."

Mrs. Yu returned and hurriedly put a plate and utensils and a linen napkin before Adam. She patted him on the shoulder and said, "We have tie-tip tonight. You rike."

Mrs. Yu had come to America from China with her sickly husband decades before Adam was born. Mr. Yu had been run over by a truck and killed shortly after they arrived. Michael had hired her when Adam was just a baby only because everyone else he knew had Mexican and South American servants and he wanted to be different. Michael always wanted to be different. He had specifically sought out a Chinese maid, and would settle for nothing else. "When was the last time you saw a Chinese maid, huh?" Michael sometimes asked of anyone within earshot. "*The Courtship of Eddie's Father*, that's when. These days, they all speak Spanish."

19

Adam never pointed out that Mrs. Livingston, the housekeeper on *The Courtship of Eddie's Father*, was Japanese. He knew if he did, his dad would only say, "Chinese, Japanese, what's the difference."

Michael Julian had declared his independence in the face of trendiness by hiring a servant of different ethnicity from everyone else's. Had it been possible, Adam was sure his father would have hired an extraterrestrial. The ultimate in cheap immigrant hired help. If you could keep them from eating the cat.

"Well, it's been awhile since you've joined us at the dinner table, Adam," Michael said. "Did the projection bulb blow out at the Nuart, or something?"

Adam said nothing. Mrs. Yu continued to place food on their plates.

"How are things?" Michael said. "What have you been up to, if anything?"

"Not much," Adam said. "I've been doing some writing."

Michael stopped eating, looked across the table at Adam. He seemed on the verge of smiling as he leaned forward slightly, almost imperceptibly. "Writing? A screenplay?"

Adam shook his head as he cut his meat. "A little poetry. A short story."

Michael rolled his eyes and sighed. "I've told you. How many times have I told you?" He picked up his knife and fork and went to work on his dinner. Stabbed and cut his meat as if it had offended him. "If you've got some talent at writing, put it into a screenplay, for Christ's sake. Anything else is a waste of time. Publishing is falling apart. Nobody has time to read books anymore, let alone poetry." He shoved a big bloody piece of meat into his mouth and chewed as he talked. "But a screenplay...if everything works and it gets produced, it's on the big screen, bigger than life. Then, it's on the shelf at the bookstore of the twenty-first century, the *video* store. Each produced script is...it's like a little piece of eternal life."

Michael Julian was a big man. Broad shoulders, thick arms, and a round belly. When Adam was a little boy, he remembered his dad being lean and muscular. But these days, his body was a sloppy, lumpy mess. As large as his body was, though, his head was too big for it, and he had no discernible neck. His head appeared to sit between his shoulders without suspension, as if he were always shrugging.

"If you can write poetry and short stories, you can write a script," he went on. "Just write what you know, then add the honey."

"Honey" was his euphemism for sex and violence. Adam had heard it all countless times before.

Michael's dark brown hair was long and thick and wild. It curled and waved just past his shoulders. Bushy eyebrows and a bushy beard and mustache that looked as if they had been purchased to match the bushy hair on his head. For all Adam knew, they had. There was a streak of gray in his beard on each side of his chin, both artificial. He thought the look commanded more respect than facial hair with no gray.

The beard and long hair helped disguise the fact that his face was not only, like his head, unusually large, but perfectly round. The facial hair, however, could do nothing to camouflage the flatness of his face. It even sank in slightly in the center, giving him an ugly profile that he never knowingly allowed to be photographed. Gossip columnist Mitchell Fink had referred to him once as "the dinner-plate-faced scribe." The tossed-off remark had so infuriated Michael Julian that both Adam and his mother had been even more careful than usual to stay out of his way for about two weeks.

"That honey sweetens the box office receipts," he continued. "Pays more than any Goddamned short story. Who the hell's gonna read a short story? I don't think anybody even publishes them anymore. But *everybody* goes to the movies."

Adam did not respond to his dad's screenplay speech. He wished the conversation had never begun, and certainly did not want it to continue. The food was good, though. Adam seldom ate at the table when his father was around, but the food made up for the company.

Saturday and Sunday breakfasts had been Adam's favorite meals as a boy. His mom always cooked them. Saturdays, she would make waffles with fresh fruit and whipped cream. Sunday, eggs and bacon and fried potatoes. The indulgent breakfasts were eaten at that table, with Adam seated in the same chair he occupied now. And with his mother seated in the same place as Gwen.

He frowned slightly as he thought about those weekend breakfasts. They had stopped abruptly when he was still a little boy, but he could not remember why.

He looked at Gwen, sitting in his mother's place, and felt a moment of *déjà vu*. It had been longer than he had thought since he had eaten at the dining room table. The last time, that spot, where Gwen sat—his mother's spot—had been empty.

✝

Mom was Emily Moessing. She had not been quite as pretty as Gwen, but much more beautiful. A bigger forehead, bigger nose, weaker chin. Long straight dishwater-blonde hair that would not curl or take on any shape no matter what she did with it. But she was not ugly or even plain. Tall, a killer smile, big brown eyes.

Adam could not hear the massive wind chimes she had hung around the patio without thinking of her laugh. She used read to Adam at night, acted out each story, made Dr. Seuss sound like Shakespeare.

If they met today, Adam guessed, Michael Julian would not give Emily Moessing a second look. She simply was not his type now. Of course, when Michael Julian and Emily Moessing met, Michael had not yet achieved his tremendous success.

They met while he was writing for a few television action series and she was working in wardrobe at Paramount. Their marriage was a good luck charm at first. Somebody bought one of his screenplays, and the movie, *Mayhem*, did surprisingly good business. Somebody saw her sketches and made her a designer. He started selling scripts for big money. The critics laughed at and eviscerated the movies, but they were hits at the box office. Emily was in big demand, worked with the biggest directors in the business. His reviews got worse…and she got an Oscar nomination. Then another. The third time, she won.

The New Yorker called Emily "the Edith Head of our time." Michael's bitter response was, "That's not the kind of head I'm interested in."

Her Oscar ate at him like a cancer. After she won it, things fell apart fast. They shouted instead of talked. Adam would find his mom crying in the kitchen or living room, sometimes with bruises on her arms, neck, or a swollen black eye.

Emily was beautiful, but not in a Hollywood way. Her beauty was authentic and shone from inside. Everyone loved her and her work, and everyone with an I.Q. higher than their shoe size agreed that Michael was a prick who pulled his scripts out of his ass.

Adam was convinced that Oscar was why his dad had killed his mom. He had no proof. Nothing solid he could show anyone. Just a certainty deep in his gut.

✝

"How's the movie coming?" Gwen asked, delicately dabbing the corners of her mouth with a napkin. Adam watched. There was no sign of such delicacy when she had his cock in her mouth. She caught him staring and smiled.

"It's coming along. Everybody's worried it's gonna piss off the *gay community*," he said as he lifted his hands and hooked invisible quotation marks in the air with the first two fingers of each. "Those dipshits never learn. Of course it's gonna piss off the queers. The cannibal serial killer's a fag, for Christ's sake, it's gonna make 'em all nuts." He stabbed his fork hard at his food, took in a mouthful and chewed, but kept talking. "But that'll mean another, what? Twenty? Thirty million at the box office? You can't buy the kinda publicity you get from a buncha Judy Garland fans picketing theaters and whining on radio talk shows. That kinda stuff sells tickets, for Christ's sake."

Gwen asked, "What if this is the time everybody decides to agree with them?"

"Never happen," he said. "This movie's already got everything going for it. Sex and guns, a couple kick-ass car chases, some kinky killings. The protests'll be a plus. And with any luck, there'll be some controversy over the MPAA rating. You know, they'll wanna give it an NC-17, we need an R for it to be a success, we'll have to cut some sex, that kinda thing. The movie's gonna make a fucking fortune, and they all know it. The only reason the studio's worried about the fags protesting is that half the people who work there are fags, and they don't want their friends talking bad about them under the hair dryers."

Adam could not hold back a quiet laugh.

"You think that's funny?" Michael asked, turning to him with a smirk.

"I was just...laughing at the way you put it."

That was partly true. Adam was repulsed by his father's harsh language toward homosexuals and racial minorities. He often referred to Mrs. Yu as a "chink" when he thought she was out of earshot. His favorite term for black people was "jungle bunnies." He practically fell over laughing every time he said it. The reason Adam had laughed at the dinner table was that he knew a great number of the people his dad worked with, and for, were indeed openly gay. And because his dad regularly attended benefits to raise money for AIDS research and to support gay rights. They were two of the biggest thorns in Michael Julian's side. A bit of him died each time he attended such a function. Ate at him from the inside out, because he did not give a damn about the charities he was donating to or the causes being supported. More often than not, he was completely opposed to them. But he knew everyone who was anyone would be there and it was important to attend, to be seen. And it was nice tax write-off. Adam found that funny.

Somewhere in the house, a phone purred.

Michael and Gwen exchanged a lingering look. He started in his chair and laughed quietly.

Adam knew they were playing footsie under the table and suddenly, no matter how delicious the food, he lost his appetite.

Mrs. Yu entered the room with a cordless phone in hand and went to Gwen's side.

"Missy Gwen, phone for you."

Gwen took the phone and said, "Hello?"

Adam poked at and cut his food, even though he was no longer eating it. His dad ate as if there were a chance the food might flee the plate. His knife and fork clacked and scraped, jaw worked hard beneath that mass of hair. Grizzly Adams eating something he had just killed and waved over the campfire a couple times.

After a long silence, Gwen whispered, "Oh, my God."

Adam looked across the table at Gwen's wide eyes and open mouth. Something was wrong.

"My daughter, what about my *daughter?*" she asked, loudly this time.

Michael put down his utensils and watched his wife, frowning.

"Oh, Jesus," she said, her voice breaking as her head dropped forward and she covered her eyes with her hand.

"Hey, hey," Michael said quietly as he got out of his chair and went to her side.

"Have you checked her grandmother's?" she asked. After a moment, "No, his mother. She thinks that girl can do no wrong, and—" She stopped and listened for a few seconds. "Yes, that's the address. If she's run away, she might be there, or at least on her way."

Adam exchanged a puzzled look with his dad.

"Oh, yes, she's hitchhiked before," Gwen said.

Mrs. Yu stood beside Gwen looking aloof, indifferent. Waiting for the phone so she could put it back where it belonged when Gwen was done.

"Yes, I wish you would," Gwen said. "And please call the second you know anything. Will you, please?" She sat up straight in her chair, took a deep breath and let it ease out of her. "Thank you. Thank you very much." She pulled the phone away from her ear, handed it back to Mrs. Yu, who immediately left the room.

"What the hell was that?" Michael asked.

Gwen wiped her eyes, although there appeared to be no tears in them. "Police in Miami. There's been a fire. Larry's house. It burned down. He was in it. He died." She sighed and shook her head slowly. "Probably drunk. As usual."

"What about your daughter?" Michael asked as he hunkered down beside her, put an arm around her shoulders.

"She's run away again. They don't know where she is."

"At least she wasn't in the house with her dad," Adam said, uncertain and cautious.

"They'll find her," Gwen said hoarsely. "She's at her grandmother's, I'm sure. If she'd been home, she might have been able to save Larry. Wake him up, get him out of bed. He sleeps like a corpse when he's been drinking. Which is probably most of the time now that he doesn't have me around to bitch about it."

"Hey, you're not gonna start blaming yourself, honey," Michael said firmly. "I'm not gonna let you do that." He leaned forward and embraced her, kissed her cheek.

"No, no, no," she said, pushing him away. "I'm not blaming myself. I'm just...angry. At him, at her. When they find her, she'll have to come live with us, you know. Right away." She turned slowly to Michael. "She's not an easy girl to live with."

He smiled. On him, it looked more like a sour expression. As if he had bitten into an extraordinarily unpleasant cheese. But Adam recognized it as a sincere smile, an oddity on his father's face.

"Hey, that's no problem," Michael said enthusiastically, stroking Gwen's hair. He jerked his head toward Adam and said, "Hell, you think it's been a barrel of dancing girls raising this clown? He's not perfect, either. He's not even normal. I mean, Jesus, he writes poetry, for God's sake." He glanced at Adam. "For all I know, he's a fag."

A supressed laugh snorted through Gwen's nose, but she managed to make it sound like an emotional catch in her throat. Adam smirked.

"You wanna go upstairs?" Michael asked. He stood, took her elbow and gently tugged her to her feet. "C'mon, let's go. You can take a couple of my pills. You'll feel better."

As he led her away from the table slowly, she glanced back over her shoulder at Adam and kissed the air silently, smiled.

"Oh!" Michael blurted. "You go upstairs, baby, I'm right behind you." He returned to the table, looked down at Adam. "If you don't have any plans, we're taking *Money Shot* out for the Fourth. The whole week. You wanna bring a friend, fine. We'll be leaving early on the Fourth, as usual." He headed out of the dining room again. Over his shoulder, he said, "Try to bring a girl, okay? Carter doesn't count. You ask me, I think it's *way* past time you two got your own place together and started a family."

When he was gone, Adam sat alone at the table. The smell of the food stirred his appetite again and he began to eat. Dinner was delicious, and the company had improved.

THREE

The next day, Adam drove over to Carter's house, only a few blocks away. He parked behind the house and walked in through the back door without knocking. He had known Carter since third grade, and often felt more comfortable in Carter's house than in his own.

Adam walked through the large kitchen, said hello to Mrs. Sanchez, the maid, passed through the dining room — there were four cardboard boxes on the table — and nearly ran into Devin in the hallway.

"Oh, my God!" Devin said, leaning against the wall to take a deep breath. "You scared the shit out of me!"

"Sorry about that."

"I'm just preoccupied." Devin held a cardboard box in his arms. It looked heavy, although it wasn't very big. He was a thin man who stood a few inches short of Adam's six feet. On that hot summer day, he wore a light blue sundress of thin, cool cotton, no stockings, which was rare for Devin, and a pair of deck shoes with no socks. His glasses rested on his chest, suspended from his neck on a thin silver chain.

"What're you doing?" Adam asked.

"Cleaning out the library. C'mon." He jerked his head for Adam to follow him back into the dining room. Devin put the box on the table with all the others. Sweeping the back of his hand over his shiny forehead, he turned to Adam and smiled. "We keep buying new books,

27

but we have no place to put them. So I'm getting rid of the ones we don't need anymore."

"I didn't think Mr. Brandis ever got rid of books," Adam said with a chuckle. "He's got the biggest library I've ever seen."

"He's got more books than he's got library. But I've been working on him. I finally got him to agree that there are at least a couple hundred we can lose. I'm taking advantage of his fit of reason before he changes his mind. I figure as long as I don't touch his collection of first-edition signed Harold Robbins novels, I'm safe."

"Is Carter around?" Adam said.

"I haven't seen him. Either he's gone, or he's in his bedroom or studio." He glanced at his watch and gasped, pressing his other hand to his chest. "Oh, God. Jeremy will be home for lunch in a few minutes." He squeezed Adam's shoulder affectionately. "You make yourself at home, sweetie. I've got to talk to Mrs. Sanchez."

Adam went into the hall and headed for the stairs to look for Carter.

Devin had been Jeremy Brandis's partner in life for over three years. Mr. Brandis's relationship with Devin had been his longest to date, not counting Mrs. Brandis. He had spent years going through one boyfriend after another before meeting Devin, who insisted on a serious, long-term relationship or nothing at all. While not a cross-dresser himself, Mr. Brandis had no problem with it. "He doesn't mind my dresses," Devin had said once, "and I turn a blind nostril to his cigars."

The summer before Adam and Carter entered the fifth grade, Mr. Brandis had announced to his family that he was gay. He regretted hurting them, but said he could no longer live a lie and needed to pursue his true nature.

This came as a big shock to Adam, who had always thought Mrs. Brandis was the homosexual. Greta Brandis was a stocky woman—not fat, but thick and solid—who never, ever wore dresses or skirts. Adam had never seen her in anything that could not be worn by a man without anyone knowing the difference. She kept her hair cut very short, and, depending on her mood, she sometimes had it buzzed. She was a photographer and her subjects ranged from celebrities to wild exotic animals in remote jungles. She had a loud, deep voice and a laugh that sounded like someone torturing a goat.

Mr. Brandis, on the other hand, was tall and slender, and while not overtly macho, there was definitely a manliness about him. He loved sports, did a lot of off-road driving and mountain climbing, and bore a strong resemblance to a somewhat younger Burt Reynolds, but with real hair. He was a very popular production designer who had worked on some of the biggest movies of the last two decades, and had been nominated for two Academy Awards, neither of which he had won.

Ms. Kindler-Brandis—the name sounded to Adam like a pricey daycare center—had accepted her husband's announcement with surprising grace. They divorced, but remained close friends and occasional roommates. Ms. Kindler-Brandis maintained their Beverly Hills home as her "base camp," as she called it, and showed up for a couple weeks two or three times a year. The arrangement suited Devin, who was a fan of Greta's work. He once had told Adam he thought she was "a divine adventurer, like Indiana Jones with a uterus."

Carter was not in his bedroom, so Adam went up to the attic, which everyone in the Brandis household referred to as Carter's "studio." Adam could hear Marilyn Manson playing loudly overhead.

The attic had served as a darkroom for Carter's mother. Since the divorce, she had used it less and less, until she finally rented a studio in Westwood. The attic had been empty ever since, until two summers ago.

Since Adam had entered high school, his father had been trying to interest him in one aspect or another of the movie business as a profession. The one constant was screenwriting, which he had pushed relentlessly since Adam was old enough to understand what he was saying. But every few months, he would come up with something else. One evening, he had a nervous, fidgety cinematographer over for dinner in an unveiled attempt to get Adam excited about cinematography. He had taken Adam to a foley session to watch as sound effects were added to his latest movie. To Pixar, where he was led through all the steps of making a movie with computers instead of cameras.

Adam had explained to his father that no matter what kind of work he did later in life, it would have absolutely nothing to do with show business in general and the movie business in particular. It held no appeal for him.

His father had sniffed dismissively and said, "Don't be ridiculous. Everybody wants to work in the movies. Most people would kill for the opportunities I'm giving you."

I'd kill for you to stop, Adam had thought.

A couple years ago, he had arranged for Adam to tour a "creature factory." Annoyed, Adam had asked Carter to come along so he would not have to endure it alone. Carter was far more excited about the tour than Adam could feign. For Adam, it had been a marginally amusing diversion. For Carter, it had been a revelation. Carter had been awed by the masks, makeup, shockingly realistic wounds and severed limbs. Had become as excited as a child and asked endless questions, wanting to know exactly how everything worked, how it had been made, how it was operated. Adam had been a little embarassed by his friend's behavior, and after awhile, even the two long-haired guys taking them through the shop seemed to tire of the rapid-fire questions.

After they left, Carter had talked about nothing else, and went back a few times, without Adam, to ask more questions. Within the month, he had taken over his mother's old darkroom, filled it with everything he needed, all purchased on his dad's credit card, and made his first mask. A reptilian face with a curved, sharp beak and bulging yellow eyes. Masks and body parts soon filled the shelves, and he was always trying to make Adam up as a zombie or burn victim.

While Adam was impressed with Carter's abilities — he had started out pretty good and improved rapidly — he simply could not get excited about the field. About six months after starting, Carter had asked him about his lack of enthusiasm.

"You just don't like movies, admit it," Carter had said.

"I love movies, Carter. I just don't like the business of making them or the people in it. Well…your dad's a nice guy, but he's an exception. My dad's a prick. If I got into the movie business, any part of it, I'm afraid it wouldn't be long before I couldn't enjoy movies anymore. Before I…became like my dad. I'd rather die than be like him. You know that."

"Yeah, I know."

"But you're so good at this, Carter! Just because I'm not interested doesn't mean you shouldn't go into it. You'd probably end up being one of the best in the business."

"Oh, no, I don't wanna do this for a living," Carter had said.

"You don't?"

"And work with pricks like your dad? Are you on crack? It's just something I like to do."

"Well, you're going to have to do something, eventually. We both will."

Carter shook his head. "It's just a hobby."

"It's sure an expensive hobby."

Carter had grinned. "That's the one good thing about the movie business. It pays my dad enough to afford all this shit."

The attic stairs were at the end of the second floor hall and were narrower and steeper than the others in the house. The door at the top bore two vintage '70s movie posters: *The Incredible Melting Man* and *The Devil's Rain*. Oddly enough, Carter had purchased all of his horror movie posters prior to his interest in the mechanics of horror movies. He had started a movie poster collection when he was a little kid, about the same time Adam had started his.

The door was locked, so Adam knocked hard and shouted Carter's name to be heard above the music. The music lowered and the door opened.

"Hey!" Carter said. He wore an enormous *T2* T-shirt—even on Carter it was billowy—and a pair of baggy, dark blue shorts. His hands appeared to have been sprayed with blood. "C'mon in."

Adam closed the door and followed Carter into the brightly lighted room. More movie posters covered the walls and slanted ceiling.

"What are you working on?" Adam asked. He went with Carter to a rectangular table stained with paint and covered with what would look to most people like junk. Adam saw the work in progress.

In front of him lay a severed male human head. No, it looked more like it had been torn off than severed. The neck ended in a dangling mass of bloody meat, veins, and a stump of neckbone. Carter had been putting on the gory finishing touches.

"Carter, that's...disgusting," Adam said, and he meant it. "Really awful. I don't know if I can look at it much longer."

Carter grinned. "Thank you. Here, look at this." He put an index finger in the mouth and pulled it open. It looked as if the head had been silenced in the middle of a scream. "And this." He reached into the mouth with thumb and finger and pulled a pliable, glistening tongue forward until it rested on the bottom teeth. Even the teeth, which were not perfectly straight—one in the front was even chipped—looked remarkably authentic. "This moves, too." He wiggled the stump of neckbone, which ended in a jagged break on the bottom. Then closed his fist on the long salt-and-pepper hair that fell all around the bald pate. Held up the head by the hair and let it dangle, face tilted slightly downward. It looked as if he had just ripped it off the body.

Adam shook his head in awe. "Does it work?"

"Haven't tried it yet."

"Are you going to try it on Devin?"

"Nah, I'm getting tired of trying stuff on him. He's too easy. You tell him bell-bottoms have come back, he jumps on a chair and screams like a woman." He shrugged. "Maybe I'll try it on Mrs. Sanchez, I don't know." He leaned back in his chair, yawned and stretched, rubbed the back of his neck with one paint-stained hand. "I've been doing this since about seven-thirty this morning. My neck feels like his looks," he said, nodding at the head on the table. He stood. "I didn't eat any breakfast. Wanna get some lunch?"

"Sure, sounds good. But there's something I thought you'd like to do with me first."

"Oh, yeah? What's that?"

"Well...it's a long story."

"Sounds mysterious."

"Not really. I'll tell you in the car."

Carter rolled his eyes. "You writers. Everything's gotta be a story. I've gotta take a shower and change clothes."

They left the attic and went down the narrow stairs. In the hall, Carter lumbered along beside Adam and asked, "Hey, got any plans for tonight? There's a showing of the 1936 Flash Gordon serial. All thirteen chapters, back to back."

"Is that the one with the flying dildos with sparklers stuck up their —"

"Hey! It was the *Star Wars* of its time! Those effects were state of the art!"

Adam laughed. "You special effects guys. Always defending your flying dildos."

While Carter took a shower, Adam sat on the end of his bed and played a game on Carter's Playstation.

Carter Brandis stood six feet, three inches tall and weighed well over three hundred pounds. Even though he had an ample belly, he looked imposing and powerful rather than sloppily fat. At least, that was how he looked to people who did not know him. If you knew him as well as Adam did, you knew there was not an ounce of imposing flesh on his genuinely large bones.

Even back in the third grade, Carter had been overweight, and had been picked on mercilessly by the other kids, which was probably why Adam — who had always been picked on for being scrawny — had approached him during recess one day and introduced himself. From junior high to graduation, Adam gained on his classmates in height but remained skinny. Carter, on the other hand, sprouted until he towered over all the other students and most of his teachers, but he got fatter as well.

Carter's biggest problem was exercise, because he got very little, if any at all. He was sedentary, spent most of his time working in the attic. But even before he had begun his expensive hobby, he had never been active, preferring to watch a movie, read a book, or just sit and talk to doing anything physical.

Adam often asked Carter to join him for a swim, a brisk walk, or a game of tennis, but he always refused. Adam did not want to be like so many other people — "You really *should* lose some weight, Carter," and, "You need some exercise, big guy, " — and tell Carter what he should do. He knew Carter was as sensitive as he. But Adam was concerned for his friend's health.

Since being with Gwen the day before, when she had told him he needed to work out because he was scrawny, Adam had been thinking, and the thinking had developed into a plan, and the plan had led him to Carter's house. He was pretty sure it would not work, but decided to try it anyway.

Carter entered the room wearing a robe and carrying a towel. "Have you ever seen Mimi Rogers naked?"

"No, she wouldn't take her clothes off, the bitch. But she gives great head." Adam kept playing the video game.

"Smartass." He threw the towel over his head and briskly scrubbed at his wet, dirty-blonde hair. "I saw her in some movie on Skinemax late last night. *Full Body Massage*. Ever seen it?"

"I've seen the box in the video store. Any good?"

"Who cares?" Carter said as he started to get dressed. "I mean, I don't even remember what it was about. I just remember Mimi Rogers naked. She's, like, one of the greatest special effects ever put on film.

Her tits are…well, they've practically got their own weather systems. Each of them. And they're real."

"You're sure?"

"First of all, the only women who intentionally have their tits blown up that big are in the porn business. Mimi's breasts are totally an act of God. They moved, for one thing, like tits're supposed to."

"You've researched this? The whole thing about the women in porn?"

"Lick me."

Adam laughed, then said, "Shit," when he was killed on the television screen. He put the control down and stood. "So, did you tape it?"

"No, but it's on again next weekend." Carter's hair was still wet, but he swept a comb through it after putting on a *Babylon 5* T-shirt and a pair of baggy black jeans that were thin at the knees. "Okay, so what's this mysterious thing you're gonna tell me about?"

"Oh, nothing much," Adam said with a shrug. "I just wondered if you wanted to come to the house because Dad's having Mimi Rogers over for lunch, and I thought you'd —"

Carter's mouth dropped open and his eyes became hubcaps. "Are you shitting me?"

Adam laughed so hard, he staggered backward and almost fell on the bed. He was a lousy liar and could never sustain a gag. Carter had a poker face and the willingness to say just about anything that might get a reaction from someone, but he was a sucker.

Carter swept his towel up off the floor and threw it at Adam. "You bitch!"

Still laughing, Adam said, "C'mon, let's go. I'll tell you about it on the way."

Carter followed him into the hall and closed his bedroom door. "On the way to where?"

"Mimi Roger's house."

"Oh, would you just — you can eat my crustiest pair of shorts!"

Adam laughed all the way down the stairs.

✝

"Holy Jesus Christ!" Carter barked, turning to Adam in the car. Once again, his jaw hung loose, eyes wide. "You…you're joking, right?

That's the only reason you showed up today, isn't it? To mess with my head?"

"Nope. No joke." Adam was grinning.

"That sorta thing...it only happens in letters to *Penthouse*." Carter's forehead wrinkled with a deep frown as he processed the new information. "But isn't that, like...incest?"

"She married my dad, that's all. We're not related by blood."

"Yeah, but still, that's...well, look, Adam, I'm not dissin' you, but...there's just something a little too...Woody Allen about it, you know? It seems a little sick, doing a woman you call Mom."

"I don't call her 'Mom.' I've *never* called her 'Mom.'"

"Even so, Adam, think about it. That's you and your dad parkin' your skinmobiles in the same garage, you know what I mean?"

Adam laughed. "Yeah, I know, it is a little weird, but I —"

"A little weird? There's hardly any difference than if you and your dad were doin' her at the same time."

"Oh no, uh-uh," Adam said sternly, shaking his head. He was no longer laughing and his smile had disappeared without a trace. "No, there's a big difference. He doesn't even know about it. And if he did, he'd probably kill me with his bare hands."

Carter turned his head side to side slowly and said, "No, man, you're kidding yourself. You're both doin' the same woman!"

"But not at the same time."

"So what's the big difference?"

"For one thing, we're not doing her at the same time, like I said. If we were, I'd never be able to get it up, and I'd probably puke trying."

Neither of them said anything for awhile. Adam was about to turn on the radio when he noticed Carter was glancing at him every few seconds with a sheepish expression.

"What?" Adam asked.

"Well, it's kinda personal, but...what's she like?"

Adam smirked. "You mean in bed?"

"Hey. Alex Trebeck. Yes, in bed."

"Well, she's better than being sodomized by a bull elephant."

"Cut the shit."

Adam's smirk became a smile as he took in a deep breath. "Here's a bombshell. She's got reloads."

"Oh, bite me, she does not. I've seen her in a bikini and those are —"

"I've felt them, Carter."

"You…you mean, her funbags have…little funbags inside?"

Adam nodded. "Back-up funbags."

"Shit. But…they move. Remember that day I was over at your house and she was wearing that T-shirt with no bra? I was so worried you'd want to leave the room before she did, because there was no way I could've stood up. Her breasts jiggled under that T-shirt, Adam. They *jiggled*."

"Looks like strides are being made in the field of funbagology, Carter."

Carter said nothing for several seconds, then let out a long sigh, as if he were exhausted. Rubbed his eyes with the heels of his hands. "I don't know, Adam. I mean, doing something like that, doing your stepmom…" He dropped his hands and turned to Adam. "You're either gonna burn in Hell or end up on *The Jerry Springer Show*."

"I'd prefer Hell."

FOUR

Adam's idea had been to take Gwen's advice, join a health club, and put some muscle on his bones, and to get Carter to join with him. Carter was reluctant at first but, still stunned by the revelation that Adam had been having sex with his dad's wife, he agreed to give it a try, especially when Adam said he would not do it without him. Adam drove them to The Spectrum, a Beverly Hills health club where his mother had been a member for as long as he could remember.

The Spectrum was a bad idea. Adam had forgotten that it catered mostly to industry types, from studio suits to actors. They left immediately.

"I don't like living around them, and *with* one of them," Adam said, back in the car. "I sure as hell don't want to sweat with them."

They went to the one place in Los Angeles where people in the movie business would not be caught dead: Hollywood. They joined Sal's Gym and Sauna, a little piece of strip mall just off Sunset. The place was as quiet as a mausoleum when Sal himself took them on a tour of the equipment. They got lockers and worked out for awhile, laughing the whole time, feeling like idiots on the exercise equipment.

On the way back to the car, Adam noticed a bookstore a few doors down in the strip mall, The Book Place. Neither had seen it before and went inside to look around.

It was a used bookstore, but with a hippyish, New-Agey look and feel. Along with the large selection of books, the store sold scented candles, potpourri, and incense. Their aromas blended into a sweet, cloying smell that made them both wrinkle their noses when they walked in.

Carter went to the magazine shelves while Adam made his way slowly up and down the narrow aisles between tall shelves of books.

She stepped in front of him so abruptly, Adam almost ran into her.

"Hi," she said, smiling.

Pale, with hair a deep red, pulled back from the sides and held with something in back, while loose strands cascaded past her shoulders. She said nothing after "hi," but did not move. Just stood there smiling crookedly. There was a dimple in her left cheek, where the corner of her mouth turned down instead of up like the right. In contrast to her dark red hair, her pale blue eyes exploded from her face in spite of her slight squint. A charming squint.

"I bet you're looking for something interesting," she said.

Adam realized he had not replied to her greeting, just stared at her. He cleared his throat and said, "Um...hi." Instantly, he realized how stupid that sounded because she had already said something else, moved forward in the exchange. He felt like an idiot.

"Do I need to talk slower?" she said.

"Oh, no. Um...I just...I was startled, I guess."

"Okay. Hi."

"Hi."

"I bet you're looking for something interesting."

"Always." He finally smiled.

"Let me guess." She looked into his eyes, squinted a little more, ran a fingertip along her lower lip. Turning, she walked deeper into the store, slowly, and Adam followed. "Elmore Leonard. Or...*no!* Something gritty but darker. Ummm...David Martin? Thomas Harris?"

"Adam Julian."

"Oh. Who's he?"

"That would be, um...me."

"Oh!" She turned to him with wide eyes. "What do you write?"

"The songs. You know...the ones that make the whole world sing." Embarassment burned in Adam's neck and cheeks. He did not know why he had said it or where it had come from, but it had slipped by the censors and was on the air.

His palms were wet, but there were no tremors in his legs yet. When he was overly nervous or stressed, his legs became possessed by the shivers. Carter said it made him look like Don Knotts in *Alien*, but there was nothing Adam could do about it.

Then she laughed! The sound so surprised Adam, he took an abrupt step backward. It was such a bright sound, so embracing. And it was not quiet.

"My mom listens to his music sometimes," she said. "Course, she also listens to the Grateful Dead."

They came to a wall of shelves at the end of the aisle. Adam recognized it as the horror section because it held the works of only two authors: Stephen King and Dean Koontz. The girl looked around at the books, spread her arms, and said, "Ah, the giants." Then she giggled. "I bet you don't know what that line's from."

"*Star Trek IV: The Journey Home*," Adam said. "That was Spock responding to Kirk's explanation of profanity. Kirk identified its source as the popular writers of the time, the collected works of Jacqueline Suzanne and Harold Robbins. And Spock said, 'Ah. The giants.'"

Her smile stalled, mouth dropped open. "That's good. That's *very* good. Alyssa Huffman."

"Never heard of her."

"She would be me." She grinned.

"Oh! And what do you write?"

Her grin tilted slightly and for a brief moment, became deeply naughty. "Things that would give both my parents strokes if they ever read my diary. Maybe I'll let you read it sometime." She looked around. "Horror? Is this where you were going?"

"I don't know where I was going. My friend and I just came in to look around, see what kind of store you had."

"The guy at the magazines?"

"Yeah. Carter."

"Well, it's a...booky kind of store. Unless you just ran out of strawberries-and-honey incense."

"In which case it would be an incensey kind of store."

She nodded. "Pretty much." She turned and headed back toward the front.

Alyssa was dressed in black. Black tank top, skirt with a slit up the side to reveal black net stockings and pseudo-Victorian-style pointy-toed boots. Against all the black, her skin was like milk. She had beautiful lips. Full, lush, Janeane Garofalo lips. They were painted a deep red, but Adam thought they would look much better without it.

They passed through the romance section. As a boy, Adam had been struck by the number of romance novels in bookstores. They almost seemed to reproduce on the shelves before his eyes. He'd decided to search for the secret to their popularity and had bought a few at random. One of the novels was called *Passion's Stormy Sea*, by Teresa Laree Montgomery. He could remember nothing about the novel except for a single phrase, which had haunted him ever since. "A mouth like a ripened fruit." It had made no sense to him. Ripened fruit? What kind of fruit? A banana? Depending on how ripened, that could be disgusting. An orange? An apple?

Alyssa's lips reminded him of that phrase. The words suddenly sprang to life. His immediate response to seeing her lips had been a desire to put his mouth over them and suck, as he would suck on a ripe fruit. A peach, a pear, any fruit. He suddenly realized the fruit itself, which had thrown him for so long, was not the point.

Her bracelets and necklaces of black and silver chittered together as she walked. A step behind her, Adam let his eyes move over her body. Tall and shapely. Loose in her movements, comfortable in her body. Dressed as if she had just returned from a black mass, ritual sacrifice, and book signing at Anne Rice's place.

"You work here, right?" Adam asked.

"Yep. I know this store inside and out. I grew up here."

"In the store?"

"Practically. My parents own it."

"You must read a lot."

"Almost always."

"Who do you like?"

She stopped walking and thought a moment.

"Wait," Adam said. "Please promise me you won't say Anne Rice."

"What's wrong with Anne Rice?" she asked, turning to him.

"Well, I guess it's a matter of taste. Like anything else. But I think people who like her work as well as people who don't can agree that it's better read than worn."

She pressed her lips together and there was a quick flash of fire in her eyes. For a moment, Adam thought he had said the wrong thing, that she was angry.

"Are you making some kind of judgment of me based on my clothes?" she asked.

He responded quickly. "Oh, no, no, not a judgment. Just an educated guess."

"Yeah, sure." The flames in her eyes crackled again as she cocked a hand on her hip. "You think because I'm wearing all black, I read Anne Rice and listen to Bauhaus and obsess over role playing games and hang out in basements with other losers and assorted children of the night. Right?"

Adam thought, *Must...get...foot...from mouth!* "Well, I didn't say that," he said.

"You were thinking it. Weren't you?"

He decided not to bother arguing. "Yes. I was. The black clothes, black nail polish...I don't know what got into me."

"How do you know I'm not, like, in mourning? How do you know my boyfriend wasn't just killed in a drive-by shooting and I'm wearing black to mourn my loss? Or maybe black reflects how I feel inside after years of sexual abuse from my father, for which my mother blames me. Maybe *that's* why I wear black."

Adam tensed, prepared himself for the worst. "Is...is any of that true?"

"Nah. It's the goth thing, like you thought. But my heart's not in it." She shrugged her shoulders and her breasts moved freely beneath the black tank top. "My friends kinda got into it and I didn't have anything better to do, so I went along with it. I'm not too crazy about the subculture, myself. There's *way* too much piercing going on, for one thing. Come to think of it, I'm not too crazy about the friends I got into it with."

The door rang open and three chatty women came into the store. Alyssa went behind the counter, found a notepad and wrote something. Ripped the page out and handed it to Adam, smiling.

"The address is where to be tonight at ten," she said. "The phone number is where to call if you can't find where to be."

"Where is this?"

"My house. Come pick me up."

Adam smiled. "To go where?"

"Anywhere. Wherever."

"No, uh…no walking through graveyards, or anything, right?"

She laughed softly and leaned over the counter, their faces close. Her breath smelled of cinnamon. "Don't worry, I've got a whole closet full of very non-Rice clothing. I'll wear some for you."

"I'm kidding. You can wear anything you want."

"Okay. And I won't make you walk through any cemeteries."

"We can walk by," Adam said. "I'm just not comfortable with actually walking *on* the dead."

✝

In the car on the way home, Adam talked of nothing but Alyssa.

"Are you outta your mind?" Carter barked. "You don't wanna mess with those goth chicks, man, they're trouble with a capital N, for 'neurosis'. They don't live in the real world. They latch on and never let go. They want your blood, man. *Literally!*"

Adam laughed. "They're harmless. They just want to belong somewhere, like all of us."

"Hey. Dr. Drew. I'm gonna start puking all over the upholstery, here. Turn on CNN if you don't believe me. They're in the news all the time. Killing their parents, shooting up their schools. Hell, without those freaks, Anne Rice would probably be writing greeting cards for Hallmark!"

"There's nothing wrong with this girl, Carter. She's not like those people. She just wears the clothes because her friends do."

"Yeah, sure, that's how it starts. That's how she'll do it to you, a little at a time. Pretty soon, she'll have you wearing black suits from the Salvation Army store. Then a shirt with ruffles and puffy sleeves. Next thing you know, you're lurking down Melrose looking like Andy Warhol's mortician."

"Nobody's gonna make me wear anything, jeez."

"They drink blood, you gym teacher, don't you watch *Dateline*? *20/20*? *The Learning Channel?* I mean, they're not, like, *real* vampires, or anything, but they drink each other's blood, I'm not shitting you! You're gonna start showing up with Band-Aids all over, it'll happen."

"Are you through?"

"Yeah. All I'm sayin' is…be careful out there, okay?"

"There's nothing to be careful about. This girl's different." Adam's voice lowered when he added, "She's special."

Although Carter tried to change the subject, Alyssa was all Adam could think about the rest of the way home, and for the rest of the day.

The sun mockingly slowed its pace as it made its way across the sky. Adam kept himself busy as time stretched. He worked on a short story, did some reading, watched a little television. He consulted the map of the Los Angeles area tacked to the inside of his closet door and found the shortest route to Alyssa's house. Above all, he lay low, avoiding his dad and Gwen.

Time still did not pass fast enough. Adam stripped, went into his bathroom and turned on the shower. As the water hissed, he put a CD into the boombox on a windowsill just outside the shower. Dave Brubeck's *Time Out*.

Ever since he was a little kid, Adam had thought "Take Five" was the coolest piece of music in the universe. It had been his mother's favorite, too. She had been a jazz lover, and it had been the soundtrack of their long days together before he started school. He had loved it because she had loved it. She used to laugh so hard when he danced to "Blue Rondo a la Turk," spinning around and around. Adam kept her collection of CDs, tapes, and records in his room. The music soothed him, made him feel safe. He turned it up and got into the shower.

Piano, sax, bass, and drums cut clearly through the shower's hiss. Eyes closed, Adam scrubbed shampoo into his hair.

A hollow *clack* sounded in the steam. The latch on the shower door.

He turned around and opened his eyes, which were stung by shampoo suds. But someone was there. The shower door closed again. He spun around and put his face under the stream, scrubbed at his eyes.

Soft hands slid over his back. Around to his chest.

Gwen. Adam smiled as he rinsed his hair.

She stepped close, so her breasts pressed against him.

It was not Gwen. The breasts were too small, body too short.

Gooseflesh crawled over Adam's arms and shoulders in spite of the hot steam. He turned around and stepped back, away from the hands. He meant to say something, but could think of nothing appropriate to say to a total stranger in his shower.

She smiled as he stared at her. Tanned and curved, she stood in a careful pose that suggested she knew it, and knew how best to show it off.

When the girl started to move toward him, Adam held up both hands and said, "Uh, look, y'know…not that I really mind, or anything, but…who are you and what are you doing in my shower?"

She moved forward again, and when Adam put up his hands, she pressed hers to them, slid her fingers between his. Locked them together. She smiled. It was an amused smile.

"I'm Rain," she said. When Adam looked confused, she continued: "I thought we oughtta get to know each other. We're gonna be spending a lotta time together."

"We are?"

"Yep. For as long as I can take it, anyway. Long as I'm here, I want to make sure there's somebody to fuck." She had a generous mouth, and it spread into a large smile now, revealing small, impeccably white teeth. "Got a problem with that?"

Cold water splashed in Adam's stomach when he realized who she was.

Gwen named her daughter Rain? he thought.

Her eyes darted over his face before she dropped suddenly, disappeared from Adam's field of vision. He felt her breath on his penis, which was already hard.

"Okay, wait a second, *wait* a second," he said as he grabbed her upper arms and lifted her. "Maybe, uh…I don't know…" He turned off the shower. "Maybe we should step out of the shower and talk."

"You don't look like you wanna have a fuckin' conversation, honey," she said, smiling at his erection.

He turned off the shower, stepped around her — skin slid together like satin — opened the door and stepped out. He grabbed his towel and scrubbed his wet hair, then his body as he left the bathroom. He heard her moving around behind him as he opened a dresser drawer and poked around inside.

It was a messy drawer, like all the others. He could not find his new underwear. Now that there was a horny naked girl in his room, the only underwear he could find were the boxers he had bought at a science fiction convention, all covered with Japanese movie monsters. Godzilla, Rodan, Mothra, Ghidra, all over his underwear. He closed the drawer, opened another.

"I like your ass," Rain said casually, getting closer. "It's a happy ass."

"Thank you," Adam said. "You should've been here last week when it was really depressed. You could've cheered it up." He found a pair of gray cotton boxers, put them on.

"Hey, you're putting away the fuckin' toys," she said, beside him now. "Got a hot date, or something?"

"Yes, as a matter of fact, I do." He turned to find a shirt.

"Why do you talk like that?"

Adam stopped, turned to her. "Like...what?"

"Like Mr. Douglas on *My Three Sons*. Y'know, on TV Land? Like you got a long stick wrapped in silk shoved so far up your ass, it's operating your head."

Adam gave it some thought. "You mean...like a ventriloquist dummy?"

She went to him, put her arms around his waist and leaned on him. "No, I mean like Mr. Douglas on *My Three Sons*. And Mr. Douglas on *Green Acres*, too, come to think of it. Coupla fuckin' hard-ons."

"Are you saying I'm a hard-on?"

"You *have* a hard-on." She laughed, then gnawed on his neck.

"But are you saying I *am* one?"

Her eyes flitted over the features of his face, over his hair. "Maybe a little uptight."

"Well, however it seems to you, I'm not uptight." He went to his closet. "I am kind of anxious to get ready for my date, though." He put on a shirt, then jeans. "Um, in fact, you might want to put on some clothes, too."

"I like being naked."

"What if your mother walks in?"

Rain frowned and walked over to Adam, stood in front of him. "Why would she just walk into your bedroom?"

"She lives here, it's her house, remember?" At the same time, he was thinking, *Oh, shit, can she tell? Is there some kind of mother-daughter mind meld thing nobody told me about?*

He tried combing his hair in the mirror, but she kept getting in his way, frowning, eyes moving slowly up and down his body.

"Have you been fucking my mom?" she asked.

Adam felt the question in his intestines. Rolled his eyes. "Of course not."

"Well, don't. She's trouble."

"You think?"

"She's a cunt. I hate her guts. How about you? What's your dad like?"

"My dad? He's like waking up on Christmas morning with a case of explosive diarrhea and shingles all over your body."

"He's...huh?"

"He's an asshole."

"Yeah, she knows how to pick 'em. Shoulda met my last dad." She slowly looked around at the things on the walls and shelves.

Adam sat on the edge of his bed to put on socks and sneakers. "Oh, that's right. I heard about your dad. I'm really sorry about that."

"About what?"

"The fire."

"Oh, that." She laughed. "You don't have to be sorry about that."

Certain he had misunderstood her, he said, "What?"

"Oops. Shouldn'ta said that, huh?" She smiled poutingly.

"What do you mean, I don't have to be sorry about that?"

She giggled and pulled him with her as she flopped onto the mattress. Put an arm across his chest, ran fingers through his hair. "C'mon, let's fuck," she said.

"I'm not dressed for it."

"So take 'em off, dammit." She pulled at his shirt. "Why'd you put 'em on in the first fuckin' place, anyway?" she asked, her voice suddenly loud and angry.

"Hey, hey, stop it, okay?" He pushed her hands away and sat up. "Are you on drugs, or something?"

"Just a little." She sat up, threw herself onto Adam and pinned him to the mattress. "Want some?" she asked. Her mouth was on his before he could reply.

Adam's lips experienced fresh new sensations as they were, for the first time ever, sucked open. His tongue was drawn out hard, its roots straining. Cheeks compressed, gums puckered. His lungs emptied as breath was sucked out of them, and he suspected teeth had shifted in his head. She ground herself against his erection while opening his jeans with her right hand wedged between them.

With a firm push, Adam got her off of him. Pulled his head back to peel their faces apart. The disengagement of their mouths sounded unearthly.

"You want some?" Rain asked.

"Some what?"

"Drugs. You were asking."

"No, I don't want any drugs. Don't you watch *Cops?* You want to show up on Fox being hog-tied and thrown in the backseat of a patrol car?"

"What makes you think I'd have to be hog-tied?" Rain asked.

"You're right. They'd probably taser you just to save time."

"I've fucked a few cops. They were all so stuck on themselves. Kept wanting to hear how big their cocks were. Average or less, every one of them."

"Was this a series of incidents?" Adam asked. "Or did you all meet at once?"

Rain lay on her back, propped up on her elbows, legs wide open. Her face was angular, sculpted. Hard. Her eyes, large and deep brown, were half-closed as they looked around the room. Delicate cheekbones and a perfectly straight nose hinted at a beauty somehow concealed, while the rest of her face remained guarded, closed up. A small cartoon mushroom-cloud tattoo was frozen in mid-explosion from the top of her left nipple.

"What, you mean was it a gangbang?" she asked. "So what if it was, huh?"

Uncomfortable, embarassed, Adam tried to think of a way to cut down the fallout from his remark. "Then you, uh…you must have been very tired afterwards."

"I'll tell you what I was. Not in trouble with my dad, who never found out his little girl had been stripping in a pool hall and selling

49

blow jobs in the storeroom. In exchange for the train, the cops fixed it for me. We all have ways of getting what we want, Mr. Douglas. Mine is sex. What's yours?"

Adam found himself chuckling. "Sorry, I'm not laughing at you. My dad…he gets them small parts in his movies. The cops. In exchange for no speeding tickets."

Rain shrugged a shoulder and cocked her head in a knowing, cynical way. "Hey. Whatever it takes, huh?"

He looked across the room at the U.S.S. *Enterprise 1701* clock on top of his dresser. "I should move my butt." As Adam stood, his jeans dropped. He didn't even see Rain move. Suddenly on her knees in front of him, she pulled down his boxers. Ignorant of morals and good taste, deeply unconcerned with previous obligations, and thoroughly incapable of giving a single thought to practicality, Adam's penis stood rigid and wet. The hot, liquid sheath of her mouth covered his erection and knocked his knees out from under him. He fell onto the bed with a loud, breathy, trembling moan.

Whatever she had done with her mouth while kissing him withered in comparison to the abilities she demonstrated on his erection. She sucked at the underside of his penis and made him press his head back hard into the mattress. She used her lips, tongue, teeth to devour him, drown him in pleasures that bordered on pain. Time disappeared, and Adam kept forgetting where he was. Entire trains of thought were sucked off their tracks and out of his mind.

He lifted his head and blinked his bleary eyes. Rain was on top of him. She seemed to hop onto his erection. Growled more as she moved on him frantically. It was not a noise that sounded like a growl. It was a growl.

Red-alert klaxons went off in Adam's head. He was not wearing a condom. He tried to sit up as he stammered, "Hey, no, uh-uh, whoa—"

Rain slammed him back down, fingernails clawed his nipples. Adam cried out in pain when her nails dug in and a couple broke flesh.

"Where the fuck you think you're goin'?" She spoke in the growl, sounded unsettlingly similar to the demon's voice in *The Exorcist*.

Disturbed by the fact that he was not using protection, Adam tried to roll her off him. She suddenly clutched his throat with both hands and squeezed.

What the hell is she doing? Adam thought.

Rain appeared to be strangling him, and it seemed she had committed herself to the task. She moved faster on him, angry movements. Arms straight, elbows locked. Her nails dug into his neck on each side while her thumbs pressed hard on his trachea.

Adam's face felt hot and puffy. A fire ignited at the closure of his throat and roared down into his lungs. He flailed his arms and kicked at first, then grabbed her wrists, loosened her hold on him almost enough to get a breath, but something threw him. Rain squeezed his cock with strong vaginal muscles, hard enough to make Adam cry out. If he were not being strangled.

Adam punched her in the side of the head and she let go of his throat, fell back, but not off of him. She bucked harder and harder, growling behind clenched teeth. It sounded like pain and rage and fear, all rolled into one dangerous sound.

Gasping for breath, coughing, Adam tried to sit up. His throat felt broken, but he could breathe again. Once up, he put his hands on Rain's ribs, ready to throw her off. But he did not.

The entire time he was unable to breathe, Rain had been riding him like Debra Winger rode the mechanical bull in *Urban Cowboy*. He had felt every bit of it, even as his vision blurred and his lungs became molten lava. Now, still gulping air into his lungs, he was about to come.

Adam embraced her. Rain kissed him, growled down his throat, rattled his organs. Her nails clawed his back as she sucked on his neck, bit him hard.

Adam's orgasm was, as far as he was concerned, amazing. But it was drowned out and swallowed up by the ferocity and trauma of Rain's. She threw him back on the bed and writhed and bucked on him. Her short wet hair seemed to stand on end as she uttered a long, senseless stream of obscenities, spat them in the same scary growling voice. Then she howled.

"Shh-shh!" Adam put a hand over her mouth. She bit it. "Ow, Goddammit, what the hell is wrong with you?"

Rain slowed down, slowly. The howling and clawing stopped. Finally, only their breathing remained. She smiled and rolled off him.

"Mmmm," she purred, "you play nice, Big Brother."

"Please don't do that."

"Don't do what?"

"Call me Big Brother."

"Too creepy for ya?" She laughed.

He propped himself up on an elbow and touched her chin, turned her head toward him. "I'm really sorry about hitting you," he said.

Rain pushed his hand away and sat up on the edge of the bed. "Hey, don't apologize. Like I said, Mr. Douglas, you play nice. And we're just down the hall from each other. Fuckin' A, huh?" She tossed a smile over her shoulder.

Did she want *me to hit her?* Adam thought as he stood. He undressed quickly, went to the bathroom and showered again. Afterward, he went back into the bedroom to find his towel.

Rain browsed through his desk drawers. "You got any pot?" she asked.

"No," he lied. "Are you, um, on the pill, by any chance?" He dried quickly, then began to dress again.

"Course I'm on the pill, Mr. Douglas. I look like the fuckin' mommy type to you?"

"Do you have any, um…you know, diseases?"

"Had my tonsils taken out when I was eight, and I got chicken pox when I was ten, that's about it. How about you?"

He ignored the question. "Could you please stop going through my drawers?"

She turned to him. "What would you hide from your little sister?"

Adam was becoming impatient. "And quit saying that," he snapped. "We are not related."

"Next time, you come to my room. That's where all the goodies are."

"There won't be a next time," Adam said. Even as he spoke, he knew it sounded harsh. "I'm sorry, I didn't mean that like it sounded, because that…well, what we just did was…pretty incredible. It's just that…well, come on, be realistic. I mean, what if Peter Brady started fucking Jan Brady? You don't think there would've been trouble? Alice would know immediately, of course, but the others would catch on. Next thing you know, they've gotta call Sam the butcher to pull Mr. Brady off a semi-conscious Peter and there's blood all over the place."

She stared at him open-mouthed, nose wrinkled. "What the fuck're you talkin' about?"

"I'm saying that what just happened here can't happen again." He sat on the bed again and quickly put on his shoes.

"But it happened, right?"

"Yes, but it's not going to happen again." He went to the full-length mirror beside his dresser.

"What if I want it to happen again?" Rain asked.

"Then I'm sorry to disappoint you." As he blow-dried his hair, Rain appeared in the mirror, behind him. Lovely, but cold, hardened. Her mouth moved, but he heard nothing over the blow-dryer's high jet-like whine. She put her hands on her hips, looked angry as she spoke.

When he was done, Adam turned off the blow-dryer.

" — see who'll suck your cock like that in prison," Rain was saying.

"What? I couldn't hear you over the blow-dryer."

"I was just explaining to you that I'll be wanting to do that again in the future, and that means we'll be doing it."

"You mean sex?"

"Yep."

He combed his hair. "Look, I'm not gonna do it. It's just too creepy, okay? Nothing personal, but you're my dad's wife's daughter."

"You just did."

"And that was a big mistake. As nice as it was, it would only cause — "

"How old do you think I am?"

The significance of her question went through him like the glimmering steel blade of a sword. He turned to her, and she was smiling. But it was not warm or funny or sexy or playful. It was a *gotcha* smile, and it was mean.

As if in class, Rain raised her hand and said, "Sixteen."

Adam ran the pad of his thumb back and forth over the teeth of his comb. It made the same sound his nerves were making at that moment, just beneath his skin.

"What…what the hell does that mean?" he asked.

"Just that I like our relationship the way it is. That's all."

"No." He pointed the comb at her. "No, you're telling me you're calling the shots here, right? That if I don't do what you want, you're gonna turn me in. Right?" He clenched his teeth angrily as he waited for her reply.

Rain retrieved a red and blue silk happy coat from the floor. Slipped it on and smiled. "You watch too many movies, Big Brother," she said as she left the room.

or the first time since Christmas, Adam used his cellular phone to call ahead and tell Alyssa he would be a little late. He had taken a wrong turn somewhere and was in the wrong neighborhood.

Adam hated cellular phones. Placed them among the most significant harbingers of the coming fall of humankind. They elevated the very concept of self-involvement to a new level with the conviction that it is necessary for everyone to be able to contact you at every second, no matter where you are or what you are doing. Adam had not wanted the phone, but when his dad gave it to him for Christmas, he had accepted it graciously and planned to exchange it.

"If you exchange that, I'll change all the locks next time you leave the house," his dad had said. "You'll have to get a job among the civilians."

"But who would need to be able to reach me all the time?" Adam said.

"I might. Or you might need to call me."

"Under what circumstances do you see that happening?"

"One of these days, your smartass tongue is going to wrap around your neck and strangle you to death, you know that? I'm telling you, Adam, you can't function in life with that attitude. People will hate you, some will punch you, your life will be miserable. So knock it the fuck off, okay?"

"Okay, I just don't think I need a cellphone."

"What if something happens? A…a family emergency. You never know these days."

"You never know these days" was one of Michael Julian's ways of saying, in code, that you were irritating him, and if you kept it up, he might blow. Its alternates included, "Now, let's just enjoy ourselves, okay?" and, "I think this is for the best," and every now and then, "Hey, you're irritating me, and if you keep it up, I might fucking blow."

But Adam was not ready to let the topic go yet. He was genuinely confused. Surely his dad was not worried about his safety or whereabouts. It had to be something else.

"You really want me to have this, don't you, Dad?"

"Want you to have it? I insist! Keep it with you wherever you go! See?" He took the cellphone from Adam to demonstrate. "It's small, flips open like the communicators on that stupid show you like so much."

Michael Julian refused to say *Star Trek*. He would use the word "star," and probably the word "trek" if he could work it into a sentence, but he would not say *Star Trek*. Back in the mid-eighties, he had written a *Star Trek* script for Paramount. The script was not only rejected, he was banned from the Paramount lot. Rumor had it that, upon reading the script, *Star Trek* creator and executive producer Gene Roddenberry was so enraged, he hired someone to kill Michael Julian, but had a change of heart later that day.

Adam had read the script and counted nearly two hundred uses of the word "fuck." The word "fuck" did not exist in the *Star Trek* universe, but obviously his dad had been unaware of that. It became even more evident he had never watched a single episode of the series when Adam read the nude shower scene his dad had written for Captain Kirk and a female alien. At one point in the script, Mr. Spock inexplicably fires "red beams of deadly laser light" from his eyes. And in a casual way, as if he did it all the time.

The script created quite a buzz. A phenomenally bad one. When Liz Smith mentioned the nude shower scene in her column, everyone started joking about it. Even Johnny Carson and David Letterman. Michael Julian had been humiliated, but somehow endured. He had bounced back quickly, and everyone loved him again when his next picture, *Violent Movie*, was a blockbuster. Michael was quick to remind everyone at any opportunity, "Gene Roddenberry's dead." But he still refused to say *Star Trek*. In the Michael Julian universe, *Star Trek* did not exist.

Adam asked, "What could possibly happen to me that would worry you so much?"

"Anything! A million fucking things! Just hang onto that and use it when you need to."

Adam's mind searched until it stumbled over one of the biggest fears of celebrities in Los Angeles, especially those with children: kidnapping. The public remained unaware of the phobia, just as it was unaware of the guards and surveillance cameras, the labyrinthine security systems. The small guns tucked into purses and the larger ones concealed beneath expensive suitcoats, carried by people who actively opposed handguns in public. People who knew guns would always be available to them simply because of who and what they were, no matter how the laws changed.

"Are you…are you actually afraid someone would kidnap me?" Adam had asked.

"Why the hell not? You know how many attempts are made every year? How many times it's actually happened? But the cops are always right on it, the story never gets out, they're good about that. Even the feds. That's why I love this town."

"Well, I'm touched that you'd worry, but…who would want to kidnap me?"

"Don't be a shithead, Adam, nobody gives a fuck about you. They'd do it to get to me, to my money. They'd do it because you're my son!"

Ah, so the truth comes out, Adam had thought. *In case of kidnapping, I can use the cellphone to foil the kidnappers' plot and save my dad a bundle in ransom. I wonder if he has kidnapping insurance. Why did he wait so long, for crying out loud?*

"And what the hell is wrong with you, talking like that?" Michael had snapped. "'I'm touched?' Who talks like that, outside of fags and Oprah? Nobody! Michael Caine, maybe, because people *expect* it of him. But nobody *else*."

The act of talking on the phone while driving—something that irritated Adam in other people—was made less bitter by Alyssa's voice. By the time he approached her house, they had been talking for about ten minutes, trying to decide what to do together.

"There's an around-the-clock Three Stooges marathon running at UCLA," Adam said as he eased up to the curb in front of her house and turned off the engine. Alyssa was sitting on the porch with her cordless phone, but she stood when Adam got out of the car. "How does that sound?"

"Nice car," she said, eyeing his convertible as she walked toward him across the lawn. "Cadillac?"

"Uh-huh. Nineteen-fifty-nine Fleetwood. Got it for my birthday. It makes my dad feel better about himself to give me expensive toys."

"I wouldn't mind just riding around in it for awhile."

"We could do that," Adam said, crossing the lawn toward her. The gap between them closed fast, until they were standing face to face.

"Well," she said, voice soft, quiet, "I guess I'll see you later."

"Yeah. Later."

They hung up and Adam slipped the cellphone into his pocket. They smiled at each other for what seemed a long time, then closed the remaining space between them and kissed. It was so unexpected to both, they laughed afterward.

Still without a destination, Adam drove them around for awhile. They ended up on the Santa Monica boardwalk in time to play a few games and get a couple chili dogs before the vendors closed. They leaned on the wooden railing overlooking the beach as they ate.

"Can I ask you a question, Alyssa?"

"Sure. I'll tell you anything."

"Why did you come up to me at the bookstore today? I mean, you just stepped right in front of me, almost like you knew me."

She shrugged. "I could tell you were different."

"Different from what?"

"From most. Customers, I mean. I can usually tell what they're looking for the second I see them. The overweight housewives who come in for a crate of romance novels. The older men, really gruff-looking, who smell like stale cigarettes and sometimes whiskey and buy westerns or war novels, maybe something by Tom Clancy. And, you know, all the science fiction geeks and horror weirdos. But you were different. As soon as I saw you, I knew you were looking for something interesting. Something…I don't know, unusual and exciting. I knew if you bought something, it would be, like…a dusty old volume from the back, or maybe some obscure autobiography."

"You thought all that? Just from looking at me? Jeez, I'm glad my fly wasn't open."

She laughed. "Maybe I didn't think it. Maybe it's more like I felt it. Hasn't that ever happened to you? You see somebody, a total stranger, but suddenly you feel something about them that seems so true?"

Adam nodded and smiled. The chili dogs were messy, but he had grabbed a fistful of napkins from the aluminum dispenser. They dabbed their mouths after a big bite.

"What went through your mind?" Alyssa asked.

"That I'd left my crucifix at home and you were going to bite my neck before Peter Cushing showed up with a wooden stake."

She laughed again, but stopped abruptly to slap his shoulder. "You didn't even notice!" she said as she stepped back and spun around once. She wore a tight red skirt, black-and-silver top with black stockings and red heels.

"You look great," Adam said, grinning awkwardly.

"Great? Just great?" She pouted a little. "Paint jobs look great. Christmas decorations look great."

"Beautiful."

"That's better."

"You look hot."

"Really? Wow, nobody's ever called me that before." He pulled her to him and they kissed, sharing bits of their chili dogs.

"So, what about your friend?" Alyssa asked after a moment.

"Carter?"

"Yeah. Does he have a girlfriend?"

"No."

"Hmm. Maybe we should introduce him to my friend Brett."

"Is she nice?"

"Well…no, not really. But she's pretty. We could introduce them, see what happens."

Adam kissed her again, and this time they did not pull apart as easily.

"Whoa," Alyssa said with a breathy laugh. "Is that a copy of *Tropic of Cancer* in your pocket, or are you just glad to see me?"

Adam laughed. "Very funny."

"Well, I need to be serious for a second. I've got to tell you something. If I don't, it'll be the same as lying to you. I don't want to do that."

Adam tensed, moved back from her a little. He could not believe the other shoe was dropping already. They had barely let go of the first one.

"Is something wrong? What's wrong?"

She shook her head. "I just don't want to lead you on. So I'm telling you right now that, uh...we won't be having sex tonight."

"I'm sorry," he said, confused. "Did I miss something? I feel like I walked in on the middle of a movie."

"I just want you to know I'm not too casual about sex."

"You only have it formally?"

She nodded, grinned. "R.S.V.P."

"I look like a dork in a tux."

Alyssa laughed as she pulled him close again. "I don't mean I'm saving myself for marriage, or anything. I'm just saying I take things a little slowly. So if that's going to be a problem for you, I'll understand. I'd hate it, but I'd understand and wouldn't hold it against you."

"What you're saying, really, is that, um, you don't put out on the first date."

"Is that bad? That's what you're going to say, right?"

Adam tried to process the sudden rush of feelings that went through him, all in the direction of Alyssa, but failed. Instead, he blurted, "Will you marry me?" It sounded jokey, and Alyssa laughed, but inside, Adam was serious, and knew if she said yes, he would drive them to Las Vegas that instant.

"I don't marry on the first date, either," she said.

"Neither do I. But it's the thought that counts, right?"

"So, with the sex thing out of the way..." Alyssa stopped, took a deep breath. "Well, maybe we could do something radical, like...get to know each other."

"Radical? It sounds downright subversive! I'll start. How old are you?"

"I'll be nineteen in seven weeks."

Relief coursed through Adam's veins like adrenalin.

They tossed the remaining bites of their chili dogs over the railing to the sand below and made their way slowly back up the boardwalk as the lights around them blinked out.

SEVEN

As he finished brushing his teeth and turned out the bathroom light, Adam could not remember the last time he had gone to bed feeling so good. Not just good, but happy. He walked naked to his bed, turned out the lamp. Got on the bed, tugged the sheet from the tangled bunch of covers beside him, pulled it over him. Closed his eyes and let a sigh slip out as his head found the right spot on the pillow. Alyssa's face hovered in the darkness behind his eyelids.

His body shook the bed with a startled jump. He thought he felt something touch him. He rubbed his eyes with thumb and forefinger in the dark. Something touched him again. His lungs stopped working. A hand came to rest on his flaccid penis. It squeezed.

In 1980, a slasher movie called *Friday the 13th* hit theaters. Produced, written, and directed by Sean S. Cunningham and starring a cast of young unknowns, it made a lot of money off throngs of teenagers who enjoyed seeing their peers slaughtered.

Adam laughed at the movie now — it was a sloppy mess in every way — but had found it terrifying when he first saw it as a boy. There was one scene Adam still could not watch if he planned to get any sleep in the near future.

Early in the movie, a young Kevin Bacon is lying in a bottom bunk in a cabin. Unknown to Kevin, a male corpse reclines in the bed above, blood still dripping from its gaping throat. Something drips on his forehead and he wipes it off with a hand, looks at it. Blood. A hand swings up from under the bed, slaps onto his forehead and holds his head down. Blood spurts as the deadly-sharp head of a hunting arrow plunges upward through his throat.

Adam hated the movie and its endless sequels, but was haunted by that particular scene, especially at night before he went to bed. Even now, when he knew better.

When the hand touched his penis, Adam flashed on the movie. The scene played out in his mind in vivid detail in a fraction of a second. His horror catapulted him from the bed. While airborne, he screamed. If asked about it later, he would insist he only shouted, but it was a high, piercing shriek, like Janet Leigh showering in *Psycho*. He hit the floor running for the door. As he pulled it open, he collided with it, and it slammed shut again. He turned and pressed his back to the door, heart about to explode, to face his assailant.

Gwen was sitting up in his bed, the bedspread and blankets wrapped around her. "Adam?" she said, groggy.

"Oh my God," Adam said as he slid down the door to the floor. Adrenaline thrummed in his veins. He could not quite catch his breath and was afraid he might hyperventilate. "Oh my God, oh my God."

"Adam, honey, are you okay?" she said.

He did not trust his legs, so he returned to the bed on hands and knees. "No, I'm not okay," he said. He climbed back onto the bed and lay beside her. "And somewhere, Sean S. Cunningham is laughing his ass off."

"Sean who?"

"Never mind."

Gwen curled up beside him, draped an arm and leg over him. Whiskey rode her breath when she said, "Sometimes I don't know what you're talking about, Adam. It worries me."

"Don't worry." His voice was still shaky from his scare. "Sometimes I don't know what I'm talking about either." After a moment, he asked, "Don't most people?"

"Don't most people what?"

"Not know what they're talking about sometimes?"

"Oh, sweetie, most people don't know what they're talking about *most* of the time."

Adam's frown deepened. "So how do we communicate? How do we accomplish anything?"

"I don't know. But it explains talk radio." She sounded sniffly.

"Do you have a cold?"

"No."

"Have you been crying?"

She did not respond.

Adam stroked her upper arm and asked, "What's wrong?"

"Oh, please, I don't want to whine and blubber like some —"

"What did Dad do?"

"Well, it's not so much what he did."

"Something he said? That's worse. I prefer the hitting. I got plenty of hitting growing up. But dad never shut up while he was doing it. The hitting alone I could handle. That pain went away and never left any scars."

"I…I'm still not sure what happened," she whispered. "One second, I was talking about going out on the yacht Saturday and…next thing I knew, he was furious. Like a fucking werewolf. Something about macaroni and cheese."

"Oh, *Kraft* Macaroni and Cheese?"

She nodded. "Yeah! I mentioned I might pick some up for the trip because it's so easy to cook and everybody loves it. I *thought* everybody loved it."

"Oh, God, did he give you the Kraft Macaroni and Cheese speech?" He laughed, sat up straight and deepened his voice when he spoke. A fair impression of his dad, inflections, tics and all: "I ate Kraft Macaroni and Cheese every Goddamned day of my life till I left home. We'd have a turkey for Thanksgiving, a roast for Christmas, an Easter ham, but even *then*, there it was. A vat of Kraft Macaroni and Cheese. Doesn't matter what the entree was, if there was an entree. It was always there. *Congealing*."

Gwen squealed laughter into her palms as she rocked back and forth on the bed.

"All I could ever taste was that Goddamned gooey Kraft Macaroni and Cheese. I vowed that when I grew up, I'd never eat it again. I won't have it in my house. To this day, I see one of those blue boxes, I can taste that shit in my mouth and I wanna puke."

"Oh, God, Adam," Gwen gasped, wiping tears from her eyes, "that's so funny. You're so good at that! Almost word for word!"

"There are variations," Adam said. "Like the story about how he almost choked to death on Kraft Macaroni and Cheese, and his little sister saved him with the Heimmlich maneuver. One Christmas, Aunt Renee said he was full of shit, it never happened. He hasn't spoken to her since. And if he's been drinking, he'll try to find somebody who loves Kraft Macaroni and Cheese and pick a fight with him."

Gwen kissed his cheek. Nibbled his earlobe. "You hate him, don't you?"

"Like Bette Davis hated Joan Crawford. I keep meaning to put a dead parakeet in his lunch."

"Sometimes I hate him, too."

Adam turned and propped himself on his left elbow, facing her. "Do you love him?"

She frowned as she watched her fingers toy with Adam's nipple. "I care about him." Her words sounded hollow.

"I don't think you can hate someone you've never loved."

"Where'd you hear that?"

"I don't know. Might have been Roger Ebert."

"Well, there are times when I really hate him. Times when I could kill him."

There was no tease in Gwen's voice. She was not joking. Adam adjusted his pillows and sat up, nestled into them. "You're serious, aren't you?"

"Mm-hm." She closed a hand around his erection.

"How serious?"

"I'm only serious about it when he hits me and pulls my hair."

"What'd he do, give up kicking? Is it Lent again already?"

"Yeah, he kicks, too."

Adam fidgeted. His dad had started beating his mother toward the end. Just before he killed her. He wondered if Gwen's relationship with Michael would take the same road.

His mind locked a tractor beam on that thought and pulled it in for closer inspection. If that was, indeed, his dad's plan, Adam would have to prevent it. He could not let that happen again.

Why would he do it, though? he thought. *They're practically newlyweds.* But Adam knew logic was the wrong approach. He would have to watch for it, and if he became certain of it, he would have to prevent it.

He had already decided to kill his dad. That would be a tasty bonus excuse.

Gwen said something. Said it again.

"What did you say?" he said.

"I asked if he was that way with your mother."

"My dad? Oh, yeah. Yeah, he...he was."

"The whole time they were married?"

"No, just toward the, um...the end." An ache filled Adam's chest, and he suddenly missed his mom deeply. If he told Gwen the rest— that his dad had started beating his mom shortly before he killed her— she would not rest until he gave her a complete explanation. But he had no solid proof, not even passable circumstantial evidence. Just that feeling in his gut. Suddenly, Adam wanted to be alone.

"What's the matter," Gwen said. "Something wrong? We can stop talking—"

"No, it's not that, it's just been a rough day, you know? I think I should get to sleep."

"Are you trying to kick me out?"

"Speaking of kicking...Dad's car was in the driveway when I got home earlier. Where'd he go?"

"Nowhere. He's in bed asleep."

Dragging on the cigarette, Adam coughed out a mouthful of smoke. "He's home? In the *house?*"

"Don't worry. He's snoring out both ends. We ate Mexican to-night."

Adam rested the cigarette on the ashtray's edge and got out of bed. "Look, Gwen," he said, "you can't be here in my bed when Dad is home, he might wake up, wonder where you are, come looking for you, I mean, God, what *is* it with you women?"

"Women?" Gwen got off the bed and stood in front of him. "What women?"

"It's just that...do you know what would happen if my dad found out we've—"

"Are you referring to my daughter?" Gwen said, suddenly sounding very much awake.

Adam froze. "I-I-I...what?"

"Have you met Rain?"

Adam nodded, fought to keep his voice steady. "Oh. Yeah. We met in the hall. Earlier. Didn't have much time to talk, but she seems like a nice gir—"

"Be careful." Her mouth turned down slightly at each corner. "She's my daughter and I love her, but she's nothing but trouble, Adam."

He tried to change the subject. "What if I'd had somebody in here *with* me tonight?"

"Then I would've left you alone." She sniffed. "Why? Do you have someone else?"

"Well, I…I think so."

"That's nice, I'm glad. I'm serious about Rain, though. She makes trouble. I doubt she'd try anything with you, though. You're too close to home. In fact, she could use a friend like you. Somebody level-headed and mature. Maybe it wouldn't be such a bad idea after all. You hanging out with her, I mean."

"You don't know me very well, do you?" Adam said with a Bela Lugosi lift of his eyebrow.

Gwen put her arms on his shoulders. "Oh, I know you better than you think I do."

Adam kissed her, held her a moment. "I'll see you tomorrow, okay?" he said.

"Sweet dreams." She gave him a peck on the cheek and left the room.

In bed, thoughts ricocheted around in his head like bullets in a western movie salloon. Was Gwen serious about killing his dad? Would Rain claim he had raped her if he told her to go screw herself? What was it about Alyssa that made her so different? Her eyes? Yes, maybe something about her eyes.

Adam drifted off to sleep, and sometime during the day's first light, he dreamed of Alyssa.

EIGHT

Mrs. Yu had a big greasy breakfast waiting for Adam when he entered the kitchen yawning the next morning.

"You trying to kill me with all this cholesterol, Mrs. Yu?" he asked as he took a seat in the breakfast nook that overlooked the garden.

She laughed, patted the top of his head. "You sirry."

While Adam was eating, Gwen entered the kitchen, joined him in the breakfast nook. She wore denim shorts, a white T-shirt with James Dean on the front. "Any later and you would have missed lunch," she said, smiling. She had a cup of coffee with her and sipped it. "How are you?"

"Tired. I needed the sleep." He sipped his coffee, passed a napkin over his mouth. "How about you? Feel any better today?"

She stared at her coffee, took a cigarette from a pocket and lit it. She looked sad. "Some, maybe. I don't know." She took a drag on the cigarette.

Mrs. Yu stepped into the breakfast nook, smiled. "'Scuse me, Missy Jurian, but Missa Jurian no rike cigalette smoke innadoors."

"Thank you, Mrs. Yu, for pointing that out," Gwen said pleasantly. "But from now on, there are some things Missa Jurian is just gonna have to get used to. I'm tired of being sent outside my own house to smoke, like a dog with fleas."

Mrs. Yu bowed her head and hurried away.

"Hey, hey, go easy on Mrs. Yu, okay?" Adam whispered.

Gwen frowned and leaned toward him. "What's wrong with *you?*"

Adam scrubbed his face with both hands, yawned. "Nothing. I'm sorry. Just lay off Mrs. Yu. You might even want to get to know her. She's had a very rough life and somehow she's managed to remain a good person in spite of it. That's more than you can say for most people who've led easy lives."

Mrs. Yu returned briefly to set a small crystal ashtray in front of Gwen, then disappeared.

"So, what did you do that kept you out so late?" She gave him a calm smile, as if to show the sudden outburst was forgotten.

"First, I was with Carter. He's making this severed head that is truly amazing."

"I'm telling you, that boy is a serial killer in the making. What about last night?"

"I went…out."

The left side of Gwen's mouth curled upward. "Who is she? What's she like?"

Adam cautiously searched her face.

She laughed and said, "You don't have to worry, Adam. You should be dating, I *want* you to date."

Adam put down his fork and smiled, pleased to hear her say that. "Her name is Alyssa. She's…different. Not like anybody I've known, really. We just met, but when I'm around her, she makes me feel like…like we've known each other a long time but didn't get around to actually meeting until this week."

"Oh, such a romantic, Adam. It's sweet."

"I guess that's better than being a *boy.*"

"Did you happen to see Rain anytime last night or this morning?"

He chuckled. "Thought you wanted me to stay away from her."

"The more I think about it, the more I think you might be good for her." She sighed, shook her head. "She just got back to L.A. and she stays out all night. She's upstairs asleep now, but I don't know where she's been."

"Did you ask her?"

"Not yet. You'll be hearing that when it happens. We always end up shouting, she says horrible things—" A deep breath as she fidgeted, "—and I suppose I do, too."

"Does she have friends around here?" Adam asked.

"A few. She did before she went off to live with her dad, anyway. A bunch of lowlifes."

"Why did you let her hang out with them?"

"Let her?" She tipped her head back and laughed. "Same reason I let the earth revolve, honey. I don't have much choice."

Having spent some time with Rain, that made perfect sense to Adam.

"She's…you just don't know her. Her dad could talk to her. I never could." She smiled at Adam again. "Maybe you'll be a good influence on her."

Adam laughed to cover his discomfort. "Yeah. I'll let her borrow my Bible. I've already underlined all the holiest parts.

"Just be careful. Like I said."

"You talk about her like she's the Incredible Hulk, or something. What are you afraid she'll do, break my neck with her bare hands and throw me down the Hitchcock steps?"

Gwen scooted her chair closer to Adam at the end of the oval table, leaned close. He smelled whiskey on her breath.

"An ex of mine, before I met Michael," she said. "He's in prison right now. At the bottom of the food chain, you know what I mean?"

"What's he in prison for?"

"Child molestation."

"Is he a child molester?"

Gwen laughed. "Of *course* not. Rain was never a child, not even at twelve."

Adam shook his head, rubbed his eyes. "I'm sorry, you've lost me."

"Rain seduced him. And when he wouldn't give her money, she cried rape. Poor Taylor. He wasn't such a bad guy. Now he's in prison, probably with some big guy;s bitch."

The image terrified Adam, made him feel nauseated. But it confused him, too. He could not understand Gwen's attitude toward what had happened. "Gwen, the man fucked your twelve-year-old daughter!"

"I think everyone will fuck her eventually. Probably before she's twenty. You didn't see her when she was twelve, Adam. She developed early. Looked like an expensive whore before she was thirteen."

"But this guy, your boyfriend, he knew she was twelve, right?"

Gwen reached over to stub out her cigarette in the crystal ashtray on the table. Instead, she dropped it in when she heard Michael's voice.

"Who's been smoking in here, Goddammit?"

Adam turned to see his dad standing in the kitchen with his attorney, Roger Menkin. Rog was Michael's age and short, midway between five and six feet. He tried to make up for his lack of height with clothes and jewelry. One of Michael's oldest friends, he had been his attorney long before Michael had become a success and amassed an army of attorneys. A freshly-lit cigarette dangled from the corner of his mouth.

"Oh, shit," Gwen breathed as Michael came toward the breakfast nook. Rog stayed by the kitchen doorway.

"How many times have I gotta tell you, Gwen?" he said angrily. "This is a non-smoking family. We've all gotta die, but nobody in the Julian family's gonna do it because their lungs don't work or they've got cancer." He reached down and stubbed out the butt in the ashtray.

Gwen stood and went to him, kissed him on the cheek. "I'm sorry, sweetie. I was being naughty." She reached down and squeezed his ass. "What brings you home so early?"

He softened quickly, put his arms around her and smiled. "My baby's health, that's what," he said, lowering his voice. "I don't want anything to happen to your lungs. You know how much I love your...lungs." They laughed together.

Chuckling, Rog said, "Am I going to be able to get you out of here, Mike?"

"Yeah, I've gotta go. I just came to pick up some stuff I left in the office." He kissed her again and started to leave, but turned to Adam. "Hey, what about July Fourth? We need to know how many to plan for. You coming? Gonna bring anybody?"

Adam cringed inside at the thought of a week on the yacht with his dad. Michael Julian went out on his yacht occasionally throughout the year, usually with assorted industry types. But every year on Independence Day, he took his family out for the week. It had been fun when Adam was a kid. Sometimes they went to Mexico, or north up the California coast to Oregon, Washington. On the night of the Fourth, Michael always shot off some elaborate fireworks. But as Adam grew older, the fighting between his parents had grown worse, and being with them for a week became less enjoyable every year. He had stopped going after his mom died, and now the very sight of *Money Shot*, as Michael had christened the yacht, depressed him.

But it might be fun if Alyssa were with him. He liked the idea, but would have to decide if he was ready to expose her to his dad yet.

"Yeah, I might go," Adam said with a nod.

"Might? What, you gonna check with your personal assistant? See what your schedule's like?" Michael guffawed. "Okay, Adam, you have your people talk to my people. But do it by tomorrow, Goddammit." He kissed Gwen again, then left the breakfast nook saying, "I'm out of here." Rog followed him out of the kitchen, and his cigarette trailed a ribbon of smoke.

Gwen sighed. "I suppose I should try to accomplish something today." She stood, picked up the coffee mug, and winked at Adam. "See you later."

After she was gone, Adam picked at his breakfast for awhile before deciding he could not finish it. He wanted to get out of the house.

NINE

It was a typical summer day in Los Angeles. Hot and humid, smog that clung to the insides of nostrils like a greasy film. And always in the air, the exhaust of cars, the sound of their engines, and the cars themselves. So many cars, endless columns of them, everywhere, stopping, going, honking.

Adam originally planned to go see Carter first, maybe even go to the gym, then drop by The Book Place late in the afternoon. But he needed to feel the way Alyssa made him feel, and he did not want to wait that long to feel it.

When he stepped into the bookstore, the bell rang and Adam smelled smouldering rose petals, a hint of honey and cinnamon. Behind the counter, a woman removed books from a brown grocery bag, stacked them on the counter until the bag was empty, then started on another. She stood up tall and straight and smiled at Adam. Her hair was thick, long, and frizzy. Once a light brown, silver had infiltrated and blended nicely, turned it the color of ash.

"Hi," she said. "How are you?"

"Fine, thanks."

"Can I help you find something?"

"Um…Alyssa? My name's Adam. I came by to see her."

She had a lot of teeth, but they were white and shiny, and the slightly crooked one in the front gave her smile a sexy bite.

"Hi, Adam," she said, extending a hand over the counter. "I'm Sunset. But everyone calls me Sunny."

Smiling, Adam asked, "Is Alyssa around?"

"Not right now. She could show up anytime. Or not. We're not much of a clock-watching family."

"You're Alyssa's mom? Nice to meet you."

Sunny wore no makeup, didn't need any. Her skin was fair, healthy, and lightly freckled.

"Guess I should have called first," Adam said.

"She'll be in sooner or later. Find something to read."

"Do you know where she might be?"

"No idea. We pretty much let Alyssa go her way. We figure the only way to learn about life is to live it, right? That's how we were raised. Where did you meet Alyssa?"

"Here, in the store."

"Ah! You must be the customer she mentioned. She hardly ever talks to us, but she mentioned you. So, you're Alyssa's suitor?"

Adam laughed at the word. "Sounds like I came to fit her for something."

Sunny slapped the counter as she laughed, made her braless breasts sway beneath her white peasant blouse. Adam was sure he would be able to see her nipples through the thin cotton if not for the colorful, intricately-beaded bolero vest she wore over the blouse.

"You're a book lover, too?" she asked.

"Oh, yeah. When I'm not reading, I'm watching a movie."

"Do you want to direct?" She laughed, shook her head. "Sorry. It just seems everyone in this town wants to direct."

"Including my dad."

"What does he do when he isn't wanting to direct?"

"He's a screenwriter."

"Ah, a writer."

"No. A screenwriter. In his case, there's a difference."

Behind her, an old black-and-white poster was tacked to a door. John Lennon in a fetal position beside Yoko Ono, both naked on a bed. The door opened and a lanky man taller than Sunny came out to the counter. The top of his head was bare. The thin reddish-brown hair that wreathed his skull fell just past the collar of his shirt. The shirt was not tucked into his jeans, but its bagginess could not conceal the pot belly that stood out on his otherwise skinny frame. Gold wire frames held thick lenses before his gentle eyes. The thick mustache was too big for his face.

Sunny introduced Adam to her husband, Mitch. As they shook hands, Sunny said, "He's Alyssa's suitor."

Adam asked, "Is that, like…a tailor, or something?" Sunny and Mitchell laughed, but did not respond. He still had no idea what "suitor" meant.

Mitch told Sunny to let him know anytime she wanted a break. He put an arm around her waist, kissed her. Squeezed her ass and sneaked a quick finger between her legs, then disappeared behind the grim John and Yoko.

Adam and Sunny chatted for awhile about books, found they both liked Carlos Castaneda and Sidney Sheldon.

"But sometimes Sheldon gets a little too metaphysical for me," Adam said.

Sunny laughed and slapped the counter again. "Would you like a cookie? I made them just this morning." From beneath the countertop, Sunny produced a plate piled with large chocolate-chip cookies.

Adam took one of the cookies and bit into it. It was delicious, but the bits of marijuana in his mouth surprised him. Made sense, though. Sunny and Mitch were hippy types, so there was nothing odd about marijuana in their cookies. But Sunny was more casual about it than most. She knew nothing about him, and yet she had given him a loaded cookie.

Then again, maybe it was a test. Perhaps Sunny was seeing what he was made of, how he would react. *Don't most parents care about who their kids are with, where they go?* Adam wondered. *That's the theory, anyway. So maybe this is Sunny's way of finding out*. It was a little elaborate, but not out of the question. He stopped chewing.

"I'm sorry!" Sonny slapped a hand to her forehead and screwed up her face. "Those have pot in them, don't they?"

He nodded.

"I forgot about that. Is it a problem?"

"The cookie's delicious, but—" He shrugged. "—it's a little early for me, and I'm going to be driving. The cookie's great, I just don't feel comfortable, um…taking it with me, in case…well, you know, in case I get pulled over for something and the cop…you know, asks to see…my cookies."

Sunny laughed as she took the cookie from him, put it with the others. Put the plate somewhere behind John and Yoko. "That was my fault. I've got to quit doing that or we'll all end up behind bars."

The phrase made Adam wince inwardly.

Alyssa came into the store a few minutes later. Gasped when she saw Adam, quickly removed her black-framed cat's-eye glasses. In the second he saw them, Adam thought her face made the nerdy glasses very sexy. Without them, he could see fear pass quickly over her eyes.

She was different, stiff. Glasses off, Alyssa gave him a quick, strained smile, then did not look at him again until they left. Talking with her mother, Alyssa's voice became tight and the spectre of a whine sometimes rose to the surface.

"I'm not saying you have to come, you know better than that," Sunny said. "I'm just letting you know that Aunt Christianne is going to be here, and I know she'd like to see you. So, if you're not doing anything, and if you're comfortable with it, you might want to be at home this weekend, or at least drop in to see her. You could bring Adam." She turned to him. "You'd love Aunt Christianne. She's a scream."

"Mom, I'm *really* sure Adam wants to spend the holiday meeting my relatives, you know?" Alyssa's tone was bitter.

"Well, it was just a thought, Alyssa," Sunny said with a dismissive wave.

Alyssa took Adam's hand in hers. He knew by how hard she squeezed that she wanted out fast. She told her mother they had to go, as if they had plans, and they left, Alyssa holding her glasses in one hand, Adam's hand in the other.

She spoke rapidly once they were in the car. "I'm sorry about that, Adam, I'm so sorry, I just went out to have lunch with my friend Brett, but I didn't know you'd be coming by the store, see, otherwise, I wouldn't have—"

"Hey, hey, you really have to lay off the caffeine, Alyssa," Adam said.

She laughed, took a deep breath. "How long were you there? With her?"

"About twenty minutes, I guess. Your dad came out of the office and said hi."

"Oh, God, both of them."

"They're nice, I like them. You're lucky. How many people have a mom who's so cool she gives their friends chocolate chip marijuana cookies?" He grinned at her.

Alyssa's features seemed to slide down the front of her skull in horror. "She gave you...oh, God, I'm so sorry, Adam."

"What are you apologizing for?"

She just shook her head. After watching the passing sights for awhile, she said, "They were both raised in the same commune. Their parents were honest-to-God hippies, and they passed it on to Mom and Dad. You know, like some kind of...bad gene."

"Hey, it could be worse. They could be Jehovah's Witnesses. Or actors."

Facing front, she said, "I hate them. I'd like to kill them."

Adam chuckled. "Yeah, there's a lot of that going around."

Alyssa made a noise that sounded like it might have been a laugh trying to get out. "You hate them, too?"

"No, I think your parents are cool. You should be happy to have them."

"No, I mean, do you hate *your* parents?"

Adam hesitated. "My dad," he said after a moment. "I hate my dad."

"You don't hate your mom?"

"No, I miss my mom. She's dead."

"Oh, I'm sorry. I didn't know that."

"You couldn't have known. And don't apologize, I'm pretty sure you didn't do it."

"She was murdered?"

Again, Adam hesitated. He wanted to say yes, she was, but decided not to share any of the dark stuff with Alyssa. Not yet, anyway. There was an airy, light-headed quality to their relationship and he did not want to damage it.

"She was killed in a boating accident." The instant he said it, he heard the voice of Richard Dreyfuss in his head: *This was not a* boat *accident!*

"That sucks."

"She was great, too. Nothin' to hate there."

"You were lucky to have her at all. I wish my parents had died in childbirth."

"Jeez, what could be so bad about them? They seemed very—"

"They're freaks."

"Hippies, maybe, but not freaks. I think hippies are pretty...groovy. They're with it, baby. They tune in, turn on, and drop acid. Make love, not Michael Bay movies, my flower child."

"Stop it," she said. She turned her face away from him and said, with some difficulty, "They have sex."

"And that's bad?"

"On the sofa? In the middle of the day? They walk around naked. The other day, I walked into the bathroom — the door was wide open, I figured it was unoccupied — and there's Dad sitting on the sink while Mom gives him...well...you know."

"A pedicure?"

"They were naked. They're always naked. I can't have any friends over because their idea of dressing for company is throwing a towel over their genitals. And even then, Dad's dick is always hanging out." She said the word "dick" the same way she might say, "Grandpa's colostomy bag."

"Yeah, that sounds a little too...natural for me."

"And they're always stoned. Naked and stoned. Letting it all hang out."

"Stoned isn't so bad."

"Hey, I've got nothing against anybody getting stoned. I don't smoke pot, but I don't mind if others do. It's a lot different, though, when the pot's in a plate of brownies Mom made and put on the coffee table like a bowl of peanuts. You know what it's like to have a friend over and then spend the whole evening thinking, Gee, I hope Mom doesn't offer Brett a hit off the bong tonight. When my parents leave town, the last thing they tell me before going is to take care of their marijuana plants. They're more worried about those than about me. I hate them, Adam."

Adam shrugged. "Maybe you're being a little hard on them. Like I said, I hate my dad. He's like this big rectum on two legs. But eighteen's a few years behind me, and I'm still living there. I guess there are things in life we all have to live with, you know?"

"One of these days, I'm gonna quietly snap, and I'm gonna get the biggest knife in the kitchen, and I'm gonna stab each of them as many times as I've wished they'd used a rubber."

"And leave me without a date?"

Alyssa turned to him and smiled. "Is this a date? Where are we going?"

"I don't know. Anywhere you want."

"Take me to my house so I can get my contacts."

"I think the glasses are sexy," Adam said with enthusiasm.

"Cut it out."

"I'm serious. They're very sexy. But they make it hard to see your eyes. I prefer to see your eyes."

She smirked and said, "You're just being nice."

Adam's surprise came out as laughter. "No! I'm serious. Your eyes…" Words got clogged together in his throat and he had to gulp them back down. He had never said such things out loud, not to mention *to* anyone. "You have beautiful eyes. They make me feel…I don't know, like touching you. And not just your body, I mean, there's something about your eyes that makes me want to reach into them. And touch you inside."

Alyssa stared at him curiously for a long time as he drove. Something was happening behind her eyes. Adam could tell, even through the glasses.

"Pull over." She turned her body toward him, tucked her legs beneath her in the seat.

"What?"

"Pull the car over."

"Where?"

"Anywhere, I don't care, just pull it over now."

Adam pulled the car over at a bus stop and shifted to Park. A sign warned that the spot was for buses only and no parking was permitted at any time. He turned as Alyssa's eyes closed in on his quickly. She held his face between her hands and kissed him very gently at first, small kisses, over and over. The kisses grew in intensity until her open mouth stayed on his. She continued to hold his face in her hands, stroked his eyelashes with the pads of her thumbs. Finally, she pulled back, just a little, and looked into his eyes with something that resembled desperation in hers.

"It was so, so wonderful of you to say that," she whispered.

"I didn't say it for points, Alyssa. I mean it. I could…" *Maybe you should quit while you're ahead,* he thought, but went on. "I could sit here and look into your eyes for hours. For…ever. If…if only we weren't parked at a bus stop."

"Oh. Then we should skate."

She started to pull away, but he did not let her. He kissed her again, then held her tightly, chin resting on her shoulder. On the sidewalk, a homeless man wearing filthy rags stood beside the bus kiosk. He held a sign that read,

LOST JOB, HOME—
WILL DOCTOR SCRIPTS FOR FOOD.

The homeless man watched them. When his eyes met Adam's, he slowly lifted his right arm, extended his fist, and stuck his thumb skyward.

"What would you like to do?" Adam asked when they were back on the road.

"How about a movie?"

"Sounds good to me."

"Or we could go back to the bookstore and kill my parents."

Adam tried to laugh, but it sounded like he was clearing his throat instead.

Smirking, Alyssa said, "Then we could go take care of your dad. And then...we could just run away."

"Run away where?" he asked, his mouth dry.

"Anywhere! Everywhere! Just hit the road and ride. Just travel the country and save others from weird asshole parents. Like Martin Sheen and Sissy Spacek in *Badlands*.

"Yeah! Or Julia Roberts and Hugh Grant in *Notting Hill*. Or...no, wait..." Alyssa laughed and he was relieved to change the subject. "What kind of movie do you want to see?"

"Let's go home and get my contacts. We can call from there for showtimes. I'm in the mood to eat popcorn and hold hands in the dark."

"Hey, if it's dark, why stop with hands?"

She touched a fingertip to his lips. "Good question."

On the way home, Adam stopped at a florist and spent some of his dad's money on a dozen red roses to be delivered to Alyssa at the bookstore. Then he stopped for a carton of frozen yogurt and went home.

The garages were closed, so he could not tell who was home. Inside, he went to the kitchen, where he found Mrs. Yu in the breakfast nook, a newspaper spread open on the table next to a steaming mug. Smoke curled from the cigarette held between her thin lips.

Adam pointed a finger at her and gasped loudly. "Mrs. Yu! Shame on you, Mrs. Yu!"

Mrs. Yu took the cigarette from her mouth, laughed and shook her head. "You funny."

"I've never seen you smoke before." He put the the bags on the table, took a seat.

"Becah yo fadduh no ret anybody smoke inna house. Missy Jurian, she light abou dat. Missa Jurian jus gonna haffa get used to some tings. I too old be smokin' beside swimmy poo."

Adam's laughter echoed off the surfaces of the kitchen. "How would you like a bowl of strawberry frozen yogurt?" He took the carton from the bag, put it on the table.

Mrs. Yu picked it up as she put down her cigarette and stood.

"No, no, Mrs. Yu, I'll get it for you."

"Oh, no. No sugar for me, doctor say."

Adam scooped some of the yogurt into a bowl, put the carton in the freezer and returned to the table. "Is Gwen around?"

"Missy Jurian go shopping. I rike Missy Jurian, she nice. I haffa give her exla dessuht."

Adam took his books and frozen yogurt upstairs. At the landing, just before he turned right to go to his room, he glanced absently down the hall to the left. Did a double take when he saw a flash of the bright, sworled colors of a Missile Pop rounding the corner at the end of the hall. Frowning, he went to his room.

Gwen was shopping. Dad was at work. Mrs. Yu was downstairs and it was the wrong day for any upstairs cleaning. The only other person it could have been was Rain.

He sat at his desk and tried to do some writing while he ate the frozen yogurt.

What would Rain be doing in Michael's bedroom? It was the only room past the corner on that side of the house, so if she went around the corner, that was where she was headed. It was Gwen's room as well, but Adam did not think that excuse would go over with his dad. Michael Julian fiercely guarded the privacy of his bedroom.

As a child, Adam had gone into his parents' bedroom only when he knew his dad was not around and his mother was with him. He used to love watching her brush her hair at the vanity. Sometimes she would put the music box that contained Grandma's jewelry on the floor and let him carefully examine the pieces. The jewelry box played "Lara's Theme" from *Dr. Zhivago*. Whenever he heard it now, Adam thought not of Julie Christie and Omar Sharif, but of the colorful, sparkling jewelry that had been worn by his mom's mother. Sometimes, Mom would lie down on the floor with him and tell him stories about some of the pieces. A couple times, she had brought out an old photo album filled with pictures of Grandma and Grandpa. Adam had tried to find some of the pieces of jewelry in the snapshots, but was distracted by the faces. They were all hard, unsmiling faces. Everyone in those old pictures looked as if someone had just said something that deeply offended them, and like they weren't going to forget about it anytime soon.

His dad had sometimes surprised them by coming home unexpectedly. "How many times have I gotta tell you, I don't want the Goddamned kid fucking around in my room!" Depending on his mood, he would kick or hit Adam, and Adam would leave the room in one of three ways: he would crawl, be dragged, or picked up and thrown out. Usually, his dad had dragged him out by the hair.

Michael Julian guarded his bedroom as if it contained his entire fortune. It did not, of course. But a small chunk of it was kept in a floor safe under the desk in his office, which he did not guard at all. Adam had been stealing marijuana, liquor, and money from his dad's office since he was a little kid. The safe, which was always packed with bundles of cash of varying amounts, had been his livelihood. His dad never gave him money, because Adam never asked for it. He just went to the safe and took it. He was never greedy and only took what he needed, and never made a visible dent in the safe's money. Michael had caught him red-handed a couple times, but was so delighted to see Adam poking around in his office—probably hoping a desire to write screenplays would rub off—he never seemed to notice.

Adam finished the yogurt and left his desk. He did not care if Rain got caught in the master bedroom, but Gwen would be the one to take the heat for it.

He went down the hall, past the stairs to the other end, around the corner. The door of the master bedroom stood open a few inches. It was always locked, so either Rain had stolen her mother's key or picked her way in.

Inside, he looked around cautiously. Gwen's cavernous walk-in closet was open and the light was on inside. In the closet, Adam found Rain sitting on the floor, an open cardboard box on her lap. She was going through its contents, mostly papers and folders and fat envelopes.

"Excuse me, but what are you doing in here?" Adam asked.

"Oh, hi, Mr. Douglas. Tree still up your butt?"

"You know what my dad would do if he found you in here?"

"Give me a spanking?"

"You'd wish. Come on, let's go."

"This is my mom's stuff I'm going through, not your dad's."

"Doesn't matter. You're in the room. How did you get in here, anyway?"

She put a lid on the box and tucked it away on a bottom shelf. Standing, Rain said, "Locks don't stop me, Big Brother. Get used to it."

"Come on, I'm serious. Out."

"You're afraid of him, aren't you?" she asked, cocking her head to one side. She looked him up and down, smiling. "And here I thought you had a tree up your ass. You're just afraid of Daddy." She left the closet.

Adam turned off the light, almost closed the bedroom door, but remembered the lock. Reached around to the doorknob on the other side and pushed the button in the center.

"Fuck that kind of thinking," Rain said as they went back down the hall.

"What kind of thinking?"

"Being afraid of your dad."

"You said that, I didn't. I'm not afraid of my dad. I think he's pathetic. Catch me in the right mood and I might pity him. But I'm not afraid of him." *Not anymore*, he thought.

"Then why play policeman?"

"Because I know my dad and that's one thing that makes him go all Carrie. I'm just trying to keep the peace, because for now, I live here. What were you doing in there, anyway?"

"The usual. Looking to see if Mom had any money or pot or pills I could take. Hey, why don't you—" Rain stopped in front of her closed bedroom door, but Adam kept going. "Hey. C'mon in."

"No, thanks."

"Then I'll come to your room."

Adam sighed as she laughed. She opened the bedroom door and went inside. Not wanting her in his room, Adam followed her and said, "Okay, but just for a couple minutes."

The bedroom looked like CNN footage of a tornado's aftermath.

"Did your luggage explode?" Adam asked.

"Mom told me to unpack. She didn't say anything about putting shit away. So, Big Brother, why do you live here?"

Still looking around the room, he shrugged. "Because it's convenient for now. Don't you have any posters or pictures? Bare walls are so depressing."

"What the fuck do I look like, a little kid?"

"As a matter of fact, you do." He meant it.

Rain wore a tie-dyed tank top with *Austin Powers 2: The Spy Who Shagged Me* written over her left breast, denim cut-offs, and nothing on her tiny feet. With no makeup, she looked her age—a cute sixteen-year-old blonde, tanned, smiling, all-American California girl. But she wore it like a pair of shoes. No matter how perfectly they fit and matched everything she owned, they would never, ever be a part of her body.

"Close the door," Rain said.

"I'm not staying."

"Fine, but close the fucking door until you go, okay?"

Adam closed the door.

Rain rested a hand on her hip. Her eyebrows rose high over her eyes and her mouth opened as if she were laughing, but didn't make a sound. "Shit, man, somebody's trained you well, Mr. Douglas!" she said.

Adam smiled. "You told me to close it, so I closed it. No big deal." He took a steadying breath and asked, "Any particular reason you wanted me to come in here?"

"Yes, there was a reason, Big Brother." The tie-dyed tank top was gone before she finished her sentence, and her cut-offs were open and on their way down her legs as she walked toward him.

"No, uh-uh," Adam said as he turned and opened the door. "No more of that." The knob slipped from his hand when Rain threw herself against the door and slammed it shut.

She leaned back against the door wearing nothing, and smiled up at him. "What board meeting are you late for, Mr. Douglas?"

"Could you *please* do me a favor and call me Adam? My name is Adam. Not Mr. Douglas. Not Big Brother. *Adam*."

"Shit. You gonna sue me now?"

"I'd just appreciate it if you'd call me—"

"You don't like me, do you, Adam?"

"Hey, I didn't say that, I don't even know you well enough to know if I—"

"But you liked fucking me, didn't you?"

Adam stopped talking. He watched as Rain tilted her head back and swept the tip of her tongue back and forth over the bottom of her smile. Cocked a leg and pressed the bare sole of her foot to the door. Even that single, simple act oozed with wet, sticky sexuality.

"Didn't you? Adam."

He folded his arms over his chest. "I did, yes. It was…pretty amazing. I still may have to notify my insurance company, I'm not sure yet, but it was amazing."

"And you'd like to fuck me again, wouldn't you?"

"I'd have to be brain-dead not to. But we can't do it again, because it's going to lead to nothing but misery and pain and ugly scenes you don't want to see, trust me."

"I'm not gonna be makin' any scenes."

"I'm not talking about you. I'm talking about everybody else. If we keep fooling around, it won't be long before everybody knows. It's a big house, but it's not *that* big. Can you imagine what'll happen then? The yelling and fighting and crying that'll go on past Christmas?"

Rain kicked a path through the clothes and towels and underwear on the floor and sat on an old cedar chest at the foot of her bed. The chest had belonged to Adam's mom, who had gotten it from her mom. Rain patted the empty space beside her on the cedar chest.

Adam smiled and shook his head.

"You can trust me, Adam," she said.

"No, I can't trust you. Or myself. Could you put some clothes on?"

Delighted laughter sprang from Rain as her face brightened. She pointed at the firm mound in Adam's jeans next to the fly. "Look who showed up!"

"Yeah, well, he can't stay, either." Adam opened the door.

"Wait, wait! I'll put something on." She searched the floor, snatched something up and slipped it on—a silver terrycloth robe that fell mid-thigh and seemed to hang on her crookedly. There was something heavy in the right pocket.

"Something?" Adam asked. "That's hardly anything at all."

"How old were you when your dad started hitting you?" Rain crossed her legs properly and sat with her palms pressed flat to the cedar, elbows locked.

Adam leaned back against the door. "I don't know. But it wasn't always hitting. Sometimes he kicked me, dragged me around by my hair. Can you believe that? Even when he was beating a little kid, the son of a bitch fought like a girl."

"Fought like a girl? You don't know what the fuck you're talking about."

"What do you mean?"

"You're right, the guy fights like a pussy, but not like a *girl*. You've never seen girls fight because we only do it when you're not around.

It's ugly and bloody and people get hurt. Fought like a girl, my ass. You know what I'd do in your position?"

"The thought of asking terrifies me," Adam said.

"I'd wait for the right time, when Mom was out of the house, and he'd find me masturbating naked on his bed. I'd get him on the bed, give him head, and then I'd bite off his cock. I'd smile at him while he bled to death. Tell him it's not such a good idea to go around pullin' people's hair, is it? Then I'd make it look like Mom did it and get *that* miserable cunt outta my life. Two turds with one boner."

"That wouldn't work for me," he said.

"Why not?"

He laughed. "I can hear it now. 'Hey, Dad, let's watch a game together. Or go shoot some hoops. Or…I know! Your favorite—I could give you a blow job!' Uh-uh. He'd kill me. He's not into that, anyway."

"How do you know? You don't know what the fuck he's into. He might take you up on it, ever think of that? Yeah, he might jump on it." She smirked. "Bet that'll fuck with your head for a few days. Don't ever think you know what kinda sexual shit people are into, because you don't. You only know what they want you to know. Most people, if they know they won't get caught and nobody will ever find out, will do fucking *anything* if it looks like it'll feel good. I say use what you got when you need to. If it ain't their thing, maybe it'll stir up a little heat they didn't know they had in 'em." She grinned.

There isn't a jury in the land that would convict me of statutory rape, Adam thought, shaking his head. *No matter how solid the prosecution's proof of her age,* no *one would believe she's only sixteen.*

"Well, even if he was into it," Adam said, "I'm not."

"Don't know until you try it."

"Try it? Is that how you found your sexual identity, Rain? Fuck a few girls, a few guys, maybe a German shepherd or two, see which one makes you squirt harder?"

Rain shrugged.

"Is there no end to your decadence, Rain?"

"No end to my *what?* Speak fuckin' English, will ya?"

"Nothing. Never mind."

"I bet you've wanted to kill him, haven't you? You've thought about it."

"Would you really bite his dick off?"

"If I had to. Most people'd do anything if they really had to."

"No offense, Rain, but...you're not like most people. And most people aren't like you."

"That's what my fuckin' mother says. I think you're a couple of shit-for-brains Teletubbies. You're livin' in Fantasyland, ridin' through 'It's A Small World' over and over."

Adam pushed himself away from the door and slipped four fingers of each hand into the back pockets of his jeans. Walked slowly toward her, trying not to step on any of her clothes. "Why do you hate your mother so much?" he asked as he sat beside her on the cedar chest.

"The fuck do you care? You gonna try to fix me? Please, Adam, be anything you want, but don't be one of those whiiining, booorrring assholes who wants to heal all my wounds so he won't feel guilty when he finally fucks me. They're *so* predictable."

"I'm just curious. I like your mother. I can't figure out what she's doing with my dad."

"You only think you like my mother, and I know *exactly* what she's doing with your dad." She turned toward him, put both feet up on the cedar chest and hugged her knees. "She's shopping. Planning her future. Which doesn't include him."

"Why would she do that?" he said. "If she was after money, she could've done a hell of a lot better than my dad."

"Maybe she's done it before and has more money than she needs already. Ever think of that? Maybe she's got a shitload of dead-husband money packed away and she just wants more. *Wants* it, doesn't need it."

"Well, you should know if she's done it before. She's your mother."

Rain nodded. "I do know."

Adam frowned. "You mean...are you saying she *has* done it before?"

She nodded again.

He did not believe it. Nodded with eyelids half-closed in a *yeah-sure* expression.

"Four times. Twice before she had me. All rich. She's got quite a nest egg put away. A great big Tyrannosaurus Rex nest egg. Might even retire after she's done with your dad."

"So, that would make the second rich man your father? Or...wait. The third?"

"I don't know who my fuckin' father is, and neither does she."

There was a perfectly natural casualness to her tone that bothered Adam. It gave her words a note of truth.

"When I was little, she took my pediatrician for free appointments and a discount on my tonsilectomy. And she didn't even have to. We could afford it."

"How'd she do that?"

Rain lowered her head. Her eyes crinkled up a little as she smiled behind her knees. "You're so fuckin' cute when you're dense. She fucked the pediatrician, Adam, what do you think?"

"No offense, but that's pretty hard to believe, Rain."

"Believe whatever you want. Just tellin' you what I know."

"How do you know?"

"I noticed Mom never went up to the window to pay like everybody else. After my tonsils were taken out, I went in for a check-up. Dr. Petrie came into the examination room, said hi to me, then took my mother's arm, and they were gone. Didn't take long before I was bored, so I left the room and walked down the hall to the next door. It was another examination room. I went in and it looked empty at first, but someone was breathing heavy, y'know? Huffin', puffin', ready to pop off a big one. They were behind one of those folding dividers, but I could see their fuzzy shadows. She was on her knees and her head was bouncin' like a ball. Up and down."

Rain rested her head face-down between her knees. The room became deafeningly silent.

Maybe it was true. If it were, though—if Gwen had been married before and her husbands had died—Adam had heard only one side of it, and that from a bratty, unstable child. It did not mean Gwen had actually murdered them. Rain would probably tell him her mother had killed JonBenet Ramsey if it would get him on her side. Part of him felt sorry for her, though. Life was hard enough on its own without going through it with a you're-either-for-me-or-against-me attitude toward everyone else on the planet.

Adam said, "Well, I like her."

"Does that mean you're not gonna help me kill her?" Rain asked.

"You're crazy." His erection had not gone away, and Adam was furious with his penis.

Rain lifted a bra from the floor on her toe. It dangled for a moment, then dropped. "You know what you need?"

"More manageable hair?"

"You need to go out with me tonight."

"What would that accomplish? Besides a possible appearance on *Cops*."

"Might accomplish more than you think. Might wake you up. Bring you back to life."

"I'm not dead," Adam said, standing.

She smiled. "Not yet."

He stepped toward the door. "Thanks for the tour of your dwellings. I'm sure FEMA will be on it in no time."

Rain bounced off the cedar chest, stepped in front of him. "Oh, no you don't. I've been good long enough. Now I want to play." She untied her belt and the robe fell open.

Adam looked at her for a moment. Small round breasts, smooth, tanned skin. His jeans got tighter between his legs. He grabbed the lapels of her robe and pulled it closed. "No. I told you that's not going to happen again."

Wearing a beautiful, sparkling smile, Rain reached into the right pocket of her robe and removed a Smith and Wesson LadySmith revolver, a snubnosed .38 Special with a scaled-down grip for the gun-totin' lady's smaller, more delicate hand. Touched the tip of the barrel to the little furrow beneath his nose and said, "Take off your clothes."

Adam's veins clenched. His bloodflow diminished. His vision darkened and he was afraid he would pass out.

Rain laughed. "You look funny with your eyes crossed like that. Now take your fuckin' clothes off, Big Brother."

Deciding it was not an ideal time to remind Rain not to call him that, Adam took off his shirt and tossed it onto the cedar chest.

Rain said, "C'mon. Everything."

"I...I can't take my pants off standing up with...with that, um...that thing in my face. Gun, that gun."

She stepped back, but still pointed the gun at him.

Adam did not want to take off his jeans. His penis remained erect, ignoring him, paying no attention to the adrenalin and fear. It seemed, however, that both of his testicles had hidden among the lobes of his lungs. He quickly removed shoes, jeans, boxers. Once free, his penis aimed slightly upward at Alyssa, prepared to return fire should she discharge her weapon.

"You've got such a friendly cock!" Rain said. "I like it when a cock remembers me."

Sitting on the cedar chest to remove his socks, Adam was struck by something that should have been obvious immediately. He thought of everything that would happen to Rain if she shot him, whether she killed him or not. And he knew.

"You're not going to shoot me," he said. Suddenly, she looked ridiculous, standing there with her robe open, holding a gun. "That probably isn't even loaded."

"Wanna try me?" Rain asked. Her grin was joyous, but she frowned at the same time. It looked almost as if she were transforming into something else. Something not so pretty. The expression bled her face of its beauty. "Come on, you wanna fuckin' find out if it's loaded, Mr. Douglas?" She held the gun with both hands now.

Adam stood as he said, "You know damned well you'd get caught if you shot me, and you don't do anything that might get you caught. You like to pretend you're such a bad girl, hot shit, sooo tough, but not tough enough to steal so much as chewing gum if there's a chance you could be caught." He took his jeans from the floor, lifted a knee to put them on. "So there's no way you'll—"

The gunshot was not as loud as Adam had expected, but it was not quiet. He dropped the jeans, bent at the waist and covered his head with both arms as something broke behind him. He did not move for awhile, just stood that way, arms over his head, staring at the floor. Rain laughed hysterically as her robe dropped around her bare feet. Ears ringing loudly, Adam craned his head around to look under his arm. Behind him, on top of the headboard of the guest bed, stood a ceramic clown holding three balloons on strings. The clown's head was gone, and red, blue, and white bits of it were scattered over the oak finish. There was a tiny hole in the wall behind the bed.

Still laughing, Rain said, "Shit! That was *too* fuckin' funny."

Adam stood and lowered his arms slowly. The ringing in his ears continued, but the fear that had tensed his muscles turned to anger. "Funny?" he croaked. "You little shit, you could've killed me!"

"We're not done yet." She put the round tip of the gun's barrel into Adam's navel and moved it in tiny circles. "On the bed. On your back."

He did as he was told, amazed and more than a little disturbed by his erection's persistence. It throbbed in the face of death, leaked fluids at gunpoint. It knew exactly what it wanted and was not going away till it was satisfied. But Adam did not want to have sex with Rain, especially while she had a loaded gun in hand.

Once he was on the bed, she crawled spider-like toward him. Kept the gun on him at all times, finger curled loosely around the trigger, as she crawled up his body and straddled him. As she slid down his erection, Adam gasped and Rain said, "Don't move. Just lay there, 'kay?"

Adam had no intention of moving. His eyes followed the gun everywhere. Winced whenever the metal touched his skin. With each position the gun took, Adam calculated where the bullet would enter his body.

Rain experimented, first moving up and down, then grinding in slow, hard circles against him. She smiled and breathed, "Oh, yeah," and continued the movement for awhile, eyes closed.

The side of the gun pressed against his chest as she leaned her weight on it for a moment. The bullet would have entered his head beneath his jaw, or maybe gone into his throat. She lifted the gun, and for a few seconds, had she fired, it would have pierced Adam's heart.

Her body's motion moved him within her. Adam felt the sensation all the way down his legs and up into his abdomen. Tried to ignore it as he watched the black, dead eye of the gun. It slid down over his belly, and Rain directed the short barrel into the small patch of fine, light hair between her thighs. Between the two small fleshy mounds beneath it.

Seconds passed before Adam realized Rain was rubbing the gun's barrel over her clitoris as she moved on him. Masturbating with a loaded handgun. Tiny chips of ice tumbled through his veins and gooseflesh rose on the back of his neck.

"Here's what we're gonna do," Rain whispered. As she spoke, her voice sometimes became a shaky whisper.

Adam's eyes having assumed dinnerware proportions, he watched the gun move up and down through tightly-curled hair to which clung beads of moisture. Each time it moved downward, the barrel pressed against him just above the base of his penis. If Rain pulled the trigger, Adam hoped he would die instantly. Death would be preferrable to life with maimed genitalia. Of course, Rain was more likely to shoot herself in the vagina. The way Adam saw it, that would not be his problem.

"You're gonna help me kill Mom," Rain went on. "But we're gonna kill both of them. An extra bonus for you, Big Brother." When she said "Big Brother," she squeezed his penis hard inside her.

Adam gasped, his eyes rolled back in his head and closed. Inside, Rain was a soft, hot, wet fist with a steel grip. He forced his eyes open, looked down at the gun. Still there, poking him, black metal glistening. But something else, something new. Finger still on the trigger, Rain's hand was developing a tremor. "Then we'll be orphans, Big Brother," she continued. "Just you and me. And their money."

If he tried to speak, Adam knew he would sound like a choking goose. It was becoming difficult to pull his attention away from the waves of sensation passing through him. He trembled in spite of his efforts to remain rigid, unmoving.

"No arguments," Rain whispered. "No bullshit. Otherwise...you know what happens."

Adam wanted to tell her to shut up, but if he opened his mouth, he would cry out in pleasure.

"Don't worry, Big Brother. We're gonna be friends." She moved to kiss him, but he turned his head away. "You'll like me once you get to know me. And, we start tonight at ten."

Rain squeezed him harder as she ground on him. A growl started deep in her chest. She slapped a hand onto the right side of Adam's ribcage and dug her nails into his skin, as if to clutch the ribs beneath and hold on for the ride.

Adam cried, "Ow, Goddammit!"

Rain did not hear him. She was lost in her orgasm, growling, clawing Adam's flesh. She stopped the circular motion and began to pound herself onto him repeatedly. Her nipples became a blur as her breasts bounced. She moved the gun barrel faster over her clitoris and her chin jutted, revealing her lower teeth. Eyes snapped open wide as she screamed.

"Will you be quiet!" Adam said in a dry, broken voice. With Rain jumping up and down on him like an enraged monkey, Adam realized there was no chance he was not going to come. "Goddammit, will you stop that!" he said raggedly when she clawed him again. He tried to move her hand, but felt something warm and slick on his skin. While Rain began to calm down, Adam looked down at himself. Blood was smeared over his ribs, on Rain's hand and her left breast.

By the time Rain stopped moving on him, Adam's penis was harder than ever and ready to explode. But she did not seem to be finished with him yet. Holding him inside her, she leaned forward and kissed him. Sucked his cheeks into his mouth so hard, the outline of his teeth became visible on his face.

Rain pulled off of his mouth, clamped her teeth on his neck and sucked hard.

A hickey, Adam thought, barely able to make out his thoughts among the thunderous throbs of his heart. *She can't give me a hickey!* "No!" he shouted and pushed her away.

Rain's mouth made a wet sucking sound when it pulled from his neck. She sat up a bit and smiled as she put the gun to his left temple. "Wanna fuck me on top, Big Brother? Let's roll." She rolled first, pulling him with her. He followed her clumsily and flopped onto her like a seal. She wrapped her legs around his waist and nudged his head with the gun. "C'mon, we don't have all fuckin' day," she said.

He pushed himself off her slowly. "N-no, no, really, I-I'm fine, I really should go." He stopped moving when she pressed the end of the barrel to his temple hard enough to hurt.

"You think I give a fuck about you?" she asked, voice raising. "*I'm* not finished yet. Now start fucking, or tell me where you want the bullet."

Those last words — *the bullet* — made Adam's throat constrict for a moment, and he felt a surge of nausea in his stomach. At that moment, he realized with relief that his erection was retreating. He was no good to her limp.

"Oh, fuck," she said angrily. Inside, she squeezed him repeatedly, and within seconds he was hard again.

Adam raised himself up on his arms, out of breath with no exertion, sweating without heat. He slid in and out a few times, hard but half-hearted.

"Goddammit!" Rain shouted, and on the word "dammit," she slapped his face hard. It was almost as loud as the gunshot. "What the fuck're you, a Hallmark card?"

One side of Adam's face burst into invisible flames. He thought there was a chance she had knocked a molar loose. Suddenly angry again, he got on his knees, pulled her legs off him and pushed her knees back to her shoulders. He slammed into her hard and fast.

"Yeah…yeah," Rain said. She reached out for his chest, fingers bent, nails searching for nipples. Adam slapped her hand away and thrust harder.

Something thunked onto the floor beside the bed, something heavy, and Adam turned his half-open eyes to the left. Rain's right hand was empty. She had dropped the gun off the bed. Adam reached in that direction, but could not stop pounding into her.

Rain saw what he was doing and croaked, "No, no, wait." She grabbed his reaching arm, dug in her nails.

That angered Adam enough to stop moving his hips and slide off her. All he could see on the floor were clothes, no gun. But it was there somewhere.

"Wait, Goddammit!" Rain shouted. Then she hissed through clenched teeth, *"Finish!"*

He leaned over the edge of the bed, left hand probing the tangle of clothes.

Rain closed her hand on some of his hair and pulled him toward her hard.

The sting of his scalp as she pulled his hair was an unpleasantly familiar sensation. Adam was on his knees again instantly. His right arm whipped around fast and the back of his fist struck Rain's face. He regretted it immediately, but she pulled his hair again, harder as she laughed. He hit her again, with his palm this time, and she laughed some more.

"Finish," Rain said.

He did. Later, he would hurt from pounding so hard, but all he wanted at the moment was to finish. He was closing in on that powerful release when Rain violently pulled his hair again. He slapped her again. "Stop it, Goddammit, or I'm gonna—"

She pulled again. Adam swung his arm back and forth, struck her with each arc. He did not know how many times. They came together, loudly, with Adam's hands on her breasts, squeezing, crushing them in his fists.

When he rolled off Rain, he got off the bed and onto his feet. Walking in a slow, small circle, he inspected his wounds. There was a lot of blood but it came from nothing more than scratches. The blood alone made him woozy. "I must be out of my Goddamned mind," he muttered to himself.

"Don't blame yourself, Adam."

He turned to her as she stood beside the bed, gun in hand. There was some swelling and discoloration around the outer corner of her left eye and her cheeks were bright red.

"I had a gun on you. Remember?" She waved the gun around a little and grinned.

Putting his jeans on quickly, Adam said, "You know, people use words like 'insane' and 'crazy' all the time. Without even thinking about it, without ever really knowing what those words mean. But *I* know what they mean." He pointed at Rain angrily. "Because *you*…are fucking crazy. You are insane, you should probably be in a facility somewhere, not walking around free, you're a *menace!*"

"I thought this was pretty fuckin' nice," Rain said, shrugging. "Just what I needed. What's the matter, too rough for you?"

"Rough? In case you hadn't noticed, I'm bleeding where you tried to gut me like a kill!"

"Aawww, you gotta owie?" She bent down and kissed the bleeding wound, licked it. Sucked on it. When she stood, there was blood on her lips. Her tongue licked it off as if it were ice cream. "Mmm. I think I got most of the fuckin' body fluids covered. All that's left is for you to piss on me." She smiled.

"That's disgusting," Adam said. He didn't put his shirt on. He wanted to wait till he could wash off the blood.

"Time for you to go, Adam," Rain said, moving closer to him. "It's my bedroom this time. Don't forget. Ten o'clock. Your car."

"I've got other plans."

"Oh, would you cut that shit out? You know how easily I could fuck you up for life today? I mean, this *afternoon?* All I have to do is go to the cops, tell them I was raped by my step-brother, and give 'em a fuckin' sample of your boybutter I got bubbling in me right now, you'd be in jail before dinner. You think your dad's gonna pay the bail? What *would* he do, anyway?"

"You won't do anything like that if you need me to help kill your mother."

"I didn't say I needed you, I said we're doing it *together*," she snapped. "I don't fuckin' need anybody. You're replaceable, Adam. But I like you a lot. I really do." She kissed him. It was another of those kisses that loosened his fillings and shortened his hair.

"Hey, hey," he said as he pulled away from her. "Have you ever kissed anyone without severing the brainstem?"

"What? Whatta you mean?"

"Well, when you kiss, you don't have to *suck* so hard. I think you put a kink in my uvula."

Rain laughed. "So how the fuck'm I supposed to kiss?"

"Well, you just…just…" *What am I doing?* Adam wondered. *Being in this room is dangerous. Hell, being in this* house *is dangerous.*

"Just go ahead and kiss however you want." He turned and went to the door.

Rain followed him, saying, "Show me!"

Standing in the doorway, Adam turned to her slowly. "If I show you…do I still have to go out with you tonight?"

She frowned. "What the fuck do you mean, course you're still goin' out with me tonight. Quit being such a prick and relax a little, would you? Don't worry, you're gonna have fun."

He left the room and started down the hall wearily. Shirt wadded in a ball in his hand. "I'll show you later."

ELEVEN

Dude, *when* . . . did your life turn into a V.C. Andrews novel?"
Carter said. He stared across the desk at Adam as if he had never seen
him before, jaw slack.

They sat facing each other at an old partners desk that had occupied the attic for as long as they could remember. Adam had told him
all about Rain, and Carter had quickly forgotten the issue of *Fangoria*
open before him.

"I like to think my life is written better than a V.C. Andrews novel,"
Adam replied.

"Maybe written better, but still trashy as hell. And definitely paperback."

"What am I going to do? I mean…I can't go to Gwen about it."

"Why not?"

"Are you high?" Adam said. "She'd go ballistic if I told her I was—
look, can you imagine me saying to Gwen, 'Rain made me have sex
with her at gunpoint this afternoon, could you have a talk with her?'
Think she'd believe something like that?"

"Hey, she might! Sounds like your story might not surprise her."

"She'd kill me.

"Look, if anybody's gonna kill you, my money's on the underage
chick."

"Rain."

"Yeah, whatever." He shook his head. "Who the hell names a kid Rain? What kind of sick bastards would do that? Was her father a weatherman, or something? I think I'm more upset about you boning a woman who would name her daughter Rain than about you boning an underaged psychoslut."

"Look, Carter, I know my situation may be funny from a certain distance, but I'm in the middle of it, okay? I really need you to be serious."

"I *am* serious!" Carter said. "She should sue her parents for that shit. Naming her after weather." He shook his head, looked down at the magazine.

Adam felt fidgety. He stood and wandered around the studio, looked at the strange objects on the shelves. "What am I going to do, Carter?"

"You're asking me?" Carter blurted. "I just found out about all this sordid shit, I need a little time to digest all the details, man, that's a three-part miniseries at least. Probably ABC."

Adam sighed as he stared back at a human face with skin that had been eaten away. Carter had researched the flesh-eating virus, printed up some pictures from the internet. He had done a great job, too. Adam never ceased to be amazed by Carter's talent. But at the moment, he was getting angry with him.

"What part of 'I'm in serious trouble' don't you understand, Carter?" Adam asked with an exasperated swing of his arms as he went back to the desk. Hands flat on the desktop, he leaned toward Carter. "If she goes to the police, I'm fornicated, my friend. I mean, if the jury finds me...what, Carter? What do you think the jury would find me?"

Carter looked at his friend with surprise and concern. He was uncertain if Adam expected a reply. "Well, I-I-I—"

"Even if they found me not guilty, that would be with me forever. You can't shake something like that. Statutory rape, jeez. Of course, being a free statutory rapist is better than being one in prison. I already have hemorrhoids, Carter, I wouldn't *survive* prison!"

"I'm sorry, I didn't know this was such a big deal with you, shit, I didn't mean to make fun of it. But think about it. Should you be takin' her this seriously, man? She's sixteen, for crying out loud. And obviously neurotic already. Maybe she's just a...I don't know, maybe she just likes to make trouble, you know? Like one of those soap opera vixens? Or maybe, hey, no offense, but maybe she just annoys the hell out of you and you're making her sound worse than she really is, you know what I mean?"

Adam ignored him, frowned as he went away for awhile into his own thoughts. After half a minute of silence, he asked, "You think mental illness would keep me out of prison if Rain turned me in?"

"Is that, like, a plan?" Carter said.

"It might be, I don't know. It just came to me."

Carter leaned back in his chair and put an ankle on his knee. "Maybe it would keep you out of prison. But you'd go into some kinda mental institution. You'd be in prison, what? Five years, probably less. Once they get you in one of those cuckoo's nests, though, they can keep you there till the day you turn into a great big pissed-off pre-casino American Indian who can lift a marble sink and throw it through the window. 'Bout how long you think that would take?"

Adam sighed. "Let's get out of here, go someplace. I'm antsy."

"Where you wanna go?"

"I don't care. Let's go to Creature Features, see if Wally's got anything new. You drive."

Carter brightened. "I get to drive your convertible?"

"No. Your car."

Carter's car was one of his dad's Mercedes. He drove them to Hollywood.

"There has to be another alternative," Adam said on the way. "Go to prison for a few years...go to a balloon factory for God knows how long, or...what? Everybody gets better choices than that. Sophie had better choices!"

"Oh, you've got another choice," Carter said. "But it would, you know...you'd have to, like...well, *you* know."

Carter looked at him, serious and unsmiling. Adam knew what he meant, and it surprised him. Carter was letting him know that considering it was not so bad. And actually doing it might be...negotiable. The very thought made Adam dizzy. And it was not an entirely bad kind of dizzy.

"Jeez, you sick bastard, you did it again," Carter said. "Got me caught up in one of your stories."

"It's not a story, Carter."

"You tell it like one. Look, man, I'm not saying I don't believe you, I'm just saying I know how you get when somebody pisses you off. "

"How many times do I have to tell you? This is not just how I perceived her. She makes the girl in *The Bad Seed* look like Cindy Brady."

"But don't you think it's a little unfair that I don't know this girl? I mean, you're telling me all this stuff about her, and I haven't even met her."

"Unfair? You should get on your knees and thank God you haven't met her!" Adam spotted an opportunity and grabbed it up. "You want to meet her tonight?"

Shrugging, Carter said, "Sure."

"So you'll come with us?"

"Come with you where? On your date? What planet is your dealer from, Adam? Huh? You strung out on pangalactic gargleblasters, or something?"

"I'm serious. I don't want to go alone with her, and you're right, you should meet her."

"What if she doesn't want me to go?"

"So what?"

"If she's carrying a fucking piece, man, I don't wanna—"

"If she's carrying a piece?" Adam interrupted.

"Huh?"

"You just said the words, 'If she's carrying a fucking piece, man.'"

"Well, yeah. So?"

"Who are you, Al Pacino?"

"No. But I still say DePalma's *Scarface* is a masterpiece, no matter *what* you say."

"Look, Carter, I don't know if she'll be, uh…carrying a piece, or packing heat, or whatever. But I think she might be safer with two of us there instead of just one."

"Think so?"

Adam nodded. "You might be saving my life, for all I know."

"I'll think about it."

In Hollywood, Carter parked in a public lot and they walked the remaining block to Creature Features Book and Video Emporium. When they walked in, a skull beside the door screamed as its eyes flickered red.

"Hi, guys!" Wally Kirk said from behind a row of glass display cases. He closed the register drawer, grinned, and a gold-capped front tooth gleamed.

Adam and Carter had been frequenting the store since they were in the sixth grade. Most of the genre movies and books they owned had been purchased there. They sometimes hung out in the store and talked movies and books with Wally even when they bought nothing.

"Where you guys been?" Wally asked. "Haven't seen you in a couple weeks."

Carter said, "Takes time to satisfy all the women in Los Angeles. We've been busy."

They went to the display case and looked down through the glass top at the merchandise inside: trading cards, buttons and key rings bearing logos of genre movies and TV shows, expensive pewter figures of characters from *Star Wars* and *Star Trek*.

"Anything new since we were here last, Wally?" Adam asked.

"You kidding? Lotsa stuff." He was fifty-nine, with unshaven steel-colored stubble on his round, chubby-cheeked face. His gray hair, shot with a few remaining streaks of black, was long and braided in back. He moved along the showcase and turned, dropped suddenly as he went down the ramp. What was left of him, the part he had brought back from Vietnam, was in a wheelchair. "C'mon over here. You guys're gonna love this. The horror movies of Herschell Gordon Lewis, all on DVD."

As they followed him to the DVD section, Carter said, "No shit? *2,000 Maniacs?*"

"All of 'em. *Blood Feast, Wizard of Gore,* they're all here."

Adam and Carter wore broad grins as they snatched DVDs from the shelves.

"Over here," Wally went on, wheeling the chair with thickly muscled, tattooed arms, "I got a digitally remastered *Conqueror Worm* under the original title, *The Witchfinder General.* The British version that was never released in America. And right here—" He took a DVD from the shelf, "—Oliver Stone's *The Hand,* with audio commentary by Stone and Michael Caine. Good commentary, too."

They were ecstatic, euphoric.

"There's a new T.M. Wright novel," Wally said. "Just arrived yesterday, in fact. And the new Stephen King, of course."

Adam checked his watch, which he was not wearing, as he asked, "A new King already? What time is it?"

They spent a few hundred dollars of their dads' money, and left the store with four plastic bags heavy with DVDs, novels, magazines, comic books, and toys.

Back in the car, Carter started the engine and pulled out of the lot. He asked, "You think, uh…well, I mean, if she's really like you say she is, you think she might, um, hit on me? Try to blackmail both of us?"

"Carter, I'm honestly surprised she hasn't nailed you already. She might do you in the backseat of the car while I drive."

"Are you shitting me?"

"I don't know, Carter, that's what I mean! She's completely unpredictable. Like a pit bull. One second it's licking the baby's face, next second it's eating the baby's face. I want you to see that, to see what she's like."

"I, uh…don't know if I want to."

Adam sighed and shook his head. "Don't bullshit me, Carter, I know you better than that. You've got such a hard-on to meet her, you couldn't stand up right now without popping your zipper."

Carter laughed. "Yeah, you're right."

Adam grinned and said, "Then come with me, dammit!"

Carter thought about it awhile. Turned on the radio and found some music. "Okay, but only on one condition."

"What? Anything."

"If weird shit starts to happen, or if my woman's intuition kicks in and I start feeling like weird shit is *about* to happen, I'm gone. You drop me off and I call for a car."

"Deal," Adam said. "No problemo, Kimosoggy."

"Then I'll go."

Adam's 1959 Cadillac Fleetwood convertible was the glossy color of a freshly-made candied apple, with a hungry-sounding V-8 engine ready to chew pavement, and fins on the back like the ones on the Batmobile in the old TV series starring Adam West. The black leather upholstery was pristine, and the original black top could not have been in better condition the day it was manufactured.

Although he did not like prolonged exposure to the sun, Adam was not immune to the siren's call of the convertible. It was heard loudest in Los Angeles, where everyone drove everywhere, freeways coiled and tangled above and beneath one another in the desert heat. In Los Angeles, where a drive to the grocery store is potentially an all-day event, a car is an integral part of life, a necessity rather than luxury. Adam discovered there was something at once exhilarating and deeply calming about driving a convertible. Especially around dusk, when the setting sun turned the dangerously high levels of deadly toxins in the air such lovely shades of red and purple.

The convertible was his father's way of assuaging his own guilt, of saying, *Look, Adam, I'm not sorry for anything I've said or done, but…here's a really cool expensive car for your birthday, okay?* Adam could live with that. But the convertible was a surprise. Something his mom would have been more likely to buy him, not his dad. He wondered if Gwen had been involved in the choice.

"This is not a car you take just *anywhere*," his dad had told him. "You don't know exactly where you're going? You take the Lexus. It's three years old and outta shape. Unless you're going someplace with a protected garage, or at *least* valet parking, leave the convertible at home. That car didn't come cheap. Anything happens to it, I'll drown you in the fucking pool like a sack of cats."

Adam had no intention of letting anything happen to the convertible. That was why he usually drove the Lexus. Going out with Rain would be no different than any other time.

"What?" Carter said as they walked through the main garage. "You're not taking the convertible? You mean I've gotta sit in that shitbucket Lexus again?"

"Yeah, I wanna go in the fuckin' convertible, Big Brother!" Rain said.

Carter and Rain walked several paces ahead of Adam, arm in arm. Adam had not turned on all the lights in the garage, and in the shadows, they looked like Laurel and Hardy without their bowlers.

The right side of Rain's face looked puffy, but any bruises she might have sustained from her time with Adam that day were invisible. He assumed she had covered them with makeup.

She had been flirting with Carter ever since Adam introduced them, and Carter flirted back, seemed to enjoy her company. Adam hoped his friend was keeping a clear head about everything. He had been warned.

Adam got into the car and opened the garage door with the remote clipped to the visor. On the other side, Carter and Rain decided who would sit where.

"You sit in the front, Carter," Rain said. "I love backseats."

"No, you're in front, Rain," Adam said.

She opened the passenger door, leaned in to give him a wicked smile. "You want me to sit up front with you, Big Brother?" she said with a wink.

"Actually, I don't want you behind me, okay?"

"Hey, that's no problem," Carter said, getting into the backseat.

Before they reached the gate, Rain found a radio station playing hardcore rap and turned it up loud. Adam stopped at the gate, killed the radio, turned to her.

"It's very important that you listen to what I'm about to say, Rain," he said. His index finger pointed rigidly upward between them. "If you are in a car that I'm driving, under no circumstances are you to tamper with the radio or the CD player. Don't even reach for it as *if* to tamper with it."

"Jeez, what's up your ass?" Rain said.

"Nothing," Carter said from the backseat. "He's always that way about the radio. He has an allergic reaction to rap."

As Adam drove on, Rain leaned toward him and puckered her mouth. She spoke through it in babytalk as she reached over and casually squeezed his genitals: "Poor widdoo *bay*-beee." Adam quickly slapped her hand away.

Rain leaned back in her seat and lowered her window. She wore a pair of red-framed wraparound sunglasses that matched the red of her lips. Short black skirt, tight purple sleeveless top. A small black bag hung from her shoulder by the loop of its long silver chain.

"It's after ten o'clock at night," Adam said. "Why are you wearing sunglasses?"

She smiled at him. "I like it dark."

"I think it's cool," Carter said. "It shows individuality. A refusal to conform. Those are admirable traits, Rain."

She turned around in her seat, got on her knees. "You think so, Carter?"

"Sure. You're a rebel. You don't accept the status quo. You're—"

"Rain, would you please sit down," Adam said. "And put on your seatbelt."

Rain turned to Adam slowly and glared. "I'm talking to Carter," she said, teeth clenched.

"Then I'm pulling over, because I'm not driving while you're sitting like that."

"Unfuckingbelievable," Rain said as she sat in the seat and put on her seatbelt. "I bet you go to church every Sunday and visit old people in rest homes, don'tcha, Mr. Douglas."

"Mr. *Douglas?*" Carter said. "What's up with that?"

Rain explained why she called Adam "Mr. Douglas," and Carter laughed. The more he thought about it, the harder he laughed. Pointed at Adam and said, "Fruh-Fred MacMurray!"

Adam ignored him, turned to Rain again. "Look, I don't even know where we're going, okay? So you've gotta tell me."

"Where *are* we going, anyway?" Carter said as his laughter subided.

"To a party," Rain said.

"Par-*tay!*" Carter shouted.

"It's at my friend Monty's house in Compton."

"What?" Adam said as Carter simultaneously said, "Oh, shit."

"What's the big fuckin' deal?"

"The big fuckin' deal," Adam said, "is that we can't go to Compton because we're not armed!"

"Jesus, what a coupla fuckin' pussies!" Rain said. Leaned her head back, rolled her eyes. "It's not that bad. He doesn't really live there, that's just where he's staying until he gets back on his feet. It's a nice little house and tonight he's having some friends over to welcome me back."

"Okay, but we're not staying long," Adam said. "We'll go in, you can say hi to your friends, then we leave."

"Who died and left you my fuckin' nanny?" Rain shouted so loudly that Adam winced.

"You were the one who wanted to go out," Adam replied, almost as loudly. "So we're out. But we're in my car and I'm driving, so we do things my way. Now, if you want to go to Compton and hang out till you get shot in a drive-by or raped by a drug dealer or employed by a pimp, you'll have to do it in some other car with some other guy at the wheel."

Rain smiled with satisfaction and said, "Well, Big Brother...we've only known each other a couple days and you're already coming outta your shell."

"Quit analyzing me and tell me where to go," Adam said.

"How about to an analyst?"

In the backseat, Carter tried to stifle his laughter, but it got out anyway.

Adam glanced over his shoulder at Carter and said, "How would you like me to kick your traitorous ass out of the car in Compton and leave you there?"

Carter's eyes widened. "Traitorous? I just thought it was funny, that's all."

Rain was looking at Adam with an annoyed frown. "You talk like a fuckin' librarian, Adam, what's wrong with you?"

"If proper English offends you, I'm sorry. You'll just have to deal with it."

"Proper English doesn't offend me," Rain said. "But people who use it so fucking condescendingly do."

A snicker from the backseat.

Adam was surprised to hear her use such a word. And correctly.

They were silent for awhile and Adam turned on the radio, found some music. The four of them did not speak again until they arrived at their destination.

A small community, Compton had a primarily black population. At first glance, it looked like a pleasant neighborhood beneath the California fan palms. With a closer look, its problems became clear. Houses and shops and even fast food restaurants had black iron bars on their doors and windows. Heavy sheets of metal slid down over the doorways of shops at closing time. Storefronts, apartment buildings, even houses were marred by graffiti, speckled with bullet holes.

Monty's house — or the house in which he was staying — was more like a cottage. On the corner of two narrow intersecting streets, it was small, once cute, now crippled and battered by its own environment. Grafitti on the door and walls, bullet holes beneath the two windows that flanked the front door. Paint curled up in narrow strips, like dead cracked skin on the heel of a foot. The street was lined with houses exactly like it.

Cars were parked all around it, some blocked in by others. There were no sidewalks on either side of the street. The road simply ended on each side, replaced by rocky dirt. The rough ground made up a tiny yard, much of which was taken up by a battered old Mustang on blocks. No lawn, no fence. The concrete walkway leading up to the porch steps was broken into chunks of gray rubble. Music with a heavy beat rattled the foundation of the little house from inside.

"This isn't a yard," Adam said as they walked around the car over the oily dirt. "It's an obstacle course."

"You're such a fuckin' pussy," Rain said.

"*Boyz N the Hood* was shot around here," Carter said to no one in particular as he looked around with interest.

A bare, yellow, anti-bug bulb in a fixture over the door bathed the small porch in the color of unhealthy urine. The concrete steps were narrow, cracked, with broken corners. An old wooden grafittied door stood behind a sturdy iron security door with a shiny brass deadbolt lock.

Rain went up the steps first and kicked the screen door hard four times.

Carter leaned close to Adam and whispered, "I think we should keep the smartass remarks to a minimum. Somebody's libel to bust a cap in our asses, know what I mean, Big Brother?"

"Knock that shit off!" Adam said. His nervousness made his voice tremble.

After more kicks, the door finally opened. Adam almost exclaimed, *Opie Taylor!* but clenched his teeth and swallowed instead.

The young man at the door was in his mid-twenties, but had the innocent, freckled face of a small-town country boy, with red crew-cut hair. He came out and picked Rain up in his enormous, muscular arms. His entire body rippled with muscles. Shorter than Adam by a few inches, his lack of height somehow made the muscles seem more threatening. Like snakes coiled to strike beneath his tight gray Tazmanian Devil T-shirt.

Still clinging to him with one arm, Rain said, "Guys, this is Monty. He's the shit, okay? Monty, these're the guys. That's Carter, and that's my new big brother Adam."

Monty stepped out past Rain, smiled and extended a hand to Carter. Monty's hand was no bigger than Carter's, but when they shook, Carter's knees wobbled. He didn't fall, but could do nothing about the look of agony on his face: head back, eyes clenched, lips sucked between his teeth.

"Nice to meet ya, Carter, how the fuck are ya?" Monty shouted like a deaf man.

When Carter tried to say hello, he cried out in pain instead.

"Oh, shit!" Monty said, laughing as he released Carter's hand. "Did I hurt ya, there, dude? Fuck, I didn't mean to do that." He pushed Rain aside, put a hand on Carter's shoulder, pulled him toward the door. "Fuck me, man, I'm sorry, I didn't mean to squeeze ya so hard, c'mon, let's get you inside and take care of that." He put his arm around Carter's shoulders, ushered him through the door. "We'll get you a beer and find you somebody who'll massage that hand with her titties, okay? Sound good?"

"Hey, Monty, they came with me," Rain said. "They're mine."

Monty turned to her and said, "Look, Rainy, it's great to see ya, but don't be a cunt, okay?" He let out a piercing, "Woo-*hooooo!*" and went inside after Carter.

Adam turned to Rain and smiled. "Welcome home."

Face suddenly ugly with anger, Rain grabbed his elbow and opened the screen door. "C'mon, let's go join the fuckin' party."

Inside, the little house reeked of alcohol and marijuana. The rap music was so loud, it was nothing more than pounding, roaring noise. Beneath it all, Adam could hear loud laughter and shouting, surprisingly audible in spite of the music. Every square inch of the house was occupied by people. Shoulder to shoulder, back to back.

Faint, night-light glows from some corners held off utter darkness. Adam let Rain lead him deeper into the house, through the crowd, which was made up of all colors. Shiny hair, shiny scalps, lots of piercings and tattoos.

"In here," Rain shouted at Adam as she pushed through a door. There was light on the other side. Inside, the noise was muffled, but not by much. Adam could still feel it in the floor.

It was a bathroom. Adam faced a bathtub filled with ice cubes and water, cans of beer and bottles of hard liquor. There were also a strip of six off-brand condoms and a torn, soggy issue of *Good Housekeeping* magazine resting on the surface of the ice.

Rain grabbed a can of beer, another off-brand, probably something made for one of the grocery chains. "Want one?" she said.

Adam shook his head. He wanted to keep his senses sharp, and what judgment he possessed in tune.

He heard two distinct sounds: wet sucking and steady tinkling. Turned to the sink in the tile counter behind him, a mirrored medicine cabinet on the wall above it. Beyond that, another door, this one wide open, and the toilet, where a petite Asian girl sat urinating as she sucked loudly on the enormous glistening erection of a tall black guy standing beside her.

"Holy shit," Adam said, turning his back to the couple immediately. He opened the bathroom door a couple inches to leave.

"What'samatter?" Rain said.

"Well, shouldn't we...I don't know, leave them alone?"

Rain looked at the couple and laughed. "You haven't partied much, have you? C'mon, let's go find Monty and Carter."

Back through the crowd, Rain stopped to take a hit off a joint offered by a Samoan guy who looked like a Sumo wrestler. When she handed the joint back, he turned to Adam and said, "Ganja?" Adam smiled, shook his head, moved on. Ahead of him, Rain stopped repeatedly — a hit off a bong, a swig of vodka out of the bottle, a snort of something — and Adam turned them down behind her. Faces began to look at him strangely, probably wondering why he had come.

"Hey, dude!" An arm suddenly squeezed Adam's shoulders so hard he was afraid his head would pop off his neck like a champagne cork out of the bottle. Monty pushed his face close to Adam's and shouted, "Rainy's talked a lot about you. Thinks you're a fuckin' prince, dude! Talks about you like you invented the fuckin' sunlight!" He laughed and patted Adam on the back so hard, Adam would have fallen over if there had been room to fall.

He frowned, thought, *That can't be true. Why would Rain talk about me that way?*

Monty said, "Let's go find a place to talk."

They caught up to Rain and she and Monty shouted at each other. Adam couldn't understand what they were saying, so he ignored them, looked around.

A black girl was sprawled and motionless on a nearby sofa. Her head had fallen back, mouth open like a deep sleeper's. A tourniquet on her left arm, tied tightly above her bleeding inner elbow. Right hand resting on the cushion, lightly holding a syringe. She wore a tight, low-cut, sleeveless top that showed off her ample cleavage, but was naked from the waist down. A platinum-haired Latina knelt before the still girl, head between her thighs. Adam watched the platinum head roll around in a lopsided oval motion. Four guys stood behind her and laughed as they watched. The girl on the sofa lifted her head, looked around with dead eyes, then vomited on herself. It soaked her black top and spattered onto the platinum hair. Neither girl noticed. The guys made sounds of delighted disgust.

As if seeing the syringe had opened his eyes, Adam noticed others on the endtables and coffee table.

"Hey!" Carter shouted behind him. "We finally made it to high society, huh?"

Deep in the crowd, male voices shouted angrily, rose above all the others.

"I'm going to the car," Adam said over his shoulder. He squeezed around Rain and Monty and headed back the way he had come.

The angry voices grew louder as the others dropped a few notches. Sudden cries and shouts came from the crowd as a disturbance broke out. Most of them hurried backward, away from something. Adam stopped, looked back. A large bald man and a larger man with dreadlocks circled each other. The bald man held a knife, the guy with the dreads nothing but pot-roast-sized fists. They shouted at each other, threw a few punches. In a blink, the man with the dreadlocks was no longer empty-handed. His right hand held a large handgun. So big, it looked like an exaggerated toy, something that might squirt water, not shoot bullets. Screams erupted.

"Jesus Christ!" was one of them, and it came from Adam. He knocked people out of his way and stepped on feet. His heart pounded in his ears, nearly drowned the cacophony behind him. He pulled the front door open and slammed into the heavy screen door. Nearly knocked himself to the floor because it was locked. Adam turned the lock, pushed the door open, threw himself out of the house. Nearly tripped on the steps and broken concrete path, ran left to go around the Mustang in the yard.

The gun fired inside once, twice. Glass broke to Adam's right. The ground swept up like the hand of God and hit him in the face.

Adam hit the ground rolling. He stopped in front of the Mustang and took a quick body inventory to see if he had been shot. Relieved to find nothing more than sore elbows and a scratched forehead, he crawled the rest of the way to his car.

A helicopter flew overhead, passed a slow searchlight over the neighborhood. Always there, a part of the night in Los Angeles, although they never seemed to find anything.

Once inside the Lexus, Adam locked his door. His hands and arms shivered with fear. Sweat broke out over his body with stinging suddenness. He was furious with himself for coming. He should have said no to Rain and stayed with it, but no, he'd caved, believed her scary little story about going to the police. He clenched his hands into fists, made the trembling stop.

A group of partiers rushed out the front door and headed for their cars. Among them, Adam saw Carter and Rain. He opened his door, got out and waved at them. "Hey! Come on! We're going!" He got back in, slammed the door, locked it again, reached over and unlocked the passenger door.

Carter fell in. His face sparkled with sweat. "Son of a bitch!" he said in a jagged voice. "Honest-to-God gunfire!"

Rain got in with no hurry and left the door open as she said, "I think Monty wants to talk to you, Adam."

"I don't care if Monty wants to crown me king of Denmark, we're getting the hell out of here." He started the car. "Close your door, Rain."

"No. You have to talk to Monty."

"What do you mean, I *have* to talk to him?"

Rain turned and smiled at Carter. "Could you let us speak privately for a minute."

"And get outta the car? You're funny."

She sighed, leaned close to Adam and breathed, "Monty's gonna help us."

"*What?*" Adam shouted.

She nodded at his door and said, "C'mon, let's step out. Just for a second."

Adam did not want to, but did, anyway. They went to the front of the car. The engine idled as they whispered to each other in the headlight beams.

"What do you mean, he's gonna help us?" he asked, trying to contain his anger.

"I mean that's what he does! He's done it before, lotsa times. And he'll give us a discount because he's my friend."

Adam pointed at the house and asked, "That buffoon in there is a hit man?"

Rain continued as if he had not spoken. "Monty, uh...I don't know, he's got some fuckin' thing for me. Normally, I'd be down with that because I think Monty's hot, but he fucks guys, too, and I don't fuck people who can't make up their fuckin' minds. I mean, you gotta have some kinda standards, right?"

Adam stepped very close to her, neck muscles taut. "Have you been fucked out of your mind? You're telling me *that* guy is going to kill your mother for you?"

"He's going to kill both our parents. For us."

"Oh, no, don't give me that *us* shit. If that guy's involved, you can count me out."

"You don't even know him!"

"I know all I need to know. Jesus, we'd be *lucky* if we got caught. We'd probably all end up dead. I wouldn't let that guy change the oil in my car, Rain, and I'm sure as hell not—"

"Hey, you guys, wait for me!"

Adam and Rain turned toward the voice. Monty rushed toward them wearing a long tan coat that flapped around his legs like a cape. It was a cool night, but not that cool. Adam did not like the look of it.

Rain said, "You gonna tell him that?"

"Ran outta vodka," Monty said as he jumped into the car, taking Rain's seat.

Rain got into the backseat with Carter.

The engine continued to idle as Adam stood beside the car, staring at the steering wheel. He wanted to go home, and intended to make that his only goal from that moment on.

"You comin'?" Monty said. "You want me to drive? I know this fuckin' neighborhood upside-down."

Adam threw himself behind the wheel and pulled the door closed. "Where are we going?" he asked as he drove away from the house.

"Liquor store," Monty said.

Adam turned right, then right again. "I saw one coming in, just a couple blocks up here."

"No, that store closes at, uh, eleven. Gotta go to another one. Make a left up here."

"Across that traffic? Uh-uh. I'll take the long way." He turned right, got into the left-turn lane at the next light and made a legal U-turn. Went back the way he had come.

Adam glanced in the rearview and saw Rain on Carter like a hungry predator, kissing him as Carter's surprised struggles weakened, finally stopped.

Monty laughed. "Hey, they look pretty fuckin' occupied, huh?"

Adam felt sick to his stomach.

"Rainy says you gotta job. Hasn't told me shit, though, so I don't know if I wanna fuckin' do it or not. Somethin' about your parents. You wanna fill me in, Adam?"

Monty turned on the radio and found a rap station, turned it up so loud it caused Adam's ears actual physical pain. He expected them to start bleeding any second. He was afraid to protest this time, let it pass. He had to shout to be heard. "I, uh...I think Rain might have been a little hasty."

"Little pasties? *What?*"

"Uh...I think she spoke too soon. We haven't decided on our plans yet."

"Oh. Well, fuck." Monty shook his head slowly. His knees bobbed and he slapped his thighs to the music as he spoke. "You gonna do your fuckin' parents, you gotta have somebody like me, dude. You get tagged with somethin' like that, man, you're fucked. You need somebody's got no fuckin' connection to the family."

"You're a friend of Rain's."

"Nah, that's no fuckin' problem. Her mom, your dad, none of 'em ever fuckin' met me. Don't know me from shit. Hey, does your dad fly?"

"Huh?"

"Your dad, does a have a fuckin' plane?"

"Oh, no. No plane, no jet."

"How about a boat? Your parents gotta fuckin' yacht, or somethin'?"

"A yacht and a fishing boat. Why?"

"That's always a great fuckin' way to get ridda more than one at a time."

"What? You mean, like…sinking it? Blowing it up?"

"Why the fuck not? Yachts explode all the time."

"They do? Where do yachts explode all the time?"

"Ever watch TV, dude? Cable? C'mon, man, that kinda shit's goin' on alla fuckin' time."

"Uh, what reason would a yacht have for exploding in real life? I mean, a yacht that's *not* on TV."

"Fuckin' explosives, dude! That's what I do, I go plant the explosives in the fuckin' yacht, they go out on the fuckin' yacht, the fuckin' yacht blows into a billion fuckin' pieces. Problem solved."

"Yeah, I can see how that would work," Adam said with a nod. Thought, *This asshole would blow himself up in his car.*

"No connections, no traces. I'm thinkin' in your case, it's the way to go."

"You think?"

"From what little I fuckin' know about it."

"How long you been doing this kind of work, Monty?"

"'Bout eight months now."

This is a nightmare, Adam thought as he asked, "Get much business?"

"Oh, yeah, fuck yeah. And I do it all. Shoot 'em, blow 'em up. Fuck, I even strangled one. Ha! But that's a long fuckin' story. I'll tell ya sometime."

"Well, like I said, Rain and I haven't decided how we want to handle this. Or if we even want to do it."

"That last part's bullshit!" Rain shouted from the backseat.

Adam ignored her. "I hope you don't mind, but I think it'll be awhile before we can—"

"Take the next left," Monty said, pointing.

After turning, Adam said, "I mean, we can't make a commitment to anything right now."

"A fuckin' commitment? The fuck're you talking about, we gettin' married? Take this right up here."

"I mean, we haven't decided anything yet. So we won't be needing your—"

"Here, to the left, this is the fuckin' place, dude."

"—services."

On the roof of a liquor store on the left corner, a giant neon clown held a bouquet of flashing balloons. At the clown's impossibly long feet, a bright sign read, CIRCUS LIQUORS. Adam parked just outside the door.

"Good, it's not fuckin' busy," Monty said. He turned to Adam and flashed an Opie smile. "C'mon in, dude. Leave the engine on."

"Huh? Oh, no, I'll wait out—"

"C'mon!" Monty shouted as he got out.

"Oh, for crying out loud," Adam complained. He looked over his shoulder. Rain's head bobbed on Carter's lap, while he slumped in the seat. Carter saw him through heavy-lidded eyes and shrugged helplessly.

"Fuck, you comin'?" Monty called.

"Gettin' close," Carter replied with a lazy laugh.

Adam got out of the car, threw the door closed and jumped onto the sidewalk that surrounded the store. Monty fumbled with a floppy piece of orange cloth.

"Figured I better bring one for me 'cause the cops know my face," Monty said, putting his hand on Adam's back. He pulled the glass door open and pushed Adam into the store, saying, "But Rainy says you're fuckin' clean as shit."

"Clean? What kind of clea—" Adam turned as Monty slipped an orange ski mask over his head with one hand and pulled a large black-and-silver gun from his right coat pocket with the other.

"C'mon, bro."

"*What?*" Adam felt light-headed, close to passing out. Everything slowed, including his heart. Even the rap beat coming from the Lexus outside slowed to a lazy thump.

Not really, Adam thought. *Nothing's really slowing down. This is just my nervous system preparing me to die.*

Monty turned, aimed his gun at the closest front corner above them, where a black surveillance camera looked down over the entire store. Fired two quick shots before the camera popped into two pieces and dangled by a cord.

Adam's muscles tensed more with each shot. His body frozen, inside he was a terrified, screaming pit of chaotic flashing images, familiar voices gibbering over one another. Voices from his past—mostly his mother's, talking over itself repeatedly—warning him about the Wrong Crowd and Bad Neighborhoods and the Danger of Guns. Not a single voice mentioned anything at all about what to do to keep from getting his guts blown out during a liquor store hold-up.

"Back up, back up!" Monty shouted at the middle-aged Korean man behind the counter. "Turn the fuck around and face the cigars! Put your fuckin' hands up on the racks! *Do it*, motherfucker!" Satisfied with the man's position, Monty looked back and said, "Hey, come hold this motherfucker for me."

Adam stood frozen about eight feet behind Monty, near the door. Couldn't even blink as he stared at Monty's gun, pointed at the back of the man's head. Monty was saying something, but Adam was underwater, at the bottom of the pool, Monty's voice an indecipherable groan making its way down to him.

"Goddammit, I said come hold this guy, you wanna get us fuckin' killed?"

Adam broke the surface of the water and suddenly everything fell back into place. Sounds and smells icily clear, time moving at its normal speed again.

"Oh, shit," Monty said. He still held his gun on the cashier as he looked over his shoulder at Adam with wide-eyed realization. "Shit, man, Rainy said you was cool! And you don't got any fuckin' metal?

That's fucked up, dude!" He stuffed his left hand into his coat pocket, glaring. Not so much like Opie Taylor anymore.

The Korean man began his turn, knees bending, head ducking. Monty took another gun from the coat pocket, and flung it at Adam. It spun through the air, a deadly boomerang, growing larger fast in Adam's eyes. He swiped at it with both hands, but it slammed into his chest and knocked him back against the door. He caught it there, awkwardly, nearly dropped it once.

"Hey, fuckmeat!" Monty shouted at the cashier. He fired his gun, but too late. The man had disappeared beneath the counter.

Adam was still holding the gun between two palms like a mentally handicapped child when he heard the *chuh-chunk* of a shotgun being racked. The man popped up from behind the counter, leveled the sawed-off barrel at Monty and fired.

I should go now, Adam thought.

The sound of the shotgun lingered heavily in the air as Monty dropped to the floor, and suddenly blood was spattered everywhere. On the floor, the counter, the racks and shelves. On Adam's shoes. It dribbled warmly down the back of his right hand. Something about the way Monty had hit the floor convinced Adam he was dead. He pushed back and opened the door.

The Korean man shouted furiously in his native tongue as he turned the shotgun on Adam.

The night had been cool and friendly awhile ago. Now it was hot, smelly, like a sick dog's breath. But the heat came off Adam's body, and what he smelled was his own fear.

Carter and Rain watched him from the backseat, their faces ghosts in the window. Rain looked tense, eyes hidden behind her sunglasses. Carter seemed about to shoot out of his skin like a screaming Independence Day rocket. He was shouting something. Adam heard his muffled voice, saw his mouth moving, but the words were garbled by the closed window, drowned by the ringing in his ears. He tried to run, but had little control over his body. With the gun in his right hand, his arms flailed, rubber legs wobbled and staggered.

Another explosion from inside the liquor store shattered glass. Bits of it rained down on Adam as he stepped off the sidewalk and ducked around the car, groped for the door handle. Rain climbed into the front and opened it for him.

" — the gun, drop the gun, drop the fuckin' gun, Adam, drop it!" Carter shouted as Adam flopped behind the wheel.

Rain sounded firm and calm as she said, "Give the gun to me."

Their voices were gnats flying around Adam's ears. He let Rain take the gun and put the car in reverse.

The door of the liquor store was now a metal frame with glass fangs. The Korean man kicked it open, lunged out of the store. Leveled the sawed-off shotgun at the Lexus.

Adam stomped on the accelerator and the car lurched backward. He shifted again, floored it, sent the car shooting across the L-shaped parking lot.

The shotgun fired. Dinging and thumping sounds made all three of them jump inside the Lexus. The windshield and driver's side windows were instantly pitted with white gouges.

Adam drove away from the street from which he had entered the parking lot, toward the street that crossed it. The shotgun was quiet for the moment, things looked like they might be okay. Adam did not wait to check for traffic, just shot into the street. Got into the right lane, slowed down a little to avoid the attention of the police.

"Where am I?" he said. Then again, louder.

"What do you mean, where are you?" Rain said.

Carter screamed, "You're on the wrong side of the fucking *street!*"

It appeared to be true. Headlights sped toward him. Things were not okay. He was driving the wrong way on a four-lane street divided by a strip of concrete the height and width of a sidewalk. Cars all around him honked their horns. Up ahead, four headlights stared him down. In the rearview mirror, two cars were coming up on the other side of the divider. In the backseat, Carter's voice rose in pitch as he yammered senselessly.

Adam slowed, let the two cars on his right pass on as the two ahead of him drew closer, closer. Tires squealed and both approaching cars wobbled. Adam could see the driver in the car directly ahead of him. A large black woman, pounding a round fist on her steering wheel, angry mouth working. Getting closer.

With a final glance in the rearview, Adam turned the wheel sharply and sent the car over the concrete divider. He and Rain and Carter left their seats a few times during the turbulence, and their heads hit the ceiling of the car.

A muffled crash sounded just behind them and Adam looked in the rearview again. Another crash, and another. Some cars—at least three, from what he could tell—had piled up in the oncoming lane he had just exited.

"Son of a bitch," Adam groaned. He felt like vomiting.

"You better slow down," Rain said. She was still calm. And surprisingly calming, as well. She turned off the radio and Adam's ears rang louder.

In the backseat, Carter sounded like a fired-up, tongue-speaking televangelist in the act of healing a fat man in a wheelchair of his gout. Occasionally, a word or two in English would tumble out amid the gibberish, usually something obscene.

Rain turned around in her seat and shouted, "Will you shut the fuck up!" She faced Adam, curled her legs beneath her and leaned toward him. "Okay, what happened? What the fuck happened in there?"

Clutching the steering wheel with shaking, white-knuckled hands, Adam glanced at her repeatedly. Tried to gauge her, figure out if his ears had been damaged by all the gunfire and rap, or if she actually had snapped at him as if everything were his fault. As if he owed her an explanation. "What are you saying?" he asked, voice hoarse. "Are you saying that I did something wrong here? Me? Back there?"

"No, I'm asking what happened. Turn right up here and get on the freeway. What went wrong?"

"What went wrong? That demonic Ron Howard pulled a fucking gun and robbed the store! That's what went wrong! He's your friend, so maybe you'd know…does he do that kind of shit often?"

"He was testing you."

"Testing me? For what, sphincter control?"

"Well, he was gonna…y'know, work with us. But Monty doesn't work with anyone he doesn't trust. So he does that. Y'know, to see if he can trust 'em. If he can work with 'em. Never had any fuckin' problem before, far as I know."

"And he never will again because he's all over the *TV Guide*s back there."

Once on the freeway, Adam began to relax, but he did not like it. He told himself he should do anything but relax, should go straight to the police and explain everything. If he did not and they tracked him down, they wouldn't believe a word he said. He saw no other sane choice. He was about to voice his decision when something Rain had said finally registered.

"You *knew* about this?" he asked.

"Yeah. I figured there'd be no problem."

"You knew he was taking me in there to rob that store and you didn't see a *problem?*"

"There was no fuckin' problem before." Rain said. "You couldn't just stand there and let him do it?"

"He threw a gun at me, you demented twat! He thought I had my own *metal*, he said. Because you said I was cool as shit."

"I wanted him to do it for us, Goddammit! I figured you could make it through one little pussy liquor-store hold-up!"

"I can't believe you kept the gun," Carter said in the backseat. "It's, it's like you've never seen a movie in your life. You kept the gun!"

Rain turned to him. "Would you quit whining, Carter! Adam didn't keep the fuckin' gun, I did."

"What the hell do you need with another gun?" Adam said. "Starting a collection?"

Rain leaned very close to Adam and whispered, "It's for us. We'll talk about it later." She licked his ear and a quiet, honey-thick laugh rolled up from deep inside her.

Adam asked, "Has anyone ever told you...that you're evil?" He did not smile.

She giggled. "Yeah, I get that all the time." Her shoes were in the backseat where she had shed them and she wiggled her toes against Adam's thigh.

"Well, they're wrong," he said, then shouted, "Evil is afraid of you. Evil hides from you. You make Evil shit its pants." Adam's chest rose and fell with rapid breaths. "I'm going to the police."

Rain and Carter both cried, "*What?*"

"I think I should go back to the nearest police station. Was that liquor store in Compton?"

Rain pulled her feet away from him and slapped his arm hard. "Are you fuckin' crazy, whatta you think's gonna happen if you do that?"

"If they trace that robbery back to me, I'm doomed," Adam said. Fear made his voice catch at times. "It won't matter what I say, they won't listen, and because of my dad it'll be big news, another Hollywood scandal. This way, if I tell the police the truth now, maybe we can prevent all that and it won't get out."

"Won't get out?" Carter asked, his voice's pitch shooting so high, he sounded like a frightened Bryant Gumbel. "Did you get shot in the head? You know better than that, *listen* to yourself! You go to the cops or get caught later, either way you're going to jail, and either way it's going to get out."

"He's right," Rain said. "Except for that part about getting caught later, that's bullshit. You got away with it. So quit the fuckin' dramatics, Hollywood Boy. You didn't get caught. You're free and clear, so no more shit about goin' to the—"

"How am I free and clear? I was in the store, there were cameras and—"

"Ever been arrested?" she asked.

"What?"

"Have you ever been arrested?"

"Of course not."

"Then you don't have a record, you don't have a mug shot for some witness to identify."

"Were there witnesses?" Adam asked.

"I didn't see any," Carter said. "But I wasn't looking for them."

Rain continued impatiently. "Look, Adam, they don't know shit about you, can't you get that through your fuckin' head? You're clean, and you got outta there alive, that means you got away with it. And even if you did have a fuckin' record, it wouldn't matter, because it's just a pissy little liquor-store shooting. You think they give a shit about those? Investigating liquor-store shootings in Compton's like investigating every single fucking car alarm that goes off in Westwood. They don't give a fuck about you, they don't know you from…well, shit, from Adam. But they will if you go to them and start confessin' your fuckin' sins. They'll arrest your ass, then you *will* have a record. And a mugshot. You'll be seriously fucked and—"

"No, it doesn't feel right," Adam said. He shook his head spastically. "Not telling them just doesn't feel right."

Carter leaned forward between the seats. "C'mon, man, you *know* she's right. They got the only guy who did any shooting. And he's probably got a rap sheet longer than Milton Berle's dick! You don't exist as far as they're concerned, you're not in the system."

"Let's just find a place where we can have some coffee and a fuckin' doughnut, or somethin'," Rain said.

Carter put a hand on Adam's right shoulder and squeezed. "Going to the cops is the wrong thing to do, Adam, you know that. Right?"

"I...I don't know, Carter."

"Let's just go chill out at Denny's for awhile, okay?"

Denny's on Sunset Boulevard was busy at all hours, and was no different that night. Innocuous music played from invisible speakers. Muted voices, clattering plates, and the cry of an infant moved through the music.

Adam and Rain sat across from Carter in a window booth, with Adam next to the window. Jaw resting on the knuckles of his interlocked hands, he stared through the glass at the nighttime activity on the Strip. Winos and junkies, some talking to themselves, arguing with memories. Prostitutes of both sexes, some indeterminate, being browsed by anonymous shoppers driving slowly by.

Adam had a cup of coffee in front of him. Carter and Rain were splitting a grilled cheese sandwich and onion rings. Three untouched glasses of ice water perspired on the table. Carter absently thumbed through *L.A. Express*, a pulpy sex weekly he'd picked up from a vending box outside.

Adam spoke in an unsteady whisper. "If he hadn't stopped to throw me that gun, he probably wouldn't have gotten shot." He turned to Rain, angry. "I can't believe you knew about it and didn't say anything. I can't believe you just let me walk into that."

"You wouldn't have gone if you knew, and then Monty wouldn't have helped us."

"Exactly how did you think that goon was going to help us? You'd trust him? He was insane, Rain, I'm telling you, stable people don't go around holding up liquor stores to win friends and influence people. They don't carry a gun in every pocket or throw parties like the one he threw tonight! That's a great bunch of friends you got there, Rain, it was like a David Lynch movie."

"They're not my fuckin' friends, okay?" she said. "I didn't know any of those people. Monty was my only real friend there," she said quietly, bowed her head. "If he's dead...I'm gonna miss him."

"Want to go back to his party?" Adam said. "Maybe you can find another one. There had to be a dozen granite-skulled social retards there with a loaded gun in each pocket. I'm not sure, but I think that party was a meeting of their union!"

Rain turned away from him. Picked up an onion ring, moved it toward her mouth, then threw it back down. Put her face in her hands and said something.

"What?" Adam asked, turning to her.

She glanced at him, hissed, "I said, that's a shitty thing to say." Her frightened, angry eyes shed real tears. Rain could not have startled Adam more had she slapped his face. The anger and hatred he had felt toward her retreated for the moment.

Carter saw the tears on Rain's face, the way Adam was looking at her, and scooted out of the booth. "I'm gonna go see what's new on the walls," he said, then walked away.

Adam lifted his coffee to his lips. His hand still trembled.

"I'm sorry, Rain," he said. "I, um...he was your friend, and I shouldn't have said that, but...I mean, considering what I went through tonight, do you think you could cut me a little bit of a break?"

Sniffling, Rain dabbed her eyes with a paper napkin. "Do you think he's dead?" she whispered.

"I...I don't know, it was...well, that close to a sawed-off shotgun...there was a lot of blood. It was there all of a sudden, everywhere it seemed, the second that shotgun went off." He noticed a drying spatter of blood on the back of his hand. Quickly dipped a paper napkin in his icewater and scrubbed it away. "I'm sorry, Rain, but I'd be surprised if he was alive." He reached under the table and used the napkin on his life-speckled shoes.

Rain picked up what remained of her half of the sandwich, held it between thumb and middle finger and carefully chose a place to bite.

Chewed slowly. "I knew Monty was crazy," she said. "But he was a nice guy, whether you or anybody else fuckin' believes it or not. He was like a fuckin' kid. I was eleven when I first met him and I think that's why we got along so well right off, ''cause we were both kids, even though he was older than me. He stole Hostess Fruit Pies and *Seventeen* magazine for me. That first summer, he drove me out to the desert and taught me to shoot an AK-47."

Adam decided to keep to himself any remarks that came to mind. He heard genuine grief in her voice—or what sounded like it—and did not want to belittle that. Monty was a dangerous low-life cretin, but Adam could not comment on the friendship Rain had had with him. Maybe Monty had changed her life in some way. That it was a change for the better was dubious, but this was the first time he had seen her express any real emotion other than anger. He must have meant something to her.

"He was always there for me, no matter where we went, where we lived," she said. "And he helped me out again tonight."

"What do you mean?"

"The gun."

"The one he threw at me?"

She nodded.

"That helps you?"

"It helps us."

Adam waited for her to continue. When she did not, he said, "Look, I don't feel like playing the Pyramid, okay? Say what's on your mind and quit—" He was about to say, *quit wasting my time!* She didn't need to hear that now. "Just don't be so mysterious, okay?"

"What's the fuckin' mystery?" Rain asked. "It's an untraceable gun."

"How do you know it's untraceable?"

"Okay, maybe it's traceable. But not to us."

"Do you know anything about it?"

Rain shrugged. "It's a fuckin' amazing gun, a Colt .45 automatic handcannon. Other than that, I don't know dick. Maybe it wasn't even his. Maybe a friend loaned it to him for the night. And maybe his friend had borrowed it from another friend, without asking. And maybe *that* guy picked it up in a house he broke into and robbed, and maybe it's registered to the guy who owns the house. The cops show up at *his* fuckin' door, not ours. The house guy doesn't know us, we don't know him, the cops come back a couple times and talk to the house guy, then go have some doughnuts, 'cause they know they got nothin'."

Adam sipped his coffee, then turned and watched Rain slowly eat a glistening, broken onion ring. She tilted her head back just a bit, lowered the onion ring into her mouth. Pulled it in with her tongue.

"Why would the cops be looking for the gun?" Adam asked. "I mean…we have the gun. Right? We do have the gun, don't we? Did I miss something?"

Rain nodded. "It's in the car, under the seat."

"Okay, so why would the cops be looking for it when they've got no reason to know it exists? It wasn't even fired."

"They wouldn't be looking for it now, you fuckin' sportscaster," Rain said. She whispered, soft as rose petals. "Y'know, if it turned up later. Like, in a murder, or something."

She smiled, stroked his leg. Her touch startled him, made him jump. Turning from Rain, he sipped his coffee again. Stared into the cup.

There it was again. Killing his dad and Gwen. The more he thought about it, the easier it seemed it would be to kill his dad. Memories kept coming back, things he hadn't thought about in years. Some little things, others bigger. Like the time Michael introduced him to Harrison Ford at a party at the house.

"This is my son, Adam," Michael had said, putting a hand on top of Adam's head. "He's a big fan of yours. Probably because you're everything he's not. I swear to God, he isn't a doer. I don't know what the hell's gonna become of him. I'll probably be supporting him the rest of my life."

Adam had been eight years old at the time. Harrison Ford had looked almost as big as he did on the theater screen. He'd looked down at Adam and smiled, said, "Hey, how's it going, big guy?" Then he had walked away.

"Okay, happy now?" Michael said. "Go to bed. *Go!* Upstairs, before the guests start to leave because of you."

Adam couldn't remember if he'd done anything to deserve that last remark. Probably not. It was the kind of thing his dad would say with no provocation, for no reason. He had run upstairs to his room and cried himself to sleep.

Other memories, some similar, others worse, came back in trickles and bursts. They made it easier to seriously consider murdering Michael Julian.

One question kept trying to occur to him: *What would Mom think?* He never allowed the question to fully take form, told himself he would be doing it for her. To avenge her death. Her murder.

"You don't seem too fuckin' impressed," Rain said. "I thought I was being pretty resourceful."

Adam nodded reluctantly. "Yeah, that…that's very resourceful. I just don't feel very enthusiastic right now, okay?"

"I don't like it when you talk that way, Big Brother," Rain said.

"Like what?"

"Real loose like that, like you could be talkin' about anything. Makes me nervous. You should be committed, Adam."

He chuckled. "That's funny. I've been thinking the same thing about you."

"You asshole. Is everything a fuckin' joke to you? Aren't you ever serious?"

"I'm always serious, Rain. Only the jokes are funny. Sometimes."

"I mean you should be committed to what we're gonna do, Big Brother, because I don't wanna spend all fuckin' summer talkin' about it. That gun's exactly what we need, and we're gonna use it. Soon." She smiled, shook her head. "You oughtta be grateful. In our original plan, you end up in prison for murder." She laughed.

"What? *Whose* original plan?"

Carter returned to the table and slid back into his seat.

Adam decided to pursue the remark later. "I still haven't said I'd do it."

She laughed a pretty, girlish laugh. "Sometimes your jokes are pretty fuckin' funny, you know that, Big Brother?"

"What're you guys talking about?" Carter asked.

"Oh, just stupid shit," Rain said casually, taking another bite of her half of the sandwich.

Adam told him what they were talking about with a silent look.

Carter said, "Y'know, I was thinking just now — " He stopped uncertainly.

"Thinking what?" Adam asked.

"Well, um…" Laughter burst out of him and he muffled it with a hand over his mouth. Shook his head, nodded, shook it again. Leaned toward them and said quietly, but with great passion and delight, "Tonight was the most fun I've ever had in my entire life! I mean, it was like a really scary amusement park ride!"

"We've done it now, Rain," Adam said. "We've sent Carter over the edge."

"No, I'm not kidding," Carter insisted. "It was…I've never felt that way before."

Adam asked, "You mean, in danger? Like maybe you're gonna get your brains blown out, that kind of feeling?"

"Yeah, that's it!" Carter pointed a finger at him. "Danger. I guess I've never experienced danger before. Real danger. It felt good! I really think it was a life-changing experience."

"Bullshit," Adam said. "An underwear-changing experience, maybe."

"No, really, Adam, I'm twice as alive now! I want to do it again."

"You're in shock, Carter. You can't do it again."

Rain sat motionless and watched Carter, smiled knowingly as she listened.

"I've always kinda felt like something was missing from my life," Carter went on. "And that's it. Danger. Excitement. I don't have enough danger and excitement in my life."

"You don't have enough *life* in your life," Adam said. "You wouldn't leave the house if I didn't go over there and drag your ass downstairs."

"Hey," Rain said to Adam. "Would you shut the fuck up and let the man talk."

Adam rolled his eyes.

"I guess what I'm saying is…" Carter moved closer and whispered, "If you guys really want to kill your parents, I wanna help." He paused a moment, frowned. Then smiled. "Yeah, that's what I wanted to say. That I want to help." He leaned back, somehow more relaxed, and finished off his half of the grilled cheese.

Rain laughed and gave Carter's arm an affectionate slap. "You're good fuckin' people, Carter."

"Thank you," Carter said with a nod and a grin. "I think you're pretty cool yourself."

Adam said, "I'm going to vomit."

They left Denny's when four obstreperous young men took the booth across from theirs, mistreated the waitress, then made lewd remarks about various parts of Rain's body. She leaned over and whispered to Adam that she wanted to leave.

"Really?" he said. "I'm surprised. I figured four guys like that would be a typical date for you."

She gave him a foul look. "You know, I'm beginning to think your dad isn't the only asshole in the family."

Adam's mouth dropped open, snapped shut again. He could not believe she'd said that. Did she know how deeply it stabbed him? Probably. She knew more than she was telling about a lot of things, he suspected.

Carter and Rain made out noisily in the backseat. Adam felt no jealousy — after all, Rain *was* the Antichrist — and yet it made him uncomfortable. Didn't feel right. Nothing felt right. Everything in his life at the moment was wrong. Except Alyssa. It was late, but he still planned to go see her after he dropped off Rain and Carter.

At his house, Adam stopped in the driveway and waited with the engine running while Rain got out. She said goodbye to Carter, but not to Adam. Carter got in the front seat and they headed for his place.

"Looks like you and Rain get along pretty well," Adam said, smiling in spite of his discomfort with the whole thing.

"I'm not sure," Carter said. "I feel a little spooky about this, Adam. I mean, it's surreal. I'm not complaining, I just want to make sure I'm not doing anything that's gonna...y'know, that's gonna hurt you. Is this gonna be a problem?"

Carter's words made Adam's shoulders feel a bit lighter. "Thank you, Carter. You have no idea how much I appreciate that. But I don't want you to get hurt, either."

"Me?"

"I've warned you about her, but I don't think you've listened. She's sixteen. You left sixteen behind the same time I did, years ago. That means you are now a criminal. In the eyes of many, a pervert."

"I know, I know, she's underage, she's trouble, I kept telling myself that the whole time, but...Adam, she's spectacular."

"Yeah, I know. I think I lost a section of my right lung the first time she kissed me. And a blow job from Rain is like having your brain massaged."

"My brain is still tingling."

"But it's *scary*, and it's not free. She'll want something for all the fun, and she'll get it. Turn on the news, see if there's anything about the robbery."

Carter turned on the radio, found a news station. "You still think she's evil?"

Adam laughed. "Still? Evil doesn't just go away, Carter. Evil is like Strom Thurman, it just hangs around and farts and slobbers and decays and makes everybody sick. And Rain is evil."

The female newscaster on the radio read a story about a twelve year old boy in Canoga Park who had raped and killed the five year old girl who lived next door. She went on to cover a story about a single father in Canyon Country who had locked his nine year old son in a small, unventilated, metal toolshed as punishment for bad behavior, and had forgotten about him, leaving him there from the late hours of the morning until dinnertime. By the time the father opened the shed, the intense heat and lack of oxygen had killed the boy. There was no mention of the liquor store robbery.

Carter turned to Adam, his expression serious. "You're really in trouble, aren't you?"

"You and me *both* now."

"I'm not joking."

"I've *never* joked about it! You're the one who's been acting like it's a joke!"

"Are you gonna do it?"

"Do what?"

"You know."

"Oh. That. I'm confused, Carter. You seem awfully comfortable with the idea of killing my dad and Gwen."

Carter shrugged. "I'm not saying it's right, or anything, but...I don't think anybody's really gonna miss your dad, are they? Besides a few studio bean counters, right? He's an amoral prick whose feet smell like the chimneys of Auschwitz. Your words, by the way, not mine."

"But what about Gwen?"

Another pause. "I don't really know her. I mean, it would be, like, a definite waste of grade-A womanflesh, but still, I don't know her. And besides, like you said...she's got reloads. I take that very personally."

In some small back room of his mind, Adam could not believe he was having this conversation. But it did not intrude on his other thoughts, or his attention to what Carter was saying. The idea felt good. He did not trust Rain as far as he could kick her, but he had trusted Carter his whole life. If he was going to do something dangerous, he wanted Carter with him.

"Why do you want to do this?" Adam asked.

"To keep you from getting caught, dipshit," Carter replied impatiently, as if it were obvious. "And because your alternative sucks. You know what would happen to you in prison? You'd get more dates the first day than you've had all your life."

"I've done my best to come to the conclusion that prison wouldn't be so bad. Or that my dad would hire Johnny Cochran to get me off." Adam gulped. Suddenly his mouth was dry, throat felt swollen. "Anything to avoid doing what Rain wants to do."

"And what *you* want to do! How many times have you talked about killing your dad? Remember our freshman year in high school? You talked about it so much I thought you were really gonna to do it. You wanted to throw him in front of a moving train and watch him come apart, remember? But we couldn't figure out how to get him to the tracks."

"But what if we get caught?" Adam said, thumping a fist on the steering wheel. "I go to prison for statutory rape, and no matter how bad it is, at least I'll come home at the end of it. With murder, we're talking the death penalty, or life in prison. Not for Rain, of course, she's a minor, but definitely for us. And Rain knows that, which is why she wants me to help, because that distances her from it. 'My big brother did it!' she'll say, and she won't be lying."

"That's why you need me. To help you, and to keep an eye on her."

Adam nodded. "Makes sense. So...you really want to do this?"

Carter grinned. "Can't wait!"

After dropping Carter off, Adam could not get to Alyssa's house fast enough. It was almost one in the morning, so he called ahead and asked her if it was okay to come so late. She and her parents were already in bed, but she would meet him at the door.

When he arrived, Alyssa waited for him in the doorway in a white Bugs Bunny T-shirt several sizes too large for her, legs and feet bare. She leaned on the doorjamb, smiling but sleepy.

Adam threw his arms around her and locked his lips over hers. He was beginning to like walking up to a beautiful girl and kissing her like that without a word or a signal.

Inside, Alyssa's house was dark and smelled of incense and mari-juana. An overhead light lit the small foyer, but beyond that, only darkness. Hunkering in a shadowy corner of the foyer was a four-foot tall ceramic Buddha that made Adam back up a step at first glance. For a moment, he thought it was a fat naked black dwarf.

Adam asked, "Are your parents Buddhists?"

"No. They worship at the First Church of Bad Taste."

It was an old house with arched plaster ceilings and doorways. Alyssa led him into the dark living room and turned on a lamp. Brass lamps, wicker furniture. Two tall plants in brass pots flanked a rect-angular window that looked out on the front yard. Nearly one whole wall was covered with bookshelves, knick-knacks on each shelf in front of the books. A brass peace sign, a red weatherbird, a little Nixon doll hanging from a gallows, some ugly Troll dolls. A glass-topped burled wood coffee table with a shiny finish stood in front of the wicker sofa, a large brass ashtray in the center. Three barely-touched joints rested on the edge, books of matches scattered around it. Against a wall, the focal point of the entire room, a big-screen TV.

"Are you hungry?" Alyssa asked. "I can fix you something."

"Hungry for you," he said, with an embarassed chuckle. It was not the kind of thing he normally said out loud. But with Alyssa, it felt right. He kissed her again, until she laughed. "What's so funny?" he asked.

"Did you have a horny night, or something?"

"No. I missed you, that's all."

She frowned, took both Adam's hands in hers. "You're shaking. Are you all right?"

Adam wanted to tell her everything, knew it would be such a relief, but feared it would soil their relationship, send her running in the opposite direction. He said, "It's been a rough night."

"Family stuff?"

He moved his head in a way that might be interpreted as a nod.

"I have an orange juice craving." she said urgently and beckoned him to the kitchen. Rather than turning on the overhead light, Alyssa went to a counter to the right of the entrance. Reached beneath a bank of wooden cupboards, switched on a long rectangular fluorescent over the counter. Then another over the sink. Even in bad light, it was a homey kitchen. Spacious, with a hardwood floor, pale stucco walls. An island in the center housed an electric range, and beyond it, more wooden cupboards and counter space, a dishwasher, and a refrigerator. Both counters and the island were tiled in glossy watercolor-yellow and -blue. Plants hung in the windows and the kitchen smelled of a mixture of rich coffees and teas. One back corner was taken up by a wooden brick-red picnic table with two long matching benches. Newspapers and crossword puzzlebooks were stacked on the table, a bag of laundry rested on a bench. In the other corner, a small desk with computer, monitor, and printer.

"Nice kitchen," Adam said.

She smiled as she opened the refrigerator. "Yeah, you'd think it belonged to normal people, huh?" She opened a carton of orange juice and took a few gulps. Turned to him suddenly and tossed an arm around his neck, pulled him to her. She dribbled some orange juice into his mouth. Adam laughed and inadvertantly spit some of it back.

"Sorry," he said, still laughing as he wiped his mouth.

Alyssa's mouth hung open in feigned offense as she bent over laughing, trying to be quiet. "You don't like pulp?"

Shaking his head, he put his arms around her again. She put the carton back in the refrigerator and closed the door with her foot.

"I love pulp," Adam said. "You just surprised me." They kissed for awhile, then Adam whispered, "Let's go back in the living room. I hated *9½ Weeks*."

They went to the sofa, lay face to face on its soft cushions and throws. Spoke in whispers, gently stroked each other's faces, hair. Traded feather-soft kisses.

Adam vaguely observed that the kiss involved no physical trauma of any kind. No internal organs were jostled or damaged, and his spine went uninjured.

Alyssa seemed tense, as if anticipating something.

"Something wrong?" Adam asked.

"A little nervous, I guess. I know it's stupid, but I keep thinking my parents are going to walk in here and catch us."

"There's nothing stupid about that. Nobody wants to get in trouble with their parents."

"That's not it, see, I wouldn't get in trouble. If they come in here and find us naked and humping, they'll probably tell us to enjoy ourselves. Or worse, sit down to chat."

"You're kidding."

"Oh, no. They want me to do my own thing."

"Fine, but do they have to *watch?*"

Alyssa laughed.

"Forget about them," Adam said.

"I can't forget about them. They're my parents. God, I hate them."

"Want to go somewhere else? Your bedroom?"

"No. It's in the back of the house next to their room. I'm fine here. Very comfortable." She smiled.

Adam reached up and turned off the lamp, plunged them into darkness again.

"That's better," Alyssa whispered.

They continued kissing and stroking as a siren wailed in the distance, approaching fast. Adam's body stiffened, overwhelmed by the certainty that it was coming for him. He expected a few police cruisers to squeal to a stop in front of the house, lights throbbing and spinning. Officers would get out, aim their guns at the house as they squatted behind open car doors. The command through the bullhorn: "Adam Julian? You are surrounded! Take your tongue out of the girl's mouth, and come out with your hands up!"

But there was only one siren, and it faded before it got close.

A car drove by outside with its stereo so loud, Adam could feel its beat in the wicker sofa. A horrible, vivid image flashed in his mind, crisp, real: Monty cruising the streets in his junky old Mustang, music loud. Body opened up by the contents of a shotgun shell, blood and bits of him smeared on the seat and steering wheel. Looking for Adam. Pissed off that Adam had left him on the floor of the liquor store in a puddle of his own fluids. Pissed off and looking to teach Adam a lesson.

"You're shaking again," Alyssa said.

"Oh, um, I'm sorry."

"Are you okay? You're not cold, are you?"

"No, I'm fine."

"Not afraid of *me*, are you?"

"Afraid of you? I'm very fond of you. I'm enamored of you. I'm crazy about you. But I'm not afraid of you, no."

With a little more kissing, Adam's mind was off his problems as much as it would be for the rest of the night.

Awhile later, Alyssa pulled her mouth from his and whispered, "So, when are we going to kill our parents and run away together?"

Adam immediately felt tense again. During the nightmare his night had been, he'd forgotten the little adventure he and Alyssa had whipped up. It tied a quick knot in his stomach. Just a fantasy, but it hit too close to home for Adam.

"Soon, and on the night of a full moon," he said in his best Basil Rathbone. "Once we get rid of them, we'll take my convertible and get out of this stupid city."

"Yeah."

"We can go, um…I don't know, you want to go north? We could follow the coast up through Oregon and Washington. Take our time. Sleep on cold beaches, eat seafood in those weathered old cafes. Stuff that just came out of the ocean."

"*Yes!*"

"Just wander. No destination. Nobody to barge in on us and chat while we're making out."

Alyssa did not laugh, as Adam had expected. Her breath was hot on his throat, coming faster than before.

"Will they catch us?" she breathed.

"Making out?"

"For killing our parents."

"Oh, never."

"And…when do we…start hunting down all those other shitty parents?"

"We could start doing that right away. Just deal with them as we find them. Travel the country helping people. Like Bill Bixby in *The Incredible Hulk*."

"Yes."

Everything changed at that moment, the air itself. Subtle but drastic, electric. They quickly undressed each other. Adam fell off the sofa and thunked onto the floor, landed on his coccyx. What should have been a harmless tumble was accompanied by an excquisitely sharp pain in his seat. He grunted and cursed, got to his feet, pants and boxers around his ankles. "Shit, piss, and corruption," he whispered, sitting gingerly on the edge of the sofa.

Alyssa laughed, then covered her mouth. "I'm sorry. Are you hurt?"

"My tailbone. I think it's a goner." He kicked off his pants and boxers, pulled off his socks. Alyssa smiled up at him. A shaft of cloud-soft light came through the two-inch gap between the drapes, fell across her bare breasts in a V-shape. Her breasts reminded him he had no condom. "Damn, I've gotta go out to the car," he muttered, reaching for his pants. "I've got a condom in the glove—"

"No, no, c'mere," she said, tugging on his arm.

They were all skin as they kissed, rubbed together. Adam's first effort was clumsy, but on the second try, he slid inside her. They both made soft, high sounds in their throats. He opened his eyes, looked directly into hers. Alyssa looked back. Adam suddenly realized what made her so different from everyone else: eye contact.

No one in Los Angeles—not in the movie industry, anyway—made eye contact with anyone else for more than a heartbeat, maybe less. Afraid of revealing that their work and lives were deceptions, they averted their eyes. Afraid of seeing something genuine in someone else's.

Eye contact meant Alyssa was being honest with him. He could trust her.

Later, they wiggled around on the sofa until they were in their original position. On their sides, facing each other, naked this time.

"This is going to sound stupid," Alyssa whispered. "But that was…scary. You know? Intense."

Adam nodded. "Yeah, it was. But it was a *good* kind of scary."

"Yeah, not like a Stephen King kinda scary, or anything. We were…really inside each other, weren't we? I mean, you were inside me, but I was inside you, too. Kind of. It was…well, it was kind of, um…"

"Hard to tell the difference?" Adam said.

"Yes! It…it's like we were *supposed* to be together. Like it was our…well, y'know, our destiny."

"You think?"

Alyssa laughed suddenly, slipped a hand between their faces and covered her mouth.

"What's so funny?" Adam said.

"Oh, that just reminded me of something silly." She laughed again. "*Our Passionate Destiny*," she squeaked between laughs. "A stupid book I read once."

"Who wrote it?"

"It was just a stupid romance novel. But the title came to mind, y'know? I read romances all through the seventh and eighth grades."

"Well, even stupid romance novels don't write themselves."

"I think it was a Montgomery novel. Teresa Laree Montgomery. I read all of her—"

Adam interrupted her with a laugh that sounded more like a cough. "You've got to be—are you serious?"

"Uh-huh. Heard of her?"

"You reminded me of her the day we met, of something she wrote. A phrase from, let's see, *Passion's Stormy Sea*. 'A mouth like a ripened fruit.' Most of my life, I thought it was the stupidest thing I'd ever read. I never knew what the hell it meant. Until I saw your mouth."

Alyssa's eyes grew large as he spoke. "That is so incredible, Adam. That…that *is* destiny."

"Yes, it's our *passionate* destiny."

They laughed, kissed some more. Held each other close as they drifted to sleep.

✝

"Good *mooorning!*"

Adam opened his eyes. Alyssa's dad stood over them wearing a wine-colored caftan with a Nehru collar, smiling with all his teeth. He held a steaming mug with a teabag string dangling over the rim.

"Uuuhh, hi, Mr….Mr. um…" Adam momentarily lost Alyssa's last name.

Alyssa jerked awake, stiffened against Adam. Made a small mewling sound as she pulled her head under the throw.

Adam cleared his throat and tried to round up some saliva. "I-I'm really sorry, Mr. um…*Huffman!* We didn't, um, no…*I* didn't mean to fall asleep here, really, I was just, um…I mean, we weren't—"

"Hey, it's cool, no problem at all, uh…Adam, was it?" He spoke quietly, smiled.

"Yeah."

"You can go back to sleep if you want," Mr. Huffman said. "But I wanted to let you know breakfast is ready if you're hungry. Hot cereal, fresh fruit, and the muffins come out of the oven any second. If you want to come in and join us, that's cool." He nodded, started to walk away, then turned back. "By the way, Adam, I folded your clothes. They're on that chair over there." Another smile, and he was gone.

Adam propped himself up on his elbows and looked down at Alyssa. All he could see were her hair splayed all around her head and her eyes peering over the edge of the throw. "He folded my clothes?" Adam whispered.

Her eyes crinkled up and she laughed. "See, I told you," she said.

Adam lay back down. "He didn't even blink. I mean, he looked right at me, no violence in his eyes. And he folded my clothes. I think that's illegal in some states."

She tossed the throw away from her face. "We're a very open family. When I come home late at night, they never ask me where I've been. But they always want to know where I'm coming from. And where I'm at. I'm supposed to think of them as equals."

"Equals. Hm. If my dad told me we were equals I'd have to kill myself."

She laughed as she sat up. Adam saw her in daylight for the first time. Pale, generous breasts. Ghostly blue veins mistily visible through translucent skin. A flat, smooth belly. The top of the patch of hair that made a V between her legs. Adam pushed her back down on the sofa and pressed his erection against her as he kissed and sucked her breasts.

"No, no, Adam, you've gotta go, really," she whispered.

Her nipples hardened on his tongue. He did not want to leave.

She laughed and said, "So much for taking it slow, huh?"

"Muffins are ready!" Mr. Huffman called from the kitchen.

It was enough to wilt Adam's normally heroic penis. Loaded guns could not deter his erection, but nearby parents rendered it lifeless. He knew it would quickly return if he stayed there next to Alyssa. He rolled off the sofa, hurried to the chair for his clothes.

"Are you hungry?" Alyssa asked as they both dressed. "I can grab you a muffin."

"No, thanks."

"Why do you look like you're in such a hurry?"

"Because if I don't go right now," he whispered, "I'm just gonna stay here all day touching you, whether your parents are around or not."

They walked to the door. Before opening it, Alyssa embraced him and whispered, "I'm so glad you came over. Last night was—" She was interrupted briefly by her own laughter. "It was pretty fucking amazing."

"It was some pretty amazing fucking, too, wasn't it?"

They agreed to get together later in the day. Alyssa told him to go before her mother, who was always naked in the morning, came out and offered him tea and a good-morning hug. Adam gave her a quick kiss and hurried out of the house.

He decided that, no matter what, he could not tell Alyssa anything. Not about Gwen or Rain, or what Rain wanted him to do. It could scare her away. He did not want to scare her away so soon after finding her.

2

VIOLENCE

"I'm a student of violence
because I'm a student of the human heart."
<u>Sam Peckinpah</u>
a director whose films are known for their violence

✝

"For the same price, I can get an actor with two eyes."
<u>Harry Cohn</u>
head of Columbia Pictures on auditioning Peter Falk

✝

"What is it to be a nice guy?
To be nothing, that's what.
A big fat zero with a smile for everybody."
<u>Kirk Douglas</u>

✝

"People keep asking me, 'What evil
lurks in you to play such bad characters?'
There is no evil. I just wear tight underwear."
<u>Dennis Hopper</u>

The news that morning reported that the twelve year old boy who had raped and killed his five-year-old neighbor in Canoga Park had not necessarily committed those acts in that particular order. Very brief mention was made of alleged evidence suggesting the boy apparently had been regularly molested by a man for years, possibly his stepfather, who had a record of sex crimes against children. But until that was followed up, it became immediately clear that the media would be taking up its torches and storming the usual castles: sex and violence in movies, television, popular music, and on the internet.

A steady stream of commentary on the rape and murder came from psychiatrists, psychologists, sociologists, and assorted members of the "Hollywood community." Most visible from that last group likely would be Jack Valenti, President of the Motion Pictures Association of America, which rates movies. Whenever it was suggested in the media that violent children were influenced by violence in the movies, Valenti came to Hollywood's defense. His mouth would start moving the instant he saw a camera and would not stop until he sounded like he was about to say something, which sometimes took as long as forty-five or fifty minutes.

Meanwhile, another group, made up of child psychologists, ministers, priests, rabbis, social workers, and parental experts stood or sat before television cameras all across the country and pontificated on the death of the nine-year-old boy in Canyon Country. Few of the story's details had been released, so they discussed hypothetical reasons a father might have for forgetting he had locked his son up in a metal toolshed that morning. They could convince neither themselves nor each other with their speculations. Unable to come up with a reason to do otherwise, they reached the informal conclusion, in front of the cameras and microphones of the world, that the single father was a monster and did not deserve to live.

Two news helicopters collided early in the afternoon while following a high-speed chase over the intricate system of southern California freeways. There were no survivors in either chopper, but no one on the ground was injured.

The subject of the high-speed chase was an ex-con in a pickup truck who had shot and killed three people while trying to rob a bank in Orange County. Overhead, the media locusts swarmed, unfazed by their loss, buzzing on, voraciously eating up images that played in living rooms all over southern California, the country, the world. The chase made television ratings soar. Before it ended in the spectacular crash everyone had been hoping for, one of the two television stations that had lost a helicopter in the crash had to evacuate everyone from the building when they received several bomb threats from viewers angry that the station was not covering the chase from the air.

The news was busy, and had no room for a little story about a liquor store shooting in Compton.

✝

After getting home from Alyssa's house, Adam took a swim, a hot shower. He had tried to lock his bedroom door before showering, but it had no lock. It had never been a problem before. The bathroom door did, though, and he used it, made a mental note to put a deadbolt on his bedroom door. He did not want Rain popping in on him whenever she pleased, like the goofy next-door neighbor in a sitcom. An evil female Kramer. And the idea of Gwen sneaking in while his dad remained in the house gave Adam the creeps.

Early in the afternoon, he went down to the living room and watched the flat-screen television on the wall for awhile. Just in time to catch the opening of *Double Indemnity* on American Movie Classics, a classic Adam had never seen. He fell into the movie immediately. Stretched out on the sofa, dug into a bowl of mixed nuts he had taken from the endtable.

Adam quickly sympathized with insurance salesman Walter Neff, seduced into helping Barbara Stanwyck kill her husband for the insurance money. Neff ends up putting three bullets into his *femme fatale*.

Rain was Adam's Barbara Stanwyck. Adam, like Neff, had been weak, had given in when he should have stood firm. Embraced Rain when he should have walked away. Then he realized something that made him close his eyes and cover his face with both hands.

Walter Neff was played by Fred MacMurray, who later played the father on *My Three Sons*.

"I *am* Mr. Douglas," Adam muttered into his palms. "Rain was right."

"Rain was right about what?"

Adam sat up so suddenly at the sound of Gwen's voice, he nearly fell off the sofa. Mixed nuts scattered over the carpet and coffee table when he clumsily hit the bowl with the side of his hand. Cursing under his breath, he got down on his knees to pick up the nuts. "You scared me," he said.

"I can tell," she said, standing behind the sofa. "You must have a guilty conscience."

Adam looked up to see if she was serious. She wore a short white skirt and a plaid short-sleeved shirt tied just above an exposed strip of her belly. Her eyes were covered by large round Jackie O. sunglasses.

"You have a hangover?" Adam asked.

Gwen walked around the sofa, got down on her knees in front of him and helped him pick up the spilled nuts.

"What was Rain right about?" she asked.

"Oh, nothing. Just a stupid nickname."

"A nickname? Sounds like you and Rain are pretty friendly." No change in her tone, very casual.

Adam shrugged and said, "I don't know. We live in the same house."

"And she has a nickname for you?"

"Yeah. She thinks I'm too uptight, so she calls me Mr. Douglas. You know, Fred MacMurry on *My Three Sons*."

"You got off easy," Gwen said. She dropped a handful of nuts back into the glass bowl on the coffee table. "She calls me 'cunt'."

Adam did not doubt it. "Why the sunglasses?" he asked, hoping to change the subject.

She shook her head slowly, but said nothing.

He gave her a black eye, Adam thought. He reached for the sunglasses, but she grabbed his wrist and pushed his hand away.

"Please, just…give it a couple days to get better," she whispered, gripping his wrist hard. A tear dropped from beneath each of the dark, round lenses onto her cheeks. "It's too ugly right now, okay?"

"Sure, okay." Adam started to pull his hand away, but Gwen took it in hers and squeezed. Anger rose from deep inside him, made him feel hot for a moment. "That…that son of a bitch. He needs to have the shit kicked out of him, you know that? He needs to—"

"Stop it," she said. "You just stay out of it, okay?"

"Oh, not me. He'd kill me. I mean we need to find somebody big enough who can kick the—"

"Stop talking like that, Adam. It doesn't suit you."

With all the nuts back in the bowl, Adam put it back on the endtable. Gwen flopped onto the sofa and he joined her.

"What're you watching?" she asked.

"*Double Indemnity* just got over. You're in time for *The Mole People*."

She leaned her head back and released a long, surrendering sigh. "I knew what I was getting into," she whispered. "Now I'm just gonna have to take it."

"He didn't waste any time with you, did he?"

"What do you mean?"

"Well, he didn't start hitting my mom until awhile before she—"

Gwen laughed bitterly. "Adam, honey, when you're a little kid, you may be able to tell something's not right in the house. But you don't know *everything* going on between Mommy and Daddy. I think he was beating her long before you noticed."

Adam wondered if that were possible. Had his dad been beating his mom all along? The possibility sent a pang through his chest. Maybe his mom had hidden it from him. It made him want to kill his dad even more.

Gwen chuckled coldly. "Hell, he started on me before we were married. But here I am."

If she's stupid enough to marry him after *he'd beaten her,* Adam thought, *maybe she deserves to die.* A second later: *No, no, that's a horrible thought. Gwen's decent, a good person. I'd think that even if we hadn't had sex. Wouldn't I?*

Adam asked, "So, is it his money, or his charm? I forget."

She gave it a moment of thought, then nodded. "Yeah. That's pretty much it. The money. Michael is fun at a party because he says whatever comes into his head, like an Alzheimer's patient. But as a husband, he sucks."

"What was your other husband like?"

"He was a lot of things, but he never beat me."

"Why didn't you stay with him?"

"Because he was always moving around. And he was a loser. I didn't stay with him because I couldn't keep up with him."

"What did he do?"

"Whatever he could find. No ambition. No drive. The only reason we moved so much was to avoid creditors."

"What about…others? I mean, you were married before him. Weren't you?"

Gwen sat up, turned toward him, frowning. "You writing my unauthorized autobiography for me?"

"Just curious."

She brushed his hair from his forehead with her fingers. "You need a haircut," she said.

"Nah. It's fine."

"Wanna go upstairs?"

He looked at her, she looked at his hair. "Sorry, Gwen. I just can't."

"What's wrong?"

"Nothing's wrong, it's just…this girl I met. The one I told you about."

Her tense face opened up when she smiled. "Oh? Is it getting serious?"

"I guess so. I hadn't thought of it that way. Serious. But I was with her this morning, and I can't wait to be with her again."

"Sounds like Adam's in love."

He considered that. "Maybe so. I don't know."

"I'm happy for you. That's wonderful."

"But it's got nothing to do with you. I mean, I don't want you to take it pers—"

"I know, I know. You don't have to tell me that." She kissed him on the cheek, then stood. "I need to change clothes. I've got some errands to run, shopping to do."

Adam stood, watched her cross the room. "Hey, Gwen. You're not…you know, upset with me, or anything. Are you?"

She stopped abruptly. "Oh, no, honey, please don't think that. I'm not, really. I want you to be happy." She smiled and left the room.

Would the vile woman Rain had described behave that way? He didn't think so.

Daytime television was too depressing to watch during the day, so he turned it off and left the living room. Halfway up the stairs, movement rushed up behind him. He turned to see Rain bounding up the stairs toward him.

Eyes round, lips parted, she stopped a couple steps beneath him, out of breath. Looked like she was about to speak. Instead, she grabbed his elbow and pulled him the rest of the way up the stairs. On the landing, she jerked him to the left, down the hall and into her bedroom. Slammed the door and turned to him.

"Monty is alive," she said.

It sounded like gibberish to Adam. "What?"

"I *said*, Monty is alive. In a coma, but alive."

Something was not right. Was the floor slanted? The walls crooked? He could not put his finger on it. "Well, that's…good. Right? I mean, he's your friend and—"

"It's no fuckin' good if he comes out of that coma, 'cause if he does," Rain went on, "he's gonna tell everything." She took a pack of cigarettes from her nightstand and lit one. "All about how you robbed the store with him. About the gun. About why we were with him in the first place."

"Why would he do that to you?" Adam asked.

"Normally, he wouldn't. The shape he's in now, full of drugs and holes, who knows? He could spill everything without even knowing it. Might even be talking in his coma. Can people do that? Talk in comas?"

Dizzy, he staggered toward a chair covered with clothes, fell into it.

"Monty can't wake up, Adam. We can't let him."

Unable to catch his breath, he clutched his shirt. "I've gotta go outside," he said, shooting out of the chair. His voice sounded like gravel being crushed. "Walk around. Or leave. Go somewhere."

Rain went to the door, leaned her back against it. "We don't have time."

"I don't want anything to do with it," he said. His heart flopped around in his chest like a dying fish. Knees trembled. Unable to leave the room, he started pacing. "I don't even want to know about it."

"No time to fantasize, Big Brother. We've gotta do it fast. He could wake up any second and start shooting off his mouth. Telling everything."

"Then you do it!" Adam shouted. "He's your friend, not mine, *you* kill him! You got me into this shit! He wouldn't be in a coma if you'd told me he wanted to rob a liquor store, because I wouldn't have been stupid enough to drive him to the liquor store in the first place!"

"Me? I'm not gonna do it."

"Fine. Then it won't get done." Adam slowed down, took deep breaths. His legs were getting worse. Making him walk like Ray Bolger in *The Wizard of Oz*.

"Hey, it's your ass, Mr. Douglas. Maybe you'll get lucky and he'll die."

The deep breaths were not working.

"Then again," Rain added, "maybe he's awake already."

A surge of blinding anger coursed through him. Next thing he knew, he had Rain pinned against the door, hands squeezing her throat. He lifted her off the floor, and her small feet dangled. Teeth clenched, spitting his words: "Rats. And snakes. *Cringe*. In your presence. Don't they?"

Rain smiled as her face reddened, eyes teared up.

"Oh God." Adam dropped her abruptly. Shocked, he pulled himself away from her, staggered to the bed. Sat on the edge of the mattress and fell back, arms spread.

Rain laughed as she walked to the bed. "No time to play," she said.

A headache dug its claws into his brain, settling in. Worse, his lungs were shrinking. "I-I think I'm…having a huh-heart attack."

"You're hyperventilating. Calm down."

"Jesus. What'm I gonna do?"

"Don't be a fuckin' bonehead, Big Brother," Rain said as she smiled down at him. "You're gonna kill Monty."

I can't believe you brought this car!" Carter said. "Why didn't you bring the Caddy?"

Adam shrugged a shoulder. "The convertible stands out too much."

"Stands out? You think people are gonna mistake all this gunshot damage for bird shit? Think you were strafed by a squadron of pigeons? What'd your dad say?"

"He didn't see it," Adam said.

"Really? Your dad didn't notice this?"

"Adam was out all night," Rain said. "The big scary daddyman was already gone when Adam got in this morning."

Carter looked back at her as she lit a cigarette, blew smoke in his direction, eyes hidden behind the wraparound sunglasses. He looked at Adam again and asked, "Is there something you want to tell me?"

"Oh, what, you're my mother, now?" Adam shouted. "I have to report to you?" He glanced repeatedly at Carter, eyes cutting beneath a frown.

Carter flinched at Adam's anger. "Hey, what's the matter with you?"

Adam did not respond, kept his eyes on the road.

159

Slumped in the backseat, Rain took a drag on her cigarette, blew a smoke ring. Poked her cigarette through the quavering circle a few times, smirking.

Carter stared intensely at Adam for a moment. "What did you mean about the convertible standing out?" He looked through the windshield, the side window, back at Adam. "We're not going to Denny's for breakfast, are we?"

Adam shook his head slowly, and explained.

"Oh, you've gotta be *shitting* me!" Carter shouted. "I can't believe you—I mean, I-I-I—what the hell did you come get *me* for?"

"You said you wanted to help," Adam said.

"I said I'd help you kill your dad! I was very specific! I didn't say a damned thing about any coma patients!"

Rain leaned forward between them, looked at Carter. "This is just as much your problem as ours. You were there."

"I didn't get out of the car!"

"You think the cops'll care about that?" Adam said.

Rain said, "You were there, Carter. You think if Monty wakes up and starts talking, he's gonna fuckin' forget about you?"

Carter rocked himself, fidgeted. Bit his lower lip, ran a hand through his hair. "I can't—you shouldn't have—I gotta get out." He reached for the door's handle.

Adam hit the console's master-lock button and saved Carter from an ugly death.

"He's in ICU at LAC/USC Medical Center," Rain said. "I don't know if they've got a cop guarding him. If so, this is gonna be a fuckin' pain in the ass."

Carter looked at her with wide, incredulous eyes. "You don't know how you're gonna do this yet?"

"I just found out a little while ago, so give me a fuckin' break," Rain said.

"Do you have any idea how you're gonna kill this guy once you get to him?"

Rain shrugged. "Pull his plugs."

"Plugs? Which plugs? You ever been within a mile of a life support system? Do you even know what one looks like?" He turned to Adam. "C'mon, tell me you're not seriously gonna do this. You know what's gonna happen? You're gonna go in there and unplug the television. He might not even be allowed visitors, you think of that? The guy's a pile of hamburger with tubes, he's not lonely."

"We won't know until we get there," Adam said.

"But they'll see you, Adam! You go in there, finish him off, come back out, people will *see* you. If you even get that far. They'll be able to identify you."

Rain said, "Right now, we don't have much fuckin' choice."

Carter glared at her. "Hey. Elizabeth Bathory. I'm not talking to you."

"I hate to admit it," Adam said, "but she's right."

"Who's Elizabeth Bathory?" Rain asked.

"C'mon, Adam, you don't really think he's gonna sit up in bed all of a sudden and hold a press conference, do you? He's not gonna come out of that coma!"

"I *said*, who the fuck is Elizabeth Bathory?" Rain said impatiently.

"We don't know that," Adam said. "We've got to make sure it doesn't happen." He swallowed, but had no saliva in his mouth.

"Goddammit, who is Elizabeth fucking Bathory? And what's this fuckin' *we* shit? I'm gonna warm this seat, you're on your own, Mr. Douglas." She flopped back, took another puff on her cigarette.

Adam looked at her in the rearview and his eyes narrowed. "Elizabeth Bathory was a sixteenth century Hungarian countess who murdered over six hundred young girls in her lifetime. She believed their blood kept her young. She tortured each of them, drained their blood, then drank it, cooked with it, and bathed in it. But next to you, Rain, she's Shirley fucking *Temple!*"

"Fuck you, Big Brother. And you too, Carter."

Carter shouted, "Goddammit, Rain, will you shut the hell up!" He turned to Adam again. "People will see you, they'll see this car, you'll be—"

"We won't be in this car," Adam said.

"What?"

Adam turned right, down a narrow side street. Took another right and stopped the car beneath a tall rectangular sign: SUREFIRE AUTO BODY—Miracles Overnight.

"I picked it out of the Yellow Pages," Adam said. "They're fast, they'll do it right away, and my dad won't know anything about it."

Adam talked to a tall, skinny guy in his twenties, tattoos up and down his arms. Told him he had called earlier about the damage done to his car by a drive-by shooter. The guy asked no questions. Gave Adam a 1989 Honda Civic as a loaner and said the Lexus would be ready tomorrow morning.

"That was amazingly easy," Carter said as Adam drove them away from the body shop in the Civic.

"What do you mean?" Adam asked.

"The guy didn't ask you about the damage."

"I explained it already."

"Yeah, but still...isn't that the law? Don't they have to report that kind of thing to the police?"

Adam shook his head. "That's doctors, Brainman. Doctors have to report gunshot wounds to the police." Adam merged into the traffic on the Hollywood Freeway, said, "ICU might be a problem. When my grandma had a stroke, they only let in family members, except kids. To get in, you talked to a nurse on a telephone, told her who you were, who you wanted to see, and she'd buzz you in. The double doors were always locked."

"They do that in all hospitals?" Carter said. "Maybe not at this hospital."

"If they do, we need to be ready for it."

Carter looked at Adam in horror, pressing himself back against the door. "We?"

"Yes. We. Us. You and me."

Carter's mouth opened into a large O and he shook his head rapidly. "Oh, no-ho-ho *way!* I'm not going in there with you. I mean, I'll help with, like, the creative end, I'll be an idea man, I'll give you moral support, *immoral* support, whatever. But I am *not* going into that hospital."

"I need you, Carter." Carter almost spoke again, but Adam held up a hand. "Just listen for a second, if they keep those doors locked, I'll need you to call the nurse on the phone to get me in."

Carter stared at him with a blank expression for a moment. "You can't use a phone?"

"You know me, Carter! I'm no good at that kind of thing. I can't lie, I can't fake anything. I get all nervous and my voice—"

"You end up sounding like a twelve year old boy whose voice is changing, yeah, I've seen your act."

"So I need you to do the phone for me. If it's there."

Carter looked out the side window for awhile. Chewed on a fingernail. "Okay, so if the phone is there, I make the call, and that's it, right? After that, I can just leave."

"Leave? Couldn't you at least…wait for me?"

"Hey. Dr. Kevorkian. I don't think you're understanding me. I want nothing to do with this. In fact, once I get out of this Japanese death box of yours, I may not get back in. I may take a bus home. Just to distance myself from you. You hear that? I would rather ride a city *bus* than be connected to this, wrap your brain around *that*."

Adam eased the car down an off-ramp to the surface streets. "You're the one who needs to do some brain-wrapping, Carter. You *are* connected to this. Monty could identify both of us!"

"How? I didn't give him my last name."

Adam's laughter was brittle, dark. "Yeah, that's the funny part. I didn't tell him mine, either."

Carter turned slowly to the backseat.

Indifferent, Rain lit a second cigarette, took her time on the first puff, and said, "Yeah, I told him who you are, who your daddies are. He was pretty fuckin' impressed. 'Specially with you, Big Brother. Monty's a big fan of Daddy's movies."

"I'm overwhelmed by a great lack of surprise," Adam said, looking in the rearview. Behind him, Rain stared at the ceiling as she smoked. "I bet you like them, too, don't you, Rain?"

"Fuck, yeah. *Bomber* was the shit. I liked *Explosion*, too."

Adam nodded. "Yeah, no surprise there, either. What do I keep telling you, Carter? We need a really good plague, like in Egypt in the Bible. But this one would only kill people who like my dad's movies."

"Fuck you, Mr. Douglas!" Rain shouted. "You're such a fuckin' snob. All you movie people are alike. You all think you're so fuckin' important. Everybody in this cocksuckin' town's an executive or an artist. Even my fuckin' mother. Makeup artist, she says. Ha!" She took a hit off the cigarette, blew smoke in an explosion of breath.

Adam said, "That's not what I mea—"

"Even *actors* are fuckin' artists," she went on, emphatically pounding the seat with a fist. "Stupidest motherfuckin' thing I ever heard. Memorize some lines, get in front of a camera, pretend to be somebody else for awhile, say 'fuck' a few times, maybe show your ass, and you're an artist! Doesn't sound like art to me. You're all a buncha fuckin' overpaid snobs. You don't know dick about real life. Or *any-thing* real. All you know is the fuckin' movies, the center of your universe. But movies aren't real. So what do all you fuckin' artists have to feel so fuckin' important about, huh?"

"Hey, I'm no artist," Carter said quickly as Adam said, "Rain, that's not what I was talking about. I meant—"

She leaned between them. "You ever been abandoned in a big city you didn't know? When you were a kid, I mean?"

Adam and Carter shook their heads.

"It's about midnight," she went on, nearly whispering. "You're all alone, it's fuckin' rainin' hard as bullets. And you know Mom's not comin' back, not tonight. You're all alone in a big strange city, and you don't know a single person." Her head turned right to left as she looked at them both. "How fuckin' important you think movies would be then, huh?"

When they did not reply, Rain sat back slowly, took a final puff and stabbed the cigarette into the ashtray in the back of Carter's seat.

For a moment, Adam's mind left the unbearable problem weighing down on him. He was impressed by what Rain had said, and to his surprise, felt guilty for making her feel the need to say it. He doubted she would ever believe that he felt the same way.

Carter asked, "Did, uh…did that happen to you?"

"When I was ten," she said.

Adam had to remind himself that Rain was still the Antichrist because, for a moment, he felt a dull ache of sympathy in his chest for her. The rearview showed her staring out the side window, smoking her cigarette.

Was it possible Gwen had done such a thing? Abandoned her little girl in a big city in the middle of the night? What could keep her from meeting her daughter and taking her home? Why would she leave the child alone on the street in the first place? Adam wondered how much his dad knew about his wife's past. Not that it would matter to him, of course.

He did not want to believe it, not coming from Rain. But it sounded so true. Could Rain be such a good actress? Could Gwen?

Los Angeles County/USC Medical Center was an enormous, pale, blocky building, and looked exactly like a hospital. Driving into and up the hospital's multilevel parking garage, Adam's nausea reminded him where he was going, what he was about to do. His legs, which had been calm for a few minutes, began to shake again.

What was he thinking? How could he be so stupid as to fall for anything Rain said? If he felt any pity or compassion for her, it was only because she wanted him to. Maybe she was softening him up for something.

Adam parked the Honda on the third level, pocketed the keys and turned to Carter. Cleared his throat and gulped before speaking. "You ready?"

Carter looked as afraid as Adam felt. "Oh, yeah. I'm ready. Sure. This won't bother me a bit. Can't you see how cool I am?"

Adam wanted to shout at Rain, scream at her. Instead, he said, "Try not to hotwire the car and drive to Tijuana with a street gang while we're gone, okay?"

Adam and Carter got out of the car and headed toward the stairs that led down to the front of the hospital. Their footsteps echoed softly.

"How are you gonna do it?" Carter whispered.

"I don't know."

"You don't—we're here, Adam! This is the hospital!"

"I suppose I could just use...his pillow." Walking was already becoming difficult, and they were not even inside yet. His legs wobbled and jerked beneath him. He clutched the rail as he went down the stairs.

"You mean...over his face?"

Adam nodded.

"But what if they're breathing for him?"

"Huh? What do you mean?"

With the stairs behind them, they stopped and faced each other.

Carter snapped his fingers a few times. "Shit, what do they call that thing, that machine that breathes for you?"

"A respirator?"

"Yeah. What if they've got him hooked up to one of those?"

"And? What?"

"Well, I dunno, could you still do it with a pillow? If he's got some machine breathing for him?"

Two men in suits approached them, talking loudly, laughing. Adam and Carter started walking again. Fast, heads down. Adam swerved a couple times, stumbled. His palms were wet and beads of perspiration dribbled down his back and sides.

The voices of the suits faded behind them. Ahead, the hospital's main entrance. Automatic sliding glass doors opened and closed, an alien mouth that ate people up and spit them out.

Adam stopped and leaned against a wall. His face glistened with sweat. He whispered, "I don't know if I can do this."

"Jesus Christ, Adam, you look like shit," Carter said. "Are you sick? You're shaking. You look like Don Knotts in *The Texas Chainsaw Massacre*. Just don't hurl, okay?"

"I'm serious, Carter, I don't know if I can do this. My body won't let me."

"Hey, I'm with your body. As Winston Churchill said to Groucho Marx, this is some seriously stupid shit. Close range? A shotgun? He's *not* comin' outta that coma. You're gonna get yourself arrested doing this. Just don't do it and tell Rain you did."

"She'd find out. She'd—"

The doors opened and spit out two uniformed police officers. Adam and Carter froze in place. Statues with panicked expressions.

One officer spoke while the other chuckled and nodded his head agreeably. They walked by without giving Adam and Carter a glance.

Adam coughed to find his voice. "I've gotta go to the bathroom," he said.

"Me, too," Carter said, nodding.

Flopping onto a bench outside the hospital, Adam said, "I can't live like this. And if I don't go in there and do this thing…this is exactly how I'm going to live. Petrified. All the time."

Carter paced in front of Adam a moment, cursed under his breath. He stopped and said, "Okay, but let's do it before I change my mind and get the hell out of here."

Adam stood and they went into the hospital.

The Intensive Care Unit in LAC/USC Medical Center was on the
third floor. Adam stopped in front of the double doors and looked
around, as Carter walked on. There was no telephone outside the
doors. Each door had a small, square window in the top, which gave
limited views of the corridor on the other side, part of a nurses'
station. The doors had no knobs or handles on the outside.

Carter came back and whispered, "You think if we both stand here
and stare at these doors like a couple methadone patients, we'll be
less conspicuous?"

Adam crossed the corridor and leaned his back against the wall.
His ears rang like church bells and his stomach burned like Hell. Legs
shook visibly as he leaned against the wall, no matter how hard he
willed them to stop. One question repeated itself in his head: *Can I do
this*?

He did not think he could. Killing his dad was one thing. But taking someone's life with his bare hands was very different. Pressing
the pillow down with his hands. Holding it there until whatever life
remained had left Monty's body. It made Adam's upper lip curl into
a nauseated sneer.

"Let's go in here," Carter said. He stepped through an open doorway just inches to Adam's right. The plastic rectangular sign against
which Adam had been leaning his head read, **WAITING ROOM**.

The waiting room contained one sofa, fifteen or twenty chairs, and a few endtables scattered with magazines. A television mounted up on the wall was tuned to Court TV. A water cooler and large chrome coffee percolator stood in the corner. Posters of kittens and puppies and sunsets offered pearls of treacle. Some plants by the windows, two shelves of magazines and paperbacks. A phone on the wall with no keypad or dial. Everything smelled of pine scented cleaner.

Adam and Carter looked from the phone to each other.

"Maybe that's it," Adam whispered.

Carter nodded. "I want some coffee."

They went to the corner and each grabbed a styrofoam cup from a stack beside the percolator.

A young man and woman sat on the sofa. He was thin and fragile-looking, with mocha skin, a narrow, angular face, close-cropped hair. Puffy eyes, moist cheeks. He had been crying. The young woman looked like she had been sleeping, or had not gotten enough sleep. She was black, too, but much darker. Her hair went in all directions, and her heavy-lidded eyes stared blankly at nothing.

Adam tried not to stare, but she was familiar. It was a gnawing, worrisome familiarity. He took his black coffee to a chair, sat down and tried to get comfortable.

An old woman sat in a chair reading a book, oblivious to everyone else in the room.

Two middle-aged women sat together, crocheting and talking. One of them was talking, anyway. A morbidly obese woman with glasses, large brown hair, and too much lipstick. Probably in her mid-fifties. She wore a muumuu that swirled with muted earth tones. Her voice was a pulsing hum of background noise about her sister-in-law's gall bladder and her cousin's arthritis.

A man in his forties, balding, chunky, in jeans and a blue short-sleeved shirt, fidgeted in a chair. As Carter took a seat, the man got up and walked to the window, where he stood and stared at the swirl of earth tones in the air.

The room was filled with tension. Adam wondered if it was just his own, or came with the territory.

"You okay?" Carter said.

"No. I'll never be okay again."

"Oh, cut it out. I'm not exactly enjoying this, you know."

"You don't have to do it."

"Neither do you."

"Now you cut it out."

On the sofa, the young man turned to his dull-eyed companion and said in a trembling voice, "I don't know how much longer I can wait. What time did she go in there?"

"I dunno," the young woman said in a low monotone.

"I can't believe they wouldn't let me in to see her."

"Family only."

"I know, but, Jesus!" He began to cry again, until his gaze fell on Adam and Carter, who watched him carefully. "What're *you* staring at?" he snapped.

Adam and Carter shrank in their chairs. They had not meant to be rude. Their stares had been absent-minded.

Adam blurted, "Bluuhhh, nothing!"

"Sorry, really," Carter said.

Adam's eyes moved to the black girl. Why did she look so familiar?

"What do you want to do?" Carter whispered.

"Go home."

"Fine with me."

Adam leaned forward, put an elbow on his thighs and held his head in one hand. Thought awhile. He sat up suddenly, put his coffee on a nearby table and whispered, "Okay, we need to find out if that's the phone we're supposed to use."

Carter put on a smile and said, "'Scuse me, um…ma'am?"

The chattering woman in the muumuu turned to Carter. "Yes, hon?"

"Sorry to interrupt, but my friend and I were wondering—" He pointed at the telephone. "—do we have to call ahead on that phone before they'll let us in?"

"No, you can just walk right in, who you here to see?" Her bright red lips continued to smile as she let her crocheting rest in her ample lap.

"Uuuhhh—"

"A friend," Adam said.

The woman waved a hand, waggled her fingers. "Oh, they won't let you in, then, you gotta be family, friends don't count, not in I.C.U., you want I can call and see how your friend is, they know me in there, what's your friend's name?" The woman set her crocheting in

the chair beside her with her purse. She was about to heave herself to
her feet when Adam and Carter said loudly and at the exact same
instant, "No!"

They startled her, and she dropped back into her seat. It startled
everyone in the room, and all eyes were on them. Even the empty
stare of the strangely familiar black girl.

The woman said, "Okay, you don't have to shout, I just thought I
could help, 'cause I been here almost two weeks and all the nurses
know me, so, you know…"

"Thank you," Carter said with a Boy Scout grin. "I really appreciate it. See, it's my friend, his brother." He pointed a thumb at Adam.
"So he'll be going in to see him."

She resumed her chrocheting, thick fingers moving delicately. "Oh,
well, that's nice, what's wrong with your brother, honey? You know,
my husband had an embolism in his head and had to have a brain
operation, and he's been in there ever since—" A nod toward the door.
"—and it happened the day we were supposed to leave for Florida,
gonna go see all them amusement parks, you know, but soon as we
got to the airport, boom, he hit the floor, out like a light, and from
what the doctor says, we probably won't be getting any vacation, not
this year, anyway, dammit all to heck and back, we planned that vacation for years, now that the kids are all gone, the honeymoon we
never had, you know, but nope, not to be, not to be, just like the new
refrigerator, not to be." She shook her head and sighed.

Adam found the sigh to be the most amazing part of her mono-
logue. Amazing because she had enough breath left to give life to a
sigh.

"With my luck, I'll end up taking care of him for the rest of our
lives, not that I haven't been doing that already for thirty-two years,
but this would be everything, the doctor said he may be a vegetable,
and I just don't know what I'd do if that was the case, but I know one
thing, Peggy, honey, you'd have to be my regular date—"

Peggy laughed a high, girlish laugh.

"—'cause I know I'd have to keep bowling, sweetie, you know I
couldn't live without my nights at the lanes—"

She went on. Adam took sneaky looks at the black girl whenever
he had the chance. He *had* seen her before. She sat slumped low on
the sofa.

Holy shit! Adam thought when he recognized her. He turned to Carter and whispered, "We've gotta get out of here."

"Why?"

"Never mind, let's go." Adam stood and pulled on Carter's arm until he stood, too, and put down his coffee. As they made their way to the door, Adam tried not to hurry but was unable to walk at a normal pace. He got through the door first. Carter was not so lucky.

"Hey, if you boys are gonna be around for awhile, you be sure and let me know if there's something I can do to help, you hear, just speak up, my name's Angie and this is my friend Peggy, here, and I know how lonely it can get waiting in a place like this, I'd probably go crazy if it weren't for Peggy, here, and—"

Carter backed out slowly, a grin frozen on his face. She was still talking when he finally got out of the room.

They walked down the corridor, trying to look casual. Adam walked as if something very cold were moving around in his shorts.

"Jeez, look at you," Carter said. "You look like Don Knotts in *Spartacus*."

"I recognized that girl," Adam whispered.

"Back there?"

"Yeah. She was at Monty's party."

Carter was not very concerned. "You're sure?"

"Positive. She was on the sofa and she threw up, and a girl—"

"Some chick was vacuuming her carpet while a few guys watched?"

Adam nodded. "She had a syringe in her hand."

"Yeah, I saw her. Why did you want to get out of there so fast?"

"She could identify us!"

"Adam, that girl couldn't identify her own reflection in a mirror last night."

"What about the guy?" Adam said. "He doesn't look familiar, but he could've been there. What am I saying? Look how upset he was, of *course* he was there, he's obviously a friend of Monty's. Maybe they're lovers. Rain said he goes both ways. That guy in the waiting room was there and *he* could've seen us."

"Hey. Oliver Stone. You need to double your dosage, you know what I mean?"

Adam groaned and scrubbed his hands over his face. They stopped walking and he leaned against the wall beside an abandoned gurney.

"C'mon, Adam, are you gonna do this, or not?" Carter said. "Because no offense, but I could be home working on my impaled eyeball."

Carter was right. Adam had to do it, get it over with. He took a few deep breaths, clenched his jaw, his fists. Pressed the sole of his right sneaker against the wall and launched himself with a strong push. Walked briskly but clumsily down the hall as his legs continued to rebel. Carter was right behind him.

"Go to the car," Adam said. "If I'm not down there in fifteen minutes, get the hell out of here."

"Who're you, Tom Hanks? You're not storming Omaha Beach, you know. If it doesn't look like a sure thing, then just get your ass outta there, Adam, I'm serious."

"Just do what I said," Adam said. A second later, he turned sharply to the right, toward the I.C.U. entrance.

Adam raised both hands, palm out, to push the doors inward, but held them close to his chest. The doors burst open and the edge of one landed in the center of his forehead. He stumbled backward as a large young woman with blonde hair and a round face emerged from between the doors. A roll of lazy flesh lolled like a tongue between her pink tube top and denim cutoffs, both of which were too small for her.

The woman gave Adam a sturdy shove and he slammed against the wall. She released a long, ulalating wail as she rushed into the waiting room, which suddenly filled with activity and loud, emotional voices.

"Shit, man, are you okay?" Carter asked.

"No. I'm gonna pass out."

"No, you're not," he said, shaking his head firmly. He put a hand on Adam's shoulder and guided him back into the waiting room. "Come sit down and—"

"Carter, I'm gonna pass out."

Still shaking his head: "No, you're not, just sit—"

"Yes, I am."

"No you're not."

"Yes, I *am*."

Four feet from the nearest chair, Adam passed out.

✝

Carter guided him to the floor easily, dropped to his knees beside Adam, shook him a little. "Adam? *Adam!* Jesus, what do I do, here?" He was suddenly overwhelmed by a sickly-sweet, rose-like odor. It clogged his nostrils and constricted his throat.

"You step aside, honey," Angie said, pushing him away from Adam, "because I did time as a nurse's aide during my Stuart's *inventing* phase, and I know my CPR." She knelt beside Adam, shifted and wiggled her bulk to get comfortable.

Carter said, "I don't think he needs CP—"

"Don't you worry, honey, I know what I'm doing, and while I'm doing it you better call a nurse or doctor or something in here right away." She put her hands on Adam's face, pulled his mouth open. Stuck a finger in his mouth, felt around. Leaned her face over Adam's with her mouth open wide.

He regained consciousness and opened his eyes.

Adam's scream was instinctive and came from his gut. It was jagged and ear-shattering, probably the most frightening thing anyone in the waiting room had heard all day.

Angie joined Adam with a scream of her own as she threw her tremendous weight backward and to her right. Everyone by the sofa stopped crying and hugging when they heard Angie's ankle break beneath her. Probably the most painful thing anyone in the waiting room had heard all day. Angie's scream was, without a doubt, the loudest.

Adam scrambled to his feet, but grabbed Carter's shoulder when dizziness swayed him. "Let's get the hell out of here."

Carter's attention was across the room. "No, wait. Come over here." Holding Adam's arm supportively, he led the way around Angie and closer to the sofa. The three young people had already forgotten about the sound of breaking bone and were crying again. The blonde cried out a single word over and over.

"My ankle, my *aaaankuulll!*" Angie shrieked. Peggy knelt beside her saying, "Oh! Oh! Oh! Oh!" The old woman who had been reading so silently and the man by the window quickly went to Angie's aid. The man went to the phone on the wall, picked up the receiver, waited a moment, then spoke to someone.

"If we help you," the old woman with the book said, leaning over Angie, "will you shut up?"

Adam and Carter watched the three people in front of the sofa. The hefty blonde woman who had nailed Adam on the forehead dropped onto the sofa, slid sideways and curled up, sobbing. The guy knelt in front of the sofa and leaned in close to whisper something to her. The dazed girl stared at nothing in particular.

"Monty!" the blonde cried. "Monty!" She repeated the name, dragged it into a longer cry each time.

Adam's eyes widened as he glanced at Carter, at the girl on the sofa. To Carter, he said, "Monty's dead?"

The blonde, the guy, and even the somnambulistic girl turned to Adam at once.

"You know Monty?" the blonde asked, voice thick with tears. She sat up slowly.

"Uuuhhh," Adam said.

Carter said, "We were, um, y'know—"

"Not well," Adam said.

"No, not very well at all."

"But we'd heard, um, you know, that he was, uh…here."

The narrow-faced guy eyed them as he got to his feet. "Who are you?"

"I've never met you," the blonde said. She stood beside her friend, taller than he, pear-shaped. "How do you know my brother?"

Adam said, "I-I-I…we…I-I-I—"

"Oh, *you're* Monty's sister?" Carter said, trying to smile without his lips trembling. "Y'know, Monty talked about you all the time. I wish, um—" He dropped the smile, cleared his throat. "I wish we could have met under better—"

The girl's wet face seized up with anger. "Monty hated my *guts*."

Carter's eyebrows bobbed up. "Oh. Well. Shit. You never would've guessed it from the way he—"

The guy stepped in front of the blonde and glared at Carter. "Who the fuck are, you? Huh, big guy?"

Behind him, the girl slurred, "The cops told us to watch for strange people comin' around. Suspicious people."

"And you two are definitely suspicious," the guy said.

Adam's vision blurred, breaths came more rapidly. Rusty railroad spikes were being driven into his skull. The pain in his head seemed to be directly connected to his stomach, where a big Fourth of July fireworks display finale was just beginning.

The guy looked at Adam. "What are you up to? Who *are* you?"

It happened suddenly, the result of his nearly incapacitating nervousness combined with the swift blow to the head. Adam bowed at the waist, as if greeting Japanese dignitaries, and vomited on the guy's shoes.

"Oh, Jesus *tits!*" the guy cried, jumping backward. He turned and clumsily wiped his shoes, one at a time, on the side of the sofa. He turned to the blonde. "Where are the cops?"

"'Cross the hall in I.C.U. Least, two were there when I left. Right after...right after..." Her large face quivered.

A nurse had arrived and tended to Angie, who would not stop screaming. Nor would she stop rolling her body back and forth, bunching her muumuu up around two dimpled slabs of white flesh.

"Don'tchoo worry, Angie," the nurse said, "the wheelchair is coming, and we'll get you to the emergency room."

There was a clear path to the door.

The guy turned to Adam, glared at him. "Go get 'em, Trudy," he said over his shoulder.

"Get what?" she said.

"The cops!"

Taking a step backward, Adam whispered to Carter, "Time to go."

"Sure!" Carter turned and broke into a run. Adam fought dizziness behind him.

"Hey, shit, wait a second!" the guy shouted as Carter and Adam left the room. They heard him shout, "Get the cops, dammit!"

"Hurry up!" Carter hissed. He reached back, grabbed Adam's arm and pulled him along.

"I'm dizzy!" Adam whispered.

"Be dizzy later!"

The dizziness receded quickly when Adam heard footsteps gaining on them from behind. A chrome foodcart rolled toward them up ahead.

"Stop them!" the guy shouted behind them.

A small middle-aged Asian woman wearing a hairnet and a white apron over her uniform peered skeptically around the corner of the cart.

"Those guys, stop them!"

The Asian woman disappeared behind the foodcart and stopped pushing it as Adam and Carter ran by.

"Stop *him!*" Carter called over his shoulder. "He's the bad guy!"

They rounded a corner, saw the elevator up ahead. Behind them, the guy's voice faded as he shrieked, "What the fuck're you—Jesus *Christ*, lady, will you get outta my fucking—back *off* you—"

"Stairs," Carter said, out of breath.

"Yeah," Adam agreed.

"Stop them! Somebody stop them!" the guy shouted to no one in particular. He was gaining on them again, but had not yet rounded the corner.

They passed the elevator, and Adam pointed to a door marked **STAIRS**. Slammed through it into the stairwell, stumbled down the stairs while Carter stopped and turned to the door. As he silently closed it, a voice shouted in the corridor outside.

"Where did they go? Jesus *tits*, where did they *go?*" The guy was angry.

Carter hurried after Adam, caught up on the second floor landing. Halfway to the first floor, they heard footsteps above them, muttering. Adam stopped on a step, looked up the stairwell.

The guy peered over the rail at Adam. "You bastards!" A moment later, muffled as he leaned into the corridor: "Bring the fucking cops, for God's sake! They're taking the stairs!" Then footsteps ratta-tatted down the stairs.

Adam went faster, somehow kept his balance and did not plunge headfirst down the stairs. At the bottom, he pushed through the door and looked around quickly, tried to get his bearings. Carter would not let him. He grabbed Adam's arm and pulled him to the left, through the main lobby, to the automatic doors.

The thick summer heat crashed into them the second they stepped outside. They picked up speed in spite of it on their way to the parking structure.

Carter groaned on the way up the stairs. "You couldn't find a lower parking space?"

Behind them, a distant, "Hey! I think they went over there!"

They did not stop running. All the way up the steps, across the third level. The only thing that stopped them was the car. They ran into it. Panting, grunting.

There was no one behind them, no one hurried toward them.

In the car, Adam started the engine.

"What happened?" Rain asked.

Adam said, "Shut up," and backed out of the parking slot.

"Don't puh-panic, Adam," Carter said. He clutched the dashboard with both hands, trying to get his breath back.

"Don't panic? Carter, I passed panic a long time ago."

"No, I mean, your driving. Don't speed. You'll be tempted, but don't. It's a dead giveaway."

Rain leaned in between them. "What's the matter? What the fuck happened?"

Adam looked at her in the rearview for a couple seconds as he approached the parking structure's exit gate. "Rain? Shut. Up."

Both Adam and Carter looked around carefully as they emerged into the sunlight.

"Maybe we're okay," Carter said.

"Not until we're out of here," Adam said as he drove out of the parking lot, merged into traffic.

Rain shouted, "Goddammit, what the fuck is going on?"

They shouted together, "Shut *up!*"

After dropping Carter off at his house, Adam drove Rain home in silence. He went upstairs to his room, flopped on the bed, and almost immediately fell asleep. An hour later, he awoke with a great jerk, ready to keep running. But no one was chasing him. He took a couple minutes to wake up, then realized he had come to a decision, as if it had happened in his sleep. In the hall, he went down to Rain's room.

There were two things Rain needed to know. First, that his finger-prints were all over the gun she was keeping, and he wanted them back. Second, he would kill his dad, but he would have absolutely nothing to do with killing Gwen.

He stopped outside her bedroom, raised his hand to knock. The door was already open an inch. Adam lowered his arm and said, "Rain? We need to talk."

No reply, not a sound.

"Rain?" He nudged the door and it eased open a foot, a little more. Poked his head into the room and looked around.

The decapitated clown was gone and the headboard had been cleaned. A large poster of Marilyn Manson covered a good portion of the wall behind the bed, including the bullet hole.

Although the room was still a disaster area, he could see more of the carpet than he had seen the last time. Had she actually picked up some of her mess, or simply rearranged it? Impossible to tell.

He stepped back and looked up and down the hall. No one was around, the house was quiet. Adam quickly stepped into Rain's bedroom and closed the door.

Where would she put that gun? he wondered, eyes darting around the room. Clothes were everywhere and hid any number of things. Adam got on all fours and swept his hands through the clothes. Back and forth over the carpet, through silky underwear, over shoes and T-shirts and jeans. No gun. He went to the big papa-san chair in the corner and plunged his hands into the mass of clothes that covered it.

Two angry voices drifted upstairs, grew louder.

Adam's hand fell on cold metal and he pulled it out of the pile. Monty's gun.

" — and you're not going anywhere until we talk." It was Gwen.

He held his breath.

"Come on, Goddammit," Gwen said. Closer now, in the hall and closing in. "In your room, now, c'mon!"

With no time to think, he rushed into the dark walk-in closet and was pulling the door closed behind him when the bedroom door opened.

"What were you thinking?" Gwen said as she slammed the bedroom door. "Just what the fuck were you *thinking*, getting involved with him? He's scum."

"I didn't get invol—"

"Close enough! You got lucky. He died."

Adam stood perfectly still and listened.

Gwen continued: "From now on, until this is all over, you have no contact with anyone, you understand? No old friends, no new friends, and no—"

"What the fuck am I supposed to do, sit in my fuckin' room all the time?"

"Later you can do whatever the fuck you want. But for now, you'll do as I say, or we're screwed, okay? Are you listening to me? You think I'm enjoying this? Huh?"

In the closet, Adam frowned as he listened, confused.

Rain spoke in an even tone when she asked, "I'm supposed to live like a fuckin' grandma while you're…doing what?"

"Whatever I have to do, just like you. Where's your pot? I need some."

"You're not takin' none of my fuckin' shit!" Rain shouted.

"You wouldn't *have* that shit if I didn't give it to you. Jesus Christ, don't be such an ingrateful cunt!"

The sound of a drawer opening.

"You're fuckin' crazy if you think I need *you* to get pot," Rain said. "I can get drugs you don't even know *exist* whenever I want, and I can—"

"But you need me to get *this*, so shut the fuck up."

"To get what?"

"All this money, stupid." Gwen sounded suddenly weary.

Sweat beaded Adam's forehead, dribbled down his spine.

"Here's a couple joints," Rain said.

Gwen lowered her voice. "Is he gonna do this, or what? I don't know if I can spend another second in bed with that troll-dick."

"He's gonna do it. He's too fuckin' scared not to."

"Well, start pushing him to do it soon, okay?"

"I am."

"You gonna use the gun you got from your friend? Who you shouldn't've been fucking around with in the *first* place?"

"Probably."

"What do you mean, *probably?*"

"I don't know, I'm just kinda makin' this up as I go along, you know? Gimme a break."

"How does my eye look?"

"Swelling's gone down a little, but the bruise is ugly. Want me to hit you again? That's my favorite part of this whole fuckin' deal, y'know. Gettin' to punch the shit outta your face once in awhile."

"No, I don't want you to hit me again. I'll wait a couple days."

A pause between them. Adam's mouth still hung open, fists dug fingernails into his wet palms.

"You keeping him happy?" Gwen asked.

"He's too fuckin' uptight to be happy, but I'm managing. Why, you wanna fuck him?"

Gwen ignored the remark.

"You do understand that if you fuck Adam, you could fuck everything. Right?"

"Don't be an idiot," Gwen said. "It wouldn't make much difference if I did, and you know it. Oh, Rain, honey…are you jealous?" She grinned. "You're not getting attached to him, are you?"

"Fuck, no!"

"He'll probably be going away after this."

"What if it doesn't work?"

"It will if we do. If not…we'll burn that bridge when we get to it."

"Can I go shopping now?"

"Shopping for what?"

"Nunna your fuckin' business."

"As long as you get your money from me, it's my business."

"I don't need your fuckin' money! I just wanna get some clothes, a couple CDs."

"Don't shop for clothes alone. Look at this shit, it's like a trailer park blew up in here. You dress like white trash, Rain, you're in Beverly Hills now, for Chrissakes. We don't want to offend any of these Hollywood fucks. When Michael's gone, we'll still be living here awhile, maybe as long as a year. For appearances. So stop walkin' around like a trailer tramp before the fashion police beat the shit out of you with their mauve clubs."

"Yeah, awright, jeez. Mauve clubs. Very funny."

"Okay, okay," Gwen said. The sound of the door opening. "Go shopping. But stay the fuck outta Walmart! I mean, go to Rodeo Drive, we can afford it."

The door closed and their muted voices grew more and more faint. Until the room was silent.

Adam's bulging eyes stared at the strip of light glowing beneath the closet door. How could he have let all this happen? He was not that stupid, not *that* desperate for sex. Was he?

That explains why I've been getting so much, he thought. *Alyssa's the only one who's not fucking me to death.* Alyssa was different. He wanted to go to her, tell her everything. But it would get worse, he was sure, and he did not want her connected. She could not know a single detail about what he had decided, at that moment there in the closet, to do.

TWENTY-TWO

The sun shone somewhere behind the ugly layer of dirt in the sky. High in the distance, an airliner climbed steadily but slowly, as if its engines could not reach full power in such polluted air.

Adam and Carter were stretched out on lounge chairs in the shade near Carter's pool. They stared silently through their sunglasses at the backyard. Birds chirped and sang loudly all around them.

It was almost four o'clock in the afternoon, hours after their visit to the hospital. After leaving Rain's bedroom, Adam had been desperate to get out of his house. He had gone to Carter's, surprised to find him swimming in the pool. He told Carter what had happened in Rain's room, what he had overheard.

Carter had not reacted in more than a minute. Just stared out over the yard, watching the noisy birds. His silence made Adam nervous.

"Are you okay?" Carter asked. "What are you going to do?"

Adam did not take his eyes off the yard. He sat in a ball, arms folded over his bent knees, chin resting on his arm. He shrugged. "I just...I can't believe Rain was supposed to fuck me...and Gwen wasn't. Gwen started on me before Rain even got here. But I know what Rain meant now about their 'original plan.' They were going to get me to kill Dad. I mean, between Rain fucking my brains out, and Gwen fucking my brains out, and on top of that, Gwen getting beaten up by my dad…I think it would have worked. But they were stabbing each other in the back over me. I'm not worth that kinda shit!"

"Don't be so hard on yourself, Adam. You're worth nothing but shit." After a moment of thought, Carter said, "Maybe Gwen was protecting herself."

Carter's remark was like a light coming on in a dark room. It made perfect sense. Adam turned and sat on the edge of the long chair, faced Carter.

"Yeah, she was probably afraid Rain was going to do exactly what Rain *is* going to do, if I don't stop her," he said.

Carter nodded. "And maybe she thought some hot sweet lovin' would make you less likely to go along with Rain and kill her." He shrugged. "And it worked. She's been your biggest problem with this all along, right?"

Adam nodded slowly while an absurd image formed in his head: standing naked and rigid in posture and penis on a giant gameboard, being moved here and there by two giant, lovely, feminine hands.

"I wonder what she'd do if she found out," Carter said.

"If who found out what?"

"If Rain found out you were doing her mom."

Adam laughed. "That's a great idea! Oh, shit, that could turn into a catfight. Wouldn't that be cool? I'll have to get out the video camera. It'd be so wonderful if they killed each other. Oh, Jesus, I wish I could get them *all* to kill each other."

"Might not be such a good idea to start trouble at home. Maybe you should get your ass outta there, get a place of your own."

Adam nodded. "That's not a bad idea." He thought about it awhile. "Under normal circumstances, that's probably what I'd do. But I think I'm gonna stay there for awhile and kill all of them."

Carter flinched, watched him carefully for a moment.

"You'll have to help me," Adam said. "You said you would."

Carter cleared his throat. "Yeah. I did, didn't I?"

"Unless you were just in it for the blow jobs."

"I wouldn't get my dick anywhere near Rain now."

Adam left the chair and walked around it slowly. "I may have to."

"Could you? After this?"

"Oh, yeah, I could. Easily. She likes me to hit her during sex. Beat her." A grin opened slowly on his face. "I think I could make her pretty Goddamned happy, if she'd give me another chance."

Carter shook his head rapidly, waving his hands in the air. "No, no, no, Adam, if you're gonna kill her later, beating her up now is just gonna make trouble for you. That's the kinda thing that'll make you look a lot more suspicious afterward."

"You think?"

"I *know*, you lumbering bumblefuck!" Carter stood, a towel slung around his neck and hanging from his shoulders. "How do you wanna do it?"

"I'd like to put them in one of those giant, flat, square things they used in *Superman 2*. Send Dad, Gwen, and Rain hurtling through space together for all eternity. But I wouldn't know where to *start* looking for one of those things, would you? So we're going to call your friend."

"What friend?"

"Billy Rivers. The guy with the exploding throat." Adam stopped, faced him. "By the way, you were swimming earlier. You haven't been in that pool since before eighth grade."

"Well, I'm kinda self-conscious about, y'know, taking my shirt off when other people're around, that's why. You know me. But since we haven't been able to get back to the gym, I figured I'd get some exercise on my own."

"That's good, Carter. I'm glad."

They went upstairs to Carter's studio to make the call. When he got an answering machine, Carter did not leave a message, just hung up. "I'm sure he's home. He never answers the phone. Let's go to his place."

Billy Rivers lived in the San Fernando Valley, in North Hollywood. On the way there, Adam said, "From now on, I think we should be very, very careful."

"Careful about what?"

"Everything. Don't do anything that might get you noticed. You know, don't be loud or obnoxious, or anything. People remember stuff like that. We don't want to be remembered."

"Yeah, right." After nearly a minute of frowning through the windshield, Carter asked, "Um, why is it exactly that we don't want to be remembered?"

"Once this is over, I'll be the only one left, they'll *have* to suspect me. For awhile, anyway, but I'll have alibis. Theoretically. I don't know what they'll be yet. Anyway, if I'm charged, there'll be a trial. The prosecution's gonna be looking for witnesses to testify against me. So we never know when we're being witnessed by a potential witness."

"A trial, huh?" Carter sounded concerned.

Adam took a look at his friend, saw the worry in his face. "Don't worry, Carter. No matter what happens to me, you'll be fine. If I end up in the O.J. chair, you won't be involved."

"I wasn't worried about that," Carter said. "I guess I didn't..." He was silent awhile. "I guess I didn't stop to think about it until now. A trial never occurred to me."

"It's good to think about it, but don't get attached to the idea. It's not gonna happen, if I can help it."

Billy Rivers lived in an apartment complex that looked like an old, run-down motel. It might have been at one time. It was called Waving Palms Estates. The palms were too short and squat to wave, even if they had a reason, and nowhere in sight could Adam find anything that might be called an "estate."

There was a small courtyard in the center of the U-shaped building. No pool or playground, just weeds standing in the cracks of an expanse of old concrete, some fossilized dog feces here and there.

A man sat outside a ground-level corner apartment in the back. His chair appeared to be of the lawn variety—the kind with a folding aluminum frame and faded strips of worn, ratty nylon stretched across the seat and back—although it was impossible to see enough of the chair to tell. The man wore a pair of horn-rimmed glasses, small purple shorts, and house slippers. His enormous belly and two sour-milk-skinned breasts, inverted triangles of flesh that sagged at opposite angles, staunchly obeyed the laws of gravity. A ballgame played on a small radio perched on the window ledge behind him.

"Looks like somebody sculpted that guy outta Crisco," Carter whispered.

"Ignore him. Don't even look at him."

But the man looked at them. He reached up and lowered his glasses on his nose. Worked his toothless gums as he peered over the top of the frames at Adam and Carter.

The man called out, something unintelligible. It had the same sound as globs of cold Cream of Wheat hitting a hard, flat surface. It hardly sounded like English. Adam and Carter hurried up the stairs. They were halfway up when the man called again, this time louder and somewhat clearer.

"Hey, you boyth! Who ya here for?" If rubber could talk, it would have the same voice. The man stared up at them, arms arest on the sizeable roll of fat that went around the middle of his body, like a large girdle of cream cheese going bad.

Carter and Adam stopped halfway up the stairs and looked down at the man. Standing, his morbidly fat belly threatened to crush his bony, knobby-kneed legs.

"What did you say?" Carter said.

"Are you deaf? I *thaid*, who ya here for?"

Carter pointed up at the second door and said, "Billy Rivers, apartment 202."

The man nodded, waved. "I'm Floyd. The manager."

They started up the stairs again.

"He's the manager?" Carter muttered.

"You think he even *owns* a shirt?" Adam whispered.

"I've only been here a few times, but always at night. I've never seen the guy before. I'd remember him."

All the apartments along that side had sliding glass doors. A dark blue curtain hung on the inside of Billy's. Carter knocked on the glass.

"That party we went to wasn't here, was it?" Adam asked.

"No, that was his parents' house. He still lived with them back then. His dad's a hack musician. Scores low-budget, straight-to-video action movies. His mom works in kiddie cartoon shows at Fox." He knocked again, a little harder.

"Why does he live in *this* place?"

The curtain pulled aside and a young man in his late twenties looked out. His eyes and mouth turned downward sadly on the outsides. He held a cordless phone to his left ear. Half his mouth smiled when he saw Carter, and he opened the door.

"C'mon in," Billy said, his hand over the phone's mouthpiece. "Just give me a sec, okay?" He turned, disappeared into the bathroom and closed the door.

The apartment was dark and thick with the smells of stale cigarette butts and marijuana. For a change, the air was worse inside than outside. Carter left the glass door open to air the place out a little.

The apartment was too cluttered and cramped for furniture. Adam noticed what the room was cluttered with and gasped. Wall shelves held every kind of face imaginable. Bloody human body parts were lined up on the floor. Prosthetics covered the tabletops, even in the tiny kitchenette. Adam turned around slowly, marveling at Billy's work.

"This is incredible," he said. "No offense, Carter, but he's even better than you. That's saying a lot, too."

"'Course he's better than me. He's a genius."

"And he's not working professionally?"

"No," Carter whispered. "That's a long story. He got his first job on some monster movie, but something happened. Nobody's sure what, but it really hurt him, I guess, changed him. I don't know if it's true, but I heard his parents pulled some strings to get him dropped from the job. They don't like what he does. They think it's too ugly. Beneath them, or something. But it's what Billy lives for. He moved out, disappeared for almost a year. By the time anybody saw him again, he'd found this place, and he...wasn't the same."

"You didn't perform an immediate intervention? This place is not a place to live. Won't his parents help him out?"

"They do. He takes their money, but I heard he hasn't spoken to them since he left their house. He saves money by living here, so he can afford to make those." He nodded at the faces on the shelves.

"Does he sell them?" Adam whispered.

"Once in awhile, to fans. But always for a lot less than they're worth." Carter shook his head, frustrated. "If he won't work in the movies, he should at least make a living off these things. They'd sell at sci-fi conventions like crack in Inglewood. He could take orders, do custom work." Carter shrugged. "Nobody knows why he doesn't. But we all think it's because of whatever happened on his first job."

"Hell, I may buy a couple myself, just to have on the shelf. We've got to get this guy out of here, Carter. Get him some work."

"Don't say anything to him about...anything, okay? He won't talk about it, and it'll just upset him. I'm serious, maybe you should just let me do the talking, okay?"

Adam nodded as Billy came out of the bathroom.

"Sorry, Carter," Billy said. "How ya doin', man?"

"Good, Billy. You remember my friend, Adam, don't you?"

Billy swept back some of his long, thin, brown hair, which fell past his shoulders. His scalp was visible on top, where the hair was thinning fast. "Uh…sorry, 'fraid I don't. But nice to meetcha, Adam. Any frienda Carter's. You guys want somethin' t'drink?" He was about six feet tall, but his shoulders hunched and his head drooped. He was so thin, his chest appeared to be collapsing.

"I don't think we'll be sticking around, Billy," Adam said, glancing at Carter.

"Yeah, Billy, we need you to help us find somebody. Remember a party you threw at your parents' house about two years ago?"

Billy frowned as he reached behind him to scratch his back. His body stiffened suddenly. Mouth dropped open, eyes squeezed tightly shut.

"Billy?" Carter said.

Billy dropped to the floor on his back and began to convulse.

"Oh, Jesus!" Adam said.

The convulsions stopped. Something moved under the tank top. Under Billy's skin. In his belly.

"Oh, *Jesus!*" Adam shouted.

Billy's flat belly exploded. Viscous blood and globs of organs were thrown up through the holes in the tank top, and splattered all over Billy.

Adam's jaw hurt because his mouth was open so far, but he did not feel it. He was too preoccupied with the tears in the fabric of his sanity. His horror became panic, and he ran from the apartment crying, "Oh, Jesus! Oh, God! Oh, Jesus! Oh, God!" Halfway down the stairs, he heard laughter coming from Billy's apartment.

"Fanfuckingtastic, man!" Carter shouted.

Below, Floyd eyed Adam on the stairs. Leaning on the rail, trying to catch his breath and slow down his heart, Adam stared back. Floyd lowered his glasses and shouted something that sounded like a spitball hitting a chalkboard. Adam ignored him and went back up the stairs.

"Hey, you okay?" Carter asked, stepping out of the apartment.

Adam was angry. Embarassed, too, but mostly angry.

"That was something new!" Carter said with enthusiasm. "His exploding stomach!"

Adam's voice was low and even, but unpleasant. "You know what's going to explode, Carter? Me, that's what, I'm going to explode if we don't just do what we came here to do and leave. Okay?"

"He does that kinda thing all the time," Carter said apologetically. "Tries new stuff on his friends, you know? I'm sorry if you—"

"Let's just *do* it, okay?" Adam said, and went back into the apartment.

TWENTY-THREE

Don't piss off any truck drivers," Carter said as Adam drove them into the desert outside of Los Angeles.

"Why?" Adam asked.

"Didn't you see *Duel*, man? You wanna end up like Dennis Weaver?"

"Carter, nobody wants to end up like Dennis Weaver."

Laughter in the backseat. Billy said, "You guys're funny."

Back in his apartment, Billy had told them it would be a very bad idea to go see his friend, Diz, on their own. "For one thing," he had said, "it's almost impossible t'find the place. And they don't like, um, strangers showin' up, y'know, unannounced." Adam had suggested they call ahead, but Billy said they would get only a voicemail system.

Quietly, sheepishly, Billy had refused to give them directions to Diz's place unless they agreed to take him along. "S'really for your own good," he had said.

Adam looked in the rearview and said, "Hey, Billy, why would Diz be upset if we showed up without you?"

"Come on, Adam," Carter said, rolling his eyes. "The guy sells drugs and guns and explosives and God knows what else. I think I'd be a little tense, too, in his position."

"Oh, no, it's not just Diz," Billy said. He leaned forward and rested his elbows on the backs of the seats. "It's his parents, too."

"What do they do?" Adam said.

"Uh, well…" He chuckled. "They just do, like…stuff."

"What kind of stuff?" Carter asked.

"The, um…well, the illegal kind."

"Sounds like a wonderful family," Adam said.

"They're all real nice folks," Billy said. "Well, um…Diz is kinda moody these days. But his parents're real nice. His mom, anyways."

"Why is Diz moody these days?" Adam asked.

"Oh, that, well…he got hurt. 'Bout a year and a half ago, he was workin' with explosives, y'know? I mean, um, it's what he does, right? Anyways, somethin' went wrong an' the thing went off. Right in Diz's face. He lost some of his fingers and, um…some of his face. He's pretty self-conscious about it. Been kinda moody ever since. For a long time, he wouldn't leave the compound, not even on a job, or nothin'. He's gettin' better, though."

Adam's eyebrows popped up. "Compound? What are they, a militia?"

Billy grinned. "Thass what they call it. To be funny, I think. Just jokin'. Alls that's out there is a buncha trailers."

"They live in a trailer park?" Carter asked.

"Oh, no, just a buncha trailers. All theirs."

Adam asked, "Why all the trailers?"

"Uh, well…" He got that sheepish look on his face again, ducked his head. "They got some businesses they run out there."

"Businesses?" Carter asked.

"What kind of businesses?" Adam said.

"Oh, I…I'm not supposed to talk about it. I promised."

Adam and Carter exchanged a worried look. Adam said, "Billy, if you don't want to tell us, that's fine, but…I really need to know if we're going to get in some kind of trouble by going out to Diz's house."

"Not as long as you're with me." He smiled into the rearview. "Mostly it's just, like, Internet stuff. Y'know, websites with illegal porn, an' stuff. Except for Mrs. C.'s. She's a…um, whaddaya call it? A doma…dominatrix. That's legal. But, um, just don't tell 'em I told ya 'bout it."

That was not the reassurance Adam was looking for. He was tired of walking into the unknown — the party at Monty's, those awful trips to the liquor store and the hospital—and wanted to know what he was getting into for a change. He did not like the sound of what Billy had said. But where else would he get explosives? Rain probably knew people who could build a bomb blindfolded, but he wanted nothing more to do with any of her friends. Or Rain, if he could help it. It was Diz or nothing.

"Is 'Diz' short for something?" Adam asked.

"Short for Dizzy. I don't know if anybody knows his real name."

"Why Dizzy?" Carter asked. "Because of the accident?"

"Oh, um, 'cause he's...well, he's dizzy. He choked on a vodka bottle cap when he was a little kid. They said he died, then, um, they were able to bring him back. But, well, he got a little brain damage. Not enough oxygen, y'know? Hasn't been right ever since. He's always just a little...dizzy. Sometimes it's worse than others, but mosta th'time he's just a little dizzy."

"Oh, my God," Adam muttered, slumping in his seat. "This is Hell, we're in Hell."

"What's the matter?" Carter asked.

"Did you hear that? They sound like the mutant family from *The Hills Have Eyes!*"

Billy cleared his throat. "Oh, um, y'know...y'might not wanna say that in, um...in front of 'em. Y'know?"

"I'm sorry, Billy," Adam said. "Don't worry, I wouldn't do that."

"No prob." Billy smiled and leaned back into the seat.

Carter turned to Adam and asked quietly, "You changing your mind?"

"No, I'm losing it."

"Why? What's the matter all of a sudden?"

"All of a sudden? Where the hell have you been all week?"

Billy leaned forward again. "So what're you guys gonna blow up?"

Carter turned to him uncomfortably. "Well, Billy, we really didn't want to talk about that, you know? That's why we asked you not to ask us that question."

Billy's droopy eyes slowly widened. "Oh, yeah, y'did, dincha? Okay, sorry 'bout that." Again he smiled and settled into the seat.

Adam sighed, spoke quietly to Carter. "This Diz guy will want to know that, too."

"Maybe not," Carter said. "He probably deals with lots of people who don't want anybody to know what they're up to."

"You think?" Adam said. "A one-eyed maimed guy with chronic dizziness who handles explosives, you think he gets a lot of business?"

Carter rolled his eyes. "Okay, so maybe to make up for the dizziness, he sells his explosives at a discount."

Billy leaned forward again. "Well, um, Diz doesn't exactly *sell* explosives. He just, um, y'know, works with 'em. I...I thought you guys knew that."

"*Works* with them?" Adam said, his voice getting louder. "I'm driving a hundred and fifty miles into the desert to buy explosives, and he doesn't *sell* them?"

"He was selling them at that party," Carter said. "Wasn't he?"

"He only did that back then 'cause he needed some fast money. He don't do it anymore. If you got somethin' you need t'blow up, he'll do it for ya. Y'know, for a fee. That's what he's best at."

"Charging a fee?" Adam asked.

"No, blowin' things up."

Adam sighed and said no more. Mentally threw up his arms and hoped everything went at least as well as could be expected under the circumstances.

✝

Like a deadly cancer steadily consuming healthy cells in a human body, Los Angeles continued to spread over the earth, eating up the desert along the way. It pushed the edge of the wilderness farther and farther from the city's glimmering center. Soon, Adam feared, there would be no desert, and all of California would be Los Angeles. Then all of the west coast. The city would continue to spread until it reached the east coast and had swallowed the entire country, then the continent, and beyond. It had long been Adam's opinion that Los Angeles should be surgically excised from the earth, like a giant infected cyst filled with pus and hair before it rendered the rest of the planet septic.

"Okay, um, you're gonna wanna take your next right," Billy said.

"My *next* right?" Adam asked. "I haven't seen a right or a left since we got off the freeway."

It had been a long trip. They had made only one stop, at a convenience store in the small town of Baker, to get something to drink and use the restrooms.

The desert surrounding Baker was humped with a scattering of large dunes in the distance on either side of the road. Wildflowers and the blooms on several different kinds of cacti and bushes provided bright colors in the shade of ironwood and yucca trees, and the occasional screwbean mesquite and desert willow. Creosote shrubs were everywhere, rising up in dark green clumps as high as ten feet.

After Baker, Billy had directed Adam to take a right off the freeway. They'd gone miles and miles, seeing nothing but desert. The road's rough pavement ended abruptly, and they went miles more along a dirt road. Adam had bought a bottle of cranberry juice at the convenience store and finished it quickly. By the time they reached the dirt road, he had to go to the bathroom.

After a good twelve, maybe fifteen miles, the dirt road dwindled to no more than two ruts worn into the ground and meandered for miles more, going around hillocks and between trees, on through the desert toward a large hill.

"Dammit, I need an SUV," Adam said. "This car isn't even mine!"

"And for that," Carter said, "you should be thankful."

The ruts led them around the hill, and what Billy had referred to earlier as a "compound" appeared as if from nowhere. It was difficult from Adam's point of view to tell how many trailers were grouped together in an especially lush part of the desert. A dozen, maybe fifteen. They were all a sandy brown, and probably blended well with the landscape when viewed from the air. A tall Cyclone fence enclosed the block of trailers, with barbed wire stretched around the top. Just beyond the trailers stood a long, tan, metal building with no windows. It was all nestled in the crook of a U-shaped crop of hills.

A small guard booth stood just inside the fence on the right side of the gate. Someone sat slumped inside.

"Stop at, um, th'gate," Billy said, "and I'll get us in." He rolled down his window when Adam stopped, leaned out. "Jesus!" he shouted. "Jesus!" Billy sounded like he was taking the Lord's name in vain.

The figure in the booth stood and stepped out. A muscular shirtless Mexican guy in cutoffs, no older than twenty, squinted at Billy.

"It's me! Billy! I'm here t'see Diz. Let us in."

Jesus nodded, satisfied, stepped back into the booth. The gate slid open slowly.

"Checkpoint Charlie," Carter said.

Adam looked over his shoulder at Billy. "Shouldn't that be pronounced, Hay-soos instead of Je-zus?"

"Yeah, s'posed to be," Billy said with another of his almost embarassed smiles. "But Jesus likes everybody t'call him…um, well, *Je*sus. 'Cause it pisses off his mom."

As he drove past, Adam glanced into the booth. Several rifles were on racks on the back wall.

"Okay, um, just go along there," Billy said, pointing.

Adam drove along one side of the block of trailers. They were in mint condition and stood on concrete foundations, but were closer together than they would be in a legitimate trailer park.

"Jus' park in front of th'house," Billy said.

Adam asked, "What house?"

Past the trailers, a large ranch-style house appeared, cozy at the foot of the hill. The desert was its yard, and a natural-looking path of flat desert rocks led to the front door from a crude circular driveway made of ruts driven into the ground.

"This is unreal," Carter mumbled as Adam killed the engine in front of the house.

Adam looked at Billy very seriously. "Okay, Billy, now think. Is there anything *else* we should know before we go in there?"

"Um…" Billy bowed his head for a moment, shook it. "No. Juss, um…well, y'know, don't mention Diz's, um, face or hands, okay? Or eyebrows."

"Eyebrows?" Adam said.

Carter cleared his throat and asked, "What would he do if we were to *accidentally* mention his face or hands or eyebrows?"

Billy's face darkened with a frown. "Oh, he don't take it too well, not Diz, no. 'Specially the eyebrows."

Adam looked at Carter and said quickly, "I think we can handle that, don't you?"

"You won't hear about it from me," Carter said.

As he emerged from the car, the heat burned his lungs, dried up his mouth and throat. The car had grown a skin of dust.

Billy led them along the stone path. Halfway to the door, Adam heard unsettling sounds behind him. Quick, heavy padding sounds on the ground. Adam turned and cried, "Shit!"

One, two…three…*four* pit bulls ran through an open gate in the Cyclone fence, toward them. Squat legs kicked up clouds of dust as thick muscles rippled. Pink tongues lolled between glimmering sets of bared fangs. All four dogs silent as death.

TWENTY-FOUR

Certain they were about to sustain serious physical injuries and possible permanent disfigurement, Adam and Carter ran for the house. Adam cried, "Holy shit, holy shit!" as Carter cried, "Fuck me! Fuck me!" They ran with arms stretched out rigidly ahead of them, like characters in a Scooby-Doo cartoon running from a mummy. Together, they slammed into the heavy dark oak door and pounded it with their fists as they screamed.

Adam: "Openthedoor openthedoor openthe—"

Carter: "Fuck me fuck me fuck me—"

Adam glanced over his shoulder. Stopped shouting and did a double take.

The pit bulls jumped up on Billy, paws leaving dusty tracks on his clothes as he talked to them cheerfully. "Hey, guys, how's it goin', huh? Huh?" Grinning, he roughed them up, let them chew playfully on his hands.

"Hey," Adam said as he poked Carter with a knuckle.

Carter stopped screaming, turned. He and Adam watched the playful dogs for a moment. Caught their breath, waited for panic to recede.

Billy shook his head and laughed at them. "Y'know, I like you guys. But you're, like, *way* big pussies."

The oak door opened as a few harsh, wet coughs sounded from behind it. Wheezy, rattling coughs. A man's voice said, "What in theeee *fuck* is going on out here?"

A narrow head peered around the edge of the door wearing what appeared, at first, to be a furry cap. It was, in fact, a black toupee sparkling with a few strands of silver. The face beneath it was in its late sixties, but the voice was older. Strings of smoke rose from a long cigarette in a short, shiny black holder clenched between his teeth. His gray eyes moved up and down their bodies one at a time.

"You all right?" he asked. "Sounded like somebody was bein' circumcised out here, Jeez-iz." He stepped out from behind the door wearing only a white towel around his waist. Beneath it, an erection pushed willfully at the terrycloth.

Oh, terrific, wonderful, Adam thought. *We're never gonna be seen again.*

Adam said, "Sorry to drag you out of the shower, but we—"

"Nah, I wasn't in the shower," he said, wheezing with asthma or emphesema. "I was workin'. I'm always workin'. Well, come on in."

Adam looked back at Billy, who was still romping with the pit bulls. "Hey, Billy?" he called. Billy had forgotten all about them. He was remarkably talented at making masks and prosthetics, but he did not give the impression of being one who engaged in a great deal of critical thought.

The man held his cigarette holder between two knuckles as he stepped back and waved them into the house. He was short and wiry, but his pasty complexion gave him a look of ill health. The nicotine-yellowed silver hair on his sagging chest and belly did not match his toupee.

Adam and Carter looked at one another. Carter shrugged. Adam gestured for him to go first.

"You been here before, or what?" the man asked.

Adam replied, "Well, we just came with—"

"I got so many comin' in and out now—you know, this bidness has just gone through the roof. I got six websites, I can do two-three videos a day, every day if I so fucking choose. I could do a lot more, but my doctor tells me to slow down a little 'cause of my pump. But still I got boys comin' and goin', I can't keep up with all the boys around here." He closed the door and turned to them in the foyer, laughing. "But we can always use some more!"

The foyer walls were bare. A small surveillance camera watched from an overhead corner. Looked directly at Adam.

The man stepped between them, put his arms across their backs, cigarette holder clamped between his teeth like Franklin Roosevelt. Led them around a corner and down a hall, his erection pointing the way. He smelled of gin.

Another camera watched the hallway.

The man said, "I seen you boys around here before? Who sent you?"

Adam gulped before saying, "We came here with —"

"You want something to eat?" the man asked. "I got all kindsa sammiches and snacks in the kitchen. Beer, soda, milk, whatever you want."

Adam said, "Uh-uh."

"Nothing for me, thanks," Carter said. His voice was dry and coarse. Neither of them had recovered yet from the pit bulls.

"Right in here." He pushed them through a door.

It was a long room, and a camera high in the corner kept an eye on it. A wall had been knocked out between two bedrooms. Four digital cameras stood on tripods facing four small, spare sets, one in each corner. The first was a sofa with an endtable and lamp at one end, a simple wooden coffee table in front of it, and a velvet painting of John Wayne in cowboy hat and kerchief on the wall. A half-empty fifth of gin stood on the endtable. The next set looked like an adolescent boy's bedroom, then a Jacuzzi, a weight room, all separated by cheap divider screens. Near the Jacuzzi, two naked boys — fourteen, maybe fifteen — shared a fat beanbag chair, leaned on each other as they passed a joint between them. They sat up when the man walked in.

He puffed on the cigarette compulsively and a cloud of smoke encircled his head. "Dougie and Brandon," he said, gesturing to the naked boys as he went to the endtable and retrieved the bottle of gin. Took a healthy swig. "They just finished a live show on the 'net. You boys ever done anything like this?"

"That's illegal," Adam muttered, frowning at the underage boys. He had not intended to speak the thought out loud and regretted it instantly.

"Illegal," the man said, voice hard as steel. "Did you just say 'illegal?' That's what I just heard you say, right? 'Illegal?' In my house you said that?"

This is really bad, Adam thought. He and Carter stammered over each other a moment. "This is a mistake," Adam said, "a terrible, awful mistake, we came with Billy, we're here to see—" His mind blanked and he turned to Carter, snapped his fingers rapidly. "What's his name, what's his name?"

Billy hurried into the room. "Sorry 'bout that, guys," he said. "Hey, Mr. C."

"Billy." Mr. C.'s suspicious eyes never left Adam. He took a couple more swallows of the gin, nearly finished it. Clamped the cigarette holder between his teeth. "I can't believe you brought somebody into my house who'd say the word 'illegal,' Billy. And in my fucking *presence*!"

No longer laughing, Billy looked at Mr. C. seriously and said, "We're here on business. We gotta see Diz. I just got distracted by the dogs, assall. Sorry about surprisin' you like that." It was the most alert and articulate he had been all day.

"On business, huh?" His eyes moved back and forth between Adam and Carter. "You sure these two're okay?"

"Oh, yeah, Mr. C.," Billy said, nodding fast. "I've known 'em for years, Mr. C., I'd, um, I'd put my life in their hands."

Mr. C.'s right eye narrowed and he plucked the cigarette holder from his teeth. "Are you two Hollywood? I know Billy's Hollywood. *You* Hollywood?"

"My dad's a screenwriter," Adam said as Carter nodded.

"I wanted to go the Hollywood route," Mr. C. said, nodding. "You know, make some low-budget teen sex comedies, maybe a slasher flick or two. I didn't have no delusions, I wasn't after an Oscar, nothin' like that. But in Hollywood, you gotta have the right look, the right clothes. You gotta be the right age, know the right people. Gotta have the right color eyes. They never let me join in any of their Hollywood reindeer games." He tipped the bottle back, emptied it. Handed it to Billy. "Get ridda this and get me another one." Billy took the bottle and rushed out of the room. "But now? Hell, now I got alla Hollywood connections I need." He grinned and his dentures clacked. "I got Hollywood connections comin' outta my ass."

"You…do?" Adam asked cautiously.

"Oh, sure. Lotta big Hollywood players buy my tapes, my CD-roms." He became animated, gestured with his arms, cut trails of smoke in the air. "They want boy porn, they come to me 'cause I'm the best." He turned to Dougie and Brandon and said, "Hey, you two hit the shower. And tell Eric and Tony and, uh, lessee, Sean, tell 'em to come in here, 'kay?" To Adam and Carter again: "Some of 'em even rent my boys once in awhile. Now that, see, that wasn't even my idea. I wasn't inta that. I play it safe, and that's a treacherous trade, the meat trade. But all these big Hollywood agents kept showin' up, flashin' their cash, tryin' to get me to let some of the boys go to this party, that party, in Malibu or Beverly Hills, whatever, and pretty soon they convinced me. You wouldn't believe me if I told you some of the big names I do bidness with."

Without missing a beat, Adam nodded and said, "Yes, I would."

"The fact is, we're in the same bidness, Hollywood and me. Difference is, they do their work out in the open, and I'm out here in the fuckin' Mojave desert with the kangaroo rats and the fuckin' sidewinders and tarantulas I have nightmares about every fuckin' night. Well, that's one difference. Another's that I'm honest about what I do, I'm not a fuckin' hypocrite. And I got less overhead and a bigger mark-up. And best of all, I got a lotta Oscar-worthy material in my archives, I can tell you that. You know what I'm sayin'? Huh?" He grinned and his dentures shifted. Voice lowered, became gravelly. "So, if there's somethin' about you two that my friend Billy doesn't know, and you're plannin' to hand me over to the feds, you keep that in mind, okay? I go down, everybody goes down. Understand? *Everybody*." He held the cigarette holder like a pen and pointed the cigarette's ashy tip at them. "That might include somebody you know. Somebody you love." He coughed up a cold chuckle, pointed the cigarette between Adam's eyes and grinned. "Ya just never know with them Hollywood types." He smiled at Adam for a long moment, with no friendliness, no humor.

Billy jogged back into the room, handed Mr. C. a new bottle of gin. Said, "Well, um, we should, uh, find Diz. You know where he is, Mr. C.?"

Mr. C. waved his cigarette again. "I dunno, he's around someplace, I think."

Billy looked at Adam and Carter, gestured toward the door. "Okay, um, guys, less go find Diz, huh?"

Mr. C. stopped them as they were leaving the room. "Hey, you boys, you ever wanna make some extra cash, I got work for ya. Two hundred bucks a session. You're just what I'm lookin' for," he said to Adam. Then, to Carter: "And I gotta line of chubby videos you'd be perfect for."

"Chubby videos," Carter said. "Imagine that."

Adam said, "We're straight."

"Fine, just whack off in fronta the camera. Pays the same either way. Nobody does nothin' they don't wanna do, know what I'm sayin'? Just as long as we get a pretty dick in fronta the camera. This is a very friendly operation we got here, and everybody's happy. Like a big happy family."

"Well, um, they'll think it over, Mr. C.," Billy said, nodding. "See ya later."

In the hall, they followed Billy. Adam was so angry, his hands shook. Drugs, guns, and explosives were bad enough. But minors being used in pornography in an isolated desert compound was more than he could take. Over the throbbing of his heart in his ears, Adam listened for the sound of helicopters overhead. Doors being smashed open by FBI agents, machine guns spraying bullets.

"Hey, thanks, Billy," Carter whispered. "But could we, like, *not* get separated in the future? Okay?"

"I want out of here," Adam said.

"Oh, well, we can't leave yet," Billy said, "'cause we haven't found Diz."

The kitchen was very roomy, separated from the dining area by a long, broad bar. Trays of sandwich sections, raw vegetables, and potato chips were arranged on the mosaic tile top. A large chrome industrial refrigerator and freezer were set into a wall. Another camera watched from a corner overhead.

A thin olive-skinned boy of about fifteen stood at the bar eating chips, sampling the dips. He had stoned eyes, wet hair, and wore only a pair of boxer shorts.

"Heya, Tony," Billy said.

"'Sup, Billy?" the boy said with a smile.

"Brandon said Mr. C. wants you on th'set."

"Shit, I gotta dry my hair." He grabbed a fistful of chips and started out.

Adam stopped him. "Hey, Tony. Are you…well, you know, are you all right?"

Tony looked at him with narrowed eyes and a smartass smirk. "All right? The fuck you talkin' 'bout, dude?"

"Well, I mean…being here. Doing this. Wouldn't you rather, you know, go back to school?"

Tony grinned. "What, and leave show business?" He hurried out of the kitchen laughing, disappeared down the hall.

"You guys, um, stay here," Billy said. "I'm gonna go find Diz."

"Hey, Billy," Adam said. "Where's the bathroom?"

Billy pointed to an open doorway. "Straight through there, end of the hall."

"Thanks." When Billy was gone, Adam turned to Carter. He was eating a sandwich. Adam slapped the back of his head with a loud smack.

"Hey, what the hell's your problem, man?"

"Your friend Billy is a retard, Goddammit, that's my problem."

"I can't believe you hit me. And he's not retarded. He's just…slow."

"Maybe he had a lobotomy, ever think of that? What did I ask Billy in the car? Huh, Carter? What did I ask Billy?"

Carter thought about it. Closed his eyes a moment and nodded. "If there was anything else we should know."

"Right. Like pit bulls and child pornography!"

Carter took another bite. "That's not really *child* pornography, is it?"

"They're minors. These guys are fifteen years old *tops*, people go to prison for this shit! Who knows how young the other ones are? Doesn't that bother you?"

Carter shrugged, chewed. "Yeah, it's illegal. But a lot of things are illegal." He sucked his teeth for a few seconds. "Doesn't look like anybody's putting a gun to their heads, does it? You were making all your own decisions at their age, weren't you?"

"That's not the point. It's just…*wrong*."

"Oh, yeah, sure, it's probably wrong." He finished the sandwich and said, "Have one of these, they're great. Some kinda sandwich spread."

Adam's surprise registered on his face.

"What? Why're you staring?"

"Nothing. I don't know. I'm going to the bathroom." He walked down the hall, less upset by Carter's apparent acceptance of Mr. C.'s livelihood than by his own. He was about to do business with Diz. That was a form of acceptance.

At the end of the hall, the bathroom door stood open a foot. Adam stepped inside and said, "Oh, my God."

A mountainous woman stood facing the rectangular mirror above the sink. Well over three hundred pounds, Adam guessed. Black leather straps studded with shiny silver crisscrossed her body. White rolls of flesh stuck out between the straps and waggled like useless limb stumps when she moved. An intricate dragon tattoo emerged from the crevasse between her great breasts. Perhaps gulping air. She applied the last of her lipstick and smiled at him in bright red, face as big around as a medium pizza.

"Hi, there. You new? I don't think I've seen you around." She spoke with an inelegant southern accent.

Adam's mouth moved a few times before anything came out. "I-I'm here with Billy. A friend of Billy's. I am, I mean. Billy and I are friends. And we're here."

"Well, I'm Mrs. C.," she said. "Is my Biwwy here? My widdoo-biddy Biwwy?"

The baby talk made him afraid she was going to squeeze his cheeks hard.

Mrs. C. dropped her lipstick into a small black bag and zipped it closed. "The room's all yours. I gotta show comin' up. You tell my widdoo Biwwy I said hi!"

Adam had to step into the hall and stand in the open doorway of a bedroom to let her pass. In the bathroom, Mrs. C. had left behind perfume fallout that smelled like Fruit Loops. In sour milk.

He turned on the ventilation fan and closed the door. Locked it. After emptying his bloated bladder, he washed the dust from his hands and face. Raised his head and watched droplets of water fall from his eyebrows onto his cheeks in the mirror.

Am I really doing this? he thought. It appeared that he was. And he was doing it out here in the fuckin' Mojave desert with the kangaroo rats and the fuckin' sidewinders and tarantulas.

Overhead, a camera watched him with a shark-like eye.

TWENTY-FIVE

When Billy introduced Adam, Diz extended his right arm to shake. All that remained of the hand were a mangled section of palm, an index finger, and a thumb. A little boy's make-believe gun.

"'Sup, m'man?" Diz said. His grip was strong, for a thumb and finger.

Adam struggled to keep it off his face, but a cold shudder ran up his body when he closed his hand on what remained of Diz's.

Diz was lanky, with long basketball legs, in jeans and a faded old blue *Predator* T-shirt. He seemed Adam's age or so, but it was difficult to tell with all the damage. Except for the softness around his middle, he was lean and tall. A black patch covered Diz's right eye with a round, panicky cartoon eye painted on the front, the pupil a tiny dot in the middle of all that bloodshot white. Scar tissue gnarled the right side of his narrow bald head. A jagged hole in his right cheek exposed his gums and broken molars. And there were his eyebrows, of course.

They had been removed from — probably blown off — his forehead, then reattached in segments. It looked as if spare parts of other eyebrows had been added to lengthen Diz's. They were crooked, far too long and high. From just above the outer corners of his eyes, they arched upward, then plunged downward sharply, almost meeting

207

over the bridge of his nose. They created an odd hybrid expression of pleasant surprise and savage rage.

"Billy-boy tells me you lookin' for my services," Diz said. He perched on a stool at the bar in the dining room. Billy brought him a can of beer. Diz popped the tab, raised the can in a toast and said, "It's the fuckin' king a beers, man," and took some big, long gulps, the can between the thumb and two middle fingers of his left hand. He pressed the remnant of his right palm over the hole in his cheek to keep beer from dribbling out of his face. Eyes closed, eyebrows high above them, unmoving, as if drawn there in Diz's sleep by a child.

This is like a Night Gallery *episode,* Adam thought.

"Uh, yeah, but actually —" Adam cleared his throat, " — we're not sure exactly what your services include."

"You tell me what you want," Diz said, "I tell you if my services include it." His voice sounded hollow and nasal when he did not cover the hole.

"Um, from what I can tell," Billy said, "they got somethin' they wanna blow up."

"Let 'em answer, Billy-boy," Diz said good-naturedly. Finished off the beer. "Get me another beer. And get beers for your buddies, too. C'mon, guys, pulluppa stool, sitcher asses down and have a brewski, huh?" Diz wobbled on his stool a bit as he smiled. He was missing a few teeth in front, top and bottom.

Carter did not hesitate to get up on a chrome-legged stool. Plucked a carrot stick from one of the trays and bit it in half with a dull pop. He left Adam with only one stool between himself and Diz.

Adam pulled the stool away from the bar, set it beside Carter, and sat facing Diz.

"You hungry, Adam?" Diz asked, waving a disfigured hand toward the food on the bar. "We got plenny a food. Mom and Pop always got plenny a food around for everybody. Prob'ly why I been puttin' onna mothafuckin' pounds, know what I'm sayin'?" He patted his belly and laughed, and the hole in his cheek made it sound somewhat seal-like: *Yorp! Yorp! Yorp!*

What there was of his left hand fished a crumpled pack of Camels and a butane lighter out of his pocket. He lit up using both hands, then pulled a small glass ashtray down the bar. Although not by choice, Diz held his cigarette like a black-and-white movie Nazi, between thumb and forefinger. Errant smoke oozed from the hole in his face. "Tell me, Adam, whatchoo wanna blow up?"

Billy brought beers for all of them.

Adam took a deep breath to steady his voice. "Actually, I…um, see, I'm not sure I…" He turned to Carter for help.

"Hey, don't look over here," Carter said. "You still haven't told me dick, I don't know what the hell you're up to."

Adam had forgotten he hadn't told Carter his whole plan. He didn't even have a whole plan yet. He turned to Diz and said, "A boat."

"A boat, huh?" Diz nodded. "What kinda boat?"

"Well, actually, we were hoping we could—"

"You say *ack*-shully a lot, don'tcha?" Diz grinned. "What the fuck's 'at mean, anyway? That *ack*-shully word?"

Adam looked around the dining room for an answer, thumbed through his internal dictionary and thesaurus. He came up with nothing. It was just something people said when they were unsure of what they were going to say next. He looked at Diz and shrugged helplessly. "Nothing. Far as I can tell, it means absolutely nothing."

"Then why use it?" Diz said with laughter in his voice. "Huh? I mean, shit, if it don't mean nothin'. 'Cause I gotta lotta respect for people who say what they mean."

Adam's shoulders and back chilled. He was sure that was some kind of half-veiled threat, but the specifics eluded him at the moment. "You're right. You're absolutely right. No point in using it if it doesn't mean anything."

"Attaboy. Now. What kinda boat?"

"We were hoping we could…*buy* the explosives, you know? From you. Then we could…bluh-blow it up ourselves."

A laugh exploded from Diz while he dragged on his Camel. Smoke burst from his mouth and the hole in his cheek. He rocked on his stool as he laughed, slapped the bar a couple times.

Gooseflesh crawled up Adam's back. When Diz laughed—eyebrows high and sinister, smoke curling out of his face—he looked like a drug-induced hallucination. An image from a silent horror movie, Lon Chaney revived from the grave, wearing excruciating face-twisting appliances. Diz looked so convincingly—and yet, surrealistically—deranged that Adam wanted to run from the house.

"Do I look like the kinda guy'd hand a loaded gun to a fuckin' monkey with rabies?" Diz asked. He laughed some more, but watched Adam, waiting for an answer.

Adam said, "I'm sorry, but…I-I'm not sure how to respond to that."

Diz stood and nodded at a camera high in the corner. "Lesstep outside, take a walk around the ranch. I don't like bein' on that sick fuck's tapes, y'know what I mean?"

Adam knew.

Mr. C. came into the kitchen, took a handful of potato chips from the bar.

As the others stood, Diz turned toward the kitchen and called, "Hey, Billy-boy-blue, we takin' a walk. You hold the fort."

"Where the fuck're you goin'?" Mr. C. asked around a mouthful of chips.

"We're gonna go sacrifice a live baby in the sunlight, then jerk each other off with bloody hands," Diz said.

Mr. C. grunted.

Diz led them out the back door into the dry, hot desert air. The hill rose abruptly before them, humped with shrubs. They started up at a slow pace.

Everything was taking longer than Adam had anticipated. If all had gone the way he had hoped, they would be on their way home by now. Even walking around outside was eating up way too much time. A feeling of urgency clutched him, and it had nothing to do with his bladder.

"No cameras back here," Diz said.

The ground crunched beneath their feet as they went slowly up the hill.

"Did Billy-boy tell you I sell explosives?" Diz asked.

"Oh, no," Adam said. "But we got that impression."

"You here by mistake, Adam? Zat the problem?"

"Only if you won't sell us the explosives."

He laughed again.

"Look," Adam went on, "it's not Billy's fault. He specifically said you don't sell explosives. It's just that — " He lowered his voice. " — he didn't say that until we were on our way here. But now we're here, and I'm just hoping you'll — "

"You don't want anybody else involved, do ya?"

"No."

"And you don't want me to know what you're gonna *do* with them explosives, do ya?"

Adam shook his head.

"And you two are gonna do this mysterious thing, whatever the fuck it is, you guys are gonna do it your*selves?*"

"Something like that," Adam said.

"What kind you want?"

"What kind of what?" Carter said.

"Explosives. What kind of explosives?"

Adam turned to Carter, who gave him a whithering look, and said, "Like I'd know?"

"Of the two of you," Diz said, "which one has the most experience with explosives?"

Once again, Adam looked at Carter, who shrugged and said, "You're looking at me again, I don't understand this. Closest I've ever come to explosives is firecrackers."

"I haven't had much, um…experience," Adam said, realizing how ludicrous he sounded. "I always hated firecrackers. Just too damned loud."

Diz chuckled. "Like I axed before, do I look like the kinda guy'd hand a loaded gun to a monkey with rabies? How fuckin' dumb do I look?" He remained relaxed and jovial, but his face looked ready to kill and enjoy it. "Know what happens I do that, Adam? Send you on your merry fuckin' way with some goodies? You fuck up and vaporize yourselves, maybe a buncha other people." He laughed his seal-like laugh between sentences, shaking his head. As if someone had told a great joke. "But then, see, the fuckin' cops get involved. They don't care about you guys, you're floatin' around in the air with the pollen, if there's that much of ya left." He stopped walking and turned to them. "But they wanna know where the fuck you got the goodies. And maybe, somehow, they work their way back here. Next thing you know, we got federal stormtroopers, fuckin' psychopaths employed by Uncle Sam, we got 'em up our asses, and the bullets and grenades are flyin'."

Adam and Carter exchanged a glance as Diz absently kicked a few rocks.

"Now when all that shit happens?" Diz said. "That's bad, Adam. People die when the feds get involved. People get maimed and crippled. And otherwise fucked up? Tell ya th'truth, I can't *afford* any a that shit, man. That's why I don't do it. Now, I got nothin' against you guys, but if you think I'm gonna sell you shit that blows up—" He laughed again, getting a big kick out of the idea, "—then you gotta gimme the recipe for your brownies, man." Kept laughing as he continued slowly up the hill.

"Okay, I get it," Adam said as he and Carter followed. "You're not gonna sell us anything."

"Yo, Adam, don't take that personally, 'kay? I'm laughin' 'cause thass just fuckin' funny, man, the idea doin' somethin' like that in my line a work, shit, man, thass like askin' a lawyer to work for truth and justice 'steada for fuckin' money, you dig?"

Adam sighed. "Then we should go, Carter. We shouldn't waste anymore of Diz's—"

"Hey, slow down, Adam." Diz put a twisted palm on Adam's shoulder. "Whattaya doin', anyway?" More laughter. That Seaworldesque *Yorp! Yorp! Yorp!* "Where ya gonna go to get what I won't sell ya? Walmart? Huh? Look, Adam m'man, you got somethin' needs blowin' up, and I blow up things for a livin'. Hell, we're so made for each other, man, we oughtta haul ass to Vegas and tie the fuckin' knot!" *Yorp! Yorp!*

Adam shook his head. "I'm sorry, Diz, but…I just don't feel comfortable with this. I don't know you, I've never—"

Diz stopped again, put an arm across Adam's shoulders. A mostly-smoked Camel dangled from his lips. The hole spouted smoke when he talked. "You think I'm gonna run to the cops and tell 'em about *your* shit? Whaddaya think this is, a fuckin' sting operation to catch you in the act of tryin' to blow up your parents? Don't fuckin' flatter yourself, m'man."

Adam stopped breathing. Turned to Diz, face open with shock.

Diz smirked, shrugged. "An educated guess, is all." He removed his arm from Adam's shoulder, fished another cigarette from his pocket, and lit it with the butt of the other. Licked thumb and forefinger, pinched the butt out, and dropped it to the ground, buried it with the toe of his shoe. "Adam, you gotta understand me, this is a business. You understand that much, right?"

Adam nodded.

"But it's a sensitive business. That's why we protect our clients. Whether they want somethin' blown up, or some kid to blow 'em off. Why we don't ask no serious questions. Most of our regular clients appreciate that and have enough good fuckin' sense to do the same in return. That's how a sensitive business like this works. Even though we may not trust each other, we fuckin' have to, otherwise there's nothin' to do but stand around starin' at each other, and no *business* gets done. Nobody wants to hand you over to the cops, Adam, 'kay? Think you can get that shit outta your head? This is what I do for a fuckin' livin', 'kay, man? Been doin' this shit since I was eight."

"Where do you learn about explosives when you're eight?" Adam asked.

"From Pop. Taught me everything he knows and I took it from there. That's what he used to do. Till he retired and went into the porn biz. The fuckin' perv."

They started walking again. The hot ground warmed Adam's feet through his sneakers. Small creatures scattered ahead of them into the shrubs and rocks.

Adam said, "You took over your dad's business? So you worked with him, right?"

"If you like sayin' it that way, fine," Diz said. "I was fuckin' employed, all I knew."

"What was that like?" Adam asked, almost whispering. "I mean, did it make you two any closer, working together? Did you get to know your dad better?"

That got a few loud, full *yorp*s from Diz. "Fuck no, man. My dad's a prick of the lowest order. The kinda prick who disgusts all the other fuckin' pricks."

"Yeah, I know the feeling," Adam said.

"Your dad a prick?" Diz asked.

"Yep. And he's close friends with all the other fuckin' pricks."

Diz laughed again. Turned to Adam and raised his right hand, palm out.

Adam stared, confused, at the chunk of meat at the end of Diz's arm. Then he realized Diz was waiting for Adam to give him a high-five. Adam swallowed his disgust and slapped the small, misshapen palm.

"Okay, Adam, tell me. What kinda boat?"

Adam did not hesitate this time. "A yacht docked in Marina del Rey."

Diz nodded slowly and smiled. "Okay, now we *gettin'* somefuckinwhere."

I **wonder who** they're looking for?" Alyssa said, watching a helicopter in the sky.

Adam thought, *I wonder if they'll ever look for me that way.* He stamped the thought out like a dropped cigarette.

Parked off Mulholland, they sat in the backseat of Adam's convertible. It was a few minutes after two o'clock in the morning and they had made love there twice. And once in the kitchen at Alyssa's house when Adam picked her up.

He had been unable to sleep, but could not stop thinking about Alyssa. He'd called her, but talking was not enough, so he'd picked her up.

Alyssa was naked in the backseat, skin glowing like sea foam in moonlight, long Daffy Duck nightshirt tossed over the back of the front seat. She leaned on him, and he leaned on her, pants down around his ankles, shirtless. Their faces were close as they stroked each other's skin. Eyelids heavy, lips puffy and red from kissing.

The helicopter flew over the blanket of lights below and wielded its sword of light against the city. Searching for someone, something.

"Will they look for us like that?" Alyssa whispered.

"Will who look for us?"

"The police."

Alyssa had brought along a few Heinekens from the refrigerator and Adam was drinking one when she said it. Some of it came back out through his nose.

"You okay?" she asked, patting his back as he coughed.

"Fine." He kept forgetting about her fantasy killing spree. At first, he had thought she was talking about his plans to kill his dad. But she couldn't possibly know about that, not yet. "Yeah, they'll probably look for us like that."

She put a leg over both of his, her fingers combed his pubic hair.

"But by then," he went on, "we'll be gone. On our way to the next state. And the next. And the next one after that."

Alyssa moved closer, played with his nipple as she sucked on his neck.

"We'll always be at least one step ahead of them," he whispered. "Right from the beginning."

"Will we get married in Vegas?" Her words burned on Adam's neck, then she lifted her head, looked directly into his eyes.

Adam's heartbeat sped up. He was afraid he had misunderstood her. Perhaps she was just joking. "Are you serious?"

She nodded her head, grinned. Sighed as she took his penis in hand and squeezed. He was hard instantly. "It's two-something in the morning." Her voice was husky and hoarse as she straddled him on her knees, skipped the slow stuff and started riding him hard. "And we're fucking in your convertible," she said, teeth clenched. "You think I do this shit with *everybody?*"

They came fast and loud. Alyssa stayed on his lap afterward, Adam still inside her. They fondled and kissed and whispered.

Alyssa whispered, "I think I'm in love with you."

Adam pulled back a few inches and looked at her. He was surprised and moved. "You think? When will you know?"

She laughed. "If I *think* I'm in love with you then I must be, right?"

He kissed her. "I was trying to sleep tonight, but I couldn't stop thinking about you. I wondered if I was misreading anything, you know? But I guess I wasn't. I feel the same way. I mean, I'm in love with you."

She touched her forehead to his, placed a hand to his cheek and kissed him a few times. He could hear the smile in her voice when she whispered into his ear, "My Adam. You belong to me now."

TWENTY-SEVEN

You haven't eaten, have you?" Diz asked.

"No, I'm not hungry," Adam said.

"You gotta have Doughboy's specialty. The Five Alarm Omelette. Killer shit."

"No, thank you, I don't need a five-alarm anything right now."

"But I already ordered for ya, man." Diz lit a cigarette.

Adam sighed, closed his weary eyes. "Okay, okay."

"Yo, Adam, you all right?" Diz's eyebrows probably would have frowned if they were not frozen in place. "You look fucked up, bro."

"Just a little tense," Adam said. "I thought we were meeting someplace anonymous. Someplace with a lot of people so no one would notice us."

"This is better," Diz said. "Everybody here? Fuckin' family. I'd die for any motherfuckin' one of 'em, and they'd do the same for me. That's why we're here, 'stead-uh someplace where everybody's a fuckin' stranger and you gotta watch yer back alla time."

"Hi, Adam," Billy said. He had been sitting at the table all along, virtually invisible with his nose buried in a *Lady Death* comic book.

"Hi, Billy."

"Where's Carter?

Adam said, "I guess I forgot to pick him up."

✝

It had taken longer at the body shop than Adam had expected, so he'd arrived late at Doughboy's Diner on ninth around ten-thirty. It was a small diner with only four customers, none of them Diz. The waitress poured him a cup of coffee. A plump, rosy-cheeked woman in her late fifties. The grandmotherly type, unsuited for the pink and white polyester waitress uniform.

"Y'all wanna look at a menu?" she asked. Her nametag read JOLEEN.

"I'm supposed to meet someone here. Have you seen a guy with—"

"You Adam?"

He'd looked at the smiling woman suspiciously, nodded.

"Oh, well, why din't y'all say so!" she said in a high, laughing voice.

Joleen had taken him to the back then, talking the whole time. She had known Diz and his family for many years, before Diz was born. Said she, her husband Bert, and Diz's whole family used to vacation together every year, till Bert died.

He had found Diz and Billy sitting at a card table in a large but cluttered storage room with a filthy concrete floor and insulation showing in the walls. A bare bulb glared above the table.

Cautiously, Adam asked Diz, "Shouldn't we…you know, be alone?"

"Y'mean Billy?" Diz asked. He stood, walked around the table and stopped behind Billy. Put his hands on Billy's shoulders and squeezed. "Look, man, Billy's my posse. Billy's on the team, you dig? Weren't for Billy, I wouldn't be here. The Billman pulled me up when I was at my lowest, man. And he's the only fuckin' reason *you're* here. Billy-boy's why you're gettin' a discount, man. The fuckin' friends of Billy discount, you hear what I'm sayin'?" He laughed, slapped Billy's shoulders once, then returned to his chair. "Speakin' of which, you bring it?"

Adam reached behind him and under his shirt and removed a folded-over manila envelope from the back pocket of his jeans, handed it to Diz. It was thick with ten thousand dollars in cash taken from Michael Julian's office floor safe. It was the first time Adam had taken enough money to create a visible dent in the contents of the safe. As long as he did not check the safe before leaving for the weekend, Michael would never know.

"Tell me, Adam," Diz said. "How do you see this whole fuckin' thing happenin'?"

"What do you mean?" Adam asked.

"Well, I bet you already seen this happen in your head a million times, right? Tell me about it."

Adam had not imagined the explosion in his mind. He suspected he was afraid to imagine it, afraid the images might change his mind.

"I don't know," he said with a sigh. "Guess I haven't given it much thought."

"Not much thought, huh?" He studied Adam's face for several seconds. "You a strange dude, Adam. I can't figure you the hell out. But I like you. You got no idea what you're doin', but you got determination, man, it's fuckin' inspiring. You prob'ly think I'm fulla shit 'cause where you come from, nobody means a fuckin' thing they say, but I ain't like that, I don't give out no praise 'less I fuckin' mean it. Ask Billy-boy, I ain't shittin' ya."

Billy said, "He, um, ain't shittin' ya."

"Now, lemme help with a little suggestion, Adam. We wire the ignition. Somebody starts the boat, ka-fuckin'-boom."

Adam shook his head. "No. I don't want to hurt anyone at the marina."

"There, see?" Diz smiled, nodded again. "Y'*have* been givin' it some thought. Good for you. 'Cause that's just what'd happen. Also? There's a chance the fuckin' engine'll be started *before* the subject or subjects arrive. See, you gotta use a timer. Set the timer to go off when the engine starts. Give 'em time to get out there. Just them and the seagulls. 'Bout the time they start breakin' out the cold ones…ka-fuckin'-boom." He cackled happily. "When ya need it done?"

It was Friday, the third. *Money Shot* would leave the marina the next morning. Then, somewhere out on the water, they would simply disappear forever.

"I know it's short notice," Adam said, "but it has to be done by tomorrow morning."

"No problem. We gonna see the boat after breakfast?"

"Sure," Adam said.

"Fuckin' A."

TWENTY-EIGHT

Marina del Rey looked like a travel brochure. Clean and windy, with boats all over the place. Masts reached skyward, sails slapped the wind. Luxury yachts gleamed out in the water, coming and going. A lot of white clothes and deep tans, caps perched on sun-bleached hair. Seagulls screamed overhead.

Diz drove a sturdy old dark blue Chevy van, something from the eighties. He had told Adam to lead the way in his car. Once in Marina del Rey, he wanted Adam to park somewhere a few blocks away from the marina. Anyplace would do, the more inconspicuous the better.

Adam led them into a strip-mall parking lot, eased into a slot in front of a Nails Deluxe Salon and a comic book shop. He got out of the Lexus and went around to Diz's window.

"We gonna have our fuckin' nails done?" Diz asked with a raspy laugh. He held up both mangled hands, all five fingers, and said, "Might be fun just to see the fuckin' look on her face, huh?"

Adam thought it was funny, but was incapable of laughter at the moment.

Diz handed him a pack of cigarettes and a book of matches through the window. "Have a smoke with Billy. I'll be out in a few minutes."

Billy had gotten out of the van the second it stopped moving. Stood at the window of the comic book shop, gazing at the display.

"Are you going to be long?" Adam asked. "Because I'd really like to—"

"Chill, man. A few minutes." He disappeared into the back of the van.

Adam lit a cigarette and joined Billy at the window of the comic book shop. Handed him the cigarettes and matches. Billy lit up. The store did not open till two, but there was plenty to look at in the window.

"You like comic books?" Adam asked, staring at several Batman comic books around a shiny model of the Batmobile.

"Yeah," Billy said. "You?"

"I practically learned to read on comic books. *Batman, Superman, Fantastic Four*, a bunch. Nothing in awhile, though." In the window, a Wolverine action figure was suspended in air by two strings, as if pouncing on something below. Superman comic books surrounded a model of the *Daily Planet* building.

"See that chick?" Billy pointed to three issues of *Lady Death* in one corner of the display. The series' demonic heroine was on the covers, her colossal breasts the focus of each.

"Yeah. But I haven't read any of those."

"Cool series. Cher optioned the movie rights. She, um, wants to play Lady Death."

"You're joking."

Billy shrugged. "They can, um, do some pretty amazing things with, y'know, special effects these days."

Adam laughed. "They won't be able to do it without you, Billy."

The reflection of a third figure appeared on the window pane. Someone tall, in a cap and sunglasses, with long hair.

"You guys comin'?" Diz asked.

Adam was utterly caught off guard by Diz's smile, his face. The eyepatch was gone and the bill of the black cap was pulled low to hide his eyebrows. A silver CBS Eye stared from the front of the cap. Adam saw his reflection in Diz's large, black-framed sunglasses. The hole was gone. Like magic, it had disappeared. Straight blonde hair fell from beneath the cap to his shoulders. In his *End of Days* T-shirt and a pair of shorts, a blue and green nylon backpack strapped to his shoulders, he looked years younger, like a beach bum. As long as he kept his hands out of sight.

"Diz, that's…astounding!" Adam said, looking closer.

Diz put an arm around Billy's shoulders and said, "M'man Billy here taught me. Don't know what I woulda done without him. Some impressive shit, huh? Damned if the motherfucker didn't give me a face again."

Billy's cheeks turned a brief crimson and he smiled at his feet.

Adam had to lean close to see the latex patch. "You're a genius, Billy."

"Oh, well, um, it's...nothin' special, y'know," he said.

Diz started walking. "Gotta make one more stop. Little grocery store back up the block? Gotta get a couple bags of groceries. Adam, y'know what kinda food your dad usually stocks the boat with?"

"Yeah."

"Thass what we gotta buy."

"Why? It's not my job to stock the shelves."

"Don't fuckin' matter," Diz said.

"You mean, we're going to buy groceries and just leave them on the boat?"

Diz nodded.

"But they'll notice that."

"It don't. Fuckin'. Matter."

Adam stopped at a crosswalk to wait for a red light. Diz and Billy passed him and headed across the street against it. There were no cars, so Adam followed them, caught up. "Why the groceries, Diz?"

"People know you here?"

"Sure, but I doubt I'll see any of them."

"You might. So. You see somebody, they say hi, you say hi, they wanna know what you're up to, just bein' friendly, and what're you gonna say?"

"Ah." Adam nodded. "Just bringing some groceries for the voyage."

"Correcto-mundo. Sounds good, makes sense, no more fuckin' questions."

"What about you and Billy?" Adam asked. "How do I introduce you if I need to?"

"I'm B.J. Billy's the Bear."

"You're joking."

"Nope."

"Look, I'm not gonna introduce you as B.J. and—"

"Then don't introduce us."

Adam walked into the grocery store ahead of the other two. Turned to his right just in time to see a Korean man pop up from behind the counter with a shotgun. Spinning around to flee, Adam fell into a smiling Billy.

"S'cuse me," Billy said.

"S'up, Adam?" Diz asked.

"Uh…" He turned to the counter again. A Korean man, yes. But the shotgun in his hands was a broomstick. Sweeping up behind the register. "Fine. I'm fine."

Diz watched him for a moment. "You look like you just hadda Depends moment."

"Really," Adam assured him, "I'm fine."

Diz grabbed a cart and said, "Okay, girls, less go shoppin'."

Later, as they walked to *Money Shot*, each carrying a bag of groceries, Diz asked, "Your family eat that much fuckin' macaroni and cheese? Thassa *shit*load of Kraft Macaroni and Cheese, man."

"My dad loves it," Adam said. It had been difficult not to laugh while throwing the boxes into the cart on a whim.

Inside, they put down the grocery bags, and Adam gave Diz a quick tour of the yacht.

Plush cream carpeting, dark shiny wood furniture and cabinets, glass-topped coffee tables. A formal dining room and a galley, six staterooms and a game room with video and pinball machines bolted to the floor and walls. A big-screen TV, hot tub, and a small but fully equipped gym.

"Shit, man," Diz said with a chuckle. "Yo daddy like his comfort, don't he?"

"Oh, yeah," Adam said.

In the kitchen, they put away the groceries. Helping Adam fill a cupboard's shelves with boxes of Kraft Macaroni and Cheese, Billy said, "This is a real nice boat, Adam. You, um, go out on 'er much?"

"Not since I was a kid. And it was a different yacht then. Dad gets a new one every couple years, sells the old one. Each one's a little bigger than the last."

"This a two hunnert footer?" Diz asked.

"Two-fifty. The last one was two twenty-five. He'll eventually end up with a cruise ship. *The Hate Boat*."

When they were done in the kitchen, Adam took them to the helm station. It looked like a compact version of the bridge of the starship

Enterprise. The black and silver high-tech instrument panel gleamed among all the dark wood and cream.

Diz sat in the pilot's seat and looked the panel over carefully. "Okay, lemme see, what the fuck we got here? Take a little longer'n I thought, but not by much."

"You're not going to do it now?" Adam asked.

He shook his head. "Tonight. Any chance somebody's gonna be here tonight? Can't have nobody droppin' in on my ass." He got out of the chair, turned to Adam.

"No one should show up here until tomorrow morning."

"Two things." Diz held up his lonely thumb and forefinger. "I need a place to put my backpack. Someplace it won't be noticed somebody does come. Second, you gotta show me the engine room, Scotty."

The backpack fit perfectly into the cupboard beneath the kitchen sink. Diz spent a couple minutes looking the engine room over, then they were out of the luxurious yacht and back in the real world. Smelling the filthy water and air.

Back at the strip mall, Diz got into the van and slammed the door. While Billy got in on the other side, Adam rested his arms on the edge of Diz's window.

"What do we do now?" he asked.

"*We*...don't do shit. Billy and I got things to do. You go home. Relax. Go out tonight, have fun." He leaned closer. "And make sure plenty of people see you doin' it. Understand? Just a little piece of friendly fuckin' advice." He smiled, started up the van.

"See ya, Adam," Billy called as the van backed out of the parking slot. "Tell Carter I said yo!" He waved as Diz drove out of the parking lot.

By the time Adam lifted his hand to wave back, it was too late. They were gone. He got in the Lexus and headed home.

He wanted to go straight to the bookstore, find Alyssa. She was the only one who could get his mind off everything. But that might not be a good idea. Diz was right—everything Adam did from that point on would either strengthen or weaken his defense should he be accused of, or even tried for, murder. Anyone he encountered would be a potential witness if there was a trial. Especially Alyssa. He did not want to put her through that.

"What the hell am I thinking?" Adam shouted. His voice bounced off the interior surfaces of the Lexus and pounded back into his head. "Do I want to put *me* through that?"

TWENTY-NINE

Helicopters stirred the dirty air over the city. Police, traffic reporters, air rescue units going to or from one of the summer wildfires that raged throughout California. Ground level, there was always a siren coming from one direction or another. Everywhere Adam looked in the stop-and-go freeway traffic surrounding the Lexus, mouths yammered silently into cellphones while eyes hid behind black lenses.

Rush hour was a few hours away, but it seemed there had been a wreck somewhere up ahead. Or maybe there was road construction. Cars drove a few yards, a few feet, stopped for awhile, then moved forward, only to stop again in a few seconds.

"Look, I told you I wanted to help," Carter said. "That means I'm involved, okay? You don't have to protect me, Adam. That Diz guy, we really don't know anything about him. You shouldn't be hanging out with somebody like that by yourself."

"Billy was there," Adam said.

"Billy has his head up his foot. He's a follower. I mean, he's a cool guy, a big talent, a good friend, but...I keep waiting to hear he ate poison applesauce in some UFO suicide cult. What do you think he's doing with Diz? He's following. If you were in trouble, Billy would be as worthless as tits on the pope."

227

"Yeah, I kept wishing you were there to protect me, Carter. Just in case."

"Smartass."

"You defended the hell out of Billy yesterday."

"I was trying to make the best of a bad situation."

"What are we going to do this weekend?"

"I don't know. Got anything in mind?"

"No, but we've got to be seen. *I've* got to be seen. Know of any parties?"

"You hate parties."

"I don't have fun in mind."

"Maybe the one at Monty's is still going on."

"Bite me."

"We'll find something. You gonna bring Dracula's daughter?"

"I told you, she's not like that."

Carter shrugged. "I thought you wanted to see more of her."

"I have been seeing more of her."

"What, in the middle of the night?"

"Mostly." Adam told him about being awakened naked by Alyssa's dad and they laughed.

"They sound like pretty cool parents," Carter said. "Hey, maybe they won't mind that you killed your family and they'll invite you to move in!"

When Adam didn't laugh, Carter said no more for awhile. They drove in silence—even the radio was off—with no destination in mind.

"I'm afraid to get her involved," Adam said.

"Involved how?"

"You know, as a witness. If there's a trial—"

"There won't be if you do it right."

"It's a possibility."

"Yeah, and it's a possibility Henry Jaglom'll make a movie people can watch without wanting to commit suicide. But it's not *likely*. Remember what Diz said when we were at his place? He could vaporize that yacht and everybody in it. Unless there are witnesses, nobody will even know they blew up. It'll look like they just...you know." He made a raspberry noise. "Disappeared."

"If we're lucky."

"No, it's not luck. Diz and his family...there won't be any middle schools named after them in the near future, but I think Diz knows what he's doing."

"I don't doubt it."

"So what do you doubt?"

"Everything else."

The traffic finally began to move, picked up speed until they were cruising.

"Look!" Carter shouted, palms flat against the window beside him. He made them squeak on the way down. "Nothing." He shouted, "My *Gawd*, there's nothing! No wreck. Nobody broke down. Everybody just slowed to a stop for no reason. It's a madhouse—a *madhouse!*" He fell back in his seat, jutted his chin like Heston and reached dramatically for the windshield. "Soylent Green is *liberals*, you damned dirty ape! Now somebody give me a Goddamned firearm!"

Normally, that would have had Adam laughing hard enough to swerve the car. But he wasn't up to it. He kept his eyes on the road.

"Okay, let's just go to the bookstore and see her," Carter said, moving past the awkward moment. "You're a couple, right? Then it would be weird if you *didn't* go see her."

Adam's eyes stayed on the car ahead and he did not speak.

"Hey. Marlee Matlin. What the hell is wrong with you?"

Adam put up a good front for several seconds, until the first squeaks of the laugh came through. It exploded from his mouth. "Marlee *Matlin?*"

In an exaggerated impersonation of the deaf actress, Carter said, "Whuh? Ah'm thowwy, Ah cahn *hee* yooo. Ah'm *dayf.*"

Adam laughed harder, barely got his words out. "Stop it. Can't you see I'm trying to brood over here?" He could not stop laughing. He was incapable of not laughing.

Carter's smile dropped off his face. "Adam?"

Clutching the steering wheel, Adam rocked in his seat, gasped for breath between bouts of coughing, hacking laughter. His face turned deeper shades of red.

"You okay, Adam?" He gripped Adam's shoulder, tried to steady him. "You're not okay, are you?"

The Lexus swerved to the left, into the next lane. Someone ahead of them honked, then someone behind. They honked for a long time.

"Shit, *shit!*" Carter grabbed the wheel and pulled the car back into its lane, steadied it. "Adam, for Christ's sake, would you stop laugh—hey, slow down! It wasn't that funny!"

Adam composed himself just enough to ease the car off the freeway. He had no idea which exit he had taken and was not sure where he was. Carter pointed to a 7-Eleven next to the freeway exit. Adam parked in two spaces and killed the engine. Melted into his seat with laughter, red cheeks wet with tears.

"Jesus Christ, Adam, what do you want me to do?"

He waved a hand at Carter. *Don't worry. Just give me a minute, okay?*

"Are you having, um, I-I don't know, some kind of, you know, breakdown?"

Shaking his head, Adam made a great effort to stop laughing. It happened very gradually. He spoke haltingly, words interrupted by dying laughter. "I was just thinking. About how many things. Could go wrong. So many things. But it'll just take one. To put me on death row. And I'll end up tied to that weird table. Waiting for the needle."

"Listen to me," Carter said. "If anything puts you on death row, it's gonna be this shit."

Adam wiped his face with his hands. His voice was shaky when he asked, "What do you mean?"

"I mean this, freaking out like that annoying chick in *The Blair Witch Project*. I'm telling you, Adam. You stay cool and calm, keep your head on, you're gonna get through this without a bump. But you've gotta bottle up all this weird stuff. Laughing like a lunatic, puking on people's shoes. That kind of shit makes people talk, Adam."

Adam massaged his temples, sighed. "Okay. Yeah. You're right."

"Look, once this is all over, you wanna go crazy, go apeshit, hey, knock yourself out, have a party. But not *now*. If you want, I can get you some pills. Something to relax you. Devin's got pounds of pills at home. I'll grab some for you when we go back to the house. Maybe some Xanax."

Adam rested his forehead on the steering wheel. "Why are you doing this, Carter?"

"Hey. I'm your best friend. And I know it's what you want."

"What I want," Adam said. "You know what I want?" He sat up. "I want to be a little kid at Christmas again."

Carter opened his door and got out. "I'm gonna go in for a Klondike Bar. You want me to see if they've got some little kid at Christmas again?"

"Smartass." Adam got out and followed him into the 7-Eleven.

THIRTY

There was no one to fill in at the bookstore that afternoon, so Alyssa had to work. Adam and Carter hung around, talked, browsed. They listened to *The Don and Mike Show* on the radio, and Alyssa made them iced tea. It was a slow day, and what few customers came — *potential witnesses,* Adam thought — did not stay long. A girl entered the store about forty minutes after Adam and Carter arrived. Alyssa introduced her as her best friend, Brett.

Short, straight, blonde hair framed her round face. A small silver ring pierced her right eyebrow. They were thin, black, arched eyebrows above a face that looked as if it had never smiled, not even once, yet there was a natural prettiness to it. Roughly the same height as Alyssa, but more muscular and tan in her black shorts and red sleeveless top.

Brett listened silently for awhile as Adam and Alyssa and Carter talked. When Adam made reference to something he had written, she asked, "You write?" Adam said he did, but had nothing published yet but a couple poems in journals nobody ever heard of. She smiled then, a small, guarded smile, and said, "That's cool." It was not much, but it was clear to Adam from the look on Alyssa's face that he had received high praise from her friend. Brett asked Carter what he did. When he told her, she said, "That's disgusting."

Carter gave Adam a look that asked, *What'd I do?*

Sunny arrived about twenty minutes later and took over for Alyssa. The four of them left in the Lexus and decided to go to a movie. All but Brett wanted to see the new horror movie directed by John Carpenter. Brett was outnumbered.

"You probably like to look at pictures of dead people, huh? Car wrecks. Burn victims."

"Why would you think that?" Carter asked.

"Well, that's the kind of stuff you make, right? Violently damaged body parts?"

"Yeah, but I don't use pictures of dead people."

"Then what do you use for models? Real body parts?"

They arrived at the theater early and took popcorn and soft drinks into the auditorium, looked for seats. Adam and Carter sat between Alyssa and Brett.

"You think I'm some kind of a serial killer because I make prosthetics and masks?"

"Is that what you call it?" Brett said, eyes looking straight ahead.

"Yes, that's what I call it. What *we* call it! I mean, it's a whole industry, you know."

"Assembly line violence."

"You're one of those anti-violence people, huh?"

She laughed. "You say that like being 'anti-violence' is a bad thing."

"Depends on exactly what kind of violence you're anti, you know?"

"No, I don't. What kind of violence do you think is acceptable?"

"None! Violence is bad, all *real* violence is bad, okay?"

Another laugh. "How can you say that and do what you do?"

"I don't use real body parts, nobody gets hurt. They've got *laws* against stuff like that, you know. I make *fake* body parts, *fake* wounds, and masks. I mean, if you've gone all this time thinking the blood and gore you see in movies is real, then I—"

"Sounds like I hit a nerve," Brett said. She was not looking at him anymore, but up at the dead movie screen.

Carter frowned. "Not a nerve, exactly. It's just...something I hear a lot."

"What? That there's something wrong with you because of the things you make?"

"Yeah, that's the one."

Brett sighed, squirmed in her seat. "You know, I really don't want to see this movie."

"Oh, relax, would you?" Alyssa leaned forward to look over at Brett. "At least *try* to enjoy yourself."

"Not a movie lover?" Carter asked.

"I just despise horror movies. The pornography of violence. I think they're sick."

"Oh, okay. So you think I'm sick."

She turned to him. "I didn't say that."

Carter put his lips together to say, *But that's what you meant, isn't it?*

"You're awfully sensitive, Carter," she said. "You should work on that."

They engaged in the obligatory exchange to determine their families' positions on the Hollywood food chain. Brett's parents were animal wranglers. Her dad specialized in cattle, horses, and camels, while her mom handled insects, spiders and reptiles. Her older sister recently started working with dogs and cats.

Carter's face brightened. "Hey, that's cool!"

"You think so? How would you like it if your dad smelled like the entire custodial staff of the Los Angeles Zoo? All the time? And my mom…she plays with bugs for a living."

He laughed. "Is that why you decided not to go into the family business?"

"That, and the fact that I hate animals."

"What? You hate animals?"

"Yes."

"What kind of animals?"

She wrinkled her nose. "All animals."

"Whoa, wait a sec. You think I'm some kind of horrible person because of the things I make…but you hate animals? What about dogs and cats?"

"*Especially* dogs and cats."

He shook his head, raised his voice a bit as he said, "Oh, you are one twisted individual!"

Adam and Alyssa stopped talking in whispers to each other.

"Something wrong?" Adam asked.

Carter leaned close and whispered. "Was this a setup? Did you plan for the four of us to go out so you could set me up with Ilsa, Nazi Queen of the Frozen North over here?"

"No, it wasn't, I swear. This was totally unplanned!"

"Then can I sit in another row?"

"What? Why? What's wrong?"

"She's, like, not even human, or something."

"Just ignore her. The movie's gonna start and you'll forget she's here."

"She hates animals, man! She's like that sick fuck in *Henry: Portrait of a Serial Killer*, she's got no feelings, no soul! And on top of that, she hates me, can you believe that? I mean, *she* hates *me*."

"You mean, Henry?"

"Huh?"

"In *Henry: Portrait of a Serial Killer*. Is Henry the one you're talking about?"

"Well, yeah, who the hell did you think I was talking about?"

"I thought maybe you were talking about Otis."

"Who?"

"Otis. Henry's dimwitted partner."

The lights dimmed and several people applauded, hooted.

"Just watch the movie," Adam whispered. He leaned toward Alyssa again. She snuggled against him under his arm.

"What's the matter?" she asked.

"Nothing. Just Carter having one of his fits of nervous self-consciousness."

Carter hissed, "Lick me."

The coming attractions began, and there was no more talk among the four of them.

✝

Carter invited them to a barbecue at his house that night when they dropped Alyssa and Brett at the bookstore. Alyssa seemed hesitant to leave Adam but he smiled, assured her that he was fine, and promised to see her that evening.

"What do you want to do?" Adam asked as he drove away from the bookstore.

"I don't know," Carter said. "What do you want to do?"

"Anything."

"We could knock over a liquor store."

"Funny." Adam had been unable to enjoy the movie because his mind had gone back into high gear, gnawed at him with all the dangerous possibilities ahead. Showed him his own death from a lethal injection. Or worse, in the gas chamber, strapped to that chair, waiting for the *hissss* of the pellets. In spite of the theater's air conditioning, his train of thought had caused him to break out in a sweat in the theater and his clothes were still damp. "I've got some serious sweatage. I need to go home and take a shower, change my clothes."

At the house, Carter went into the living room to watch some television on the flat-screen. Adam went upstairs to his room, wedged the chair against the door, turned on Brubeck and took a shower. As he scrubbed himself dry with a towel afterward, he heard shuffling outside the bathroom. Wrapped the towel around his waist, turned off the music, and charged out of the bathroom. "Goddammit, Rain, would you stop—"

Michael Julian stood in the center of Adam's bedroom holding the chair that had been propped against the door.

Adam's shock was a baseball bat to the forehead. It had been years since his dad had come to his room. Michael stood there with wet hair, in a forest-green bathrobe. Four fingers of his right hand hooked beneath the wood slat across the top of the chair's back, holding it a few inches from the floor. Apparently, he had just come from the shower as well.

"How long have I been telling you about those Goddamned horror movies you're always watching with Carter?" Michael asked. "Looks like they finally got to you, huh? Afraid some big scary guy's gonna come in and hurt you?" He grinned, laughed. Put down the chair.

Adam gave no reaction. Just tucked his towel a little tighter in back. His face was blank. It was his Dad-face.

Michael's smile jerked and twitched, crumbled. "What are you saying, you're afraid of someone? You want a lock on the door? You can get a lock if you want. I just never thought we'd need locks. We're supposed to be a *family*, Goddammit. What are you afraid of? Huh?"

Adam stared right into his dad's eyes, which never held still for an instant. Except for that, they were like the glistening acrylic eyes

Carter put into the sockets of his severed heads—startlingly real in appearance, but empty. Dead.

"Rain's been coming in here," Adam said. *What am I doing?* he wondered.

"She has?"

"Yes."

Michael shrugged. "So?"

"I don't want Rain to come in here. Not unless she's invited."

A laugh snorted through Michael's nose. "Why? Afraid she's gonna show you her titties? Probably do you some good. I mean, do you even *know* any women?"

Adam did not move. Not even an eyelid.

Still grinning, Michael said, "Okay, what's the problem with Rain? I don't think there's much chance of her coming in here in the middle of the night to rape you. But, uh—" Another laugh through the nose. "—that wouldn't do you any harm, either."

Still, Adam did not react.

Tilting his head back, rolling his eyes, Michael said, "Jesus H. Christ, Adam, when are you gonna get a fucking sense of—"

"She did that already."

Michael's teeth clacked together when his mouth closed. Eyes widened a little beneath his furrowed, bushy brow. He cocked his head and said, "What?"

"She raped me. Rain. At gunpoint." He smiled inside and thought, *Why not? Maybe I'll feel better.*

Taking a step forward, Michael said, "She...*what?*"

"She raped me at gunpoint. A loaded gun. She even fired it once to prove it. It wasn't the first time we'd had sex. But I didn't want to, so it was rape."

Michael shifted his weight from one foot to the other. "You...what're you...*what?*"

"See, I've been having an affair with your wife. Then when Rain moved in, I started having sex with her, too. It was against my better judgment, but it was...pretty incredible." He chuckled, shook his head. "I mean, I've got some wild oats to sow, right?"

Michael's darting eyes calmed down until they were still enough to meet Adam's eyes.

"But I knew it would only cause trouble. And I was right. She's sixteen, you know. A minor. The second we had sex, she had something on me. I mean, statutory rape. She's done it before. To one of her mother's boyfriends. He's in a prison hospital now, undergoing rectal reconstruction. So she had me. What could I do? If she said 'dance,' I had to ask her which steps. And that…God, that got me in a lot of trouble. I…I ended up robbing a liquor store against my will. Can you believe that? A guy standing right next to me…he was shot with a sawed-off shotgun. Right there. He was a friend of Rain's. See, she…Rain told me we were going to kill you and Gwen. The two of us, Rain and I. If I didn't go along with it, she'd turn me in. She also told me her mother goes from rich husband to rich husband, all of whom end up dead. Said you were next." He shrugged. "I didn't know whether to believe it. I mean, consider the source, right? But this time, Rain wanted to kill her mother, too. So she told me I was going to help kill you and Gwen. She got this guy to help us. Some kind of, I don't know, a bisexual thrill junkie. Claimed to be a hitman. Took me into a liquor store and pulled the guns. It was supposed to be a test to see if he could trust me. The Korean guy behind the counter pulled a shotgun and shot him. But the gunshot didn't kill him. So I had to go to the hospital to…do it myself. But he died, so I didn't have to. Then I learned something. I overheard Rain and her mother talking. And wouldn't you know it? They're in on this whole thing together."

Michael slowly lowered himself into the chair beside him, but never took his eyes from Adam's. His lips were parted. Deep creases mapped his forehead. He appeared to be in pain. Cramps, maybe.

"They wanted to set me up," Adam went on. "I'd think I was helping Rain to kill you to keep myself out of prison. But actually, they planned to fix it so I'd go to prison for the murder, or they were going to kill me themselves. Rain was pulling one over on her mom, though, because she wanted us to kill *both* of you. I think that's why Gwen hit on me in the first place, because she suspected Rain was going to try to use me to kill her. Maybe Gwen thought I wouldn't do it if we were…you know. Involved."

Michael put his elbows on his thighs, his chin on the knuckles of his big knotted-together hands. "But…why?" Michael asked, voice low.

"For your money. What else? They're hustlers, Dad. Both of them. They've had this in mind all along. The fire that killed Rain's dad? Rain made some weird remark about that, and I've been thinking maybe there was no fire. Maybe there was no *dad*. I don't know, you can't believe a word either of them says. When I realized what they were doing, how they were using me, I guess I kind of...lost it." Adam bowed his head a moment. His skin felt like it was rippling from all the crackling nervous energy just beneath. He had to move before his nerve endings sprouted through his flesh, wriggling like hungry maggots. Slowly, he paced a circle around his dad.

"First," he continued, "I wanted to kill them. But...well, you probably won't be very surprised to hear me say that we've never, you know, gotten along very well. You and me. You know that. I'm not interested in what you do. I hate what you do. And you're not interested in...anything about me. Besides that, you killed Mom. I don't know how you did it, but it wasn't an accident. Mom was a strong swimmer."

Michael watched him circle until he could not see Adam anymore. Then turned to the other side and waited for him to come around again.

"You just couldn't stand it, could you?" Adam asked. "You couldn't stand the fact that she was more talented than you. That people liked her but couldn't stand your guts. So you killed her. And for that...I want to kill you." Adam's breath shortened as he continued. He was mortified by what he was saying. Tried to breathe evenly, didn't want to sound stressed. "So I've decided to kill you all."

Adam stopped in front of his dad and they looked at one another. His voice was level, but kept skipping out like a distant AM radio station, so he swallowed or cleared his throat now and then. "So. Tomorrow. While you. And Gwen. And Rain. Are out on the yacht. It will blow up." His throat felt thick, hot. "I hired a guy. A professional. Tonight, he'll wire the yacht. With powerful explosives. Tomorrow. Out there on the water. You'll all be. Vaporized."

Michael did not even blink. It was the longest Adam could remember ever maintaining eye contact with his dad. The longest he had seen him hold still and remain silent. The longest his dad had ever listened to him. And it was the first time Adam ever noticed that he had his dad's eyes.

Michael Julian rose slowly without looking away from Adam. "I don't believe it." He licked his lips, stepped forward.

Adam's instinct was to step back immediately, but he did not move.

A bead of water from Michael's wet hair zigzagged down his forehead. "Goddamned son of a bitch!" he shouted.

Adam teetered backward, a tree about to fall. Caught his balance.

"I don't fucking *believe* it!" Michael's hands pounded down on Adam's shoulders and squeezed.

Adam made a small, whimpering sound in his throat, so terrified he wanted to cry.

"I really thought you didn't give a fuck," Michael said. He gripped Adam's shoulders painfully hard. "I thought you…well, sometimes I thought you hated me. Didn't care if I lived or died. I just, I can't believe you were actually *listening*." He flashed his teeth in that hound-like smile of his.

A frown moved in like a fog on Adam's face, rolled over his features. *What's wrong with him?* he wondered. *Has he lost his mind?*

Adam said, "Well, uh—" He had to swallow again. Never finished.

"It's incredible." Michael said. "I'm amazed. *Stunned*. And you did it just like I told you. Write what you know, then add the honey. Sex, violence, tits. And fuckin' *teen* tits! You know what that's worth at the box office? At the video store, too." He spun away from Adam and cried, "Jesus H. Christ!" He paced around the chair, around Adam. Ran fat fingers through his wet hair.

"Might have to juice it up a little," he said. "That hospital scene sounds like a good place for a whammy. Maybe we could blow it up, I like that. I don't think anybody's ever blown up a whole hospital in a movie before, especially one full of people. Your character has to kill this guy, you've already got access to explosives because you're planning to blow up the yacht, so you use it on the hospital. Yeah. Good spot for a health insurance joke, too. Shit, that's good! That idea's got room for plenty of fucking honey! It's classy, too, high-end. Still needs a third act, but that'll come. Shit, we could get…y'know, I bet we could get Jennifer Love Hewitt. Finally get those juicy tits of hers out in the open where they belong." He glanced at Adam occasionally as he paced, eyes wide and fiery. "She says she'll never do nudity, but you know what that means, don't ya? It means the same when any of 'em say it. It means they'll never do nudity till somebody gives them enough money and perks or they're desperate for work. Give 'em enough money and perks, they'll show you how many weights they can dangle on clamps from their pussy lips."

Adam had turned to stone. Cold and hard and course. No organs, no soft tissue, just stone throughout. If he tried to move, he would shatter into a cloud of pebbles and dust.

"How about the father?" Michael asked. "Whattaya think of Kevin Spacey, huh? Women love that little faggot. You know, that's who this movie's gonna pull in, the fucking women. You make a movie about water boiling in a pot and put some tits in it, men will break down the Goddamned theater doors. Women wanna see something that'll make 'em think, give 'em a challenge, something smart to talk about, and Spacey's got that written all over his dick-sucking lips, he just brings it to the table with him. Jesus, thinking and talking. That's all women ever wanna do. Wish they could do both at the same fuckin' time."

Adam had stopped breathing. No longer had lungs. Or a heart or stomach. Only his eyes still worked. A paralysis of stone. Rock on.

"Nah, what am I thinking, it's too early for casting. Got anything on paper?"

Adam did not respond. Could not. The slightest movement would shatter him.

"Once we got a script, who knows who the fuck could be right. Hell, for all we know, it could end up being a Schwarzenegger picture."

The name sounded like a deafening gong in Adam's mind. He willed himself to move. Suddenly, he *wanted* to explode. Disappear. Cease to be. *Schwarzenegger?*

"He's looking for meatier roles. Doesn't matter, the fuckin' Kraut can't act, but he's still a hell of a draw. I mean, if that piece of devil shit didn't kill his career, he ain't goin' *nowhere*. But maybe he's—" He froze. Put a hand on top of his head, as if to keep it from popping open. Turned slowly to Adam. "Oh…oh, Jesus, what if…what if we could get Tom Hanks? Tom fucking Hanks! He's been talking about trying something new, something besides that Jimmy Stewart shtick of his. Shit, what'm I talking about, it's too soon for that."

Michael turned and charged toward Adam, open arms outstretched.

Adam wanted to jump onto his bed, bounce once on the mattress, dive headfirst through the window and shatter his body on the concrete below.

"We've gotta get this on paper," Michael said, clutching Adam's upper arms. "We can pound out a treatment on *Money Shot*, have it done by the time we get back. I'll set up a meeting with, uh, lessee, maybe we should take it over to Harvey Weinstein at Mirimax. That ugly fuck owes me one. And it's got a Mirimax kinda feel to it, don'tcha think? But we need that treatment. And, uh…well, it's incredible, Adam, really, a fanfuckingtastic idea. But we'll have to make a few changes, y'know? I mean, it's perfect that you used us as a model. That's what I was talking about, write what you know, and that's what you fuckin' did, you sneaky bastard, and you did it *beautifully*. This is one of those ideas where everything just falls into place, I'm not kidding, you just wait, this'll slide out smooth as shit through a duck. But we'll have to make the father, I don't know, something else. People don't like movies about people who work in the movies. Too inside, too inaccessible to the general public, they don't understand. We'll make him something hot, something current, maybe a…Bill Gates type? Lots of money and power. Jesus, this is incredible!"

Michael wrapped his arms around Adam and squeezed him tightly. Laughed a loud guffaw into Adam's ear, pulled back and grinned. His eyes softened suddenly and filled with…something. Not tears. Nothing tangible. His grip on Adam's shoulders became gentle as he frowned. "You don't…really think I killed your mother…do you?" Michael whispered.

Adam had no tongue, his throat was gone. Had no idea what expression remained etched into his stone face. Somewhere inside his head, he screamed.

"I mean…you've said some pretty shitty things to me, but…*that* would hurt. We, uh…your mom and I weren't getting along, you knew that, but…I loved her. More than life, Adam. She *was* more talented than me. God, she was a fucking artist. And everybody loved her because she was…just a good person. The kind of person you don't find in this town. Somebody you just, right away, you just want to *know* her." He dropped his arms and turned away slowly, heavily. "She just couldn't shake the Goddamned booze and pills. Finally killed her. I told her not to go swimming." He shook his head once. Turned to Adam again.

Adam's eyes felt ready to shoot from their smooth, stone sockets. They were Adam's only means of expression, the only way he could respond to what his dad had just said.

Michael became defensive for a moment. "Oh, come on! Don't look at me like that. You knew about your mother. Everybody knew. Drank champagne like it was tapwater. Took more pills before lunch every day than the entire cast of *Valley of the Dolls* did in the whole movie. But, she was…a force of nature. Sober or not."

Michael rubbed a hand across his face. Dragged fingers through his beard and sighed. Looked at the expensive waterproof watch Joel Silver had given him last Christmas. "Fuck, I gotta go. Got a meeting with Cher in half an hour, you believe that?" He started toward the door, but slowly, looking repeatedly back at Adam. Smiling. "That goofy cunt's optioned the rights to some fucking comic book character. A female superhero she wants to play. Wants to talk to me about doing the script. Sheena, Queen of the Plastic Surgeon's Office, or some shit like that. Xena, Infomercial Princess, I don't know." He laughed. Stopped at the open door. "You bringing someone with you tomorrow?"

"I'm not coming." Flesh and bone again, just like that. His voice sounded muddy, as if he'd just woke.

Michael's face fell. "What? Why the hell didn't you say so?" His voice rose as he went on. "That's why I came in here in the first fucking place, to find out if you were—" He stopped, bent his head forward. Took a breath, spoke quietly. "Hey. You've gotta come now. We've got work to do, right? What the hell you gonna stay here for? There's nothing to do here."

"I met a girl," Adam said.

"A…a girl?" He took a few steps toward Adam. "Well, why the fuck haven't I met her? I mean…look, Adam, I know I'm not the best father in the world, but you've gotta hold up your end, too, you know? You could throw me a Goddamned bone once in awhile. Fill me in a little, okay? How long have you been seeing her?"

"This week."

"Is she hot?"

Adam's numb lips spread into a smile as he nodded.

"Son of a bitch! Who are you and what the fuck have you done with my son?" Michael's body rocked with laughter. "You gonna see her today? Is that why you showered?"

Adam nodded.

"Why the hell don't you bring her?"

"She has to work. I'm going to stay here with her." He smiled again, but did not feel it. It was not his mouth, but an alien creature squirming around on the bottom half of his face. "And fuck her brains out." They were not his words and sounded wrong when spoken in his voice. It was something Michael would say. Something he would appreciate, which was why Adam said it.

Michael stepped over and punched Adam's shoulder. "Goddammit, you're gonna have more fun than me!" His stiff index finger nearly touched the tip of Adam's nose. "You better save some squirt for that treatment, you hear me? I wanna see a solid first draft by the time I get back. I'll be making some notes, too. We can talk about it on the phone." He put his palm to the side of Adam's face. "That was the best fucking pitch I've ever heard, you know that? I'm not shittin' you. I'm proud of you." Patted his cheek hard a few times. "We're gonna write a fuckin' movie together! How about that, huh?" He hurried to the door again, turned back and said, "And remember what I said about a Bill Gates type." He grinned. "You have fun. But you'll be hearing from me in a couple days, so be thinking, okay?"

Still smiling, Adam nodded.

"See you later."

As his dad pulled the bedroom door closed, Adam said, "Goodbye, Dad." He took three slow steps toward his bed, then fell heavily onto the mattress. Pressed his face into the pillow and sobbed.

The next morning, 11:37.

While Adam and Alyssa lay naked in his bed, sleepily nibbling cold Pop Tarts and each other, *Money Shot* was sixty miles off the coast of Marina del Rey.

Loud music pounded from the yacht. Inside, Gwen and Rain stood at the bar laughing like schoolgirls. Gwen mixed a pitcher of margaritas as Rain finished one off.

Michael Julian was about to do some fishing, but wanted to get a bite to eat first. They had left the house early that morning, and he had skipped breakfast. His stomach sounded like road construction. He went to a cupboard to find some crackers or potato chips. He opened the cupboard door to a rushing wave of blue boxes. They spilled out in a heap around his feet.

Michael glared down at the orange noodles pictured on the sides of the boxes. His upper lip curled back over his teeth. He lifted his head and shouted, "Who brought all the Goddamned Kraft Macaroni and Cheese?"

Divers would never find all of him. Nor would more than a few pieces of Gwen, Rain, and the three-man crew ever be recovered. Small, tattered, fish-eaten pieces. In the beat of a heart and a gout of raging flames, they were gone. So was *Money Shot*.

In minutes, only a few small pieces of burning debris remained on the ocean's surface. The flames would die quickly, until all that remained was the sound of the water, the sullen cries of the gulls, and a single piece of burnt, soggy, blue cardboard with charred edges around a picture of macaroni and cheese.

THIRTY-TWO

I can't believe who's here," Carter whispered. He turned around in the front pew, looked over his shoulder at the crowd. "Cameron, Tarantino, Woo, Frankenheimer. Schwarzenegger, Willis, Nic Cage...Jodie—wow, Jodie Foster! David Kelley and Michelle Pfeiffer...damn, she looks hot in black. Course, she'd look hot in a duck suit."

Adam sat between Carter and Alyssa. She held his hand, stroked his thumb with the pad of hers. He was disturbed. Not by the large turnout, but by the fact that he felt no emotion himself. He had expected something. A feeling of loss, of being alone in the world, or at least some regret, a little guilt for what he had done. But he felt nothing. He searched himself for any sign that he was moved by the loss of his dad and two women with whom he had been intimately involved, even though he had brought about that loss himself. But again...nothing.

He did not want his nothingness to show, so he kept his eyes front, sunglasses on. Stared at the three caskets lined up before the two columns of pews. At the photograph of Michael and Gwen Julian taken at their wedding. The other of Rain as a toddler playing in a pool—it was the only one that could be found—naked even then, practicing her moves. At the mountains of flowers around the caskets that filled the church with their heavy fragrance. Adam looked as if deep in thought, pummeled by grief. He was wondering what to do for lunch.

Michael Julian had not had a religious hair on his body. And he'd had a lot of hair. Adam doubted his dad had mumbled even the smallest, most insincere, throwaway prayer in his lifetime. But he had left instructions that his funeral be held in the Church of the Good Shepherd in Beverly Hills because it was considered *the* church of the stars. It was well-tended, the oldest church in Beverly Hills and located just around the corner from the town's other houses of worship, the shops on Rodeo Drive. Mission-style, small, it seated only six hundred, but the modest church had seen a lot of action.

Elizabeth Taylor had married Nicky Hilton there in 1950, the first of her long line of ill-fated unions. In 1926, wailing mourners, mostly women, filled the street to bid farewell to screen lover Rudolph Valentino. Another crowd had gathered there in 1998 to say farewell to Frank Sinatra. Inside the humble little church or out, it was more common to be moved by the spirit of Hollywood than the spirit of God. It was not the services that drew thousands of camera-clicking tourists to the church each year. It was the list of famous names who had been baptized, married, or eulogized in the church. Now, added to it for posterity, was the name of Michael Julian.

"Jesus Christ!" Carter said.

"Is *He* here?" Adam asked.

"No, Spielberg's here! I didn't know they were friends."

Adam sucked his lips between his teeth and bit down on them. To keep from smiling. He remembered the night his dad had gone to the premiere of *Schindler's List*.

Back in the late eighties, Michael Julian had been hired by Spielberg to do a little uncredited script-doctoring on *Indiana Jones and the Last Crusade*. Michael had been ecstatic, certain that a relationship with the blockbuster director would bring respect to his work and lift him to the top of the Hollywood ladder. He saw the uncredited job as a stepping stone to writing the sequel to *E.T. the Extra Terrestrial*. Spielberg had rejected Michael's ideas of a lesbian shower scene, as well as his mystifying introduction of spontaneous human combustion into the Indiana Jones story. Michael was never asked to work with Spielberg again. But that did not stop him from figuratively spreading the director's buttocks and puckering his lips loudly whenever the opportunity arose. Otherwise, he spoke of Spielberg with contempt.

"What'd I do to deserve this?" he had asked the night of the *Schindler's List* premiere. In and out of the bedroom, pacing the hall in various stages of dress, nervous and agitated. "That little merchandising prick had better go back to his dinosaur puppet shows and live action cartoons or he's gonna be out of a job. Kids're his core audience. Why do you think he *has* so many? They're like the ultimate captive audience for him, they *have* to go to Daddy's movies. But kids don't like this shit. *Nobody* does! Jews suffering in black and white for four Goddamned hours. Who the hell needs that? That's the kind of crap people pay money to avoid, not to see. Outside of maybe Simon Wiesenthal and Jackie Mason. That's not entertainment, it's career suicide. I'd rather go to my own fuckin' funeral."

Well, Dad, here you are, Adam thought.

A black sequined figure appeared before Adam and he lifted his head. Blinked a couple times. His back stiffened with surprise when he realized it was Cher. She looked like Morticia Addams dressed by Bob Mackey. The amount of plastic surgery she had undergone would have her looking like Vincent Price at the end of *The House of Wax* in a few more years. Beside her and a step behind stood a young man of about twenty, with wavy black hair, a square jaw, puffy lips. Face blank, he scanned the crowd, waiting patiently.

Sniffling, Cher leaned forward and hugged him. Told him how sorry she was, how much she had admired Michael, that she had looked forward to finally working with him on her movie *Lady Death* after admiring him for so long. When she left, her perfume lingered awhile.

"That was the most terrifying moment of my life," Carter said with a tremor in his voice.

"This month, that's saying a lot," Adam said.

"She's not giving the eulogy, is she?"

"Probably would if it would do anything for her career. But no, she's not."

"Thank God. Her eulogy for Sonny was so long, they had to hold the funeral in three parts."

"It wasn't that it ran long," Adam whispered. "She had to keep stopping for costume changes."

Looking over his shoulder again, Carter whispered, "This place is packed. I had no idea so many people liked your dad."

"Nobody liked my dad. They're here for Gwen, or for the press. Or both. Most of these people don't even like each other." Adam had seen a few reporters arriving outside earlier. Fortunately, there were not very many. He planned to avoid them, afraid he would not look mournful enough on camera.

The caskets were beautiful. Bronze with brass handles, lined with white satin. An enormous and unnecessary expense, considering how little was left of the deceased. But Michael's instructions had been specific, and the caskets, plots, and headstones at Forest Lawn had been purchased years ago.

The night before, Rog had told Adam that Michael had provided identical burial arrangements for him as well. It was the first time Adam had heard of it. The last place he wanted to go for his final rest was that Technicolor necrophilic theme park, Cadaverland, otherwise known as Forest Lawn. He thought it was the most nauseating tourist attraction in Los Angeles, and that said a lot. A landscaper's wet dream full of dead celebrities.

"I don't want it," he had told Rog. "Put Rain in it. I don't want to be buried. I'd like to be cremated. I want my ashes to be put into a douche and sneaked into Angelina Jolie's bathroom. Do you have papers you can draw up for that?"

Rog had not found that funny. Not even a little.

Adam wondered what Rog and the other attorneys had been thinking. Did they suspect anything? He didn't think so. No one had referred to the explosion as anything but "the accident." But he had to watch his behavior around them, appear properly distraught. Douche jokes about human ashes probably weren't a good idea.

He turned to Alyssa. "Ever seen so many celebrities under one roof, outside of a Scientology crab feed?"

"What?"

"All the celebrities here. It's like an awards show. Somebody should have Bruce Vilanch write some jokes."

"Hadn't noticed. Are you okay?"

He lifted her hand to his lips and kissed it. "Better than I would be if you weren't here."

The service was mercifully short, but felt nonetheless like a small eternity to Adam. He tried to get out of the church as quickly as possible, but had to stop several times for handshakes, condolences, and a hug from Doris Roberts, whose role in *Fistfighter*, as the hero's mother, had been small but funny, and very popular. It had been one of Michael's biggest hits.

Adam, Alyssa, and Carter started down the cement steps in front of the church, but stopped after only three.

The vans lined up in front of the church on Santa Monica Boulevard, some double-parked, made the block look like a giant *TV Guide* listing grid. CBS, NBC, ABC, CNN, Fox, *Entertainment Tonight*, *Hollywood Extra*, *Rough Cut*. There was even a camera from *The Daily Show* on Comedy Central. The convertible was parked across the street and around the corner on Bedford Drive. The ominous clot of infotainment personnel and equipment blocked their way.

A hand settled on Adam's shoulder. He turned to find Jack Nicholson beside him, looking grim in a black suit and sunglasses. Adam had not seen him inside, but was glad he'd shown up. While Adam was growing up, Jack had come to nearly every one of Michael's parties, and spent time with Adam at each one. Never talked down to him or treated him like a kid. He'd spent most of one party upstairs with Adam and Carter, maybe ten years old at the time, playing video games and eating junk food. Michael had been infuriated, but said not a word to Jack about it.

"I'm real sorry about your dad, kid," Nicholson said. "Never got to work with him, but he threw a hell of a party."

Adam introduced Alyssa. Jack leaned around Adam and smiled, took her hand and gave it a gentlemanly squeeze. Once Adam blocked Alyssa's view of him again, Jack's eyebrows rose on his spacious forehead and he gave Adam a quick thumbs up. The four of them countinued slowly down the concrete steps.

"Look at this shark tank," Jack said, surveying the media crowd. "You got somebody to run interference for you?"

"Dad's publicist wanted to stick to me like glue. I told her to leave me alone."

"Stick with me and I'll keep 'em off you."

The reporters saw Jack first and a few moved toward him. When they saw Adam, they converged on him like piranha on a bloody chunk of meat just dropped into the water. Adam held tightly to Alyssa's hand as Jack put his hand on Adam's shoulder again, steered him. The movie star held up his right arm, didn't hesitate a step. "S'cuse us, s'cuse us."

Adam kept his head down, tried to ignore the reporters. He could not understand why so many had come. Screenwriters, even successful bad ones like Michael Julian, simply did not get that much media coverage, in life or death.

Then he heard the questions.

"Do you think someone murdered your family?"

"Is it possible a bomb could have been put on board the yacht?"

"Could the explosion have been intentional?"

Adam went numb from the very center of his being to the tips of his fingers and toes. The sunny day darkened for him and he felt dizzy. Jack stopped, clutched Adam's arm. From behind, Carter grabbed Adam's shoulder and squeezed hard. The gesture silently screamed, *What are they talking about?*

"You okay?" Jack asked.

Adam's eyes were wide behind his sunglasses.

"He hasn't felt well all day," Carter lied. "I'd better get him home."

They picked up their pace and Jack raised his arm again. "Okay, c'mon, people, show a little restraint, for Chrissake," he said. "This is a funeral, remember?"

At the car, Adam and Alyssa got in the backseat. They had decided it would look better for Carter to drive them to the funeral, and Adam certainly was in no condition to drive back. He wondered if Carter was.

As he got behind the wheel of Adam's convertible, Carter asked Jack, "What were they talking about back there?"

"The reporters?" Jack asked. "Who knows? I doubt *they* know."

As Carter started the car, Jack wished Adam well, gave him a standing invitation to drop by.

Carter glanced repeatedly at Adam's reflection in the rearview mirror with troubled eyes. "Think we should take Alyssa home now?" he asked.

He knew Carter was just as eager as he to talk, figure out what the reporters had been going on about. That would be impossible as long as Alyssa was with them.

"Trying to get rid of me?" she asked with a playful smile.

"Oh, no!" Adam said. "It's just that—"

"Hey, look, you don't have to explain anything to me, okay? I understand. I want to do whatever's best for you. If you want me to stay with you every second I will. If you want me to leave you alone, I'll do that, too." She leaned close and whispered, "Even though I'd rather stay with you every second." Adam started to speak, but she continued. "I know this is a tough time for you, no matter how you felt about him. It couldn't have been an easy thing for you to do, and I'm so proud of you. But I'm not sure what to do. I've never dealt with death before. I'm afraid if I try too hard I'll smother you and you'll get sick of me, but if I leave you alone, I'm afraid…this will just end. You know? Fade away."

"If I had my way, Alyssa, you'd move in with me."

"Are you serious?"

"Yes. But this would be a bad time. I've got a lot of…family things to take care of."

"I know."

He pushed the words out fast, wanted to make sure she knew he was not just making excuses, brushing her off. "The house has been full of attorneys ever since this happened, and I don't think the siege is over. I'm not saying I don't want to see you, because I do, I want to see you often and…and naked, but I don't know when all this is going to—"

Alyssa shut him up with a kiss. "You had me at 'naked.'"

A moment later, Adam leaned forward to tell Carter to head for the bookstore. But they were already halfway there.

Adam's first test of nerves after *Money Shot* went up in flames had been a visit from a Coast Guard investigator. A tall, muscular, stern black man named Hammond came to the house to ask Adam some questions. They went to the dining room, where Mrs. Yu brought them coffee.

"Why weren't you on the yacht with the others?" Hammond asked.

"My girlfriend had to work, so I stayed here to be with her."

"Did your father have any enemies? Was he feuding with anyone? Business associates? Family?"

"A lot of people don't like him. Didn't, I mean. In his business, that just comes with the territory."

"Relatives?"

"He has family in Spokane. Grandpa died a few years ago, but Grandma is still alive. Last I heard, anyway. I think she's in a rest home. And he has a sister there, too. But they haven't spoken in years. I only met them once, when I was a kid."

It went on for about fifteen minutes. When Hammond was finished, he gave Adam his card and condolences and left abruptly.

Is that it? Adam had wondered. *Is that all I have to deal with?* If so, he figured he had nothing to worry about. But, of course, there was more.

Next, a uniformed officer from the Marina del Rey Police Department, Officer Miguel Ruiz, had come to the house to ask questions of his own. Medium height, average build, very nondescript. He apologized for having to question Adam at such a bad time, but said it was unavoidable. Once again, they talked at the dining room table. Officer Ruiz turned down coffee in favor of tea, and Mrs. Yu provided a tray of shortbread cookies.

"How long did your father have that yacht?"

"Two years at the most. He buys a new one every few years."

"How long has he been doing that?"

"As long as I can remember."

As they talked, Officer Ruiz ate one shortbread cookie after another, sometimes speaking with a bite of cookie creating a lump in his cheek. "Any other boats?"

"A fishing boat."

"What kind?"

"I couldn't tell you. I'm not into fishing, and I never went with him."

"Did you ever go out on the yacht?"

"I used to. Every Fourth of July. But I stopped after my mom died."

"Was your father an experienced boater?"

"He's been doing it for a long time."

"But was he...no offense, but was he any good?"

"He thought he was."

"What do you mean?"

"Well, Dad was...sometimes he was more willing than able."

"Give me an example."

"Once, Donald Sutherland went fishing with him. Dad made a bet that he could make better trout almondine. I don't know why. Far as I know, Dad had never made anything besides toast, and I think Sutherland's a pretty good cook. But he was determined to prove he could make a better trout almondine."

"What happened?"

"He burned up the kitchen and most of the dining room."

Officer Ruiz repeated Hammond's question about possible enemies. Adam repeated his answer.

"What about his wife?" Officer Ruiz asked.

"What do you mean?"

"Did she have any enemies?"

"Gwen?" He frowned. "I can't imagine Gwen having any enemies. Everybody liked her."

"Any old boyfriends? Ex-husbands?"

"Her husband was killed in a house fire recently. That's why Rain was living with us."

"Is it possible she was having an affair?"

Adam shrugged. "Possible, I guess. But I don't think so."

"What about your dad? Could he have been seeing someone?"

"That's more likely. But he wasn't as far as I know."

"More likely? Was he ever unfaithful in the past?"

"With Gwen, I don't know." Adam remembered his parents arguing about a woman when he was nine or ten years old. And again a couple years later. He didn't know if his dad had been unfaithful, but it seemed likely.

"What about Rain?"

"I didn't know her very well. She ran with a pretty rough crowd."

"Was she into drugs?"

"She drank a lot. And she was always high on pot."

"Did you meet any of her friends?"

"Not personally, no. But Gwen was always telling her to stay away from them. I don't think it did any good."

"Do you know the names of any of her friends?"

If the police looked too closely at Rain's friends, they might discover Monty had been killed during the liquor store robbery. If they decided to look at the security video, they would see that Adam had been there for the robbery as well.

"No, I don't," he said. "If she mentioned any names, I don't remember them."

"You mentioned your mother. I'm curious. How did she die?"

"An accident. She went out on the fishing boat with Dad and…drowned while swimming."

"Were you there?"

"No."

"Anyone else?"

Adam shook his head. "Just the two of them."

"Tell me, Adam, what do you think happened on that boat Saturday? Do you have an opinion? A guess?"

Adam bowed his head for a moment. "I wish I knew. But I have no idea."

Officer Ruiz nodded, closed his notebook. Popped another cookie into his mouth.

"Do you guys know yet?" Adam asked. "What happened on the yacht, I mean?"

"Not exactly. It looks like nothing more than an accident, but we don't know all the specifics yet. We've got experts looking over the remains of the yacht. Divers looking for more. They'll figure it all out."

Adam was surprised by how calm he had remained during both interviews. He'd feared he would be a nervous wreck, but had sailed through them with unexpected ease. He had believed every answer he had given, had not allowed his mind to wander beyond the questions being asked. And he had pulled it off.

Of course, marijuana had helped. He had been riding a buzz since the barbecue at Carter's house on Friday night. Without it, Adam knew he would be unable to function socially. He was in a permanent state of nerve-ripping suspense until the phone call came from the Coast Guard. After that, Adam's tension still didn't ease. He waited for a knock at the door. An unsmiling cop, handcuffs ready, to read him his rights.

When reporters started showing up at the house, Adam packed a few things, drove his convertible over to Carter's late one night, parked it in back, and stayed there until the funeral on the following Friday. Rog had delayed the service until divers had rounded up all the pieces they were able to find.

Adam temporarily moved into the unoccupied bedroom across the hall from Carter's, which served as a catch-all for junk Carter had collected over the years. During that week, Alyssa spent every spare moment with him. Devin pampered him like a sick child. Even Carter's dad hovered over him like a mother hen, and personally turned away reporters at the door and on the telephone, saying Adam was not there.

Brett spent a good deal of time with them, too. Her face soured during her first visit to Carter's studio. She walked along the shelves looking disgusted, but at the same time smirking. Alyssa, on the other hand, was delighted by Carter's creations and had to touch everything, laughing and squealing like an delightedly disgusted little girl.

"Carter, you're a genius," Alyssa said. "And an artist! You're an artist *and* a genius!"

"Artists and geniuses are sometimes very disturbed," Brett said.

"Oh, you're *so* Dr. Laura, Brett," Alyssa said with a dismissive wave.

A few minutes later, Alyssa tapped Brett on the shoulder from behind. When Brett turned around, Alyssa screamed and held Carter's severed head in front of Brett's face by a handful of its hair. Her scream was shrill, piercing, the scream of a fifties B-movie queen fleeing a giant bug.

"Holy shit!" Carter barked as he dropped the back issues of *Fangoria* he was stacking on a shelf.

Adam flinched, but not only from Alyssa's scream. For just an instant—arm outstretched, bloody-necked head dangling by the hair from her fist, Alyssa's eyes impossibly wide, screaming mouth stretched into a too-large, toothy grin—she looked like someone else. Some*thing* else. A chill settled over Adam's shoulders and the skin on the back of his neck shriveled.

Her scream dissolved into an insane cackle.

Brett jumped back and bumped a shelf. "Are you PMSing, or *what?*"

"Hey, it scared you!" Carter said. He smiled with satisfaction.

"It didn't scare me," Brett insisted. "Her stupid scream startled me, is all."

Still smiling, Carter said, "The head scared you or you wouldn't have jumped back."

"It did *not* scare me."

"Yes, it did."

"Did not."

"Did so."

"Did *not*."

"Did *so*."

During that week, an odd relationship developed between Carter and Brett.

"She hates me," Carter had said to Adam Tuesday morning in the studio. Just the two of them.

"Has she said she hates you?"

"Nobody comes right out and says, 'I hate you.' It's the little things she says, the way she behaves."

"I don't know what to tell you, Carter. I can't very well ask Alyssa to tell her best friend to stay home."

"She thinks there's something wrong with me."

"Carter, we *all* think there's something wrong with you, that doesn't mean we hate you."

Adam was joking, but Carter looked a little hurt.

"I'm kidding," Adam quickly said.

Carter relaxed, but still looked unhappy. "It's true. She thinks there's something wrong with me because of what I do." He waved vaguely at the shelves.

"You know how most people are."

"I thought she'd be different because she's Alyssa's friend."

Adam smiled, chuckled.

"What's funny?" Carter asked.

"You know what your problem is?"

"You're gonna tell me, right?"

"You *want* her to like you."

"Bite my ass."

Adam's smile grew. "Yeah, I think that's it. You've got wood for her, don't you?"

"She hates animals, Adam. Dogs, cats, all animals. How could I like a girl like that?"

"I can think of two reasons right off the top of my head."

Carter's defenses crumbled quickly. "Yeah. Is her chest well hung, or what? They're incredible." After a moment, he shook his head. "But she hates me."

Adam rolled his eyes. "Jeez, Carter, close mouth and engage brain! Do you think she'd be hanging around with us so much if she hated you?"

"That's just because she's Alyssa's friend, and Alyssa hangs around with us because of you."

"Okay, whatever you say. But if you were smart, you'd warm up to her. Get to know her. Put a little effort into it, you lazy bastard."

Over the next few days, Adam had noticed Carter first talking to Brett more, trying to engage her in conversation. Then the two of them began to wander off together when Adam and Alyssa were talking quietly to one another. On Thursday night, Adam found them making out on the old paint-spattered leather sofa in the studio. Carter had not brought it up, so Adam said nothing.

Sunny called Alyssa in to work at the bookstore only when she had no other choice, and even then for no more than an hour or two at a time. Adam had driven her to the store early Wednesday afternoon. Mitch's car had broken down while on a buying trip, and Sunny had to teach her pottery class at the Knowledge Pond. Adam had to meet with some of the attorneys that afternoon, and was dreading it. He dropped Alyssa off and was about to drive away to go back home when he heard Sunny calling him. She rushed to the convertible and handed him a platter covered with aluminum foil. Told him how sorry she was about his loss, got a little sniffly as she hugged him.

"That's for you, from Mitch and me," she said, as Adam set the platter on the seat next to him. "I hope it can make the pain a little more tolerable."

Adam had no doubt it would. At home, he'd removed the foil to find a pile of large chocolate-chip cookies. Another sheet of foil separated them from a mound of brownies. All of them had been made with ingredients from what Sunny called "Mitch's herb garden."

At night, Adam and Alyssa slept in the room he had commandeered. They slept eventually, anyway. But Adam did not look forward to that sleep. Each night, his nightmares grew worse. He had been able to keep them to himself until the night before the funeral.

He remembered only fragments of the nightmares. Sometimes his dad came to him, sometimes Gwen or Rain. Their naked, fish-eaten bodies dragged ropes of seaweed and intestines as they shuffled toward him, creatures from an episode of *Tales From the Crypt*. Empty eye sockets, teeth falling out of their fish-eaten grins. But they were never angry, always smiling, sometimes laughing. And they always told him, without ever speaking out loud, that they were waiting for him. That they would be witnesses to his execution, and would be waiting to greet him on the other side.

Sometimes, they were accompanied by police officers who pointed their firearms at Adam and screamed repeatedly, "On the ground! Hands behind your back!"

The worst was a nightmare in which Rain lay sprawled on her own casket, torn body in pieces, connected by the finest threads of muscle, flesh, or slime. Mastburbating with a dead fish. The fish became a handgun. Rain fired the fish inside herself.

He had awakened from that one with a shout, sweaty in the cool darkness of early morning. Alyssa had nearly fallen out of bed with fright, but quickly recovered and asked what was wrong. He'd been unable to tell her. It was too revealing, too risky. He had let her hold him instead, the side of his face resting against her warm breast. Spent the rest of the morning listening to Alyssa's heart beat, unable to go back to sleep with the funeral looming over the coming day.

Compared to his nightmares, though, reality was anticlimactic. There were no mangled, grinning corpses. No screaming police officers with guns drawn. Only eager reporters asking questions about bombs and murders. And the relentless ghosts of his own guilt haunting his sleep.

✝

On the way back from the funeral, after dropping Alyssa off, Adam and Carter listened to the news on the radio. The service at the Church of the Good Shepherd came up a few times, although the real story seemed to be the celebrities who attended rather than the people being buried. There was no mention of the explosion being intentional, and the words "murder" and "bomb" were not used. But the newscaster did say, "A police investigation is underway."

"They were just fishing," Adam said. "If they had something, it'd be all over the radio."

"They were just *hoping*, you mean," Carter said as his shoulders slumped with relief.

At Carter's house, they entered through the back door. Devin was seated at the kitchen table, talking on the phone. He wrapped up the conversation as soon as he saw them.

"Adam, I'm really sorry for not going to the funeral with you," Devin said, standing.

"You know I understand, Devin. Don't worry about it."

It was the third time Devin had apologized. On the few occasions Devin and Mr. Brandis and Michael Julian had been together, Michael had been, as usual, less than civil. He had thought he was being funny, of course, when he'd made ugly remarks about Devin's dress and asked if he was wearing a cup under there. Mr. Brandis was in New York, but even if he had been home, Adam was sure he would not have attended the funeral, either. And Adam would have understood that as well.

"If you're hungry," Devin said, "I just made a delicious fruit salad for lunch."

"None for me, thanks," Adam said.

Carter said, "Maybe later."

They went upstairs and changed clothes. Ten minutes later, they were in the studio, sitting at the partners desk. Carter worked on his severed hand while Adam did some writing on his laptop. It was like any other summer day, but instead of music, they listened to a news station on the radio. If anything about the investigation changed suddenly, they wanted to hear about it right away rather than being surprised later by a phone call or a knock on the door.

That night, with Carter at the wheel of his dad's Mercedes, Adam and Carter took Alyssa and Brett to see David Lynch's *Eraserhead* at the Nuart.

"This is sick!" Brett said almost ten minutes into the movie. "Everything about it is sick! Even the furniture is sick!" She kept up a running commentary of derision, questioning the sanity of anyone who found the movie less than repugnant.

Finally, Alyssa whispered to Carter across Brett's lap, "Would you please kiss her and shut her up!"

Carter's eyebrows popped up. "Oh. Yeah." He had been surprised by the idea. But pleasantly surprised.

Brett was silent for the rest of the movie.

Afterward, they had hamburgers at Tommy's, then went back to Carter's place.

That night, after an orgasm that made the hairs on his head dance in their follicles, Adam fell asleep with Alyssa's head on his chest. He awoke shortly after four in the morning, but not from a nightmare. Went to the bathroom, got back into bed and stared into the darkness for awhile. He had slept for over three hours but could not remember dreaming at all. His sleep had been deep and uninterrupted, restful.

Maybe it's over, he thought as he snuggled up to Alyssa. *Maybe I got away with it after all*. With Alyssa's skin against his and the sweet smell of her in his nostrils, Adam drifted back to sleep.

Y ou're not going to believe this," Adam said, coming into the studio with fresh-made roast beef sandwiches on paper plates and a bag of potato chips.

"Yeah, I'll probably believe it," Carter said from the desk. He did not look up from the severed thumb he was painting.

"Maury Povich wants me on his show."

Carter looked up. "Is he gonna have the Menendi on, too? I hate theme shows."

"Eat me."

Eyes on the thumb again, Carter muttered, "I bet Maury's audience would've laughed."

It was Thursday, six long, lazy days after the funeral.

Adam put the sandwiches and chips on the desk, where he had left the laptop open and online. On the screen, two fat, naked midgets, male and female, were having noisy sex in the missionary position on a bed. In red above the streaming video, the word **MIDGETCAM**.

"Have you checked out this cam?" Adam asked. He turned up the volume so they could hear the panting and moaning of the midgets.

"No. That chick with the beer bottle was really getting on my nerves."

Adam sat down, saying, "You're missing all the action."

Carter left his chair and came around the desk, looked over Adam's shoulder.

Adam had logged onto the Midgetcam an hour ago and bought a membership with his Visa. The cam remained dead for the first twenty minutes, and Adam and Carter had grumbled about what a waste of time it had been. Just when Adam had been about to leave the website, a small, naked, wrinkled woman with purple hair and a ring in her nose appeared and began to masturbate with a beer bottle. Adam had muttered that she looked like E.T. Carter had disagreed, saying she looked like the baby E.T. would father if he impregnated Katie Couric.

Adam had gone downstairs to make sandwiches. That was when Devin had told him about the phone call from one of Povich's producers.

"Munchkinsex," Carter said.

"Why don't we do it in the Yellow Brick Road?" Adam said with a chuckle.

"Is there a Dorothycam? I wanna see her get nailed by the Tin Man." He went back around the desk, pulled the paper plate toward him. "What's this about Maury Povich?"

"His producer called and talked to Devin. They're doing a show on the kids of recently dead celebrities."

"Recently dead is right. The funeral wasn't even a whole week ago. They must want you to cry on camera, or something."

"Have you seen all you want of this?" Adam asked, nodding toward the laptop. "If so, I'm going to check out Amputeecam."

"Yeah, go ahead. That one I've gotta see." Carter took a bite of his sandwich. His forehead creased slowly as he chewed. "Could you use a little more horseradish on the next sandwich? This first bite only incinerated one of my lungs."

"Pussy."

"Hey, you're not really going on Povich's show, are you?"

"Hell, no. Are you kidding? It's a freak show." Once he had logged onto Amputeecam, he clicked on **JOIN**, then filled out the form. Hit the **ENTER** key.

Three rapid knocks. Adam and Carter turned to the door as Devin came in. He looked worried.

"Adam, there's a police—"

The rest of the words fell on him in an avalanche of fear and dread. Each word clear and sharp, a shiny razor that sliced into his flesh.

" —detective here to see you, from Marina del Rey," Devin said.

Adam resisted the urge to lock eyes with Carter. He pushed away from the desk, stood.

"I told him you might not be up to it," Devin said. "He said it'll only take a few minutes, but it's up to you. He can come back later, if you want."

"Thanks, Devin. But I'd rather just get it…over with."

As he followed Devin out of the studio, Adam glanced over his shoulder. Carter gawked at him, mouth open. "Keep your filthy hands off my sandwich," Adam said, closing the door.

✝

The days since the funeral had been so sweet and invigorating, Adam had nearly lost sight of the dark possibilities that lay before him. His worries had been drowned in sex and laughter and one movie after another. He had been too busy getting to know Alyssa to think of the future. Too busy enjoying the phenomenon of being surrounded only by people he liked and cared for, whose company he enjoyed.

A few times, he had caught himself tensing inwardly, in anticipation of his dad walking into the room and making a cruel remark. Each time, he had to remind himself that would never happen again. It would be awhile before he broke himself of it, but he was impatient, wanted it to go away immediately and forever.

He and Alyssa were inseparable, as were Carter and Brett. Adam and Carter were on their own that afternoon only because Alyssa had to work and Brett had a dental appointment.

Adam had half-expected another visit from a police officer with a few more questions. He knew it was probably just routine, nothing to worry about. Certainly nothing to panic over. But his nervous system was already setting off its alarms. Sweaty palms, dry throat, pounding heart, wobbly legs.

Downstairs, Adam followed Devin into the living room.

✝

"I'm Detective Wyndham of the Marina del Rey Police Department."

"Hi."

They shook hands briefly.

"Sorry to bother you, Adam, but this should take no more than a few minutes of your time. I simply need to ask you a few quick questions, then I'll go. We can talk more later, once you've had a chance to collect yourself." His voice was soft, gentle. Almost, but not quite, effeminate.

"Sure."

The living room smelled of fresh coffee from a sterling silver service on the coffee table. Devin had set out some sliced homemade banana-nut bread.

Wyndham sat at an end of the sofa, leaning forward with elbows on his spread knees. He looked in his late forties, but trim and fit, and the healthy glow on his narrow face could hide a few years. Thick sandy blonde hair cut short and parted severely on the left. Black horn-rimmed glasses sat on his sharp, straight nose. Thin lips beneath a neatly-trimmed mustache a shade darker than the hair on his head. The beige suit he wore came from one discount chain or another, but the notebook he held looked expensive. Bound in fine brown leather, fat with pages and dividers, like a Dayplanner.

Wyndham's cold, stone-gray eyes made solid contact with Adam's and left them only when necessary. He smelled faintly of some aftershave that had been around forever, the kind youth advisors and guidance counselors slapped onto their cheeks and necks.

Adam sat in a chair, right ankle resting on his left knee. Devin remained standing, hovered in the background. A nervous mother waiting for the pediatrician to give his diagnosis.

"I know you were already asked some of these questions last weekend," Wyndham said. "But if you don't mind, I'd like to run through them again."

"Sure," Adam said.

Wyndham opened the notebook. Adjusted his glasses and tucked his lower lip between his teeth as he read silently for a moment. "You told Officer Ruiz that a lot of people didn't like your dad. Is that true?"

"Well, I don't mean everybody hated him. In the movie business, nobody really likes anybody. Or trusts anybody. You never know who's out to get your next job, or your whole career. That's what Dad always said, anyway. The way he says it is, 'You never know who your next job is coming from.' It's like, everybody's friendly and smiley, but at the same time, everybody knows better, and nobody's safe."

"Can you think of anyone who didn't like him enough to kill him?"

"You mean somebody he works wi—er, worked with?"

"Let's start there."

"No. I've thought about it, but I can't imagine anyone...well, doing that."

Wyndham looked at the notebook again as he picked up a slice of banana-nut bread. Put it on a paper napkin, folded the napkin over to cover half the slice. Lifted it to his mouth and delicately took a bite without spilling a crumb.

He couldn't stand it, Adam thought when he saw Carter cautiously entering the living room.

"Is it all right if I sit in on this?" Carter asked.

Wyndham quickly put his bread on the coffee table, stood, and shook hands with him. "By all means, sit down. I was going to ask for you, anyway."

Adam closed his throat before he could gasp audibly. Why would Wyndham want to question Carter?

Carter sat on an ottoman. Glanced once at Adam.

Seated again, Wyndham said, "You told Officer Ruiz that your dad did not get along with his family. Do you know why?"

"I don't know. He never talked about them. Whenever Mom mentioned any of them, Dad always clammed up, went cold. I know his sister stopped talking to him when they disagreed over something that happened in their childhood. But the others...I never knew what caused the bad blood between them, and it seemed like such a forbidden topic, I never asked."

Wyndham nodded. Took another bite of bread, chewed as he studied his notebook. His jaws slowly bunched into tight knots, then released. Bunched, released. "I have some names here, Adam. I'm going to read through them, and I want you to tell me if any of them sound familiar. All right?"

Adam nodded.

He turned to Carter and Devin. "If either of you recognize any of these names, please speak up." Eyes on the notebook again. "Waldo

Cunningham?" He did not lift his head, but his eyes peered over the top of his glasses at Adam.

"No," Adam said.

Wyndham turned to Carter, Devin. When they shook their heads, he said, "Cecelia or 'Sissy' Noofer?" Another negative. "Just speak up if something rings a bell." He put the last piece of bread in his mouth, chewed. Brushed his thighs with four fingertips to remove crumbs that weren't there. Read the names a little faster. "Nathaniel Cunningham. Wanda Marsden. Dennis Martin. Marianne Ford. Jack Edgerly. Mistress Montana. The Rev—"

"Mistress?" Devin said.

Wyndham lifted his head, slender eyebrows high.

"Mistress as in…dominatrix?" Devin asked, wincing slightly. As if worried he had asked a stupid question.

The detective smiled gently and said, "That's all it says. Just Mistress Montana." He cleared his throat before continuing. His tongue swept back and forth between cheek and teeth, searching for stray bits of nuts and bread. "The Reverend Barry Quine. Ola Blake. Dr. Leopold Buttrick. Kyla Kortzeborn." He leaned back slowly on the sofa, looking at Adam. Waiting.

Mistress Montana, Adam thought repeatedly. The name was a seed wedged tightly between two teeth. Something about it bothered him, even frightened him. But he tucked it away for the moment. Shook his head and said, "No, none of them sounds familiar. Should they? I mean…who are they?"

"Just two, actually. Something we're looking into." Wyndham closed his notebook and stood. Turned to Devin and smiled. "That is the most delicious banana-nut bread I have ever tasted. Without exception."

Devin brightened, stood quickly, hands clasped before his lavendar blouse. He beamed with pride. "My mother's recipe. I made several loaves this morning. Let me send one home with you."

"Oh, no-no-no, I couldn't do that. But I—"

"Oh, please, it's no problem at all! I'll be right back." Devin hurried out of the living room, trailing a faint scent of jasmine.

Adam stood. A moment later, so did Carter, lips pressed tightly together. He looked around as if uncertain where to put his eyes. Adam hoped Carter stayed quiet, just waited till Wyndham was gone before opening his mouth. And he hoped the detective did not notice Carter's nervousness.

"Um, if you don't mind my asking," Adam said, "what kind of detective are you?"

Wyndham smiled, holding his notebook at his side the way a pastor holds a Bible. "Homicide."

Adam locked down, became still. Held everything in. "Then...you don't think it was an accident. Did you find something?"

Wyndham bent down, took his cup of coffee from the table, and finished it off in a swallow. Put the cup back on the table. "The investigation has reached a juncture that could be very revealing. Or it could lead nowhere at all. That remains to be seen."

"Do you have an idea who might have —"

"I am sorry, Adam, but I cannot discuss the investigation in any detail. We need time to build our case. But first...we need to find all the pieces."

Adam nodded. The more he thought about the detective's last two sentences, the deeper his frown grew. "What, um...what case?"

"This case. The case that will determine whether or not your family was murdered. And if so, by whom. And why."

Adam nodded. "Okay. That case."

Wyndham's eyes were very busy. Back and forth between Adam and Carter.

He knows something, Adam thought. His stomach suddenly lurched, as if he were on a rollercoaster. His palms became moist, clammy. *Don't shake hands. He's a detective. He'll detect sweaty palms.*

"Those names," Adam said. "They all belong to just two people?"

Wyndham put his hands together in front, held the notebook with both of them, elbows locked. Nodded once. "That is correct. Two people." His eyes kept bouncing between their faces.

What the hell is taking Devin so long? Adam wondered.

The silence in the living room was opressive, smothering.

"What have you fellas been doing with your summer?" Wyndham asked.

Adam shrugged. "We're into movies," Adam said flatly. It sounded stupid even as it came out of his mouth. They were in Los Angeles. Every waitress and busboy was an actor, and even the homeless were shopping scripts around town. Everybody was into movies. "I mean, we like to go to them. Collect them. Old ones, new ones."

Wyndham nodded once. Said nothing for a long while.

Adam could see the fear just behind Carter's face, verging on breaking through. But only because he knew him so well. It was not visible to the detective. He hoped.

"Personally," Wyndham said, "I like the outdoors. I'm especially fond of the desert."

Adam's colon convulsed.

"I find the wildlife fascinating. Particularly the reptiles." He chuckled. "I'm a bit of an amateur herpetologist. The desert is filled with fascinating reptiles. I'm never happier than when I'm out there. Patiently waiting to see what comes out from under the rocks. Maybe a lizard. Maybe a snake." Mouth closed, he smiled.

Adam wondered if the detective could hear the shrieks of panic inside him. *Devin must be* making *that fucking bread!*

Wyndham tipped his head back. "Do you fellas ever spend any time out in the desert?"

Carter's eyes shot toward Adam.

"We're pretty much city boys," Adam said, smiling a little. But not much.

Again, Wyndham smiled and nodded a single time.

Devin returned with a loaf of banana-nut bread wrapped in rose-colored cellophane and tied with a silver ribbon. "Here you go, Detective Wyndham. Enjoy."

"I can't thank you enough, it is absolutely delicious," Wyndham said as he took the loaf. "I may have to come back for the recipe, if you're willing to part with it."

Adam thought, *For God's sake, give it to him later!*

Wyndham turned to Adam and Carter. "I'm sure I'll see you again soon. As the investigation progresses and more information is gathered, it is likely I will need to ask you more questions."

"Sure," Adam said.

"You don't have any plans to leave town in the near future, do you?" He glanced at Carter. "Either of you?"

Carter turned his head from side to side stiffly as Adam said, "No. We don't."

"Good. Sorry to have bothered you. And I am truly sorry for your loss, Adam." He reached beneath his coat and produced his card, handed it over to Adam. "If there is anything I can do, if you need anything at all, please call me."

Before he left, Detective Wyndham gave them another smile. And a wink.

It was a hot day, capped by a layer of carcinogenic filth that obliterated the blue sky, masked the mountains in the distance, and turned the sun's burning shine into a dull, cloying glow. Everything was corpse-gray, even the clammy air.

"We haven't been watching the news," Carter said. "If we had, I bet we would've known there was trouble."

"I have been watching the news." Adam said. "And listening to it, and reading it. But not all the time. It gets depressing after awhile."

They were in the Mercedes, on their way to see Billy Rivers. Adam had called Alyssa, told her he would not be able to pick her up when she got off at two. She had not asked for an explanation, so Adam had not provided one.

After Wyndham left, Adam had wanted to turn on the television, tune in to some local news. Carter insisted they go see Billy and find out if anything had happened out in the desert that they should know about.

A chilling thought materialized in Adam's mind and came out of his mouth before he had a chance to examine it. "What if we're being watched?"

"What?"

"What if we're under surveillance?"

Carter searched the rearview mirror as he turned onto Ventura. "You think we shouldn't go see Billy?"

"I don't know. How would that look? I mean, if they're following us, and we go to Billy's...do you think they'd connect him to the desert?"

"Maybe. I didn't know how close he was to Diz and his family until we went out there. He's like their Renfield, or something, it's creepy. If the cops know anything about Diz, then they probably know Billy, too."

"Then what should we do?"

"I could call him," Carter said. "But he screens his calls, and if I left a message on his machine—nah. Bad idea."

"Do you think we're being followed?"

"How the hell should I know if we're being followed? It was your idea. Usually, the whole point of following someone is to stay out of sight so they don't know they're being followed, so if they know what they're doing—"

"Just drive around for awhile," Adam said. "Keep an eye in the mirror, see if there's one particular car that stays with us."

"What kind of car?"

"Something...cop-like."

Carter turned and glared at him for a few seconds.

"I don't know, something that looks dull and drab, you know what I mean? Don't plainclothes cops like Wyndham drive the kind of cars spinster aunts drive?"

"Maybe in the movies. In real life? I dunno. Did you see *Enemy of the State?* They could be following us with satellites, for all we know."

Adam rolled his eyes. "Okay, forget I said anything. It was probably a stupid idea, I'm just being paranoid. Let's go over to Billy's."

"Hey, I'm not being a smartass. I'm serious about the satellites." Carter slowed and parked at the curb outside Gravy Train's, a small hobby shop where he bought many of the ingredients needed for his gory hobby. "I'm gonna pick up a couple things while I'm here. You stay outside and see if anybody hangs around, okay?"

They got out of the car. Adam leaned against the wall beside the shop's entrance while Carter when inside.

Ventura Boulevard was one of the Valley's main arteries, its traffic constant. It ran seamlessly through one town after another, towns set apart only by their names: Studio City, Sherman Oaks, Encino,

Tarzana, on and on. The vehicles traveling the boulevard ranged from the most battered and abused to the most shimmering, most expensive.

No one slowed or stopped any distance behind them. Traffic raced by in both directions. Adam looked up and down the sidewalk. A blue-and-white patrol car slowed to a stop at the corner. The uniformed officer at the wheel waited for an opening in traffic. Pulled out, turned right. Adam realized he was staring baldly at the patrol car and turned away, pulse quickening. Looked at the intricate miniatures displayed in the hobby shop's window. The patrol car's reflection slithered over the glass and disappeared.

Back in the car, Carter drove in silence for awhile. Went around a few blocks.

"Nobody's following us," Adam said.

"Any helicopters?"

"No helicopters. Let's go to Billy's."

There seemed to be no surveillance on Waving Palms Estates. At least, no one was staring from inside a parked car. That was how Adam imagined someone who was watching the apartment complex would look. A dark shape sitting in a parked car.

That's just in the movies, Adam thought, disturbed by how detached from reality he found himself to be. It seemed everything he knew, or thought he knew, had come from movies or television. Suddenly, he felt uncertain about what he knew and did not know. Of how things worked in the real world.

"Oh, great," Adam muttered as they stepped into the courtyard and started up the stairs. "It's Jabba the Manager."

Floyd watched them from his lawn chair, naked but for Bermuda shorts and flip-flops on his feet. Another ballgame played on the radio. He leaned forward as if to speak, but said nothing. Just watched them.

"Ignore him," Carter whispered.

They stopped outside Billy's apartment. Carter rapped his knuckles on the glass door.

There was a shuffling sound below. Wet breathing. "He ain't there," Floyd said.

Adam and Carter turned around slowly, looked down.

Floyd's loose, rubbery lips pulled back over his gums into something that approximated a smug grin. He offered no further information.

"Is he coming back?" Carter asked.

"Oh, no. He ain't comin' back. The *po*-leeth came and took away all hith thtuff."

They did not move or look at each other.

"The...police?" Carter asked. "You're sure?"

Floyd nodded enthusiastically, still grinning. "Oh, yeah, they wath the *po*-leeth, awright. Uniformth and everything. Two of 'em, not countin' the two guyth from the FBI. Cleaned out hith apartment. Carried everything out in bockthes wearin' rubber gloveth."

"Oh, Jesus," Adam breathed. "Let's go."

Carter was already moving along the rail, watching Floyd. "What did he do?"

Floyd shrugged as his tongue squirmed in its cave. "Dunno. I figgered you guyth'd know better'n me."

"No," Carter said as they went down the stairs. "We don't know."

Floyd waddled toward the foot of the stairs to meet them. "I thaw 'em haul off a couple computers, figgered maybe he wath lookin' at that kiddie porn. Y'thee that on the newth all the time. But hell, I dunno what he did. Figgered *you'd* know better'n me, 'cauthe I never—"

"We *don't* know," Carter snapped as he brushed by Floyd.

They crossed the street, got into the Mercedes.

Floyd stood and watched them, elbows jutting at his sides.

Carter turned on the radio, already tuned to a news station. "Maybe we should go over to Billy's parents' house."

"If the cops cleaned out his apartment, what makes you think his parents' house would be safe? Maybe they're just waiting for him to show up there."

"But what do they want him for?"

"How the hell do I know?"

"If the police and the FBI—can you believe that? The fucking FBI?—if they know about Diz's place in the desert—"

"That's not necessarily the case," Adam said.

"But if they *do*, why haven't we heard about it on the news?"

"You sound like Floyd."

"Compare me to that toothless manatee one more time and I'm gonna kick your ass out of the car."

"No, that's not what I mean. Just because it's not on the news doesn't mean it hasn't happened. But there might be something in the newspaper. Let's get one."

Carter drove around a block, headed back the way they'd come on Ventura. They went to DuPar's, a coffee shop in Studio City, and bought a paper from the vending machine outside on the way in.

They had left two perfectly good sandwiches to go stale in Carter's studio and were still hungry, so they ordered lunch with their coffee. Waiting for their orders to arrive, they combed the newspaper for some clue as to what had happened to Billy. The lunch crowd was gone and the dinner crowd would not start showing up for a few hours.

The *Los Angeles Times* provided them with nothing.

"But *Bizarro* was funny," Carter said.

The waitress brought Adam's Denver omelette and Carter's Reuben.

Relief settled in as Adam took a bite of the omelette and chewed slowly. If there was no story, there was no danger. Not yet. He asked, "What do you think happened to Billy?"

Carter shrugged. "Maybe drugs. Isn't that why they take all your stuff? If you get caught selling drugs?"

"I guess so. I'm not sure. Did he sell drugs?"

"He always had plenty of wacky weed around. He always gave it to me, but maybe he sold it, too. Maybe that's how he financed his habit."

Adam remembered the beautifully crafted masks and body parts in Billy's apartment. They were more than a hobby to Billy, as with Carter. He thought the word "habit" was appropriate.

"I'm gonna call his parents," Carter said.

"You think that's a good idea?"

"What could it hurt? Billy and I are friends. There's nothing unusual about me trying to track him down."

"At his parents' place?"

"Well...I haven't done it since he moved out. But so what? So fucking what?"

Adam could see Carter stirring up his courage, working himself up to make the call in spite of his fears.

"Yeah, I'll call, and if I get the answering machine, I just won't leave a message, and if somebody picks up, I'll just ask if Billy's there, that's all." He wiped his hands on a paper napkin and slid out of the booth. Went to the pay phone at the front of the diner. Made the call. A couple minutes later, he hung up and returned to the booth, looking frustrated. "He's not there."

"Who answered?"

"I'm not sure. Some woman."

"Did you ask her if she—"

"Yeah, yeah, she said he wasn't there and she didn't know where he was or when he would be back."

Suddenly, the omelette took on an unpleasant flavor. Adam drank a couple swallows of weak coffee to get the taste out of his mouth.

"If this has something to do with Diz's place," Carter said, "it would have to be in the news, wouldn't it? I mean, something that big? Especially if Mr. C. was telling the truth about his Hollywood connections. Reporters would be all over it." He watched Adam. Waited for a response. "Well? Wouldn't they?"

Adam stared at the slowly growing ring of moisture around the bottom of his sweating glass of icewater. He boarded a train of thought that took him places he did not want to go.

Carter went on eating as Adam drew inward for a few minutes.

"Maybe not," Adam finally said.

"What? Maybe not what?"

"A raid on a place like Diz's would be a big operation. It would involve the DEA, the FBI, not just local cops."

"Shit, just like Floyd said, the FBI."

"Maybe the BATF, too."

"The BA *what?*"

"Bureau of Alcohol, Tobacco, and Firearms. If they didn't want any press coverage, I'm sure they could avoid it. For awhile, at least."

"Why would they avoid it?"

"Think about it. Those Hollywood connections Mr. C. mentioned? Famous people, maybe even some important people. He's probably got files on all of them. If the feds just wanted to close him down, they might make a big show of it. But if they wanted to get his clientele, too, they'd have to be very quiet. Otherwise, they'd have time to disappear."

"You think maybe...the place *has* been raided?"

Adam shrugged. "It's possible."

"But that doesn't mean they know anything about us, right? It's not like we signed a guestbook, or anything."

"We did something worse than that. We walked around under all those damned security cameras."

"So what? We were there once, and not very long. That's not gonna connect us to blowing up—" Carter's voice dropped to a whisper. "It's not gonna connect us to anything else, right?"

Adam sighed. "I don't know."

"Maybe none of this has happened, anyway, right?" Carter was talking to himself as well as to Adam. "I didn't recognize any of the names that detective read. Did you?"

As things fell into place in his head, Adam's skin shrank. "Mr. C.," he muttered.

"What?"

"One of the names on the list...Cunningham. What was it, Waldo? Waldo Cunningham?"

"So?"

"Maybe that's the C. in Mr. C. Cunningham. And that other name...Mistress Montana...that one's been bugging me ever since I heard it."

"Why?"

"I didn't know, at first. But I think I do now. Let's go back to your place."

They said very little on the way back. Listened to the news, but heard nothing relevant. At Carter's house, they went straight upstairs to the studio. Froze outside the door and listened.

Someone grunted on the other side. Quiet but intense. Adam and Carter locked frightened eyes for a moment. Then Carter rolled his, opened the door and went in.

On the partners desk, Adam's laptop was still online. A thin, pale, blonde woman sat cross-legged on an unmade, dirty-looking bed on the monitor. The stump of her right arm, amputated at the elbow, was moving in and out of a plump, rosy-complexioned woman with no legs who lay writhing before her.

"No problem," Carter said. "It's just the horny amputees."

Adam sat at the desk and muttered, "Can't leave them alone for a minute."

"They're such cut-ups."

"That'll probably cost me an arm and a leg," Adam said. He typed the URL of a search engine that specialized in finding pornographic websites, waited a moment for it to open. Typed "Mistress Montana" and hit the **ENTER** key.

"What are you doing?" Carter asked.

"I told you about meeting Mrs. C. in the bathroom at Diz's?"

"Yeah."

"Did I tell you what she was wearing?"

"Oh, yeah. Scary."

"Didn't Billy say Diz's mom was a dominatrix? That she had a website?"

"I don't remember. Why?"

Adam scrolled down, scanning the results of the search. Carter pulled his chair around the desk and sat beside him.

"Ah-ha," Adam said. He clicked on a link that read "Mistress Montana's Underworld." Seconds later, a small window opened in the center of the screen informing Adam that no connection with the website's server could be made. He tried again, with the same result.

"You think Mrs. C. is Mistress Montana?" Carter asked.

"It's possible. If so, and Mr. C. is Waldo Cunningham…" He left the sentence open as he clicked on a link to another mistress's site. It opened quickly.

"What're you doing?"

"If she has a site, maybe she advertises somewhere. I want to surf around, see if I can find a banner. I want to see a picture of her."

"You think her website is shut down?" Carter asked.

"If Mistress Montana is Mrs. C. and that boy farm out in the desert has been raided, yes, the website is down. Here."

Carter looked over Adam's shoulder. "The Dungeon Shop?"

"An online store. S and M supplies, sex toys. And links to kinky sex sites." He pointed to a rectangular banner at the bottom of the screen. It was a link to Mistress Montana's Underworld, and provided a picture of the mistress herself.

"Free Willy," Carter said.

Adam's cheeks bulged as he exhaled. Mistress Montana was Mrs. C.

Carter did not have to ask. The expression on Adam's face was enough.

"What do we do now?" Carter asked.

"Nothing. We can't do a Goddamned thing except wait. And see."

Never before had time moved so slowly for Adam. It occurred to him that the longest summer of his childhood had moved faster. That even *Pearl Harbor* had moved faster, and with a performance by Ben Affleck.

The news had never taken up as much of Adam's time before. He listened to it on the radio, watched it on television, read newspapers, scanned news sites on the Internet. While searching for a story about a den of drugs, explosives, and child pornography being raided in the desert, Adam absorbed other news without even trying. Political and civil unrest around the world, natural disasters everywhere, political and show business scandals, murders, rapes, child molestations, and ominous drops in the stock market, as well as in box office receipts and television ratings. It was endless, all of it depressing.

He spent as much time alone as he could. His worries turned him inward, made him quiet and brooding. He did not want to inflict that on anyone else. When he was with Carter, they spoke very little. When they did, it was usually to rehearse their planned stories should the worst happen. When they did not, their silences were clamorous with dread.

Since Wyndham's visit on Thursday, he had been unable to sleep. No nightmares, but only because he could not sleep long enough to have them. Just long enough to drool on his pillow a bit before jerking awake. He woke Alyssa each time.

He did not want to chase her away, but feared she would start asking questions. He knew his behavior was probably normal under the circumstances, but was still afraid it would give him away, somehow reveal his guilt.

He supposed smoking marijuana did not help the paranoia he already felt about possibly being arrested, going to prison, being sentenced to death. But that and Xanax were all that kept him from ripping out his hair, screaming his head off and crawling out of his skin like a shedding snake.

Somehow, Alyssa sensed he needed to be alone. She made excuses for not coming over the next few days. Adam loved her for it. No one had ever read him so accurately, known him so well.

But how would she react if he were arrested? The question haunted him. Adam did not care what anyone else thought of him. He knew if he were arrested, it would be all over the news and most of the world would assume he was guilty, but he didn't care. His only concern was Alyssa. Would she be able to continue caring for someone who was capable of having his own father killed, as well as the other five people in the immediate area? Or would she turn her back on him, try to forget she had ever known him, and live the rest of her life darkened by the shadow of their relationship?

The second possibility made Adam feel cold.

While Alyssa gave him some time alone, Rog dropped by the Brandis house on Sunday afternoon to talk with Adam. They sat on the patio at a table under a large blue umbrella, Adam in denim cut-offs and a burgundy T-shirt with Bela Lugosi as Dracula on the front, Rog in a peach Versace suit, a tall glass of iced tea in front of each of them.

"Have you given any thought to what you want to do with the house, Adam?"

"What I want to do with it? Why, is it making trouble? Should I have a talk with it?"

Rog chuckled. "Have you thought about selling it?"

"No."

"Maybe you should."

"Why?"

"It's a big house. Costs a lot of money to keep it up. Staff, security, property taxes. Watering the lawns alone costs a small fortune. You need to start thinking about it. If you're going to be on your own—"

"Wait a second, why should I sell the house? With the money he left me and the interest on his—"

"I'm not telling you to sell the house this week, Adam. I'm simply saying you need to think about it."

"Already?"

"I don't see any point in putting it off. The money and investments your dad left you…I know it sounds like a lot, but it won't last unless you make some changes. With no income, the house and property will eat that money up fast, and you won't—"

Adam became impatient. "What do you mean, no income? Dad said he never had to work again if he didn't want to. He's still got money coming in from the first hit he ever had, how can there be no income?"

"Your dad said a lot of things. It's true, he could have stopped working and lived on his residuals and investments if he wanted. But he couldn't have lived like he'd been living. To live like that—the house and the boats and all his cars and parties and everyone he employs—he had to keep selling scripts for big bucks. And now…well, he's not around to do that."

"Maybe I'll start selling scripts," Adam said. It had come out of his mouth before forming as a thought. He was about to take it back when Rog leaned forward with interest.

"Are you serious? Do you have a script?"

"Well…no."

"Your dad always said you had a real talent for writing."

Like he would know, Adam thought.

"He told me you'd written some great short stories and he thought you had a knack for screenwriting," Rog went on. "But he said you weren't interested. Have you changed your mind?"

A cold hand closed on Adam's throat. He took a drink of tea.

"You okay?" Rog asked.

Adam nodded, composed himself. "He said that? About my writing?"

"Oh, yeah. Talked about it a lot."

"When did he ever read anything I wrote? He wasn't interested in my writing."

Rog chuckled. "Maybe you never showed it to him, but he read everything you wrote. Probably some you didn't want anyone to read. He used to sneak into your room while you were gone and read your stuff on the computer. He'd kill me if he knew I told you that." He looked down at his drink, half of his mouth smiling. "I mean…if he were around." Lifted his head again. "He said you're a wonderful storyteller. That your style is very visual. That's why he thought you'd make a great screenwriter. *Have* you changed your mind?"

Adam was numb all over, afraid if he moved, he would knock something over, or hurt himself without realizing it. A storm of conflicting emotions crashed inside him.

"Adam? You okay?"

"Yeah. Fine."

"If you have a script, I can give Barry a call. He'd be happy to represent you."

Barry Venin had been Michael's agent. An anaconda with a weave.

Was it possible his dad really had been interested in his writing? That he had *liked* it?

"Adam? Are you feeling all right?"

He had no idea what kind of expression he wore on his face. He could feel nothing. "Yeah. Fine."

"You're sure? I didn't mean to upset you."

As Adam spoke, his voice gradually dissolved to a whisper. "I'm not upset, I'm just…I didn't know Dad had read anything I'd written. I didn't think he was interested."

"Well, you know how your dad was. Not too big on praise. He was always afraid he'd give somebody a bigger head than his. Couldn't have that. But he was a fan of your work and hoped you'd take up scripts. You know what his dream was?"

Adam did not move or speak.

Rog's affectionate smile showed off shimmering orthodontal artistry. "Well, you know, ever since Paul Verhoeven butchered *Thugz*, your dad's wanted to direct his own scripts. Writing and producing just weren't enough after that. I dropped in on him one night at the cabin in Vancouver when he was working on *Eviscerator*. We shared a bottle of tequila, got fractured and sentimental. He said he wanted the first movie he directed to be from a script written by his son."

A noise blurted through Adam's lips. It could just as easily have been a laugh as a sob. His emotions suddenly felt so external and out of his control, he was not sure which one might go off next.

"Your dad would be happy to know you at least have an interest. Let me know if you want me to set up a meeting with Barry."

Adam nodded once.

Rog checked his watch, gulped down the rest of his iced tea. "Gotta fly. Look, Adam, I'm not saying you're broke, but you need to make some adjustments to avoid it in the future." He stood, put on silver-rimmed sunglasses. "Give it some thought, okay? I'll come around next week, we'll grab lunch, talk about it some more."

Adam nodded, said, "Okay." But he did not stand.

"You feeling okay? You look a little...I don't know." He frowned. "Have you lost weight?"

He shrugged. "Maybe. I haven't been sleeping well."

"You want to see someone? I'll make an appointment for you right now." He reached beneath his suit coat and produced a tiny tortoise-shell cellphone.

"No. I'll be okay."

Rog replaced the cellphone reluctantly. "You know you can call if you need anything, anytime. Okay?"

Adam nodded. "Thanks, Rog."

When he was gone, Adam went into the poolhouse. In the bathroom, he closed and locked the door, sat on the toilet seat. Planted elbows on his knees, buried his face in his hands. He waited, expecting tears, sobs. But they did not come. The only release he could give the searing rush of emotional pain that had come so dangerously close to the surface in Rog's presence was a long, agonized groan.

On Wednesday, Alyssa and Brett decided they had to go to Disneyland. Brett had never been, and Alyssa's last visit had been nine years ago. Adam was not fond of the idea, and Carter said he would rather someone rip open his chest and spoonfeed him bites of his own lungs. Adam did not like amusement parks, Carter hated crowds. But the girls insisted, so they went. Adam, Carter, and Brett shared a joint before leaving, and Alyssa drove the Mercedes.

Another hot day, still no sign of sun or sky. The air was moist and clinging. The happiest place on earth was bloated and quivering with tourists from all over the world who had paid forty bucks a head for ages twelve and up, thirty for children between three and eleven, to be dazzled, amazed, distracted from the smothering banality of their lives. The park crawled with pale white skin, lumpy with fat, revealed by Bermuda shorts and Mickey Mouse tank tops. Everywhere, children cried and screamed and laughed and shrieked, fought with each other and whined and shouted at their parents. People who probably insisted they were actors wandered around the park in bizarre costumes, posing as giant misshapen animals and cartoon people with oversized heads and terrifying expressions of glee frozen on their huge faces. Babies and toddlers wailed in horror at the sight of them, but they pressed on, skipping and dancing their way through the park from child to child.

For awhile, Donald Duck followed them around playfully, tried to make them laugh.

"I think he's creepy," Alyssa said.

Brett added, "I think they're all creepy."

Finally, Carter turned to the duck and shouted, "Hey! Did you just grab my ass? You *did!* What kind of pervert are you, anyway? Huh? Jeez, get away from me, you sick duck!"

Donald avoided them for the rest of the day.

Their favorite attractions were the Haunted Mansion and Pirates of the Caribbean. Lines were long but moved fast, and they managed to go through each twice. The second time through the Haunted Mansion, Alyssa slipped her hand into Adam's shorts and stroked his cock as they kissed. He made her stop so he would not come all over himself.

Beneath the cool bluish glow of artificial moonlight in the Blue Bayou Restaurant, they ate Monte Cristo sandwiches that oozed grease. Across the bayou, ersatz fireflies flittered between the tall weeds and sad branches of weeping willows, while boats from Pirates of the Caribbean floated quietly by.

"We haven't been to Tomorrowland yet," Brett said over lunch. "I want to go on Space Mountain."

Carter laughed. "Better not eat too much, Adam."

Alyssa turned to him. "You get sick on rollercoasters?"

"No, not sick," Adam said. "I just don't enjoy them."

"How can you not enjoy rollercoasters?" Brett asked. "They're so much fun!"

"I don't like being thrown around that way by a big metal...thing. At those speeds. I don't trust them. You never know when it'll jump its tracks and fly through the air like a missile full of people."

"That doesn't happen," Brett said, annoyed.

Adam asked, "Can you prove that?"

"Can you prove it does?" she said.

"I asked first."

Alyssa leaned close. "But you'll go with *me*, won't you?"

Thus began the campaign to coax Adam into joining them on Space Mountain. It went on through a second visit to Pirates of the Caribbean. Continued in Fantasyland, where they took Mr. Toad's Wild Ride, Peter Pan's Flight, and Pinnochio's Daring Journey. But it was not their persistence that made Adam give in. It was the nightmarish indoor boat ride, "It's a Small World." The treacly song played over and over and over while, on colorful platforms, dolls and stuffed animals wearing traditional clothes from every corner of the earth moved demonically all around them. The dolls reached out stubby arms, flailed them up and down, back and forth, as if hexing them, faces wide with happy evil. Delightedly possessed toys from Hell's closet. It was more than a ride, it was a cheerful torture. A battering ram to the psyche. Sharp fingernails dragging over the surface of a chalk board, but on an epic scale. It broke Adam down, fractured his will. Crushed his spirit.

"Okay, okay," he said. "I'll go. I'll hate it, and I'll probably shit my pants, but I'll go. And if I *do* shit my pants, I don't want to hear one word about it."

The walk to Tomorrowland was filled with dread for Adam. His first rollercoaster ride had been there at Disneyland, when he was six or so. The Matterhorn. His gut had twisted the moment he laid eyes on the ugly artificial mountain that towered over Fantasyland. He had told his parents he did not want to go on the ride, and his dad had become angry. He had ridiculed Adam while they waited in line, called him a pussy and a coward. By the time they reached the gate, Michael Julian had told his son he would have to wait for them while they went on the ride, alone and unwatched, so any pervert who came along could just run off with him, and they might never see him again, so if he had anything to say, he had better be quick about it. Afraid of being left alone, Adam had gone with them. The ride had paralyzed him with fear, but he was able to scream, and he had. Continuously, until the ride was over. His dad had tormented him about it all the way home.

Why didn't Mom stop him? Adam wondered. He examined his memory of that day and had no doubt that she had been there. Michael would not have taken him to Disneyland alone. Adam remembered seeing reflections of his own crying face in the lenses of his mom's huge round sunglasses after riding the Matterhorn. But he couldn't remember her comforting him, or intervening when his dad had so relentlessly teased him.

Space Mountain rocketed them through darkness at a frightening speed. Stars shone all around them, creating the illusion they were shooting through space. Each seat in the train was equipped with its own computerized sound system that played a futuristic soundtrack synchronized with every twist, turn, and nauseating drop of the ride. Adam had hoped the darkness would help by not letting him see anything. But if possible, it made the ride worse. Others on the train laughed and squealed, delighted by the speed with which they whipped sharply, corkscrewed, plummeted. Adam pressed his lips together, ground his teeth, tried to keep from screaming. It did not work.

He was not certain at what point he started screaming. Nor was he certain when his scream had unexpectedly became a long, pained wail. Tears blew from his face as they spilled. A burning sensation worked its way up from his chest to his throat as the wailing sound he made collapsed into a fit of sobs. Adam cried harder than ever before. With his tears came a pain he had not known was there, buried deep in the ground of his soul. It rose from its grave a ravenous ghoul and savagely clawed and ate its way through him.

The moment it began to subside, Adam wiped his eyes with the backs of his hands, took long, deep breaths. Calmed himself in time for the ride's end.

No one had noticed. None of them knew he had broken down during the ride. In keeping with his wishes, they did not say a word about Adam's puffy red face when they left Space Mountain.

✝

Late the following day, Adam drove them all the way to the southern end of the San Gabriel Valley in the convertible to see a double feature at one of the few drive-in theaters still operating in southern California. Or in the entire country, for that matter. Fewer than a dozen cars faced the screen. No one was interested in seeing movies outdoors anymore. Adam figured it would not be long before this drive-in closed as well.

They had not checked to see what was showing before leaving Carter's house. Two action pictures were running for the week. Bad ones. The first starred Jean Claude Van Damme, the second Steven Segal. They spent more time making out than watching the movies. When they did watch, Adam and Carter kept up a running commentary of vulgar criticism, mocking the accents and performances of the two muscular stars.

It was almost three-thirty in the morning when they got back to Carter's house. Adam felt as if the smoggy air had stuck to his skin and hair like viscous sewage, so he took a shower. He intended it to be a quick one, but the hot water felt so good, he lingered, eyes closed. Enjoyed the sensation. Let it loosen, if not untie, some of his knots.

As he rinsed his hair, Adam felt something touch his sides. He looked down to see two delicate, feminine hands sliding across his belly from behind.

Rain, Adam thought.

He pulled away from the hands with a jagged scream, tried to spin around. His feet went in different directions. The shower tilted and his ass hit the floor with a loud thunk.

Sucking in gasps of air, Adam's eyes moved up the bare legs that stood before him, over the flat belly, full breasts, past the graceful shoulders and neck. Alyssa's hands pressed over her mouth.

"Adam, sweetheart, I'm sorry, I didn't mean to—"

He got up, took her in his arms, held her tight. "No, don't apologize. *I'm* sorry. For scaring you."

Alyssa turned off the water, took his hand and led him out of the shower. She tried to dry him with a towel, but their kisses got in the way. They were still wet when they got into bed. Alyssa closed her hand on his erection, guided him into her. They finished quickly, but did not stop.

Dawn was beginning to warm the sky when they finally became still. Adam watched Alyssa for awhile, wondered if he could ever express all the affection he felt for her. He spoke rapidly in a whisper as he held her close.

"My dad's attorney says I need to sell the house, but I'll be able to get a nice place anywhere I want, and I want you to come live with me. We'll get out of L.A. and live…I don't know, maybe by a lake someplace, or by the ocean. Anywhere we want. I don't care where it is as long as it's not here and we're together. I love you so much, Alyssa, I could explode. I don't know what I'd do if I hadn't met you, if you weren't here with me, I'd probably—"

"Shh, shh." She cuddled against him with a sleepy smile and made a small contented sound in her throat. "There's no rush, Adam. I'm not going anywhere. Don't worry. We've got all the time in the world for our plans."

Perhaps they did. Adam relaxed beside her, realized how tired he was. Alyssa was asleep in less than a minute. Her breath purred through lightly closed lips each time she exhaled. Adam slowly drifted off, happier than he could remember ever being. Feeling as if nothing could possibly go wrong in his life.

✝

Adam awoke at eight minutes before eleven the next morning, alone in bed. He felt rested and was grateful he had been allowed to sleep. He had fallen into the routine of starting each day by turning on the radio and checking online for news. But the sounds of laughter and splashing that came from the open window to the right of his bed made the news seem even more unappealing than usual. He hadn't seen or read anything to cause him even the smallest concern up to that point. The feeling of urgency with which he had been waking each day had dissipated, and he decided to put off his search until after he had gotten something to eat.

He got up and went to the window. Saw Carter and Brett playing around in the pool. Carter was actually *playing*, splashing around with Brett like a little kid. It made Adam smile. Alyssa sat at the white table beneath the blue umbrella, reading a paperback and looking creamy in a black bikini. The sky was a chalky blue, clearer than it had been in weeks, although a thin yellowish layer of smog remained. The sun shone harshly, and Adam could feel the heat of the day through the window's screen.

He put on a pair of black swimming trunks and went downstairs. Down the hall to the French doors that opened on the patio. He ran by Alyssa and jumped into the pool, folding himself midair into a cannonball. His unexpected splash made Brett scream.

"It's alive!" Carter shouted in a Colin Clive voice. "It's alive, it's *alive!*"

Alyssa jumped in and embraced Adam from behind, kissed his neck. "Good morning," she said.

He turned around and kissed her on the mouth. "Hi. Thanks for letting me sleep. I needed it."

She nodded toward the table and said, "There's food if you're hungry."

He saw a platter of doughnuts and muffins on the table beside a bowl of fresh fruit, a coffee service.

Alyssa swam away as Carter approached.

"Did you check the news?" Carter whispered.

"I'll do it later."

A gray beachball bearing the wrapped face of a mummy floated by. Carter picked it up, bounced it off Adam's forehead.

Adam plucked the ball from the air. "Anybody for a game of Marco Polo?"

"What're we, a bunch of nine-year-olds?" Carter said. "Grow up, Adam. Act your age. Marco Polo. Jeez." He shook his head. "Let's go under and pants the girls."

Adam stayed in the pool until his stomach churned from hunger. He went to the table and poured coffee, plucked a glazed doughnut from the platter with a paper napkin and took a bite. Alyssa joined him as he sat at the table and picked up her book. It was a paperback copy of one of Lillian Jackson Braun's *The Cat Who...*mysteries.

"I thought only old ladies with blue hair read these," he said, putting the book down again.

"I'm much older than you think." She leaned toward him and lowered her voice. "Remind me next time I suck your cock and I'll take my teeth out." She took a seat and bit into an apple loudly.

"Music!" Carter shouted as he got out of the pool. "We need music! Any requests?"

"You'd ignore them, anyway," Adam said.

Carter went into the poolhouse. Thirty seconds later, R.E.M. played from the speakers mounted under the eaves. A couple minutes passed, but Carter did not come back out of the poolhouse.

Floating on her back in the pool, Brett shouted to be heard over the music. "What're you doing in there?"

"Coming!" Carter called from inside. He burst through the open door of the poolhouse holding a stubby rifle.

Adam recognized it immediately. A Super Soaker Battle Droid Rifle, black plastic painted to look like stressed metal. Adam started to duck, but was too slow. A powerful blast of water hit him square in the face and knocked him over backward in the chair.

"My book!" Alyssa shrieked. She snatched the paperback from the table and put it protectively behind her back. She was standing when a stream of water hit her in the side of the head. Laughing, she quickly hunkered down behind the chair.

Carter ran along the side of the poolhouse as Brett climbed out of the pool. He fired again and the water hit Brett directly between her breasts. She fell back into the pool with a yelp. Carter disappeared around the corner and his villainous laugh faded to the other side of the poolhouse.

"He's snapped!" Brett shouted as she climbed out. "See? I was right, there *is* something wrong with him."

"What's with your friend?" Alyssa asked with a laugh.

Adam said, "Brett, I think. I've never seen him so happy."

Brett joined them by the table, looked around. "Where'd he go?"

"He's probably going to get on the roof of the poolhouse and shoot at us from up there," Carter said. "He's got more guns upstairs. Come on."

They hurried into the house and passed Devin on the stairs.

"What are you doing?" Devin cried, spinning around. "You're all wet! You're dripping!"

"We'll only be a second, I promise!" Adam led the laughing girls into Carter's bedroom and went to the closet. Got down on his knees, fished through a mess of stuff in a corner. "Here!" He handed Alyssa a green and yellow Super Soaker, Brett a pink one, but could not find a third. He stood, left the closet. "Fill those up in the bathroom. There might be another one across the hall."

He went into the room that had become his and opened the closet. It was not a walk-in, just deep enough to hold a rack of hanging clothes. The shelf above looked ready to give way beneath the weight of board games and fat hardcover books and cardboard boxes filled with out-grown toys and old report cards.

And one silver-and-red Super Soaker. The barrel jutted from a stack of yearbooks and magazines. Adam grabbed it and pulled. "Oh, shit," he muttered as everything on the shelf slid forward and rained on top of him. He stepped back a moment too late to avoid one of the large hardcover books. Its spine hammered him once on the top of his head before falling to the floor. He tripped on a cardboard box the size of a toaster and fell backward onto the floor. The Super Soaker flew from his hand and landed on the bed.

Adam grumbled as he stood, surveyed the mess. Mrs. Sanchez would handle it.

He took the watergun off the bed, stopped at the window. Looked out to see what Carter was up to, see if he had noticed they were gone yet.

Just as Adam had predicted, Carter was crossing the slanted shingle roof of the poolhouse. As he neared the edge that overlooked the pool, he dropped to his hands and knees so he would not be seen. Crept toward the edge, wearing a large, eye-crinkling grin. He shook with laughter as he carefully peered over the edge.

Adam turned away from the window to go fill the silver-and-red Super Soaker. Did a double take when he saw movement down by the pool. Had Alyssa and Brett gone back down already?

Carter saw the movement, too. Pulled back quickly to remain unseen.

Adam frowned as his eyes adjusted to what he was seeing. Two men, both in dark blue. Uniforms. Small objects attached to their belts. Cops. They took long, quick strides. Behind them, Detective Wyndham. And Devin behind him.

Adam saw what was about to happen as clearly as if it were happening already, and he dropped the watergun.

On the poolhouse roof, Carter moved forward suddenly. Swung his right arm over the edge of the roof. Aimed the short rifle downward and shouted, "Die, alien scum, *diiieee!*"

The uniformed officers had their guns drawn before Carter finished his battle cry. They raised their guns in a burst of shouting. Both guns fired and Adam cried out simultaneously. The stream of water from Carter's Super Soaker hit the sidewalk with a *splat* that was swallowed by gunfire. At least one bullet found its target.

From the bedroom window, Adam saw a faint pink vapor rise for an instant just above the back of Carter's head. A gush of dark red ran from his face to the wet concrete. Carter collapsed heavily and the Super Soaker slipped from his hand, landed on the concrete in a clatter of broken plastic.

Adam screamed as Carter slid forward over the roof, dropped limply through the air head-first. Even through the sound of his own scream, Adam heard Carter's neck break at the bottom of the nine-foot fall.

One of the uniformed officers cried, "Oh, Jesus!" as Wyndham shouted, "God *dammit!*"

Adam was there in a blur. He would never be able to recall going from the bedroom to the patio. One moment, he was pushing himself away from the bedroom window. The next, his arms were being held behind him on the patio as he screamed incoherently and struggled against strong hands to get to Carter. Devin knelt beside Carter, wailing.

"Adam, *Adam*," Wyndham said sternly behind him. He sounded like an impatient adult speaking to a temperamental child. "There's nothing you can do. Come on inside."

Handcuffs snapped into place on Adam's wrists. He stopped struggling, allowed himself to be dragged backward into the hall.

Wyndham shouted angrily through the French doors at the officers, "Get an ambulance over here, for God's sake!" He turned Adam around, gripped his elbow. Led him down the hall toward the front of the house. "Adam Julian, you have the right to remain silent."

The detective spoke clearly, succinctly. But it was gibberish to Adam, who sobbed as he staggered beside Wyndham.

"Anything you say can and will be used against you in a court of law."

His head thundered, eyes throbbed.

"If you cannot afford an attorney, one will be provided for you."

Adam heard none of it. All he could hear was his own voice amplified to an impossible level inside his head: *I killed my best friend! I killed my best friend!*

3

HOLLYWOOD

"You can take all the sincerity in Hollywood,
place it in the navel of a fruit fly, and still have room enough
for three caraway seeds and a producer's heart."
Fred Allen

✝

"Movies are like high school with money—
everyone's absolved of responsibility, actors in particular,
and you run around behaving like you're four."
Anthony LaPaglia

✝

"Nobody's interested in sweetness and light."
Hedda Hopper

✝

"Half the people in Hollywood are dying to be discovered.
The other half are afraid they will be."
Lionel Barrymore

✝

"I wish you didn't have to be famous to be successful."
Milla Jovovich

Tell me, Mr. Julian. Did you kill Michael and Gwen Julian and Gwen's daughter, Rain Cardell?"

"No."

"Did you hire someone to kill them?"

"No."

"Were you aware of any conspiracy to kill them?"

"No."

"All right, then. Prove it."

Adam lifted his head. Met the gaze of the small woman who stood before him. Even though he was seated in a large, plush, leather-upholstered chair—it seemed to swallow him when he sat in it—Rona Horowitz was still no taller than he.

She leaned back against the edge of her sprawling desk, folded her arms across her chest. In her early forties, full black hair pulled back, a few stray strands of it dangling loose. She wore a charcoal-and-red suit, black stockings on her stubby legs. That word accurately described her whole body: stubby.

"I thought I was innocent until proven guilty," Adam said.

"Maybe on *Judging Amy* or *The Practice*. Not in the here and now." She went behind her desk. A raised platform on the floor increased her height by several inches. She sat and opened a decoratively carved wooden box, removed a long slender beige cigarette, put it between her wine-colored lips. Took a long fireplace match from a tall lavendar glass cylinder and struck it against a sparkling gray quartz paperweight. Lit her cigarette and puffed. Shook the match out, dropped it into a wastecan beneath the desk.

It was a well lit, cheerful office on the thirty-eighth floor of a Century City high-rise. Mocha-colored carpet, blonde wood and clear glass. It felt like midafternoon in there, not after midnight on the night of the day Adam's life had ended. That was how he thought of it. A complete end to his life, but one that had left him unmercifully alive.

Horowitz opened a folder on her desk. "As of this afternoon, Mr. Julian, about half the people in Los Angeles think you are guilty of murder. Forty-two percent of those think you hired someone, and twenty-six percent think you did it yourself. Seventy-nine percent of those who think you're guilty think your motivation was money, whether you did it yourself or not. Eighteen percent think you did it for kicks. And based on your pictures on television, it seems a small percentage of all subjects surveyed believe you were a regular cast member on *Home Improvement*." She smiled at him.

"A survey?" Adam asked. "You took…a poll? About *me?*"

"That is correct. And if I represent you, I will be taking a lot more. If that bothers you, Mr. Julian, this is a good time to say so." Her voice, deep and whiskey-rich, was level and controlled. Everything about her seemed controlled.

"I don't understand. What do polls have to do with representing me in court?"

"You are correct, you do not understand. If I represent you, Mr. Julian, it will be in *and* out of the courtroom. I will speak to the press for you. I will appear on television in your stead. I will be your mouth, your eyes, your ears. I will be you by proxy."

"And what would I be doing in the meantime?"

"Whatever I tell you to do."

Adam tried to lean forward in the chair, but the seat was so deep, any movement looked awkward. He ground his teeth as he clutched the edges of the fat armrests and pulled himself out. Perched stiffly on the very edge of the chair.

"Are you uncomfortable?" Horowitz asked.

"You know damned well I'm uncomfortable." He was quiet, but there was anger in his voice. "That's what this chair is for, right? Get people off balance? Make them clumsy while you sit there on your highchair at that aircraft carrier of a desk looking like you were in that suit when it was pressed."

Horowitz smiled, nodded. "Am I to take that to mean I do not meet with your approval?"

"Am I to take it that to mean you expect me to just hand over control of my whole life to a total stranger?"

She stood, arms straight at her sides. Elegant fingernails touched the glass desktop with soft clicks. "I need to explain some things to you. The first is that whether or not you like me is irrelevant. If we had a few years to get to know each other, I am sure we would discover things in common, things we might admire about one another. But we would have to do it under guard, because you will be going to prison soon without proper representation. Our time is short. So we will have to do things my way or not at all. Do you understand, Mr. Julian?"

"Stop calling me that," Adam said. "Jesus. My dad is…I mean, was Mr. Julian."

Horowitz stepped over to a sideboard that ran along a row of floor-to-ceiling windows behind her desk. Threads of smoke trailed after the beige cigarette between the first two fingers of her left hand. She picked up a small yellow watering pail with her right, the old-fashioned kind with a spout that dribbled water at the end. Potted plants grew everywhere. They hung from the ceiling, took up shelf-space, stood on the endtables that flanked the sofas. She slowly watered the plants lined up on the sideboard as she spoke.

"I know your life has changed suddenly because of the deaths of your family and your friend," she said. "But you seem to have no comprehension of exactly how much your life is going to change from now on. It will change, and change again, and then continue to change. Sometimes on an hourly basis. This thing is not even twenty-four hours old, and yet, only a small, negligible percentage of people surveyed thought you were an actor on *Home Improvement*. Do you see the significance of that, Adam? It means that only very stupid people do not know who you are. You are already a celebrity. The public simply has not decided what it wants to do with you."

She ran out of water with two more plants left. Walked back along the sideboard, replaced the pail. Made her way slowly around the desk. "You do not like to be called Mr. Julian? How will you feel about being called a murderer by David Letterman? Or Conan O'Brien? They will not be that blunt, of course. They will just make funny jokes about you cruising for chicks with O.J. and being in the same support group as Kyle and Eric Menendez. Soon, the very mention of your name will sound like a setup for a punch line. And everyone will laugh because it's just a joke, right? But how will *you* feel about it?" She hopped up onto the edge of the desk and crossed her ankles. A quick, girlish movement that dropped years from her age for a split-second.

Adam said, "I wouldn't like it, but I could—"

"*Wouldn't* like it? You speak as if what I am saying is speculation. These are not ifs, Adam, these are whens. And I can think of at least one *who*. Who will play you on *Saturday Night Live?* Week after week? In long, embarassing sketches that go nowhere? Have you thought about that yet?"

"What's that got to do with—"

"These are rhetorical questions, Adam. Please stop interrupting me. Do you know that any day now, you will start getting bags of mail? Great big bags of it. It will come from people who hate you and want to see you fry, many of whom will volunteer to pull the switch. From people who want to save your soul and ensure you of eternal life. And there will be many, many declarations of love and proposals of marriage." She took a deep drag on the cigarette. Smoke came out her mouth and nose as she continued. "Women who are convinced of your innocence. Women who are convinced of your guilt and want to marry you, because of it, not in spite of it, because they happen to be freaks. There will be a lot of freaks, Adam. You will be very popular among their people, an icon in their culture. Next, you will start getting e-mails from them. Then phone calls. Before you know it, they will be showing up at your door. Some of them will be uncommonly beautiful women. Most of them will not. Some will want you to carve your initials into their genitals with a rusty blade. And some, Adam, will be very dangerous and they will want to hurt you."

When she paused a moment, Adam sighed impatiently. "Are you a defense attorney or a bodyguard?"

"Oh, but we have not even gotten to the trial yet," Horowitz said. "All of this will happen during the months before the trial. You will be the only topic discussed on *Rivera Live* for that entire year, unless the president is assassinated, in which case it becomes a horse race. Your face will be on the cover of every magazine, newspaper, and tabloid in the country. One night, you will go to bed knowing they are defending your innocence. The next morning, you will learn over breakfast that the tabloids are claiming you had a sick sexual relationship with your stepmother and everybody wants you to get the death penalty."

Adam's heart skipped a beat and he shot to his feet. "What?"

"I am not finished."

He remained standing. Thought, *False alarm, false alarm, please let it be a false alarm.*

"These things *are* going to happen," she went on. "I anticipate them and deal with them. I prevent them if I can, exploit them to my client's benefit if I cannot. I control all outgoing information. No one gets photographs, video, or audio of my client unless I approve. My client talks to no one unless I say so. And *then* my client talks only as I instruct and says only what I tell him to say. I create and maintain an image for my client from the moment I take on the case until it is finished. I determine what the public thinks of my client. I create an image in their minds and a feeling in their guts."

"What does public opinion have to do with this?" Adam asked abruptly. "They're just people on the street, they don't have anything to do with this. It's the jury that decides—"

Horowitz raised her voice just enough to shut him up. "That jury is chosen from people on the street. *They* are the ones who will decide whether or not you go to death row, get to be everybody's favorite love-doll in prison for the rest of your life, or get to go home and eat Doritos in front of the television." She leaned back and put out her cigarette in a large round marble ashtray on the desk. Lowered her voice as she continued. "I get to them first and shape their opinion early. And opinion has everything to do with this, Adam. What do you think the law is? A list of rules? Speed limits? Tax deadlines? Those things do not make up the law. They have nothing to do with it. Law *is* opinion, Adam. Our opinions. The opinions of others. A businessman compliments his secretary every day. Her clothes, her hairstyle, her perfume. It is the businessman's opinion that he is being nice, making his secretary feel good about herself. But it is his secretary's opinion that she is being sexually harassed, and she takes it to a judge. It is the judge's opinion that there is sufficient reason to examine the woman's opinion with a trial. Several people are chosen, based on the opinions of the legal representatives on each side of the case, to decide whose opinion they like better, the secretary's or the businessman's. If someone does not like *their* opinion, they go through the whole process all over again. Opinions, nothing but opinions. What is the pinnacle of success for a law student? Become an attorney, eventually a judge, then get appointed to the Supreme Court. And what do Supreme Court justices do? They write opinions."

Adam sat on the front edge of the chair again, careful not to let it suck him backward into its gullet. Horowitz was making sense. He did not want her to make sense. He wanted to dismiss her glibly, rudely, to go home and take a nap and wake up to find it was all a dream, to find that there's no place like home, there's no place like home.

Horowitz uncrossed her ankles, dropped from the edge of the desk. "You are in big trouble, Adam. Like it or not, opinions are all you have. That is why Mr. Menkin called me. Because I know how to control opinions. He managed to track me down in the Caribbean, where I was just starting my first vacation in eight years." She leaned back against the desk and folded her arms again with a sigh.

Adam's anger was growing. He did not want to listen to another word the smug, stubby woman had to say. All he wanted to do was sleep. And never wake up again.

"Are you trying to make me feel guilty for interrupting your vacation?" he asked.

"Not at all. I am trying to decide if you are *worth* interrupting my vacation. So far, I would have to say that you are not." Horowitz pushed away from the desk and walked slowly in a wide circle around Adam. "You have no grasp of your situation. You do not comprehend the depth of the trouble you are in. If you do not know how desperately you need me…then as far as you are concerned, you do not need me at all. In which case you are a waste of my time. Of course, that might change. It is very likely, in fact. You are still in a state of shock. Not only have you lost your family, but you witnessed the death of your friend."

"It wasn't a death!" Adam shouted, turning in the chair toward her. He lost his balance on the edge and slid back into the chair's waiting maw. "He didn't have a fucking stroke, he wasn't hit by a bus! He was murdered!"

"I am very sorry about what happened today, Adam. I can only imagine the pain you must be in. I cannot erase it or bring back your friend. Should I decide to represent you, however, I can promise that the police officers who did it will be ruined. Utterly and completely. They will pray for someone to do to them what they did to your friend." She stood before him, hands joined behind her now. "If we play our cards right, they might even do it to themselves."

It was a pleasant thought, driving the police officers who had shot Carter to shoot themselves. But Adam knew it was nothing more than a sales pitch. Rona Horowitz was known as one of the best, but she could not be that good. No one was that good.

"When did you last eat?" Horowitz asked, going back behind her desk.

He thought about it. Could not remember. "I don't know."

"How about a burger? A cold sandwich, perhaps?"

Adam shrugged.

She picked up the telephone awkwardly, touched a button, did not appear accustomed to using it as she put it to her ear. "I will order."

After ordering a roast beef sandwich and a chef's salad, Horowitz told Adam to make himself comfortable on the sofa, then left the office. Rog was waiting in the outer office, where she had banished him before talking to Adam.

He could hear them speaking in hushed tones beyond the closed door as he crossed the office to the sofa. It was worse than the leather chair. The fat cream cushions were feather-soft. His knees rose as his middle sank into the sofa. He put a sneakered foot on the edge of the glass-topped coffee table with blonde-wood frame. Leaned his head back, let his eyelids drop. He opened them again immediately.

The whole day had been a nightmare from which he had been unable to wake. Like a nightmare, it had lapses in logic, gaps in which details blurred or were blacked out completely. Confusion hummed inside his head, and every time he closed his eyes, he saw Carter's blood splatter the concrete, saw him drop from the poolhouse roof. Heard his neck break.

Adam had cried until his chest ached and his stomach was sick. He had sobbed and blubbered enough to make the two winos and six or eight Neanderthalian guys in the holding cell decide to leave him alone. He did not know how long he had been behind bars. He had dreaded the possibility of going to jail, but once in the cell, he'd hardly noticed it, remembered very little of the experience. Mostly the smell of urine, a residual whiff of which still hovered around him.

Everything had seemed to move so fast, and yet time felt frozen in place. He remembered standing in front of a judge. His skull had been crumbling under the throbbing weight of a headache he was certain would kill him. His voice had cracked when he said, "Not guilty," when Rog cued him with an inconspicuous nudge. During that time, he'd heard "one million dollars" mentioned a few times. Some discussion about whether or not Adam was a flight risk. But his heart was screaming too loudly for him to absorb anything.

He had ended up in a hospital room. Or perhaps it had been an examination room in a doctor's office, he was not certain. A silver-haired doctor who smelled of pipe tobacco had examined Adam. A nurse had given him a shot and his brain had melted. It had not yet congealed and reclaimed its proper shape. The doctor prescribed some happy pills and Rog stopped by an all-night drug store to pick them up on their way to Horowitz's office.

Adam did not know how long Horowitz was gone. Maybe he had dozed on the sofa. It did not occur to him to look around the office for a clock.

When Horowitz returned, she carried a brown grocery bag by its rolled-up top. Stopped at her desk to pick up the folder.

"My assistant just arrived," she said. "He is going to make coffee. Please take your foot off the coffee table and do not put it there again." She pulled an ottoman over to the coffee table and sat across from Adam, put the folder on the floor. From the grocery bag, she removed a small white bag and set it on the table. "This is yours." Then a square Styrofoam container with a plastic fork taped to the lid. She detached the fork, opened the container, tore off the lid and tossed it aside. A small packet of dressing and two packets of saltine crackers were tucked into the corner of the chef's salad. "If you are anything like most people in your situation, you have not eaten all day. Your blood sugar is low. You feel tired and irritable. I need you to be able to think clearly and listen carefully to everything I say. So even if you do not feel particularly hungry, I would appreciate it if you would humor me and eat."

Adam struggled forward in the sofa and reluctantly opened the white bag. Removed a small bag of potato chips, a stack of napkins, and his sandwich rolled up in butcher paper. He smelled the cold beef as he unwrapped it, and his stomach stirred.

Horowitz tore off a corner of the dressing packet with her teeth, plucked it off her tongue with finger- and thumb-tips. Squeezed the dressing onto her salad. "By the way, I was not serious earlier, when I insisted you prove your innocence."

"I thought proving my innocence was your job."

"No, it is the prosecution's job to prove. It is my job to shed doubt on the prosecution's case. I need prove nothing. But that is in the future. We should not get ahead of ourselves." She crumbled two saltine crackers in their cellophane packet, then opened it and scattered the crumbs over her salad. "The tragic gunplay involved in your arrest will buy you a lot. But it will not save your neck. I will need more than that to save your neck."

Adam said, "You don't believe I'm innocent." It was not a question.

Horowitz closed her eyes a moment, sighed. "We need to make something very clear. I told you the law was made up of opinions? Well, for the duration of this process, the only opinions that matter are everyone else's. Ours are insignificant right now and we need to set them aside. It does not matter whether or not you like me, and it does not matter whether or not I believe you are innocent. For the purposes of our meeting here, I do not care if you have killed more people than Stalin. I am interested only in finding something about your case that will allow me to use the existing system to keep you off death row and out of prison. If I find that something and become your attorney, I will be paid handsomely. My exposure will go through the roof. I will be able to increase my legal and public-speaking fees, and my book advances will experience a sudden weight gain. Consider *that* the next time you wonder what I think."

She took a bite of salad. Lettuce crunched between her teeth. "You are familiar with my work, yes?" she asked.

"I've seen you on television," he said. "I haven't exactly followed your career. I hardly ever watch Court TV." He bit into half of the thick sandwich and hunger exploded in his stomach. The roast beef was tender and delicious.

"You know I successfully defended Stephen Allen Grange."

Adam remembered the name. One of the early school shootings. Grange, a junior at a Wisconson high school, had opened fire in the cafeteria at lunchtime with a 9mm automatic pistol, killing twelve and injuring at least twice that many. He had been held back a year and was nearly eighteen, so it was decided to try him as an adult. Luckily for Grange, his mother's brother was one of the biggest, richest, most powerful producers in Hollywood. Uncle Bigshot had hired Rona Horowitz to defend his nephew. Adam remembered none of the details, except that Grange was found guilty but insane and put into a mental facility, where most likely he would spend the rest of his life. It was considered quite a victory for the defense, because Grange had avoided execution.

Adam had always assumed it was concern for his sister and nephew that had motivated the producer to pay for the boy's defense, that he had hired Horowitz to keep his nephew off death row. After listening to Horowitz, he was not so sure. He remembered only one brief mention of the producer's connection to the killer and the fact that he was paying the boy's legal fees. It had been in an article in *Premiere*...or had it been *Entertainment Weekly*? Other than that, the producer had been left out of all the trial's press coverage, which had been extensive, and no significant public association ever developed between him and the young mass murderer. Maybe his motives in hiring Horowitz had been self-serving after all.

Adam recalled some of her other clients—a rap singer charged with murder, a studio executive accused of drug dealing, a fading television star whose girlfriend's suicide looked suspicious—but Grange had brought Horowitz the most attention. Adam imagined her fees and advances had tripled after that case. He wondered how much they would go up if she succeeded with him.

He did not respond until he had chewed up a couple bites of his sandwich. "Yes, I remember that. Why? Are you trying to impress me? I thought our opinions don't count."

"They do not, and I am not trying to impress you. Just trying to make a point. Grange was easy. He was not caught on videotape."

Adam stopped chewing. "Videotape?" he asked around a mouthful of roast beef. "What videotape?"

She held up a small, cautioning hand. "Don't panic. Chew your food. Just listen."

A tall, slender, dark-haired man in his mid-twenties entered the room carrying a wooden tray. It held a brown pitcher of coffee, two mugs and spoons, packets of sugar, artificial sweetener, a small pitcher of cream. He placed the tray on the coffee table and stood. He wore a long-sleeve powder-blue shirt, a black-and-red tie, black pants. The shadow of oncoming whiskers darkened the lower half of his narrow, pale face. "Can I get you anything else?" he asked. He had a deep, rich voice, but spoke softly.

"That will be all for now, Lamont," she said.

Lamont? Adam thought. *Some parents are just plain evil.*

As Lamont headed out of the office, Horowitz said, "There will be press. Shave, and carry a clean razor with you at all times, just in case. Until further notice." When he was out of earshot, she shook her head with pity. "His facial hair grows faster than the federal deficit."

She poured coffee into one robin's-egg-blue mug, poised the pitcher over the other and looked at Adam. He nodded, she poured. Stirred some cream into her coffee, sipped it. "Now, listen. Two days after your father's yacht exploded, the FBI raided a compound in the desert."

Adam ducked his head to bite into the sandwich again. It was not hard to separate himself from what she was saying. He had already separated himself from everything. His feelings of guilt had shifted since Carter's death. Diz's house in the desert and Adam's reason for going there now seemed distant and insignificant.

"This compound was the location of a great deal of ongoing criminal activity," Horowitz continued. She put the folder on the coffee table and opened it, flipped a few pages aside. "Eighteen underage boys were found on the premises, all of whom were there to be sold as prostitutes, and/or photographed and/or videotaped while engaging in sexual acts with adults and/or other minors. Agents discovered large amounts of drugs, guns, ammunition, and explosives. The weapons and explosives ranged from the most common and inexpensive to the most sophisticated and destructive. It was quite an operation, run by a man and woman. Waldo Cunningham and Cecelia Noofer, although they have several identities. Working individually and together, they have criminal records that go back decades. They have been arrested before, and they will be arrested again. People like Waldo Cunningham and Cecelia Noofer are a penny a gross. The only thing to be accomplished by arresting them is to slow them down, maybe stop their activities for a little while. Normally, not a terribly significant collar. Except this time, child pornography was involved."

After only four bites of her salad, she slid it aside. Produced another beige cigarette, this one from her pocket, and lit it with a tiny onyx lighter. Pulled an ashtray toward her over the tabletop. The smoke from her cigarette smelled like burning tires. "Child pornography is currently a very hot crime," she continued. "The Internet has heightened awareness of it. It gets ratings, it sells papers, and politicians love to denounce it. It gets votes. The federal agents assigned to the case quickly established from business records taken from the desert compound that Mr. Cunningham and Miss Noofer had been doing business with some very famous people."

Adam remembered Mr. C.'s warning: *I go down, everybody goes down.*

"There was no discretion used in keeping the books," Horowitz said. "They were filled with the names of politicians, a couple televangelists, and many from the film, television, and music industries." She inhaled a mouthful of smoke, blew it out.

"Do you expect me to be surprised?" Adam asked.

"There is more. Apparently, Mr. Cunningham did not like the looks of his situation after being arrested. His attorney informed the feds that Mr. Cunningham had important information regarding a recent prominent death that was *not* an accident."

Adam thought he already knew everything she was going to tell him, but that caught him by surprise. Suddenly, the roast beef sandwich was not so delicious.

Horowitz held the cigarette over the ashtray, tapped it a couple times with her index finger. "Mr. Cunningham offered to share that information with the authorities in exchange for some serious leniency. Urgent meetings ensued. Some kind of deal was struck, but the specifics have not been released. They are irrelevant, anyway. The important thing is that Mr. Cunningham identified you and your friend Carter. He said you had hired his son Nathaniel, aka Diz, to blow up your father's yacht."

How had Mr. Cunningham found out? Surely Diz would not have told him. Or would he? Perhaps they sat down each evening and discussed the day's business. That seemed unlikely after what Diz had said about his dad. But how else would Mr. Cunningham have found out?

Adam felt a tremor in his legs. How was he going to lie his way through everything? With Carter around, he might be able to do it. Carter had been like a battery, Adam had drawn energy from him, strength. Without him, Adam felt lost.

"Mr. Cunningham had put a copy of the security camera tape on which you and Carter appear into a safe in case he needed it later," Horowitz said. "He gave it to the feds once everyone had agreed on a deal. The tape shows you and Carter Brandis at the desert complex just two days before your father's yacht blew up."

He put the sandwich down, wiped his hands on a napkin, checked to see if they were shaking. Covering his closed mouth with a hand, he belched quietly. Sipped his black coffee. All the while, his mind ran frantically through the story he and Carter had agreed upon.

Horowitz leveled her gaze at him during a weighty pause. "I have not seen the tape, but it does exist. Your presence at the compound is not in question. Whether or not I represent you, Adam, depends on what you were doing there."

Adam frowned, drank some more coffee. He was thinking of his story, and at the same time trying to understand Horowitz's statement. "Why does it matter that much?" he asked.

"I do not take on a client unless I am reasonably confident about my chances of winning in court," she replied. "This case looks very good. Your numbers in the polls are impressive. Except for this. Something like this, Adam, could tip the scale sharply. So I need to know before we go any further."

Adam leaned forward, forearms on his denim thighs. "We went to see Carter's friend Billy that day. Billy Rivers."

"Carter's friend? Not yours?"

"I'd met him before, but I didn't really know him. Carter talked about him a lot." Every time he spoke his friend's name, something deep inside him twisted and hurt. "They made prosthetics, masks. You know, movie gore stuff. Carter knew Billy pretty well, really admired his work." Adam stared at the sandwich on the coffee table. It looked ugly, sickening. "Billy got some of the materials he used from this guy named Diz."

"Exactly what kind of materials?"

"I couldn't tell you. I don't know anything about that stuff. Whatever it was, Billy had to get some more and needed a ride, so we gave him one. I gave him one."

"That was a long ride," Horowitz said.

"A lot longer than I expected. It pissed me off, too. I didn't say anything, though, because Carter liked Billy so much. I didn't want to make trouble. But he's such a Goddamned idiot. Billy, I mean. We got out there and I couldn't believe it. Neither could Carter. We thought we were going to this guy's house, but it was like some kind of…installation."

"You had no idea what went on there?"

"We didn't even know there was that much of a *there* there. I didn't want to go inside, but Carter said if we didn't, Billy might forget we were waiting for him. So we went inside."

Adam told her about his encounters with Mr. and Mrs. C., about Diz. He told her everything but his true reason for going there.

"It sounds as if you like Diz," Horowitz said.

"Yeah, he seemed like a pretty good guy. I felt bad about his…well, his whole life. I mean, I couldn't believe what was going on there, or that those people were his parents. I couldn't get out of there fast enough. I saw security cameras everywhere. It was bad enough just being there, but to be on those tapes…you know, tapes Mr. C. could look at anytime he wanted…that was creepy."

Every word was true. Even there, perched on the lower lip of Rona Horowitz's man- eating sofa, he shuddered at the thought of the place.

"How long were you there?" Horowitz asked.

"I don't know. Probably not very long, but it felt like forever."

"Less than an hour? Less than half an hour?"

He nodded. "Less than half an hour. Probably twenty minutes, no more." Adam knew they were there longer, over an hour. But once Diz had taken them outside, they were out of range of the cameras, so there was no proof they had stayed longer than twenty minutes.

"Mr. Cunningham and his home video are why you were arrested this morning," she said. "The Marina del Rey police were brought in, and they found Mr. Cunningham's story convincing enough to charge you with murder and arrest you. And that, I am sorry to say, did not go as well as they had hoped, I'm sure. Have you heard from Diz since the day you met him?"

"No."

"Not even by phone? E-mail, perhaps?"

Adam frowned. "No, I said he seemed like a good guy, I didn't say we were pen pals."

"Glad to hear it. He is the one the police should be looking for. In fact, they are."

"Diz wasn't arrested with his parents?"

"The FBI learned of the Cunninghams' desert operation from a tipster who wished to remain anonymous. They now suspect that tipster was Diz. It seems Diz had planted explosives all over his house. They were set to go off when a specific series of touch-tones sounded over the phone line. Diz apparently wanted to be able to set off the explosives from a healthy distance. The last time his parents saw him was the day after you met him. The day after that, all the phone numbers at Diz's house were changed, something Mr. Cunningham does every month for security purposes. Diz forgot about that, or he miscalculated. Either way, he did not have the new numbers. Instead of blowing up his parents, he turned them in. Perhaps he thought there would be gunfire during the raid and the explosives would be set off after all, killing federal agents along with his parents. That particular theory is quite popular with the FBI right now and they are terribly upset with Diz. They are eager to locate him and explain to him the error of his ways. They believe he is accompanied by Billy Rivers, who has disappeared as well."

Adam took a moment to absorb it all. "You mean Diz was…you mean…" *You mean, while I was hiring Diz to kill my dad,* Adam thought, *he was planning to kill his* own *parents?* He asked, "How does that add up to me hiring Diz to blow up the yacht?"

"It does not. Not for me." Horowitz closed the folder and set it aside. Slid the salad in front of her again and took another bite. "For some reason, Diz told that story to his father. That you had hired him to blow up your father's yacht. Perhaps Diz was somehow covering his own posterior."

Adam thought, *Or maybe Billy pulled his head out of his ass just long enough to stick both feet in his mouth.*

"Maybe Diz didn't tell him anything," he said, "and he's full of shit."

"That is a healthy and vibrant possibility. Do you keep a journal, Adam?"

"Yes."

"Is there anything written in it that I should know about? Do you have any skeletons in your closet that will be dragged out into the light during the course of the investigation and trial?"

"What do you mean?"

"The District Attorney's people and the feds will be going over all your belongings with microscopes. That includes any written material. Journals, address books, computer files. They will probably memorize your garbage."

"Why the feds?"

"Because your visit to Diz's house has connected you to the criminal activity that took place there. They will be looking for drugs, guns, child pornography. Will they find any?"

He made a bitter snorting sound and rolled his eyes. He suddenly felt uncommonly loose, relaxed and at ease. Probably because of the injection he had been given that afternoon. Had there been more than one? Or perhaps it was because he felt so confident about what the feds would find in their search. He had emptied his room of anything illegal or incriminating. He had burned a lot of it, and put the rest—some pot, a little cocaine he had tucked into the back of a desk drawer a few years ago, and some drug paraphernalia—in Rain's room, where it would be presumed hers if found.

"You are not answering my question, Adam," Horowitz said. "Is there anything about you I need to know? Anything at all, good, bad, or neutral. Do not feel shy or embarassed. I am not here to judge you, I am here to protect you. But I am unable to do that unless I can anticipate anything that might come up."

"I…I'm not sure what you're looking for."

"Are you addicted to any drugs? Are you an alcoholic? Were you molested as a child? Are you gay? Have you starred in any porn films? Do you drug your dates and have sex with them while they are unconscious? Are you an habitual shoplifter? We will cover everything eventually, but right now, I am interested in anything about you that might show up on the news in the next twenty-four hours." She poked at the salad with the plastic fork.

Adam thought about her questions and chuckled. "Considering I grew up in Beverly Hills around people in the movie business," he said, "the weirdest thing about me is that the answer to all those questions is no."

"If you have something to hide, it will be the first thing reported about you tomorrow morning, I promise. Tell me about it now, and there is a good chance I can prevent that. If you cannot be absolutely open with me, Adam, we are wasting our time."

"I told you," he said. "There's nothing. I'm a boring person. I smoke a little pot now and then. My darkest secrets are that I like Disney cartoons and as I was entering adolescence, I had a brief crush on Madonna. My biggest crime, I guess, is that I'm a smartass."

Horowitz nodded, breathed smoke. "It may not be a crime, but it is certainly no secret. We will need to work on that. You cannot go around mouthing off to people when you are under suspicion of murder, Adam." She killed her cigarette in the ashtray and stood. "The most important thing you can do right now is get some sleep. You will need it. Is there someone you can stay with tonight?"

"I'll just go home," Adam said, standing.

Horowitz picked up the folder and went to her desk. "No, I prefer you stay with friends tonight."

"Well, I guess I could go to my girlfriend's house. I'm pretty sure her parents wouldn't mind if I—"

"Who is your girlfriend?"

Adam crossed the office, stood before her desk as she took her seat. He did not like the tone of her question. "Her name is Alyssa. What difference does—"

"Is she famous? A celebrity?"

His eyes narrowed. "What?"

"You need to stop questioning everything I say, Adam. We have no time for that. I have explained my methods in a nutshell, the rest is on-the-job training. From now on, your job is to be my client. That means doing as I say. If you are not happy with that, complain about it tomorrow after you have had a little time to think about what a godsend I am in your life. Now. Do you have any celebrity friends?"

He shook his head, confused. "You've got to be kidding."

"Wherever you sleep tonight will be news tomorrow. We might as well make the best of it by having you taken in by a concerned friend who does not want you to be alone. Preferrably a celebrity with a very positive public image. Perhaps even wholesome. Do you have any friends like that?"

It infuriated him. He wanted to break something. "You want me to call my friend Dick Van Patten? Maybe my pal Doris fucking *Day* has a spare room up in Carmel."

"Do you actually know the Van Pattens?"

"Hell no, I don't know the fucking Van Pattens!"

"You really are a smartass, Adam. You strike me as a very witty young man, as well. But you will pardon me if I do not laugh at your jokes—" She bounded to her feet and seemed about to come across the desk and assault him. " — *because I do not have the fucking time and neither do you!*"

Adam flinched when she shouted.

Horowitz pulled back, stood straight. "Now, please give me the names of some people you actually know."

"I know a lot of celebrities, but not well enough to ask if I can stay the night."

"Surely among all the industry people your father knew — "

" — there's not a single person I'd spend the night with! And there are no *wholesome* people in Los Angeles. I don't know where you call home, but in Los Angeles, there's nobody who fits that description." A name came to mind unexpectedly. "Oh, wait. Maybe there's somebody I could call. At the funeral, he said I could come over anytime. Jack Nicholson. He's not exactly wholesome, but he's — "

"You *are* joking," she said.

"No, this is for real. He said I could — "

"All right," she said, sitting. "I will put you in a hotel."

"What? I'm serious. He came to all my dad's parties. He used to come upstairs and play video games with Carter and me."

"Are you seriously suggesting that it would be good for people to get up in the morning and turn on their televisions and radios and log onto the internet and open their newspapers to find that accused murderer Adam Julian was taken under the compassionate wing of his dear friend, the man who took an ax to his family in *The Shining?*"

"Jesus Christ, you don't think he really goes around with an ax and — "

"Images create perceptions, Adam, and perceptions create opinions. People might enjoy watching Jack Nicholson's movies and following his bad-boy exploits in the gossip columns. But I guarantee you they would not leave their teenage sons in his care."

Adam chuckled. "Then you're not as in touch as you think you are."

"Jack Nicholson is out of the question. End of discussion. I know nothing about your girlfriend or her family, so you cannot very well stay with them."

"What the hell is that supposed to — "

"I will put you in a room at the Peninsula Beverly Hills Hotel. You will stay there for awhile. It would look bad if you stayed in your own house. That should be too painful for you. One of my drivers will be assigned to you immediately. You have finished driving for awhile. I will have people in the suite next to yours. I or someone on my staff will be within slapping distance of your mouth at all times, so do not give us a reason. Under no circumstances will you leave the hotel without me." She cocked her head, almost playfully, and there was a twinkle in her eye. Quietly, she said, "And when you return to this office tomorrow morning at eight o'clock sharp, Adam, you will speak to me and the people on my staff with respect. You will lose the attitude and the swearing, and you will do it in your sleep tonight. That kind of thing has a way of slipping out in interviews, even in the courtroom, and it is deadly. If I think for one second that you are not going to cooperate, or that you are somehow endangering the success of this case, I will drop you like an overpriced long distance plan. I will be honest, Adam, this is a gem of a case. But I do not need it if it means putting up with a rich whiny smartass Hollywood brat who probably thinks discipline is nothing more than a category of dirty pictures on a pornographic website."

Adam's cheeks and neck burned. She had not raised her voice, and yet he felt he had been shouted down. He cleared his throat and asked, "What do you want me to say?"

She smiled, and it transformed her face for a moment. Made it younger, pretty. "Absolutely nothing unless I say otherwise."

Adam's suite in the luxury hotel was cavernous, and it made him uncomfortable. Too much space and color. He considered sleeping in the closet. As it turned out, he did not sleep much at all. Closing his eyes continued to be a mistake. He spent most of the night watching softcore porn movies he found difficult to follow.

His telephone rang early the next morning, and a woman told him a car would be coming for him soon. He showered and dressed. His clothes felt almost billowy on his body. Rog was right—he had lost weight.

Adam was driven through a rear entrance to the underground garage beneath Horowitz's building by an amiable middle-aged black man named Leo in a chauffeur's uniform. Lamont awaited him there, and took him upstairs in a service elevator.

"How's it going, Lamont?" Adam asked, thinking, *I bet school was one long beating for him.* He was tall and scrawny, hatchet-faced. And, of course, his parents had given him the gift of that name.

"Very busy," Lamont said. "The phone hasn't stopped ringing. Reporters are everywhere. Practically crawling up out of the sink drains, like the spiders in that movie."

Adam smiled. "*Arachnaphobia.* Cool movie. First time I saw it, I itched for two weeks."

"I watched it with my mother. She had a stroke and died."

Adam laughed.

"No, I mean she actually had a stroke and died while we were watching the movie."

"Oh, God, I'm sorry, I thought you were joking. I wasn't laughing at—"

"I know. I should be more clear about that in the future. A lot of people react that way."

"Do you think the movie actually caused the—"

"Oh, no, of course not. We just happened to be watching it when it happened. Mom hadn't been well in years. She had me late in life and the birth nearly killed her. She always said she hadn't been the same since. *Arachnaphobia* just happened to be on HBO that evening, and she had the big one in front of the television set. Of course, had I been working for Rona at the time, I'm sure we would have come to an undisclosed, out-of-court settlement with Mr. Spielberg."

"You were close to your mother?"

"Well, yes. Most of the time. She was crazier than a bedbug. And vindictive? But, what are you gonna do, huh? She was the only mom I had, and I loved her."

"What about your dad?"

"Haven't seen him in ten years and I hope the son of a bitch is dead and rotting."

✝

When Adam walked into Horowitz's office, she looked him over with concern. Studied the *eXistenZ* T-shirt and bluejeans he had worn the night before. "Do you always dress that way, Adam?"

"Hey, all my clothes are at my place, and at Carter's."

"Do they all look like that?"

Adam looked down at himself to make sure he wasn't wearing anything too awful. "Well, kind of. Yeah."

Horowitz wore a delicate black headset with a tiny microphone that curved down her cheek to her mouth. She hit a button on her phone base, waited. "Hermione, this is Rona. How soon can you be over here for a quick meeting? I have a client in need of an overhaul." She lit a beige cigarette with one of the fireplace matches as she listened. "That will be perfect. See you then." She hit another button on the phone, turned to Adam. "Hermione will be here in an hour to fit you for appropriate clothes. We will have you properly dressed by noon."

"My suitor," Adam muttered to himself with a private smile, remembering what Sunny had called him the first time they met. Louder, he said to her, "I won't wear just anything, you know."

"What you are wearing now proves otherwise. You will wear what I think is appropriate."

Horowitz ushered him into a conference room adjoining her office. Over a dozen well-dressed men and women were seated around a long table, waiting for them. Notebooks and folders lay open before them beside steaming coffee mugs. A small buffet of fresh fruits, pastries, toast, jam, and coffee had been set up on a sideboard against more tinted floor-to-ceiling windows. Horowitz insisted Adam eat, at the very least, a banana, then introduced him to her staff. The names blurred and he did not even try to keep them straight in his head. Everyone seemed impatient with the introductions, anyway, as if they wanted to get on with it.

One man stood out. Instead of a suit like the others, he wore a green and yellow plaid shirt, jeans, and expensive-looking cowboy boots. A black cowboy hat lay upside-down in his lap. He sat in a back corner, separate from the others, slumped in a chair, left knee bent, right leg extended. Arms interlaced above a round belly. He looked like a middle-aged Wilford Brimley. His mustache was not as bushy, his hair a lighter shade of brown. But he was bald on top, wore wire-framed glasses, had the same crotchety downturning of the mouth, as if he were trying to decide how to respond to a rude remark.

"This is Max Vantana," Horowitz said when she got to the man in the corner. "A man who, were it not for his good nature and fine moral character, could bring all of Hollywood, New York, and Washington, D.C. to their knees before lunch. He is my investigator. He is the best in the business and he works only for me. You will be talking to Max a lot. If you lie to him, he will find out. If you are hiding something, he will uncover it."

Max's nod was barely perceptible. His eyes said, *I got your number, boy.*

After the introductions, Horowitz handed out a few assignments and half the people at the table left. The other half listened and took notes as she led Adam through every move he had made in the past two weeks.

✝

Hermione was a chilly British woman in her sixties who wore too much makeup. While she took Adam's measurements in Horowitz's office, Horowitz described the kind of clothes she wanted for Adam. Used phrases like "conservative but relaxed," and "not quite hip, but not out of touch with what is." Adam wondered with dread what freakish Halloween costumes might be conjured with such incantations.

By noon, as Horowitz had predicted, he was dressed in a dark blue Armani suit. He would not admit it to the stubby attorney, but he had never looked so good in his life. Not even at his senior prom. Which he had attended with Carter because neither of them had dates.

"By this evening," Horowitz said, "your closet will be stocked. The clothes will be matched and numbered. Each time you make an appearance before the press, I or someone on my staff will tell you which set of clothes to wear by number. Otherwise, you may wear anything you like. As long as it is among the clothes in your closet. You will *not* wear anything but the clothes given you. Do you understand?"

He nodded.

"You have an appointment with a hair stylist in forty-five minutes."

"Well, I'd like to see my girlfriend. I thought we could have lunch togeth—"

"Sit down, Adam." She pointed to the hungry chair, then seated herself behind her desk.

Adam sat on one of the chair's curved armrests.

"Please do not do that," Horowitz said. "Sit in the chair."

Adam slid into the deep chair with a sigh of resignation.

"You need to put yourself in my position for a moment, Adam. It is not only my job to get you out of the trouble you are in, but to protect you from any further trouble, as well. Therefore I have no choice in this."

"In…what?"

"For the duration of this case, you will be unable to see your girl-friend."

"What?" He tried to stand. "Who do you think you — what do you mean, I can't — what the hell are you — " He battled the chair's jaws for freedom, quickly gave up. "You've gotta be fucking kidding me," he said angrily.

"Alyssa's parents grow, use, and apparently sell marijuana," Horowitz said. "Did you know that?"

"Well, I…how did *you* know that?"

"I told you Max was the best."

"But she's a witness," Adam said. "I was with her when — "

"And she will be processed and dealt with like any other valuable witness. But until the trial is over, there will be no relationship. This is not negotiable. If you think I take any joy in it, Adam, you are quite wrong. I know I am only causing you more pain, and I am very sorry. You have every right to be angry. But it is necessary. Once you are able to look at it objectively, you will know I am right. What if the police were to bust her parents in the middle of all this? You would be involved by association, even though you would have nothing to do with it. The press would dine on that for weeks. Months. You might not survive it. This is your life we are talking about. It would be irresponsible of me to allow the relationship to continue."

Adam's mouth hung open. He could not decide what to say as his mind leaped forward to imagine weeks, months, a year, maybe more without Alyssa. It was incomprehensible. "I can't believe you think you can — " Adam wriggled and jerked, fought his way out of the chair. Stood and stepped toward the desk. He shouted, "Jesus H. motherfucking Goddamned Christ! All I've heard from you is what *you* want and what *you* say. Well, I've got something to say." His hand trembled as he pointed at the chair, arm rigid. "Get rid of that fucking chair! And if you don't want to get rid of it, bring one in that a human being can sit in and get out of, for crying out loud! Because I am not sitting in that fucking chair or on that fucking sofa again! Ever!"

Horowitz sat up, spine straight. "Are you finished?"

Adam sighed again, a weary, restless sound. "Okay, I'm sorry. I shouldn't have — "

She already had the headset on, hit a button on the telephone. "Yes, Sarah, you need to set up a tab for new client Julian, Adam. Profanity. One hundred dollars per word. Release the standard memo, make sure Max gets a copy." Horowitz tapped a button on the phone and turned to Adam, stood. "If you do not like that chair, use the one in the corner. Just move it over here."

It was a very simple, wooden, straightback chair with no armrests and pale yellow cushions in the seat and back. He carried it over and seated himself.

"From now on, every time you swear, you will be fined one hundred dollars. If you ever raise your voice like that again, to me or anyone on my staff, I will leave you to twist in the breeze at the end of your rope. I suspect you talk like that all the time, correct? Did you talk to your friend Carter that way? To your mother? The surprising thing is that they let you get away with it. Most people do not appreciate being spoken to in that manner, Adam. They must have loved you a great deal to put up with it. I, on the other hand, do not. Perhaps in Beverly Hills, that kind of behavior is a way of life. But you are not in Beverly Hills anymore. Your hotel may be, but *you* are not. You are going to be watched by the world. So, remember. One hundred dollars per word. Fines will be applied to your bill. Any more shouting, we go our separate ways." She tossed him a small spiral-bound notebook, then a pen. He caught them clumsily. "Make a list of the things you want brought to your hotel room from your house and Carter's," she said. "Then you can go back to the hotel for lunch. The stylist will be coming to your room."

"Wait a second," Adam said. "I...I can't just...stop seeing Alyssa without explaining it to her. I need to talk to her before I—"

"I am not telling you to stop caring for her, Adam. But you may not contact her. I will send her a note explaining that you are focusing all your time and energy on your defense. I can send flowers, if you like. If you truly care about each other, this will not damage your relationship. You will probably come to appreciate one another more because of it. Get started on that list."

She left the office.

Adam had once found himself on the Century City Chamber of Commerce Homepage while surfing the internet aimlessly one afternoon. It claimed the Century City Chamber of Commerce was one of the most "relationship-driven chambers" in Los Angeles. Still stunned by Horowitz's orders, Adam thought, *I'm relationship-driven, too. I want mine back, dammit!*

His list was a bit longer than it would have been were he not being held hostage. He intended to contact Alyssa in one way or another, and included a couple things on his list that would make that possible.

✝

Lamont knocked on Adam's hotel room door halfway through *Wheel of Fortune* that evening. He carried a suitcase, while a teenage boy behind him carried a satchel and a cardboard box. He could have been Lamont's little brother.

"Adam, this is my personal assistant, Gerald," Lamont said as he put the suitcase on the bed.

"Wait, you're Rona Horowitz's personal assistant?" Adam asked.

Lamont nodded. "Yes."

"And *you* have a personal assistant?"

He shrugged his Anthony Perkins shoulders. "That's just the kind of job it is, Adam." The lower half of his face was again dark with growing stubble.

While Lamont opened the suitcase, Gerald put the satchel and box on the floor. Adam turned to him and they shook hands.

"Nice to meet you," Adam said. He glanced back toward the door. "Do *you* have a personal assistant?"

"Nah," Gerald said apologetically. "Just a beeper."

"Is that everything on my list?" Adam asked.

"Of course not," Lamont said. "Nobody said you'd get everything on the list."

"Then what am I not getting?"

"No clothes. She says you knew that and shouldn't have bothered putting any clothes on your list." Lamont propped his hands on his hips and leaned close to Adam. Dropped his voice. "I should point out to you that when she tells me to tell you something like that, it means you're being chastised. She likes to keep that sort of thing to a minimum."

"Oh, she's pissed, huh?" Adam said.

Lamont rolled his eyes. "You are going to be trouble, aren't you? You're determined to make all our lives miserable. Including your own, by the way. Which I don't understand. Don't you realize what an opportunity this is for you? This town is filled with people who would kill to be where you are."

"Yeah, that's what they think I did to be where I am, that's the fucking problem."

Lamont rolled his eyes again, sighed. Over his shoulder: "Wait for me in the hall, Gerald."

Gerald left the room.

Lamont extended an index finger in the direction of Adam's face, spoke quickly in a hoarse whisper. "Quit thinking of this in terms of 'guilty' or 'not guilty,' Adam. That's out of your hands, anyway. Much like Christians put their problems into the hands of Jesus, you need to put yours in the hands of *your* personal savior, Rona Horowitz. As far as you're concerned, Adam, she is God. Also like God, she doesn't make mistakes. She won't steer you wrong, she wouldn't know how." Lamont walked slowly around. Looked the room over, tried the television. "You've got nothing to worry about with Rona in charge of your life. Believe me, Adam, she will probably treat it with more care and respect than anyone ever has or ever will again. Most people aren't lucky enough to experience that kind of life-affirming validation. That's what she does, you know. She's not just an attorney. She validates people during the most traumatic, soul-destroying times of their lives."

"Does she have you under hypnosis?"

"Some people walk away from that experience in the best emotional shape they will ever know. So stop thinking about the stupid-ass inconveniences and start thinking about all the things you *can* do because of the position you're in right now."

"Such as?"

"You can reinvent yourself. Be whatever you've always wanted to be. This experience is whatever you put into it, Adam."

"What if I decide I don't want her to represent me?" Adam ask.

Lamont rolled his eyes. "Oh, please. You may be a troublemaker, but you don't strike me as an imbecile. Besides, Rona would make your life a living hell."

"Like it's not already," Adam muttered. "Does she know you go around bragging about her like this? Like a disciple?"

"I shouldn't be saying any of this. It's not my place. But I get so fed up with you people that it's hard to hold my tongue. You come in here so angry and resistant, as if you're being forced at gunpoint to let maybe the best criminal defense attorney on the planet win your freedom for you when you know damned well that otherwise you'd be a dead man walking."

"Okay, so what should I do? Just sit back and smile when she tells me I can't see my girlfriend anymore?"

"Yes. You might not like it, but she doesn't do anything without a reason, a good one. You can be very sure that if she doesn't want you to see your girlfriend, then it's for the best. Sometimes she doesn't explain her reasons. She doesn't have to."

"She did this time," Adam muttered.

"Probably because she wanted you to know she has no choice. Look, she's in charge, you do what she says. You do that, and everything will be fine. Rona will win another high-profile case, you will come out of this a celebrity with the future of your choice ahead of you. But if you give her trouble…well, nothing good will come of it, Adam. Trust me on this."

"Just let her run my fucking life, huh?"

"Exactly. Be thankful you still have one. And stop swearing, or you'll be broke before the trial. This conversation alone has cost you three hundred dollars, and we're not done yet."

"Don't tell her," Adam said.

Lamont chuckled. "No way that's gonna happen."

"If you're so afraid of her, then why take a chance pissing her off by telling me all this?"

"Four hundred dollars. And I only did that because you're cute."

Adam's eyebrows rose.

"Don't panic, don't have a sexual identity crisis, or anything, jeez-Louise, I know you're straight," Lamont said. "You're so straight, my teeth envy you. But still cute." He turned to the suitcase, removed an unfamiliar laptop computer. "Rona wants you to start writing everything down. Your impressions, your reaction to the legal system, your hopes, your dreams, your passions, your pains, anything that comes to mind. Write it down on this."

"That's not my laptop. I asked for *my* laptop."

"Your laptop has a cellular modem. Rona doesn't want you on the internet."

"Why does she want me to keep a journal?"

"She wants material for the ghostwriter to work with so the book can be written quickly."

"Ghostwriter? Hey, if anybody writes a book about me, it's going to be me!"

"You're a writer?"

"Yes."

"Good. I'm sure Rona will want your input. But the final decisions are hers."

"Yeah, we'll see."

"Do you write scripts?"

"Fiction."

"Your publisher?"

"Well, my fiction hasn't been published, but—"

"Then you're not a writer."

"Yes, I am. I've written three—"

"I don't care what you've written. Anyone can do that. If it's good enough to be published, then you're a writer. Rona has some of her biggest outbursts over little things like that, so be careful. As I was saying, I didn't bring your laptop because of the modem. Rona wants me to remind you that you are to communicate with no one until she says otherwise. If you want to reach someone, tell me, or Rona herself."

"I can't use my phone?"

"Haven't you tried it yet? When you pick up in here, the phone rings next door, you're connected to whomever is over there playing Solitaire or watching dirty movies."

"You mean…I'm stuck here? I can't go anywhere, talk to anyone, I can't even dress myself?"

"But what a way to start your writing career, huh?"

"What do you mean?" Adam asked.

"Writing a courtroom drama about yourself! Publishers will assassinate each other over it. You'll be like a young Dominick Dunne. Only hip, and without those little pervert glasses. And all the exciting events will actually have happened to you. You won't be writing about it, you'll be writing *of* it." He glanced at his watch, turned and hurried toward the door. "I have to go."

"Better shave first, Lamont," Adam said.

He stopped, touched his face. Turned to Adam with panic in his eyes.

"There are razors in the bathroom," Adam said. "Help yourself."

From the bathroom, Lamont shouted over the hiss of running water. "I really appreciate that, Adam. I'm going straight to her office from here, you saved me a lecture and some points."

"No problem," Adam said.

"Okay, now remember," Lamont said as he came out of the bathroom a few minutes later with a smooth, clean face. "If you want to get in touch with someone, let me know."

"You or Rona, right?"

"Yeah, but I know her schedule, her moods, what sets her off and makes her happy. You don't. It's always safer to talk to me first, even if it's just to run something by me."

"How do I reach you?"

"You won't need to. We'll be seeing a lot of each other. I've really gotta fly. No swearing and drop the attitude, you're working on those, right?"

"Shit, yeah."

As soon as Lamont was gone, Adam got the satchel from the floor, put it on the bed. Knelt beside it as he pulled on the zipper, opened it wide. The satchel was Carter's, probably older than both their ages combined, tan leather, brittle and cracked. Faded X-Men decals on the sides. Carter had put them there in the fifth grade, when he'd started using the old satchel to carry around all his X-Men paraphernalia. Lately, he had been using it to carry sketchbooks, projects in progress. It was that satchel Carter grabbed when they decided to go sit in a coffee shop at two or three in the morning.

In a zippered compartment inside the satchel, Carter kept a small handheld PC, about the size of a VHS cassette, equipped with a cellular modem. If someone had searched the bag carefully, the computer would not be there. But it was so small and slender, it might have survived a cursory glance.

Adam smiled as he closed his hand on the lightweight slice of plastic, unnoticed by Horowitz. He e-mailed Alyssa, instructed her to meet him in the Movies chat room at Yahoo. Then he waited, with no idea how long it would be before Alyssa found his e-mail. He channel-surfed with the television remote for awhile. The Superstation was showing a marathon of the old black-and-white series, *The Outer Limits*. Adam tossed the remote aside and lay back on the bed. Got comfortable so he could watch the show while he waited. And promptly fell asleep.

✝

He awoke four hours later, washed his face. Switched from the Superstation to Letterman on CBS. His computer — actually Carter's — was still online, and he had mail. Two notes from Alyssa. The first was excited, asked where he was, what had become of him, and why the strange e-mail address. The second, sent less than five minutes ago, simply said she was still waiting for him in the chat room he had specified.

Adam had neglected to tell her not to e-mail him, and wished he had. If Horowitz discovered the computer, he did not want to give her any proof that he had contacted anyone. He especially wanted to avoid involving Alyssa.

He went to Yahoo, logged onto the Movies chat room.

She was there, using the nickname he had given her. Adam was Nick666 and Alyssa was Nora666. There were sixty-two people in the chat room. Usually, more than half were kids much more interested in shouting obnoxiously in capital letters — "BRITNEY SPEERS IS THE MOST BODAYSHUS BABE WHO EVER LIVD!" — than in reading what anyone posted. In the rush to be the funniest, hippest, most informed or disgusting, no one would notice them.

Alyssa posted, "I miss you so much! I'm so sorry about Carter I didn't even know what happened till I got out there I didn't think I'd ever stop crying! Are you sure you're okay?"

"I'm better now that I've got you online."

They chatted for two hours. Adam did not want to end their conversation. She knew him, he could be himself with her. His life was suddenly filled with strangers. Alyssa was the only part of his real life that remained. But he knew if he did not end the conversation, neither would she, and they would still be chatting when the sun rose behind the smog in the morning.

"I have to go," he typed. "Need to get up early in the morning."

"To do what?"

"Prepare for the trial. Whatever that means. Won't be able to see each other for awhile."

"How long is 'awhile?'"

"I don't know. However long it takes. I'm sorry, Alyssa, it's not up to me. My life is in the hands of an uptight Munchkin who smokes beige cigarettes that smell like burning goat turds."

"LOL!" Alyssa replied. It stood for "Laughing Out Loud." "You mean R.H.?"

"Yes. You know how, at a circus, a little tiny car will pull into the ring, and then about a hundred little midget clowns pile out of it? Well, she's the one at the wheel kicking them out because they refused to wear the clothes she wants them to wear. She's got me wearing Armani suits. As long as you don't tell ANYBODY, we can stay in touch this way. Don't even tell Brett. And don't talk to the press. You're not obligated to answer ANY questions. By the way, have you heard from R.H.?"

"Heard from her? No. Should I?"

"Eventually. She's going to tell you I can't see you anymore—but DON'T BELIEVE IT! It's a long story, I'll tell you everything later. Don't tell her about chatting with me. Just act upset and get rid of her."

"There's no way I can see you? I miss you so much!"

"I think about you all the time. Every second."

"You're all I can think about, too. I want you on top of me, I want you inside me."

Someone using the nickname Barnstormer said, "Get a room, Nick and Nora. This is a family chat room!"

They agreed to meet in the chat room at noon the next day. If he was not there, Adam told her to keep checking until she found him. He did not know what his schedule would be yet, so he wasn't sure when he would be able to get back online.

They declared their love for one another in front of sixty faceless strangers, and said their goodnights. Adam went back to sleep thinking of Alyssa. And hoping that if he dreamed that night, it would be of her and nothing else.

FORTY

Adam dreamed of kissing Alyssa. They stood in a naked embrace, sucking each other's tongues as if for life. She pulled away from him and said, "Adam. Wake up."

He tried to pull her to him again, but his arms slid through her as she disappeared.

"Time to wake up, Adam!" The voice was female, but not Alyssa's.

Adam looked down. Horowitz stood where Alyssa had been, squat and naked and frowning, but somehow—and this made Adam cringe—not unattractive.

"Breakfast is getting cold," Horowitz said.

The dream vanished and Adam opened his eyes. Horowitz's face hovered over him like a balloon in the Macy's Thanksgiving Day Parade. He realized he was lying naked under a sheet, on his back with a tingling erection pointing at the ceiling. He rolled over and grabbed the blanket, pulled it over himself. Sat up and hugged his knees. "Out of one nightmare and into another," he said, groggy. "This is like a Brian DePalma movie."

"Shower and dress quickly," Horowitz said.

Adam looked at his bedside digital clock. The green numbers changed to 4:59 A.M. "It's only five o'clock," he said. "I've got another—"

"No, you do not. Get up immediately." She walked to the open double doors, turned to Adam. "We have a big day ahead of us." Leaned toward him slightly, a doorknob in each hand. "Actually, you have a big day ahead of you. There has been a development that re-quires our immediate attention. Now, hurry and come to breakfast." She pulled the doors closed as she backed out.

"Son of a bitch," Adam said as he got out of bed.

"I heard that," Horowitz called from the next room.

He rolled his eyes on the way to the shower. Muttered under his breath, "You…you…treacherous twat."

"I heard that, too."

He froze, cringed, and gooseflesh bubbled on his shoulders.

✝

Two months after his arrest, Adam Julian was all over television. For the first three weeks, one of his few outings showed up on televi-sion repeatedly. Newscasters spoke over footage of Adam leaving his hotel, entering the courthouse for his arraignment, leaving the court-house after his arraignment, or entering his hotel. In the clips, he wore a gray Armani suit with a plum-colored shirt and black-and-gray tie. Adam was afraid people would think he never changed his clothes. For three weeks, it was all the public saw of him, except for the high school photograph some news outlets used occasionally. Both CNN and Court TV used the footage in promos of their ongoing coverage of the story. CNN's was a grainy black and white, in slow motion, accompanied by melancholy strings and ominous, dirge-like drums. Court TV was calling their coverage "Murder in Beverly Hills," which made no sense to Adam because the actual murders had taken place off Marina del Rey.

The trial would not start until February, but it was already a highly-anticipated television event. Right after Adam was arrested, Michael Julian's movies began to show up everywhere. They ran on premium channels, broadcast networks, and all points in between. Two of them, neither intended to be a comedy, showed up on Comedy Central. TV Land was planning a marathon of episodes Michael had written for various television action series. Even American Cinematheque had scheduled a retrospective of Michael's movies to be shown at the Egyptian.

Horowitz's prediction about the four late-night television talk show hosts pulling Adam out like a rubber chicken whenever they wanted a laugh had not quite come true. Not yet. So far, Adam's name had been mentioned only twice, most memorably by Craig Kilborne, who admired Adam's "cool and collected" Armani suit, "which appears to be the only clothing Adam Julian owns." One night, he held a mock telethon to raise money to buy Adam Julian some new threads. Nothing the talk show hosts had said made Adam feel as if he were under attack. The frequency of the jokes dropped significantly in the second month. But Horowitz had promised him that would change.

"Maybe it won't," he had said.

"In that case," Horowitz had replied, "you would be a rare exception to the rule, and so far, nothing about your case is exceptional."

"What does that mean?"

"It means that yours is a relatively straightforward case with no surprises." She cocked her head and lifted a brow. "Unless there is something you have not told me."

Adam's television appearances were not nearly as frequent as Horowitz's. She had appeared at least once on all the morning happy-talk shows, five times on *Larry King Live*, and Adam had lost track of how many appearances she had made on *Rivera Live*. He had been surprised to see her on *The View*, the morning talk show hosted by Barbara Walters and her giggling sleepover of female cohosts. Horowitz did not strike Adam as the coffee klatch type.

One evening, Horowitz had come to Adam's room to go over some of the details of their story. They talked as she shuffled through a stack of folders and papers on the table. Horowitz often seemed capable of doing two separate things at the same time, like carrying on a conversation while reading through folders. But her multitasking had little endurance. As usual, she became preoccupied with something before her on the table, all talk forgotten for the moment.

Adam had stared at the television from his chair and channel-surfed as he waited for Horowitz to come back. Stopped on *Larry King Live*, where she had been a guest two nights before.

"What's Larry King like?" Adam asked, not expecting a reply.

He did not get one.

"Did he hit on you? I've heard he hits on most of the women who come on his show. A lot of people think he's a sleaze, but I really think the poor old dork honestly forgets he's married. Did he fart a lot?" He flipped over to CNBC, where Geraldo Rivera was talking to Gloria Allred. "How about Geraldo? Does he primp a lot? I've always imagined him as a primper."

A moment later, Horowitz lifted her head and said, "Pardon me, were you saying something?"

"What about Barbara Walters and her band of merry hens?" He laughed. "I bet you couldn't get off that show fast enough."

Horowitz frowned. "What on earth are you talking about?"

"*The View*. I was just wondering what they were like. You know, those talk show women. Are they like Stepford hosts? Do they giggle and yip like that all the time?"

"Are you serious?"

"Sure. Does Barbara Walters smell like mothballs?" He chuckled. "Do bronzed, oiled-up musclemen carry her everywhere on a canopied litter?"

Horowitz bowed her head as her shoulders bounced, and Adam realized she was laughing silently. When she spoke, there was no sign of it. "I do not know any of them. We hardly speak off camera. Sometimes they invite me to parties. Sometimes I go, sometimes I do not."

"What about Larry King? What shade of gray is he in real life, anyway?"

"I am speaking of all of the talk show hosts. I did not know the ones who came before them, and I will not know those who come after. You probably know more about them than I. They are simply people whose jobs allow me to go on television to further my client's cause."

"Okay, if you say so," Adam had said. He had continued channel surfing then. "But I bet Barbara Walters smells like mothballs."

Furthering Adam's cause was something Rona Horowitz did with amazing skill. He marveled at the transformation she underwent before the television cameras. In person, she was abrupt, rather chilly, not exactly uptight, but not someone to bring words like "relaxed" and "laid back" to mind. When she spoke in person, her words were clipped neatly around the edges and arranged perfectly, and even the most casual remark sounded like a prepared speech. She was angular, intense, sometimes distracted, always acutely alert. Television softened her, rounded her gently and made her quite pretty. Her voice was smooth and low, soothing, reassuring. She came across as a pleasant, intelligent, independent, confident woman, compassionate and fair, and devoted without reservation to her cause, which was Adam. When he watched Horowitz on television, he sometimes forgot he was the person she was talking about.

On *Larry King Live*, she said, "Adam first lost his mother in a swimming accident, then his father, stepmother, and stepsister in that awful explosion. And just days later, after all that pain, all that death, he watched helplessly as two uniformed officers of the Marina del Rey Police Department, Officer Stanley Pembroke and Officer Warren Buchwald, came through Adam's friend's house like stormtroopers and put two bullets through the brain of Carter Brandis, Adam's best friend since childhood, who was armed with nothing more than a squirt gun. On top of all that, he is accused of murdering his family. I don't know about you, Larry, but I'm not sure I could hold up under all that. But he is a strong young man, willing to cooperate fully and for as long as it takes, because he is innocent of these charges and because he believes in our judicial system."

To Geraldo Rivera, she said, "I have no doubt that Adam Julian's name will be cleared in court. You're an attorney, Geraldo, and I'm sure you share my great respect for juries. Well, once the facts are laid out, I don't think there's a jury in the world that would convict him."

On *The View*, she said, "Adam is just a boy who has lost his father…and has no mother to comfort him." It drew a simultaneous "awww" from the five cohosts and brought Meredith Vieira to the verge of tears.

Whenever she appeared on a show that took calls from viewers, Horowitz planted callers. Adam had recognized Lamont's voice on *TalkBack Live*: "If your client is innocent, then who really killed Michael Julian and his family?"

"That is a very good question, sir, and you aren't the only person asking it, I assure you. My client would also like to know what happened to his family, whether it was murder or a freak accident, and I think he has a right to know. Until Officers Stanley Pembroke and Warren Buchwald came storming into his house to shoot Carter Brandis to death, Adam had been told by Officer Miguel Ruiz of the Marina del Rey Police Department that the explosion was an accident. But if the worst an officer of the Marina del Rey Police Department does to you is lie, I suppose you should consider yourself quite lucky."

Adam shared the headlines with what comedian Lewis Black of *The Daily Show* called "Uncle Waldo's All-You-Can-Eat Summer Camp for Wayward Boys and Guns-N-Drugs Emporium". The raid on the desert compound was a blockbuster story by itself. It contained enough lurid sex, drugs, and guns for a dozen network miniseries and made-for-television movies. But its link to Adam, and the existence of Waldo Cunningham's client list, which authorities refused to discuss with the press, sent the media into a frenzy.

Reporters spoke of it as if it were an actual slip of paper with names listed on it, locked away in a secret safe. It became the Holy Grail of the tabloid papers, and it seemed an unspoken conclusion that, sooner or later, someone with access to that safe would cave under a wad of money offered by some fat, oily, sweaty-palmed tabloid reporter, and those names would fly with the leaves on the wind.

In the meantime, speculation was rampant. Betting pools sprang up on the Internet, where suddenly Michael Jackson pedophilia jokes were resurrected to a new life and were becoming so elaborate as to take on plots, themes, and characters. Names of celebrities, politicians, and religious leaders were tossed around as possible clients of Cunningham's in serious tones as well as in jest. Some were whispered, others laughed at out loud.

Six of the underage boys found in the compound had been reunited with their parents on *Good Morning America*, *Today*, *Oprah*, *TalkBack Live*, and *The Rosie O'Donnell Show*. One of them fled his parents outside 30 Rockefeller Plaza after their appearance on *Today*, disappeared in the crowd, and had not been seen since. Another sneaked out of his parents' Chicago hotel suite late at night as they slept after appearing on *Oprah* that day. He, too, remained missing.

Two unofficial biographies of Michael Julian were in the works, one by a former lover, another by some pseudonymous hack who wrote half a dozen movie novelizations and breathless celebrity bios a year. A third, written by Michael's first agent, already had been turned down by all the major houses. "Too bitter," explained an anonymous publishing source to a reporter at the *New York Post* column "Page Six."

The *National Enquirer* and other tabloids like *Star* magazine, the *Globe*, the *New York Post*, and even closet tabloids like the *Los Angeles Times*, *Newsweek*, and *Time* interviewed a string of women who claimed to have been Michael's lovers, one of whom said she had made love with him the day before his death, and another who claimed she once had heard Adam threaten Michael's life.

One tabloid even brought up the death of Adam's mother and implied, with all the subtlety of stampeding rhinos in Nieman-Marcus on Christmas Eve, that it might not have been an accident. The story had cut through Adam's numb haze and punched him in the chest. The idea of his suspicions being proven correct—being validated, as Lamont might say—in front of the whole world almost, *almost* made Adam happy. But he lacked the emotional muscle to be happy.

Adam had lost weight since his arrest. "You look like someone the Donner Party threw back," Lamont said one morning. "Start eating better or Rona will put a funnel in your mouth and forcefeed you."

Horowitz had begun to frighten him by the second week. She was irritating at first, sometimes infuriating, but he had expected that to pass. He'd expected her to become more of a real person who might have to break wind once in awhile, or who got the occasional zit or cold sore. But that did not happen. Her facade had been impenetrable so far.

Several times, Adam had found it necessary to sit himself down and have a stern talk with himself, to tell himself that Horowitz could *not* read his mind or see into the future, that she was *not* some kind of malevolent all-knowing goddess from the pages of a dusty book of mythology.

Like God, Horowitz moved in mysterious ways. Much of the time, Adam had no idea what she was talking about, but she always ended up making sense. She was capable of making the most mind-bogglingly insightful observations, and often appeared to possess an intellect equal to that of Sherlock Holmes. But within the same minute, she could exhibit stunning absent-mindedness. When she looked at him, Adam felt she could see through him, into him, see his heart beating. Until her blue eyes narrowed a bit and twinkled with a smile that did not involve her mouth. Whenever she did that—and it was usually when he needed it most—she put Adam at ease, an immediate reaction which lasted much longer than the smile itself.

Dr. Locket, a trim dignified man in his fifties with the shiniest shoes Adam had ever seen, took blood and urine samples every few weeks. Sometimes he adjusted Adam's dosage, or replaced one medication with another. The pills kept Adam stable, but it was a false stability. Enough for him to maintain control of his hostility, but not enough for him to feel confident about that control.

His therapist, Dr. Remini, who looked like a dressed-up Betty Crocker, met with him three times a week for a sample of his neuroses. More than anything else, they talked about movies, so it was not unenjoyable. She was a lover of old movies and they shared several favorites. But it seemed to Adam they should be talking about more important things. When he said as much, Dr. Remini said, "Everything you say is important, Adam. You should always remember that."

"I mean, shouldn't we be talking about me, or something?" he had asked.

"We're always talking about you."

✝

Adam stepped out of the bedroom fully dressed about twenty-five minutes later, and Horowitz offered her unsolicited critique of his economy with time. The suite's living room was rich with the smell of bacon, eggs, and coffee, and the news was on television. He heard his name mentioned and stepped in front of the set, but the picture winked out. He turned around to see Horowitz putting the remote on the coffee table, striking in a black and white suit with a '40s flavor, and a sparkling diamond-and-onyx salamander brooch on the left lapel.

"Help yourself," she said, and went to the table, sat down to her breakfast, which she had already started.

Lamont was already at the table. His suit coat was on the back of the chair and the sleeves of his canary-yellow shirt were rolled almost to his elbows. He ate as he read a newspaper from a stack of papers on the floor beside his chair.

The comforting breakfast smells were marred by the ugly stink of Horowitz's cigarette, which smouldered in an ashtray beside her plate. "I knocked," she said, looking over some papers scattered around her breakfast. "But you did not—" She lifted her head suddenly, looked around. "Where is my fork?"

"Did you take it into the bathroom with you?" Lamont asked.

Horowitz went to the bathroom and returned with her fork. Sat down again. "But you did not answer."

Breakfast was set out on the sideboard. Adam got a plate. "That's because I was asleep," he said, dishing up scrambled eggs. "Which I usually am until about seven o'clock. What were they saying about me on the news?"

"I woke you early because we need to talk. We need to talk because of what they were saying about you on the news."

Adam poured himself a cup of coffee and sat at the table.

Horowitz said, "It seems a young newspaper reporter —"

"Editor," Lamont said. "Of a junior college paper in Oregon. Now he thinks he's Matt Drudge."

"This young editor saw something on the Internet that he found interesting. Something that became even more interesting under close scrutiny. It was in a chat room late one night."

Adam stopped chewing, closed his eyes. It did not look good, not at all. But the eggs were delicious.

"He became convinced that you and your girlfriend were chatting on the Internet under the names Nick666 and Nora666. With no clue what he had on his hands, this young newspaper editor mentioned it in his column. Students at the college began to look for Nick and Nora in the chat room. Everyone wondered if it really could be the teenager accused of murdering his rich and famous father and family. But whenever anyone tried to chat with the couple, Nick and Nora would stop chatting, or even leave the room. Lately, it seems they have been using a private room to chat. But before that happened, word spread very quickly. It was all over the Internet in the click of a mouse. I am really quite surprised you did not notice it, Adam. Someone at the *Los Angeles Times* did. They broke the story this morning. It is everywhere. Unlike all the reporters in the western hemisphere, who are *here*, outside this hotel."

It was worse than he had thought.

"We just chatted," Adam said firmly. "We didn't talk about the case. I didn't even tell her where I am. Mostly we talked about stuff she was doing. Movies, books. We'd listen to *The Don and Mike Show* on the radio together. That kind of thing. We didn't even pay attention to the other people in the chat room. Just each other. Maybe we said hi to a couple people, I don't know. Once or twice, people have started chatting with us. But we go there to chat with each other, so we avoid them, we don't even notice them."

"Ah, young love," Horowitz said with the twitch of her brow.

"I suppose you're going to take away the handheld, now. To keep me off the 'net."

"Of course not. You cannot very well chat with people on the Internet if you have no access to it. I will have the laptop you requested brought in later today."

He stopped eating again. Put down his fork. "Wait, uh, chat with…with people?"

"Yes. I want you to continue your chats with your girlfriend."

"She has a name," Adam said, annoyed. "Alyssa."

"Go on meeting with her at the same time and place. But I want you to chat with other people as well. In fact, it will be important that you spend more time chatting with them than with each other. Be friendly, answer questions. Make it clear that you cannot discuss the case, but chat with them about anything else. And get along with them, Adam. Do you understand? Do not pick or get dragged into any fights. You need to be everyone's buddy."

"What is the big deal?" Adam asked. "It's just innocent chat, for crying out loud! There was nothing dirty. If we get horny, we go to a private room. I don't see why anyone would be interested in anything we said. It's not a big deal."

Lamont looked up from the newspaper. "It's a big deal because it's *you*, you ninny."

"The night we met," Horowitz said, "I said you were already a celebrity, the public simply did not know what to do with you yet. So far, we have been lucky. They still do not know what to do with you. That means we have time to make up their minds for them. You are the son of a famous Hollywood screenwriter, accused of murdering your family, and your best friend was shot to death in front of you by two police officers. But you have no…hook. You have nothing to set you apart and make you unique in the eyes of the public. What happened to your friend has gotten you a lot of sympathy, but it will not last. They have no reason to feel any animosity toward you, but neither do they have any reason to like you, to identify with you in some way. Kyle and Eric Menendez had the fact that they were brothers. With Amy Fisher, there was sex. And forbidden sex, at that, because she was underage."

Adam was chilled by an unavoidable thought of Rain.

"You, Adam," Horowitz went on, "will be the first celebrity accused of murder with whom everyone can chat on the Internet."

Adam stared at her for a long moment. "You've got to be kidding."

"You know I do not kid, Adam," she said.

"We'll be laughed right off Court TV. They'll put a laughtrack on the trial."

"Not a chance. There may be some heat to take for it, but it will be minimal, and *I* will take it. That is why you pay me the big bucks. The public, on the other hand, will eat it up. Your accessibility alone will work tremendously in your favor. But you will drop the 666 from your nicknames."

"Why? Everybody's already seen us with those—"

"Not everybody. You will drop it because you have enough problems without aligning yourself with the Beast of Revelation, Adam."

"And how can I be a celebrity accused of murder when I'm not a celebrity?" Adam asked.

Lamont said wearily, "You *are* a celebrity."

"But I wasn't a celebrity when I was accused of murder!"

"Being accused of murder was what *made* you a celebrity," Lamont said.

"Your father was famous," Horowitz said. "Fame is hereditary."

Adam turned to her and asked, "Do you know how many cretins…how many lunatics and nutburgers I'd have to deal with if I did something like that?"

Lamont chuckled as he got another newspaper from the stack.

"Within a couple days," Horowitz said, "we will have a website up with full-time webmasters and a chatroom. That way, we can kick out or ban the unsavories. I have someone working on it right now."

"A website? Are you having some kind of neurological problem I should know about?"

"I told you he wouldn't like it," Lamont said.

Horowitz turned to him, irritated. "And I told you it would not make a difference." To Adam again: "I am not asking for your approval. I will hold a press conference tomorrow. You will be with me, but you will not answer questions."

"Why tomorrow?"

"We want to give them a day to talk about it, think about it. Not too long. Just long enough." She put her fork down noisily on the plate. Folded her hands beneath her chin, elbows on the table. "You have made an effort to curb your conversational profanities, and I appreciate that. Although you owe me, to date, over twenty-two thousand dollars on top of my regular fee. But your attitude has not changed. I still do not think you have fully grasped the severity of your situation."

"No, Spock, it has grasped *me*." Anger bubbled low in Adam's voice. "By the balls."

Lamont *tsk*ed as he made a note on his yellow legal pad.

"Tell me, Adam, do you always talk to and behave around people the way you talk to and behave around myself and Lamont?"

Adam put the last of his breakfast, a lump of hash browns with eggs on top, into his mouth. Slid the plate aside as he chewed, dabbed his mouth with a napkin. "I don't know what you're talking about. What way?"

"In a smartass way," Lamont said.

Horowitz said, "Thank you so much, Lamont, but that will be enough."

Lamont set aside the last newspaper, sat back and watched them like a tennis match.

Horowitz pushed her plate aside and lit another cigarette. "I cannot put my finger on it. It is nebulous, but unmistakable. The same attitude that has kept Robert Downey, Jr. from becoming a star."

"Drugs are what have kept Robert Downey, Jr. from becoming a star," Adam snapped.

"Not true," she said with a shake of her head. "He had plenty of time to become a star before his problems with the law. Then he could have used those problems to his advantage, climbed them right to the top. They were the keys to doors of opportunity. But he kept doing drugs because he could not catch on in Hollywood. The drugs were his way of dealing with failure, not the cause of it. He is a failure because whether he is acting or not, he is simply irritating. In much the same way you are. It does not test well, Adam. People do not like it."

"He's kind of like a Bill Murray without the charm," Lamont said.

Horowitz pointed a finger at Lamont. "Exactly."

"Smug."

"Yes, there is a great deal of smugness there."

"I'm smug?" Adam asked, shocked.

"Like he's already seen it all, done it all," Lamont said.

"Yes," Horowitz said, looking into Adam's eyes. "You are very smug, Adam."

"Hey, I come from the kingdom of smug," Adam said. "They give out awards for smugness, it's an olympic event. I know smug, and I'm nothing like those people."

"Perhaps not," she said. "But you are smug nevertheless. In a different way. You are smug in your disillusionment."

"What the—um, what does that mean?"

"Lamont is right. You behave as if everything is old news to you. You believe in nothing. Everything is a joke to you, fodder for your snide remarks. You rejected Hollywood because it represented your father. You hate everyone in the business and everything it stands for. But you are angry, as well."

"Yes, there's a lot of anger," Lamont said. "Maybe because he loves movies so much."

"Ah, yes, there is something to that, I think, Lamont. He loves movies, even though they represent everything he has been rebelling against. Everything he knows, he has learned from movies. Which is why he is not handling this process very well. The movies never show the boring parts. Or the ugly parts. Like not being able to see your girlfriend."

Adam said, "Would you at least pretend you know I'm in the room?"

"Perhaps that is at the root of your problem, Adam," Horowitz said. "Your inability to resist the thing you claim to hate has created a great deal of conflict in you, I think. You mask that conflict with a snide, too-cool attitude, saying whatever pops into your mind that might get a laugh and take attention away from your own weaknesses in the face of your inner battle, no matter how much damage it might do to the feelings of others. And on top of that, you are bottling up your emotions."

Adam pushed his chair back from the table, but did not stand. "I've got a therapist *and* a psychiatrist, I don't need to be analyzed by an attorney!"

"No, I will leave that to them." She leaned toward Lamont. "I would, however, like to discuss that with Locket and Remini. Schedule a conference call this afternoon." She stood and walked slowly around the table, trailing cigarette smoke. "I know you are upset about having to let Mrs. Yu go, Adam, but you have no choice. There are no

options. It is not a matter of someone deciding to do this, it is something you simply must do, like paying your taxes and getting older.
The sale of your house is being arranged. Until then, the staff has
been dismissed and the house closed up. I am very sorry, but it is no
one's fault. There is no blame. But even if there were, we would not
have time to deal with it. We have time for nothing but your upcom-
ing trial. Please put it behind you as quickly as possible, Adam, so
that we can get on with this process. Will you do that?"

Adam nodded once.

"Your attitude has done us no harm as yet. But the moment you
leave your cocoon here, all you will have is everything I have tried to
teach you, everything I have told you. And you have not been paying
attention. You still do not understand how important that is. Even
though I will be standing right beside you, I cannot very well tell you
what to say in front of the whole world, can I? In spite of my best
efforts, and those of my staff, you are not prepared to face what awaits
you outside this hotel, Adam."

Adam's shoulders sagged wearily as he asked, "Then what do
you want me to do? Tell me! You never really talk *to* me, have you
noticed that? You talk around me. In the general vicinity."

"Are you unable to ask questions?" Horowitz asked. "To speak
up? For some reason other than to make a smug observation or an
ugly remark? You have not become involved in this process. You do
not care." She stopped beside him. "You have to care, Adam. Your
life is at stake." Walked around the table again in the opposite direction. "You need to be humbled. I think that will happen as soon as
you step outside tonight."

"Tonight? I thought the press conference was tomorrow."

"It is. Tonight, we are going out to dinner. We are going to let the
world take a look at you and see what they think."

A grin split his face open. "Are you serious?" He was ecstatic. The
thought of leaving the hotel, just going outside, made him feel giddy.

"Yes. We have an eight-thirty reservation at *Chinois*. Photographers
and scribes will pursue us like Rwandan death squads. They will be
on you every second, Adam. And when that happens, I want you to
look around. Look at their faces, their mouths. Pay attention to the
way they behave. And think about what your life would be like right
now without me. *Then*…remember everything I have told you, and
do it."

Suddenly in a jubilant mood, Adam didn't even consider a sarcastic remark. He nodded and said, "Okay. I will."

"You have lost weight," she said. "I am putting you on a diet and a rigid exercise program. We want you to look *sym*pathetic, not just pathetic. The hotel has a wonderful gym. You will never go there alone, but it will get you out of the room a few times a week." She gathered up the papers on the table, handed them to Adam. "Copies of your chat with Alyssa."

"Copies?" He took the papers, frowned as he looked them over. "From where?"

"Our college newspaper editor in Oregon logged all your chats as soon as he suspected your identities," Lamont said. "The *Times* printed segments of it."

Adam's face screwed up into a mask of confusion. "They printed it? In the newspaper? B-but…why? It doesn't have anything to do with whether or not I killed anybody. Why would anyone want to read that? It's just chat."

Horowitz smiled. "It's perfect," she said.

Max walked Adam down to the gym shortly after one that afternoon. Each wore sweats, Adam's blue and white, Max's green and blue. "I'm not just doin' this to be friendly, y'know," Max said on the way. "The Queen Mum has decided we gotta buff you up a little. Gave me a list of the machines you're s'posed to work on." Adam could not decide if Max had a faded southern accent or simply spoke lazily. "If I can't get you to do it, she's gonna bring in one of them personal trainers. You know the typa guy I'm talkin' about? Perfect hair? Every move he makes is a pose and all he talks about is his body? This muscle, that muscle, how much he can press. Drive you crazier'n a shithouse rat in no time. So if I were you, I wouldn't give me any trouble."

The gym was empty, the equipment looked abandoned. They slowly made their way from one machine to the next. Max loosened Adam up with small talk before getting serious.

"How well did you know Gwen?" he asked.

Adam's guard went up. "What do you mean?"

"Know anything about her past?" Max asked.

"Only what I've told you. She was married before, her husband died in a housefire recently."

"Ever heard of a woman named Rhonda Chasen?"

Adam thought the name over, shook his head. "No. Should I have?"

Max sat up and turned on the bench toward Adam. "How about Jennifer Gordon? Ruth Schaffer? Elizabeth Ryan?"

Frowning, Adam sat up and turned on the bench to face Max. Adam's muscles burned, but he did not mind. It meant he was still capable of feeling something without coming to pieces. "They've got something to do with Gwen?" he asked.

"They *were* Gwen. Or Gwen was them. Whichever."

"What? That…that's insane. Why would she need four—"

"I was just lookin' for information on Gwen Cardell, nothin' else. But these couple names kept poppin' up. Then a couple more. Confused the hell outta me at first. Took me a couple days of pokin' around, but then I tripped right into it, and it was a hell of a fall. Seems your stepmama was at least four wanted women, not counting who she was when she died. She was wanted in four states under four aliases. Still is, a-course, 'cause they don't know she's gone. Far as I can tell— I gotta dig a little deeper—she had bank accounts under those aliases, including Swiss bank accounts and one in the Cayman Islands."

"What's she wanted for?"

"Oh, lessee. Extortion, conspiracy to extort, murder, conspiracy to murder, armed robbery, grand theft aut—"

"Murder?"

"Oh, yeah. It's like a Whitman's Sampler of criminal charges."

"Who did she murder?"

Max's droopy face hardened a bit. "Nobody. She's only been *accused* of murder. You understand the difference?"

"Innocent until proven guilty," Adam said with a nod. "When I mentioned that to Rona, she said it was a myth."

"Seems that way sometimes. But just 'cause it *seems* like a myth on television and in the newspapers and even in the courts don't mean it's gotta be a myth in our heads. That's where it all starts, in our heads."

"Who was she accused of murdering?"

"Wanna take a guess?"

Adam shook his head once. He hoped his face did not reveal the fact that he had a pretty good idea what Max was going to say.

"Husbands," Max said. "Wealthy ones. Four of 'em. That I know of so far."

Adam's eyes wandered away from Max. For a moment, he was hunkering in Rain's closet again, listening to her conversation with Gwen. He had told Horowitz nothing about it, of course. He'd considered, briefly, telling her absolutely everything about his relationships with Gwen and Rain, about Rain's threats, and what they had said while he was in the closet. But it was all so much like a bad novel, he was certain she would never buy it. Besides, the story did not hold together well if he left out the fact that he, Adam, was considering killing his dad at the time, too. That he had decided to commit murder. He had sworn to himself he would not confess to the crime, and making that admission would be tantamount to a confession. Instead, he had told Horowitz and her staff everything but those particular details.

Now he knew for sure that Rain had been telling the truth about her mother's habitual widowhood.

"Dad was going to be the fifth," Adam muttered, not meaning to.

"Sure looks that way, don't it?" Max smacked Adam's shoulder with a big hand. "Less go back to the room," he said. "We gotta talk."

Rain told the truth about Gwen, Adam thought, going back to the room with Max. *Then she probably told the truth about everything else, too. Every rotten ugly thing. Like being dumped in an unfamiliar city at night by her mother when she was ten.*

Neither spoke going up in the elevator, and they were in the room nearly a full minute before Max finally broke the silence between them.

"Is there somethin' you're not tellin' me, son?" He sat on the sofa, put his feet on the coffee table, crossed at the ankles.

Adam stood in the middle of the room, a young buck frozen by the glaring headlights of an oncoming Peterbilt. "Whuh-what do you mean?"

Max shrugged. "Just askin'. Seems she had a little routine she followed with each husband. She'd marry a man who not only had a lot of money, but a teenage son, too. I'm thinkin' she'd seduce the son, convince him the old man's beatin' her, or somethin' like that, and talk the boy into killin' his daddy for her. Looks like she might've knocked off one of the sons when she was through with him, too. But that's all speculation."

Don't show anything, keep your face exactly as it is, Adam thought. He felt heavy all of a sudden and lowered himself into a chair. "Do the police know this?"

"Not yet. They're not lookin' for nothin' on your stepmom. She's a victim. They're lookin' for anything they can find on *you*."

"Will they find it?"

"Dunno. Maybe. If so, it'll be a big mess unless we pull the reins on it first."

"What happens then?"

"Once the D.A. gets his paws on this? Well, he ain't gonna do *you* no favors, I can tell ya that. They'll use it against you, a-course. Say she seduced you, talked you into it, you did it for her. But something went wrong. You killed them all when it was only supposed to be your daddy. Or maybe you liked her idea so much, you decided to kill 'em all and keep Daddy's fortune to y'self. Somethin' like that."

Adam became aware that his mouth was hanging open and he closed it. "And what would we do?"

"If that happened?" Max looked up at the ceiling for a moment, lower lip tucked thoughtfully beneath his mustache. "Well, first of all, Rona'd butcher you like the fatted calf and we'd have ourselves a helluva barbeque." He smiled.

Adam sank back into the chair.

"You think I'm kiddin'?" Max asked.

"No."

"That's some pretty heavy news. She'd be mighty upset she found out you'd been keeping it from her. So, uh...y'say you knew about Gwen's past?"

"I said that? I didn't say that. Did I? No, I didn't. I mean, no, I didn't know anything about Gwen's past," Adam lied, avoiding eye contact. He had not known all those details, so it was not a complete lie. He met Max's eyes and asked, "What about Rain?"

Max shrugged. "Dund exist, far as I can tell. No Social Security number, no records of any kind. She's stayed outside the system."

Adam knew that was not possible. Rain might have pulled a train for some cops to dismiss an offense once, but surely she could not have done that with *all* of her offenses. There had to be some record — an arrest for vandalism, theft, giving Santa a blow job in the middle of a shopping mall, something.

"Well, you didn't know. That's what I needed to find out." Max stood. "We didn't have this conversation. *Comprende?*"

"You haven't told Rona yet?" Adam stood, too, feeling a little fear for the man.

"Just put it all together m'self. Figgered I'd run it by you first. See if you knew anything about Gwen's resume. If you did, we was gonna have to figger out the safest way to break it to her." In the doorway, he turned to Adam. "Like I said before, anything comes to you, you got my number."

Adam nodded and said, "See ya."

✝

That evening, Adam took a shower before dressing for dinner. His conversation with Max dominated his thoughts. He wondered if there was some way he could use Gwen's past and what he knew about Rain to save himself. Could the revelation that Gwen had been a serial husband-killer, used properly, get the case dismissed and Adam's charges dropped? He had no idea. Everything he knew about law he had learned from Steven Bochco, David E. Kelley, and *Night Court* reruns.

But his worries had not dampened the excitement of going out that night. He was so anxious, he'd chewed his fingernails most of the afternoon, something he had not done in years. While he was excited about getting out of the hotel, he had not forgotten Horowitz's warnings. He knew second- and third-hand what animals reporters could be, but had not experienced it himself. Maybe Horowitz was wrong. It could happen. Maybe they would turn out to be more like a bunch of Camp Fire Girls than a Rwandan death squad.

Adam was drying his back in the steamy bathroom when someone knocked on his door. He slipped on the hotel robe and went into the living room. No one ever knocked. Everyone walked in and out of the room like it was an airport terminal. "Who is it?" he asked.

A small, timid voice spoke on the other side of the door. He went to the door, put his eye to the peep-hole and gasped.

It was Alyssa.

FORTY-TWO

They barely made it to the bed. While Alyssa took off her shoes, jeans, and shirt, Adam closed and locked the bedroom door, then wedged a heavy chair beneath the knob.

Afterward, coming down, they lay on their sides, fondled one another.

"What are you doing here?" Adam asked with a grin. "How did you find my room?"

"Some guy named Lamont called me this morning, said he worked for your attorney. He said you needed my help and a car would pick me up at four."

"And you fell for it? My God, it could have been anybody!"

"Oh, please. Like I'm gonna ask him for some identification over the phone, or something? You're too paranoid. It didn't feel hinky to me. So here I am."

"I'm glad."

"Yes, you were." She smiled. "Feels like you're already getting glad again."

Adam pinched her nipple and waggled her breast. Alyssa broke into giggles and tried to pull away, but he held her close. Kissed her, mid-giggle.

"All those reporters outside are here for you?" she asked.

"I think so."

"Are they always there?"

"I don't pay any attention to them. I don't even watch them on TV anymore."

"If you never come out of the hotel, and they know that, then why do they stay?"

"In case I do come out, I guess."

"And you're going to reward them with an appearance tonight, huh?"

"How did you know?"

She rolled onto her back, stretched her arms and legs. "Lamont. That's why I'm here. I'm going out to dinner with you tonight."

"A date!"

"Yeah!"

"In front of the whole world."

"Uh-huh. It'll be like I'm dating Ricky Martin, or something."

"Except *I'll* have sex with you," Adam said with a chuckle.

She rolled on top of him, lay there with her nose touching his. "How bad can it be? Sounds like it might even be fun."

"What, being stalked by the press? Rona talks about them like they're the coming Apocalypse. Tonight will be my baptism by fire. Did Lamont tell you about our following on the Internet?"

"I saw it on the news when I got up this morning." She smiled. "I was so, I was like…I'm famous, but nobody knows it's me! And I can't tell anybody!"

"How long can you stay?"

"I don't know."

Adam gently pushed her off him and sat up, got serious. "You know what's going to happen after tonight, don't you?"

"I get to move in here with you?" Alyssa asked with a grin. "This bed is heaven."

"No, I mean, you're going to be a celebrity, for one thing. As soon as you step outside of the building with me. You're already a celebrity on the Internet, they just don't know who you are. As soon as they find out, some of those reporters down there are going to camp outside your front door, follow you around, look into your life. And your parents' lives."

Alyssa sat up, too. "I'm going to be linked to my parents in the press? Shit."

Horowitz already knew about Sunny's and Mitch's drug activity. Introducing Alyssa to the media would leave them vulnerable to discovery. Adam thought, *Rona knows that. Why would she do this if it's going to be a problem?*

"Didn't anyone tell you I was coming today?" Alyssa asked.

"Believe me, I'd remember that. Nobody even hinted."

"You think they're trying to keep it from you?"

Adam laughed. "That's all they do here. I only know what Rona wants me to know."

The first two fingers of Alyssa's hand walked sneakily across Adam's thigh. "You're not as glad as you were a few minutes ago," she said, a pout in her voice.

"Stick around." He smiled as he lay back. "I feel some gladness coming on."

✝

Horowitz lit one of her beige cigarettes and inhaled deeply. The pleasure of it relaxed her whole face, as if it were her first smoke in a long while. She sat in a chair in Adam's suite facing the open doorway of the bedroom, where he was dressing for dinner. Alyssa was doing the same thing in the suite next door.

"How many times do I have to tell you not to concern yourself with these things?" she asked.

"I'm thinking of Alyssa. I don't want to do anything that'll screw up her life."

"I spoke with Mr. and Mrs. Huffman this morning and explained the situation to them. They are quite willing to curb their illegal activities until the trial is over."

"You just called them up and said, 'Hi, this is Rona, and look, I know you're potheads, but could you knock it off until this thing blows over?'"

"All you need to know is that the problem has been taken care of. When will you learn to trust me?"

"It's not that. I just don't want to make trouble for her. Or humiliate her in front of the entire planet." He was quiet for a moment, then muttered, "She's all I've got left."

"Alyssa will be fine. I discussed it with her, she knows what she is getting into."

"Does she know you talked to her mom?"

"No, and you will not tell her. Just forget we discussed it and enjoy yourself tonight. Look, Adam, I do not have time to explain each and every detail of this case to you as we go along. If you have questions, talk to Lamont. Or Max."

"But you're the only one who doesn't say, 'Talk to Rona.'"

"I am not keeping anything from you. Anything important, anyway. If something comes up that I need to discuss with you, I assure you I will. Meanwhile, you need to work on improving your health, healing your wounds. You need to save your energy for when you really need it. And you *will* need it Adam, I assure you. I hope you will see that tonight."

By the time Alyssa entered the room, Adam was finished dressing. She looked beautiful.

"It's a Chanel," she said, showing off the black-and-white dress provided by Horowitz. She stepped close to him, put her hands on his chest and stroked his lapels. "And don't you look all handsome and studly. Like a movie star."

"Take that back!" Adam said with mock indignation.

Horowitz stood and said, "I need to change for dinner. Please exercise self control after I leave. There will be no sex before dinner. We do not want your clothes and hair mussed, and besides, Lamont will be here soon to get you. I will see you downstairs in a few minutes. Remain calm, do not panic. And remember everything I told you this evening, both of you. All right?"

Adam nodded and Horowitz left.

"I can't believe she just told us not to have sex," Alyssa said, shocked.

"Stick around long enough, you'll hear her tell me how to fold the paper when I wipe."

Lamont knocked on the door later and the three of them went downstairs. Horowitz waited in a corner of the lobby.

Adam did a double take when he saw her. She never wore anything but business suits, which he had come to think of as her uniform. But tonight, she wore a lovely peach dress. It was conservative, but displayed a hint of cleavage and gave her a shape he had not known she possessed.

"You both look wonderful," Horowitz said with a quick twitch of a smile. "Our car just drove up. The reporters outside have thinned out quite a bit. They will be *so* disappointed to hear they missed us."

Just outside the doors, the late-summer heat and thick, damp air immediately began their assault on Adam. After spending most of the last eight weeks inside the air-conditioned, pleasant-smelling hotel, he almost had forgotten what the air outside was like.

As Horowitz had said, there were not many reporters waiting outside with their cameras and microphones and tiny cassette recorders. Maybe a dozen. They looked so bored, so lost. Standing there with nothing to do. Nothing to report.

They were halfway across the sidewalk and the driver was opening the rear door of the limousine when the reporters noticed them. They sprang to life and rushed toward them in a flurry of footsteps and voices. Adam caught fragments of their shouted questions.

"Mr. Julian, are you—"

"Who's the girl with—"

"Are you Nick and Nora?"

"—that you murdered your father and —"

"Who do you think blew up the—"

"In you go," Horowitz said.

Alyssa and Adam got into the limousine first, followed by Lamont. The reporters immediately aimed their questions at Horowitz, who spoke as she slowly eased into the car.

"Excuse me, I am sorry, but we are not—no, really, I am sorry, we are not answering any questions right now," she said pleasantly, smiling. "We would like to have a quiet dinner out this evening, and we hope you will respect that. Thank you. See you tomorrow at the press conference." The driver closed the door solidly. She sat facing Adam and Alyssa.

"A quiet dinner out?" Adam asked. "Were you going for a laugh, there?"

"They like it when their targets are civil, or even friendly with them," she replied. "So few are these days. They are such a sad lot, reporters. They have fallen so far out of touch with the people they originally were supposed to represent that they have forgotten what it is they are supposed to be doing. They are grateful to those who show them a little respect. Whether they deserve it or not. Always remember, Adam, you get more flies with honey."

"I hate honey." He leaned forward and looked out the window to his right. In the last gray light of day, the reporters and cameramen scattered, most of them talking on cellphones.

"Will they follow us?" Alyssa asked.

"They will try," Horowitz said. "But they are already putting the word out. Tonight, the city of Los Angeles will undergo a tabloid dragnet. Those phone calls will lead to other phone calls, which will lead to more phone calls. Alerts will be sounded. Everyone from doormen to busboys will be looking for you two, hoping to be the first with the news, worth a handsome bonus from whatever paper or columnist or infotainment show keeps them on a retainer. There are always some photographers and press types outside *Chinois*, but by the time we arrive, their number will have doubled at least. And there will be many more by the time we come out."

"Can't we go out the back way and avoid them, or something?" Adam asked.

Horowitz gave him a quick, harsh look of distaste. "We did not come out tonight to *avoid* them. I thought you were paying attention, Adam. This entire evening is for their benefit."

"Well, I hope they enjoy themselves," Adam said.

It was common to see photographers and entertainment reporters loitering in and around restaurants frequented by celebrities. Wolfgang Puck's *Chinois* on Main was such a place. Its small, simple, white-and-turquoise storefront in Santa Monica was so unobtrusive, it was easy to miss on the first pass. But not tonight.

"Let me guess," Adam said, looking forward through the open divider and the limousine's windshield. "That's our welcoming committee."

The limousine slowed as it neared a shifting clot of people on the sidewalk in front of the restaurant. Stopped just before it reached the crowd.

"I took the precaution of assigning two of my security men to the restaurant," Horowitz said. "I anticipate no trouble, but I believe in being prepared. You will recognize them when you see them."

Leo got out of the limousine and walked around to the door, opened it for them.

"Follow me," Horowitz said. She got out first.

Adam squeezed Alyssa's thigh. Put his right foot out of the car. Rose as he leaned out.

Hands holding microphones consumed his field of vision in an instant. Faces with rapidly working mouths surged toward him. "Mr. Julian" was repeated so many times in the space of a second, it ceased to mean anything, became gibberish. Their questions fell in on him like the walls of a collapsing mine shaft, the rubble of words piling up around him, on him. They pressed in, swallowed up his air like swirling, lung-blackening coal dust.

Adam quickly lost all self-consciousness, unaware of the slack in his jaw, the panic in his oversized eyes. Cameras whirred and flashed, urgent voices yammered on. Question after question. But he could hear none of them. His body shrank inward and he tried to press his shoulders together to keep from touching the photographers and reporters as they moved in closer, closer. He frantically looked for Horowitz, but it was as if she had disappeared. He spun around, prepared to throw himself back through the car's open door.

The limousine was gone. He was separated from it by more microphones and cameras and jabbering mouths. They surrounded him. Kept moving in, microphones stabbing at him.

Look at their faces, Horowitz had said.

Pale beneath the restaurant's outdoor lights. Eyesockets scooped empty by black shadows.

At their mouths. Pay attention to the way they behave.

They were a staggering, groping band of black-and-white George Romero zombies. Filthy teeth with bloody bits of flesh stuck between them, lips moving in a frenzy over them. Their voices groaned, darkened lips formed words garbled by swollen tongues: *What have you done, Adam Julian? What have you done?*

Then, Horowitz had said, *remember everything I have told you. And do it.*

What had she told him? What was he supposed to do? He could not remember, could not think. His breath came faster and faster as they moved in on him even more, leaving him no space, no room to move, no way out. He turned his head in bird-like jerks, looking for Rona, Alyssa, Lamont, Leo, anyone familiar. All he saw were the cameras, the greedy faces of babbling strangers with hungry mouths eager to take bloody, jagged bites out of his life.

A large hand gripped Adam's right elbow. A male voice said, "This way, Mr. Julian."

Adam turned to the large man in a black suit who had appeared beside him and said, "Thank you, oh, Jesus Christ, thank you so much."

Smiling, Horowitz sang out, "If you would just let us have a peaceful dinner, I will answer all your questions tomorrow."

The crowd quieted down and seemed to back off a step. Cameras continued to snicker and whisper.

The man clutching Adam's arm said, with no warmth, "Excuse us, excuse us, please." Pulled him past the staring faces and jackhammering jaws.

They were inside the restaurant and the crowd was gone. Like stepping indoors out of a terrible storm. He leaned against a wall, breathless, as Alyssa took his trembling hand, stood beside him. Horowitz appeared in front of him, looked him over curiously.

"Well?" she said. "Do you understand now why I have worked so hard to prepare you for this?"

"I...I..." Adam gave up. He could not speak. His legs were so weak and shaky, he could barely stand. He simply nodded.

Beside him, Alyssa hugged his arm to her. Her brow furrowed above wide eyes. "Are they always like that?"

"Oh, no," Horowitz replied. "In cases like this, they are typically much worse. When we leave, there will be at least three times as many, and they might not be so civilized."

Adam had eaten at *Chinois* a few times. Always at his dad's insistence and against his own will. Not because he disliked the food, but because he disliked eating with his dad. It was always busy, lunch or dinner. Tonight was no different.

The restaurant had been decorated by Puck's wife, Barabara Lazaroff, in fuchsia, green, and black. Tile and brick walls, stone floors, and the oddest tables Adam had ever seen in a restaurant—turquoise and serpentine-shaped, they looked like giant squiggles of confetti.

Adam recognized a lot of faces in the crowd. Some looked familiar but he could not give them names. Most were faces he had been seeing around all his life. Charlton Heston and his wife dining with another couple. Jerry Bruckheimer with a boisterous group. Susan Sarandon and Tim Robbins. A producer here, a director there, an actor from some prime time hospital soap opera. There were others, but Adam's eyes skipped over them, a flat rock on glassy water. All of them laughing and talking and drinking.

Until they saw Adam. The noise level dropped gradually as heads turned and eyes lifted toward him. The room did not fall silent, but all the chattering voices lowered except one. A boisterous female voice: " —guy said, 'Well, if I put it in any deeper, your *mother* will, too!'" She blatted loud laughter at her own joke, then prattled on, oblivious to the shift of attention in the room. Adam recognized her as an actress, but could not recall her name. There was something else about her that danced on the periphery of his memory, but he was too humiliated at the moment to give it any thought. His face burned under the scrutiny of so many eyes. Alyssa squeezed his hand. He had forgotten for a moment that she was there and felt relieved.

Then the moment crumbled. Eyes turned away. Voices rose again. People talked and laughed, utensils clattered, and ice chimed in glasses.

Adam felt better once the four of them were seated at their squiggle. Horowitz sat across from him, Alyssa beside him. Most of the tables around them were occupied by celebrities of one kind or another.

No, make that other *celebrities,* Adam thought. *I'm a fez-wearing, secret-handshaking member of the lodge now.*

Wolfgang Puck came to the table to say hello to Horowitz. They were old friends. She introduced Adam and Alyssa. Puck shook Adam's hand firmly and smiled. "You're in good hands, my friend," he said. "You see, I am always very good to Rona when she comes to my restaurants, so when people find out I really can't cook, she will defend me."

They all laughed, even Adam. But it was only a sound he made, nothing more.

After they ordered, Johnny Cochran came to the table. More laughing and smiling and handshaking, then he chatted with Horowitz for a bit. Adam listened to their conversation for a few seconds to see if Cochran would rhyme. He did not.

The loud actress Adam had noticed earlier was seated at the next table over, facing him, still being shrill. He watched her over Horowitz's shoulder. A spiky-haired brunette in her mid-twenties. He had seen her before, a relatively new actress who had gotten a lot of attention for her "fierce beauty and whiskey voice," according to *Premiere* magazine. And for her frequent nude scenes in second- and third-rate movies. It was also said around town that she gave spectacular head and rimjobs. Recently, while channel-surfing, Adam had

369

caught her undressing in a women's-prison/martial-arts movie. But something else was familiar about her. He could not pinpoint it.

Jack Nicholson came to the table during their meal and greeted everyone.

Alyssa raved about the food, but Adam could taste nothing. He gave some of his barbecued salmon to Alyssa so it would appear he had eaten more than he had.

Someone at the loud actress's table dropped a glass and it clattered against a plate. She guffawed and clapped her hands several times.

Adam wondered if she was drunk, messed up on drugs, or just having a good time with her friends. She had been in rehab last winter, he recalled. After going crazy and doing some damage on a set, where she punched her director in the face and broke a production assistant's finger. But that was not what he was trying to remember about her.

Adam finished eating well before the others, with more than half his meal still on his plate. Tension had crept into his guts, squeezed soft tissues and caused them to cramp. He removed the napkin from his lap, tilted his head forward to dab his mouth. Put the napkin on the table beside his plate. Lifted his head and locked eyes with Melonie Sands, the loud actress whose name he could not remember earlier, *that* was it, Melonie Sands. It was her name's significance that had eluded him until that moment.

She was smiling, so Adam returned it, but reluctantly.

Melonie was one of the women Adam had been hearing about who claimed to have been his dad's lover at one time or another. Wasn't she? There had been so many. He leaned toward Horowitz. "That woman at the table behind you," he said, "Melonie Sands. Isn't she the woman who claims she heard me—"

Horowitz nodded. "Ignore her. And eat your salmon." She pointed at his food with her fork. "I expect you to eat all of that, by the way, so return the napkin to your lap, please."

Adam wanted to snap at her, but thought better of it. She had told him to be extremely conscious of everything about himself, from the expression on his face to the position of his feet. "You know that private little time of the day when you are sitting on your toilet moving your bowels and breaking wind and picking your nose, when you know that no one in the whole world can see you?" Horowitz had asked him a few weeks ago. "That is when they are watching you the closest, and do not forget it."

Horowitz gave him a wink to remind him she was on his side. To tell him to have fun, relax. It made him smile and relax a little.

Melonie Sands continued to stare at Adam, but her smile was gone.

"Do you know her?" Alyssa asked.

"No, I don't." Adam put the napkin back on his lap and took another bite of salmon.

"Want some of my Cantonese duck?"

Adam shook his head.

Alyssa watched the actress for a moment. "I saw her in some made-for-cable titty movie."

Adam nodded.

"What's wrong with that chick, anyway?" Alyssa asked.

All of Melonie's facial features seemed to have pulled in toward the center of her face. The "beauty" part of her "fierce beauty" was gone, leaving only a fierce, glaring face. And she was glaring directly into Adam's eyes.

One of the women at Melonie's table yelped like a kicked Chihuahua when Melonie stood clumsily and knocked her own chair over backward. She hurried around her table toward Adam, shouting, "You should be in prison, you son of a bitch! You daddy-killing son of a bitch!"

There were a couple muted screams. A woman from Melonie's table shouted, "What the fuck're you doing, Mel?"

Adam glanced around him, saw Horowitz's two security men converging on Melonie. But she did not bother to go around Adam's table to get to him, as the security men anticipated. Instead, she pushed Horowitz aside with her left hand while raising her right. It held a knife with a glimmering silver blade. Adam kicked frantically at the floor to slide his chair backward as Horowitz's chair tipped over sideways with her in it. Melonie leaped onto and across the table. Dishes clattered, a couple more women screamed. Melonie swung the knife down hard as she slammed into Adam and knocked him backward.

Adam saw a flash of the blade's gleam, felt the knife hit his chest as he toppled over. On the way down, the back of his head hit the back of the chair behind him and he lost consciousness. He did not even have time to wonder if he would ever wake up again.

Over his fussy, important-sounding opening theme music and footage of Adam getting out of the limousine in front of *Chinois* the night before, Larry King said, "Tonight—accused of murdering his father Michael Julian, writer of such Hollywood blockbusters as *Explosion* and *Catastrophe,* as well as his stepmother and stepsister and three crewmen on the Julian yacht *Money Shot,* Adam Julian makes his first public appearance since being arraigned—and an attempt is made on his life by a woman who claims to be his dead father's former lover! We'll have a major discussion about this bizarre turn of events in the crime story that has riveted the globe. Joining us for this weekend edition of *Larry King Live,* attorney for Adam Julian, and a long-time friend of this show, Rona Horowitz. Deputy District Attorney of Los Angeles, Raymond Lazar. Also joining us, celebrity chef Wolfgang Puck, whose Santa Monica restaurant, *Chinois,* was the site of last night's incident. And bringing us the inside scoop from Hollywood, columnist Janet Charlton. Joining us later in the hour, the lovely actress Morgan Fairchild, who plays Rona this week in a USA Network movie based on one of Rona's previous cases."

"What, no psychic?" Adam snapped. Sprawled on the sofa in his hotel suite, he stared at the television, remote aimed and ready to fire. "No juggling act? Couldn't get Dame Edna Everidge to comment on the case, huh, Larry?"

Adam's chest was badly bruised by the butterknife with which Melonie Sands had tried to stab him, but the skin was not broken. His head, on the other hand, still hurt. He had sustained a mild concussion from hitting his head on the chair and had required a couple stitches to sew up the ugly gash.

Two police officers had responded to the call from *Chinois*. Melonie Sands had resisted arrest with such fury, it had been necessary for the officers to use pepper spray. She had screamed obsceneties at Adam all the way out of the restaurant.

Max walked into the room leisurely, looked around. "Who you talking to?"

"Larry King."

"I see. Upset with Larry, are you?" Max went to the bar, got a can of diet Barq's root beer from the refrigerator. He kept the refrigerator stocked with them, his soft drink of choice.

Adam said, "I'm disgruntled with everybody. Everything."

"Zat so?" Max popped open the can and took a seat. "Lemme get this straight. You're staying in a luxury hotel suite, you gotcherself a real perty girlfriend, and you got an attorney's gonna save your ass from God's own woodshed. And you're unhappy with everything?"

Normally, Adam enjoyed Max's company. His lazy drawl could not conceal his quick mind. But now, he made Adam angrier than he already felt.

"You talk like she's doing this for free, or something," Adam said.

"'Course she's not. But you get what you pay for."

"I don't even know what she's doing! I haven't seen her since the press conference."

"How'd that go, by the way?"

"Oh, it was…fine, I guess. It was my first press conference, I've got nothing to compare it to. Scary as hell, that's for sure. All those people focusing their undivided attention on *me*. And their cameras. I didn't even speak, but they acted like Rona wasn't there, like I was just standing up there all by myself. She kept telling them I wasn't going to answer any questions, and they kept shouting questions at me. Like I said, it was the only time I've seen Rona all day. I didn't exchange more than two words with her. Everybody keeps talking like I should be so grateful. But for what? What is she actually doing for me?"

"Ain't you been watchin' television, son? She's doin' it right now." Max gestured toward the television, where Horowitz was explaining what had happened the night before.

" — then knocked my client over in his chair and stabbed him in the chest with a table knife. He received a concussion from hitting his head on a chair when she knocked him down. It was a frightening experience, Larry, not one I'd care to go through again. But I'm happy to say Adam was not seriously injured. He required stitches and is resting quietly now."

Larry King started to speak, but he was interrupted by Deputy District Attorney Raymond Lazar, a man in his forties with a streak of white in his thick black hair. "Larry, wait a second, let me say this. What happened last night was unfortunate, no doubt about that. But Ms. Horowitz has been on television all day talking about this as if it has something to do with this case, and it does *not*. What happened last night has *no* bearing whatsoever on the fact that Adam Julian has been charged with the murders of six people, including his own family."

Adam rolled his eyes. It irked him to hear Gwen and Rain referred to as his "family."

"I have not said it does, Ray," Horowitz said. "But I think it points out a problem that gets far too little attention these days — the fact that the concept of 'innocent until proven guilty' is in grave danger of extinction. This is a symptom of — "

Adam turned to Max. "A table knife?"

"You want her to go on television and say some girl knocked you over with a butter knife? Table knife sounds better, don'tcha think? Notice she didn't mention you weren't exactly stabbed, either. I'm sure it hurt like hell, but it didn't go in. The way she mentioned the stitches, I liked that. Sounds like the stitches were for the stabbing, not your head."

"But the details have been reported, right?" Adam asked. "I mean, everybody knows by now that I wasn't really — "

"Everybody knows what Rona wants 'em to know, and nothin' else. By the time she's done, nobody'll remember you been charged with murder. They'll be too busy feelin' sorry for you 'cause you've had such a bad summer. And now, everybody in the country wants to chat with you on their computers." He waved a beefy hand in the direction of the television.

" — reaction has been tremendous, and nearly all of it has been positive," Horowitz was saying. "People are being very supportive, and I think it's just what Adam needs right now. He has lost every-thing, Larry. He lost his entire family, and thanks to Officers Stanley Pembroke and Warren Buchwald of the Marina del Rey Police De-partment, he lost his best friend in the whole world. He's finding some new friends online now, and I think that will help the healing process."

"What is she talking about?" Adam asked. "I've only been online once since the press conference, but the chat room was so full, I couldn't get in."

"Like I said, everybody knows what Rona wants 'em to know, and nothin' more. Don't worry. She knows what she's doing."

Adam tipped his head back and sighed. "I just want to have a life again. And get out of this fucking room."

"You got out last night. Look what happened."

"Not just out of this room, out of this city. I'd like to take Alyssa and go away."

"Won't matter where you go now. You ain't gonna get away from this."

"Maybe when it's over. If…well, you know."

"If you get off, you mean? Oh, I think chances of that're real good."

"That's not a lot of comfort when I'm stuck in this fucking room day and night," Adam grumbled. "I can't make phone calls, I'm not allowed to — "

"Well, maybe you shoulda thoughta that before you killed your family," Max said loudly.

"Goddammit, they weren't my family!" Adam shouted. "I wasn't even related to them, just my dad, and he — " Adam was about to tell Max that his dad had not been much of a dad, that he was no more "family" than Gwen and Rain. He froze for a moment, realized what he had said, how it must have sounded. What Max must be thinking.

Max watched him carefully, interested. Head back, eyebrows raised. Waiting for Adam to finish.

Adam closed his mouth. "It just bugs me…when people refer to Gwen and Rain as my family. Because they weren't." He leaned for-ward on the sofa. "And I didn't kill them. You know I didn't kill them. Right, Max?"

Max leaned back and smiled, raised his can of root beer as if proposing a toast. "Hey. I just work here." He sipped his drink, but did not take his eyes off Adam.

As **a boy,** Adam had spent a Christmas with his dad's parents in Washington. It had been snowy and bitterly cold, and there was always a crackling fire in the fireplace. He had made snowmen with Grandpa and baked cookies with Grandma, wrapped presents with his mom. Discovered the enveloping sense of security and belonging created by walking in from the gnawing cold to a warm house that smelled of pies and woodsmoke. He had wanted to go back every year, but his dad had stopped speaking to his family after that visit, and Adam never returned. The holiday never had been the same for him after that Christmas of snowball fights and roasted marshmallows. He considered it his only true Christmas, and every one since — all spent in Los Angeles — a pathetic imitation.

With the trial looming, Christmas seemed like a half-forgotten childhood fairytale. Without Carter, it felt more like a festering wound than an approaching holiday. Christmas songs scraped his nerves raw. The thought of shopping for gifts constricted his lungs, made him feel light-headed. Other than Alyssa, he no longer had anyone for whom to buy Christmas gifts. He dreaded shopping for her, cringed at the thought of stores and crowds and all those depressing, tawdry decorations. Wondered if she would understand if he said he wanted to ignore the holiday. Except for her, Adam wanted to pretend everything in his life did not exist.

He found himself lashing out at people, even Alyssa. Not just being sarcastic, but hurtful as well, without meaning to be. He caught himself each time and apologized, and each time, he was surprised by how angry he felt, how suddenly the anger had welled up in him. Dr. Locket adjusted Adam's medication more frequently. Dr. Remini extended their sessions. Everyone was understanding and forgiving of his outbursts, even Horowitz. It irritated him, made him feel pampered.

Mrs. Yu now worked for the family of an Oscar-winning composer of movie scores in Bel Air. The Julian house had gone on the market in mid-October. Adam had gone back for the last time — Lamont had managed to avoid the attention of reporters by driving him there in the middle of the night — to decide what would go into storage and what would go with him once he found an apartment. Mrs. Yu dropped by the hotel a couple times each week to see him, usually with food — a batch of his favorite cookies, a Tupperware bowl of her lasagna. She reassured Adam repeatedly that he should not feel guilty about having to let her go. Worse than the guilt, though, was the loss.

Putting the house up for sale seemed to close the door on everything his life had been up to that point. In some ways, that was good. But it made him feel suspended in midair, high above the clouds. At any moment, he could begin his fall, and with clouds in the way, he would not even know where he was headed. Just down. Fast.

His insecurity made him feel dependent on Alyssa, and he did not like that, resisted it. He did not like the idea of putting that much pressure on her. Alyssa was his girlfriend, not his mother.

Lamont sneaked her into the hotel a couple times a week, always in the late, secret hours of the night. Horowitz had said if the press ever suspected, it would have to stop. "If the press learns your girlfriend is sneaking into your hotel room to have sex with you, it will not be enough for them. Before the day was out, they would have you conducting orgies in here with Charlie Sheen and a harem of high-priced hookers. Reporters are really quite easy to handle once you understand them completely. You may not think so, Adam, but they have been very good to you. Even if you were proven guilty of murder, it would not matter to them at the moment because they genuinely like you, which is exactly what I wanted. But let them smell sex on you and all bets are off. It drives them into a frenzy. Like sharks and blood. Once you are in your own apartment, things will be different."

"Hey, excuse me," Adam replied angrily, "but I don't like your suggestion that sex is the only reason I ever want to see Alyssa, because it's not."

"If all you did in here was crochet afghans and exchange recipes," Horowitz said, "it would not matter. A tabloid would report it, the press would run with it, the story would be everywhere, and all those soccer moms who think you are such a good boy would change their minds about you in a second."

"Soccer moms?"

"Yes. They are your biggest supporters according to the polls. Mothers who see in you something of their own children. If you were running for president and the election were held right now, there is a good chance you would be the next leader of the free world."

Shortly before putting Adam's house on the market, Horowitz had her staff looking for an apartment in a secure building near her office, in Beverly Hills or Century City. It would help keep the press at a distance and provide him with some peace in a place of his own.

"Wait a second," Adam had said. "What if you find a place and I don't like it?"

"When this is all over, you can live wherever you like. For now, you need a place close by and closed to outsiders. You are not in a position to be picky, Adam. And you should know by now that my taste is impeccable. No need to give it another thought. I will let you know when we have something."

Horowitz was right — the press did, indeed, like Adam. They liked Adam and Alyssa even more, and often referred to them by their Internet nicknames, Nick and Nora. In her press conference after the discovery of Nick and Nora, Horowitz told them Adam had, against her instructions, sneaked a computer into the hotel so he would be able to contact Alyssa. The idea of young lovers separated by tragic circumstances staying in touch on the Internet under assumed names when Adam was not even supposed to have a computer was irresistable. The Lifetime network contacted Horowitz about acquiring the rights to make a television movie of the Nick and Nora story. She told them they would have to wait until after the trial.

"How much were they offering?" Adam had asked.

"Our conversation did not get that far. We are not entertaining offers. The public is on your side for now, Adam. If you start selling your story, the press will report how much money you make on each deal, and the public will turn on you like a pack of cornered dingoes."

For awhile, the fact that Adam was accused of murder was all but forgotten as reporters played up the online love story. As a result, Adam and Alyssa became so popular online, they had no time to chat with one another. The website Horowitz had set up for them — carefully disguised as just another online chat site called Chatterfactory.com — racked up a million and a half hits on the first day.

Adam and Alyssa were surprised by the variety of people who showed up to chat with them. From teenagers and investment bankers to senior citizens and unemployed college drop- outs. A group of housewives who usually met every day in another chat room made Chatterfactory.com their online hangout. Texas_Babe, PsychoMom, Couponcutter, CheetosLuvr, and Peanut were there every time Adam logged on.

"You're way too cute for people to be accusing you of murder, sweetie," PsychoMom said one afternoon.

Peanut said, "You remind me of a boy I dated in high school."

"How long ago was THAT?" Texas_Babe asked.

Adam typed, "LOL! You're making me blush."

"Hands off — HE'S MINE!" Alyssa shouted.

"Show a little sympathy, Nora," Couponcutter said. "We're old, married, and have children — let us have a little fun!"

Many people who came to the chat room assumed the women knew Nick and Nora personally because they were so familiar with them in conversation. None of the housewives said anything that might discourage such thinking. People knew that if they missed Nick and Nora, then Texas_Babe, PsychoMom, Couponcutter, CheetosLuvr, or Peanut would be able to get a message to them. They became famous by association, even if only there at Chatterfactory.com, and they squeezed every drop of attention they could from it.

Adam was caught off guard by the support he received from people who came to the chat room. He had expected foul-tempered troublemakers to log on for the sole purpose of calling him a murderer. Instead, they told him how sorry they were about the awful things that had happened to him. Many of them told stories of how they had lost their own families, and assured Adam they knew what kind of pain he was experiencing. Some jokingly offered to kill Assistant District Attorney Raymond Lazar, while others promised to remember Adam in their prayers. There were troublemakers, but they were attacked so viciously by the others in the chat room, who were always quick to defend Nick and Nora, it was rarely necessary to kick them out. They usually left on their own.

Horowitz had been right about the mail. One day at her office, she took him into a small conference room where two women and a man were sorting through piles of mail on a large oval table. Different perfume scents clashed in the air, mixed to create a sickly sweet, vaguely nauseating odor. Fat mailbags leaned against the walls. Two green plastic garbage bags were filling up, and more waited in a yellow box on the sideboard.

Stunned, Adam gawked at all the envelopes, jaw slack. "This is all...for me?"

"Some of it is for you and your girlfriend," Horowitz said, "but the bulk of it is addressed to you alone. Many of the letters have been scented with perfume, which accounts for the room's sickening odor."

Adam slowly shook his head. "What could all those people possibly have to say to me?"

"You are getting more letters of support than I anticipated," she said with a quick, proud smile. "But there is a great deal of hate mail as well. We take the threats very seriously. All packages addressed to you go straight to the police for the bomb squad to open. So far, there have been no explosives, but we will continue to take the precaution. However, there have been a number of sex toys and worn panties. And one dead rat."

Adam gasped. "A dead rat?"

"There was no note, but it was the consensus of the room that someone was expressing strong disapproval of you."

Mouth still open, Adam's eyes moved slowly over the piles of unopened mail, bags of discarded letters. He shook his head again. "You're throwing it away?"

"Yes. It has been my experience, Adam, that this kind of mail can be very upsetting to someone in your position, not to mention distracting. It is my policy to have my staff handle it and save my clients the bother. Of course, if you feel strongly about it and would like to take some of the mail with you to read —"

"Oh, no. It kind of gives me the creeps, to tell you the truth."

Horowitz nodded. "It should. They write as if they know you, when of course, they do not. All they want is to know you read their words, good or bad. That they had some kind of contact with you. Like the diseased woman in the Bible who sneaked up on Jesus just to touch the hem of his robe to be healed."

Adam turned to her with a wincing frown. "You're comparing me to Jesus?"

"Of course not. But the same principle applies. They just want to touch the hem of your fame, and hope some of it will rub off on them."

✝

Adam's story was not the only one making news.

A fuss was made over a large plaque bearing the Ten Commandments that had been put on the wall at a public high school in Iowa. The new principal had decided to hang the plaque just inside the main building so it was the first thing anyone would see upon entering. When the principal was told he could not hang the Ten Commandments in a public school, he refused to remove the plaque. Within a week, he had appeared via sattelite on *Good Morning America*, *Today*, *Hardball with Chris Matthews*, and *Larry King Live*. The school board acted quickly. The plaque was removed and the principal was fired. On the following Sunday, an uncle of one of the students was caught trying to set the school on fire. He claimed the school had defied the will of God and should no longer stand. The arson attempt landed him in a mental institution.

A man dying of cancer in Austin, Texas, filed a lawsuit against his doctor, who had estimated, upon diagnosis, that the man had only four to six months to live. That had been nearly a year ago, and the man, furious that he had not yet died, was suing his doctor for malpractice.

An overweight teenage girl in Arizona who had been hiding her pregnancy from family and friends for eight months gave birth in a shopping mall restroom with the assistance of her boyfriend, who was not the father of the child. They left the prematurely-born infant in the restroom's garbage can, covered with paper towels, where it died before being discovered by a janitor minutes later. After leaving the restroom, the couple continued shopping, and in anticipation of losing weight, the girl bought some new clothes in a smaller size. They were arrested in a checkout line at Sears when the janitor, who had seen them leave the ladies' room, pointed them out to police. Barbara Walters landed an exclusive interview with the couple on *20/ 20*. The show won the week in ratings. The girl insisted she had been unaware of her pregnancy and surprised by, and unprepared for, the birth. She and her boyfriend had simply left the baby in the trashcan while they hurried to buy some diapers in the mall.

But only one other story matched the coverage of Adam Julian: the raid by FBI, DEA, and BATF agents of Waldo Cunningham's compound in the Mojave Desert.

E!, the entertainment channel, found an eighteen year old boy named Marcus Lozada, who claimed he had worked at the compound until he became too old for Waldo Cunningham's clientele. During his extensive interview, Marcus claimed to have been "rented" by Tom Hanks, Robin Williams, Harrison Ford, Eddie Murphy, Regis Philbin, Sean Connery, Tom Brokaw, and Madonna. Within twenty-four hours, it was discovered that Marcus was actually twenty-six years old, an ex-convict, and a fraud. He worked the streets as a prostitute and sometimes sold drugs, and those streets were the closest he had ever been to the Mojave Desert. He could not even identify Waldo Cunningham in a photograph. Long, impassioned apologies were quickly delivered, and lawsuits were filed by outraged celebrities. A week later, Marcus had a job as a VJ on MTV.

The FBI refused to name names, but gossip columnists and comedians speculated about the celebrities who might have been purchasing Waldo Cunningham's wares. The story throbbed on television and the Internet and in newspapers and magazines for months. But not much came of it, just as Adam had expected.

He did not know which celebrities and politicians had done business with Waldo Cunningham, but because they were celebrities and politicians, he had expected none of them to be identified publicly or dealt with by the authorities in any significant way. Within the entertainment industry, wagons were being circled, Adam was sure. Deals were being struck by attorneys. Careers were being saved. The politicians would do whatever politicians did under such circumstances, which probably was not too different from what was done in the entertainment industry. When necessary, Hollywood could have very tight lips. Something as serious as the desert raid could make everyone fall silent, whether they knew anything about it or not. If there were any arrests, Adam was certain they would not involve familiar names. He was surprised when his prediction proved to be inaccurate.

The Palm Springs home of a heavy metal musician whose career had peaked in the early eighties was raided by FBI agents based on information found in Waldo Cunningham's records. The musician was arrested for possession of marijuana, heroin, and child pornography.

Agents tried to arrest an actor who had shown great promise in the late seventies, but whose addiction to drugs and alcohol had led him to beat all his wives and burn all his bridges early in his career. He had made a string of awful low-budget straight-to-video action pictures, but even those had dried up by the mid-nineties, and the actor had been forced to sell his Brentwood home and move to the Valley. The news of Waldo Cunningham's arrest apparently had been more than he could take. Agents found the actor hanging in his shower. They found marijuana, cocaine, and pornographic literature and videotapes purchased from Cunningham.

Two days after resigning unexpectedly, a California congressman's home was raided and he was arrested. Among the illegal pornography taken from his house were videotapes of the congressman himself having sex with some of Waldo Cunningham's boys. One of the tapes disappeared and resurfaced on the internet days later.

There were a few others. Another third-rate actor, a screenwriter, a nationally syndicated radio talk show host based in Los Angeles, where he was despised by the celebrities he mocked and ridiculed on his afternoon program. Even a minor executive at a small movie studio. Names that were just barely recognizable. No one too big or important. But they kept reporters and tongues busy.

After attacking Adam in *Chinois*, Melonie Sands became more famous than she ever had been as an actress. She was fined, sentenced to community service, and required to go into rehabilitation for her substance abuse. When not picking up garbage beside freeways in an orange jumpsuit, she did the talk show circuit. From show to show, she apologized to Adam and the world for her behavior. It had been brought on by alcohol and drugs, which she claimed she was addicted to because she had never dealt with her molestation as a child at the hands of her father. Beyond that, she was unable to talk about

Adam or how she knew him because she was going to be a witness for the prosecution in his trial. In recounting her tribulations on *Oprah*, Melonie Sands made the overweight host cry, and they shared a long hug.

"If they are putting her on the stand," Horowitz said as she and Adam watched Melonie on CNN, "then things are even better for us than I thought."

FORTY-FIVE

During the first week in December, Adam moved into a furnished two-bedroom apartment on the twenty-third floor of a high-rise on Wilshire Boulevard in Westwood. The first thing he unpacked was the flat-screen television. Once they had it on the wall and hooked up to the DVD player and sound system, they flopped on the sofa and he turned it on with the remote.

Boxes and suitcases still cluttered the living room, waiting to be unpacked.

"What do you think?" Alyssa asked.

"Of what?" Adam thumbed his way from channel to channel.

"Your new apartment, bright boy."

"It's okay, I guess. It smells funny."

"Smells like it was painted recently."

"Great. The fumes'll probably kill me in my sleep."

Frowning, Alyssa sat up straight beside him. "Are you all right?"

Adam turned to her. "Yeah. Why?"

"I don't know. You seem...different."

He turned back to the television. "Yeah, that's what people tell me."

"Is it the apartment? I like it." She smiled.

He shrugged, shook his head. "I don't know."

"You don't like it?"

"No, it's fine."

She took a breath to say more, but slumped silently beside him instead.

Adam turned, watched as two small, vertical creases appeared between Alyssa's eyebrows. He put an arm around her and said, "Sorry for being so weird. I just feel like I'm…floating. Believe it or not, I was getting pretty used to the hotel room. Now I've got to get used to this apartment. I keep thinking when this is all over, I can go home and relax. But I don't have a home anymore."

She nodded her head against his shoulder. "You're not being weird. Anybody would feel that way. Your whole life has changed."

"What happens when I get used to this place? Am I going to have to move again?"

"No, I think you'll be here awhile. At least till the trial's over. For now, this is home."

Adam sighed. "It doesn't feel like home. Sure as hell doesn't smell like home."

Alyssa pulled up the short black skirt she wore, swung a leg over Adam. Straddled his lap and sat facing him, grinning. "Then we'll make it feel like home. *Our* home."

"Oh, I don't think Rona will approve of you living here." Adam slipped his arms around her narrow waist. "I would. But I don't know about Rona."

"Then I won't move in until after the trial. It'll just feel like I live here."

"What if I…well, I mean, what if the jury…what if they convict me?"

She touched her nose to his and whispered, "Do you really, honestly believe that any jury in the world would go up against your attorney? If I was on that jury and didn't know you, I'd be afraid to find you guilty. Just because of her. She's a pit bull."

"Guess I'm just not as confident as you."

"Let's not even think about the trial. Let's just think about today, okay? Let's make this apartment our home, even if I can't live here. We'll start by getting a Christmas tree and some decorations." She grinned. "And one of those logs that burns green and blue flames."

Adam's upper lip curled back slightly, as if he suddenly felt sick. "Christmas," he said with disgust. "Sorry, Alyssa, but I really don't feel like Christmas this year. It's not even here yet and I'm already sick of it."

"Well, I'm not going to let you sit here and worry and turn into an old man. You don't have to go shopping if you don't want to. I'll take care of everything. We'll turn this apartment into a Macy's display window. And we'll listen to Christmas music and roast marshmallows and Chet's nuts and —"

Adam was surprised by his own laughter. "You really want to roast marshmallows?"

"We can do it naked if you want." She reached down and unbuttoned his jeans, opened the zipper. Adam laughed and wriggled on the sofa as she tugged his jeans and underwear down, freed his hardening penis. Pulled the crotch of her panties aside and rubbed him between her lips. She slid him inside her suddenly and they both gasped. As she moved her hips, slowly at first, she began to sing "The Christmas Song" in a breathy voice, smiling.

Adam sat up, pushed her down on the sofa and got on top of her. He tried to sing "Here comes Santa Claus!" but only made it through the first few words. Their gasping breaths became synchronized with their pounding movements.

Christmas was forgotten.

✝

On Wednesday night in the third week of December, Alyssa and Brett came to Adam's apartment to watch the annual broadcast of *Rudolph the Red-Nosed Reindeer*. All the unpacked boxes had been removed from the living room. Adam had put them in his bedroom, where he unpacked things as he needed them.

The living room was dimly lit by a torchiere lamp in one corner, and a twinkling Christmas tree in another. The entire apartment smelled of the forest. Alyssa had brought a yule log with her and it burned with green- and blue-tinted flames in the fireplace.

Adam and Alyssa were cozy on the sofa, Brett stretched out in the recliner, as they watched the Christmas show. They were half-heartedly singing "Fame and Fortune" along with Rudolph and Herbie, the elf who wanted to be a dentist, when keys chittered in the locks on the door. Adam turned to the entryway, eyes wide.

"Who is it?" he called. He unraveled himself from Alyssa and stood.

The door opened. Horowitz's heels clacked on the entryway's marble-tile floor, fell silent on the living room carpet. She carried her black leather briefcase. Max and Lamont came in behind her and Lamont closed the door.

"I am sorry to cut your evening short, ladies," Horowitz said, "but you will have to go now." She sounded no more stern than usual, but anger burned in her face and eyes, lips trembled ever so slightly when she pressed them together. She boiled just beneath her smooth, unblemished skin.

Alyssa and Brett quickly got to their feet.

"Hey, wait a second," Adam said angry. "They just got here, we're watching—"

Horowitz snatched the remote control from the arm of the sofa and fired it at the television. "Not anymore," she said, handing the remote to Lamont. She put the briefcase on the coffee table, released the latches with a sharp clack, but did not open it. Instead, she turned to Alyssa and Brett, who stood next to Adam. "Have a good evening, ladies."

Alyssa gave Adam a quick kiss on the lips. "Call me."

Furious, Adam muttered, "Goddammit," as he followed them to the door. "I'll call you when we're done and you can come back over, okay?"

Alyssa turned to him and smiled, kissed him again. "Okay. And don't be mad. It's probably important."

Adam closed and locked the door, spun around and went back to the living room. On the coffee table, the lid of the briefcase stood open. Across the room, Horowitz opened the glass doors of the cabinet that held the VCR, DVD player, and sound system. Slipped a cassette into the VCR, nodded once at Lamont.

"Goddammit, can't you at least call first?" He was close to shouting. "I mean, what's so important that you have to barge in here like a—"

The flat-screen filled with the black-and-white overhead view of a liquor store. A man in a ski mask aimed a large handgun at the Korean cashier behind the counter. The camera was behind and above the front counter. Behind the robber, back to the glass doors, holding another large handgun between both hands, stood Adam Julian.

✝

Adam thought he had seen Horowitz's anger before—he could still hear her shouting over her desk at him during their first meeting—but he was wrong. What he had seen in her before had been nothing more than annoyance, irritation, impatience. Real anger— what he saw in her then as she stood before the frozen image of Monty lying dead on the floor of the liquor store as Adam backed out the door—fired from her eyes in white-hot beams like the tank-melting death ray from Gort, the alien robot in *The Day the Earth Stood Still*. Adam could feel its heat on his skin, expected to smell the harsh odor of his own hair being singed.

"Think before you speak, Adam," Horowitz said quietly, a slight tremor in her voice. "You have used up all of my patience. Lie to me now and you will have to find another attorney."

Max went to Adam's side, put an arm across his shoulders with a long sigh. Led him to the recliner and whispered, "Son, this'd be a good time to sit down, make yourself comfortable, and take us through all the parts of your story you left out the first twenty or thirty dozen times you told it." He pushed down firmly on Adam's shoulders, pressed him into the chair.

Horowitz stepped over to Max's side and they stood before him, waiting.

Adam did not know what to say, where to start. He had to be very careful if he were going to avoid revealing the final truth: that he was guilty as charged. With the stiff wariness of someone walking through a minefield, he told his story.

He started by telling them of his two sexual experiences with Gwen. Head bowed as he spoke, staring at the carpet, he told them how Rain had raped him at gunpoint, then threatened to blackmail him by crying statutory rape to the police. He did not bow his head in guilt, but to allow himself to go into explicit detail, which he was too embarassed to do while looking at Horowitz and Max. He told them everything, right up to the day he huddled in Rain's closet and listened to her and Gwen. He spent the most time on the nightmarish liquor store robbery. When he was finished, he slumped in the chair with a sigh, exhausted.

Horowitz and Max stared at him for a long time. Her arms folded across her breasts, his bushy eyebrows knotted together over his glasses and thumbs hooked in the front pockets of his jeans. They turned to one another questioningly. Max's lower lip curled out from beneath his mustache as he looked at Adam again. As Horowitz walked around the chair, anger crackled around her body like static electricity.

"How did you find it?" Adam asked.

"We didn't," Max said. "The D.A.'s office did."

"How did they find it?"

"They found it because *we* did not find it first," Horowitz said. She stood in front of Adam again. Fished a beige cigarette and a lighter from the pocket of her lavender suit jacket. "And we did not find it because *you* did not tell us about it." She stabbed the cigarette into her mouth, lit up, and blew smoke from her lungs as if she were blowing out a cakeful of candles. Walked around the chair again, a shark circling its prey.

Adam said, "I...I really wish you wouldn't smoke those things in here. I mean, they really stink."

Max put a hand on the recliner's armrest and leaned close to Adam. Whispered, "I'd only speak when I was spoken to if I was you, son. For tonight, anyways. You don't wanna push your luck tonight, trust me."

Horowitz stopped in front of the fireplace, tapped her cigarette over the colorful flames. With her back to Adam, she said, "There are no words to adequately describe how angry I am right now." Turned and glared at him. "Do you know why?"

"Because...I didn't tell you everything."

"Everything? You told me hardly anything. You left out the entire second act. What kind of writer are you, Adam? Your father would be ashamed of you."

"I'm sorry," he said. "I should have told you. I was afraid."

"You were afraid to tell me?"

Adam nodded.

"Well, now you can be *very* afraid. Because even if you are not arrested for this, if that tape gets out before I have a chance to prepare for it—" She spun around, waved an arm and let it slap to her side. "For all I know, it could be on the Internet already. That tape could crush everything I have done so far." Turned to him again. "You have a pristine image right now, Adam, that could be ruined by this tape."

"Why don't you just tell the truth?" Adam asked. He glanced at Max for a reaction, to see if he had made a mistake by speaking.

"The truth about what?" Horowitz asked.

"About me. That I didn't tell you everything until now because I was afraid. I figured if I didn't tell you, it would never come up."

Horowitz's nose wrinkled and her eyes squinted, upper lip peeled back over her teeth, as if she had just licked something foul. "How could you be so stupid as to think that, Adam? You had to know there were security cameras in there. You looked directly at one of them before your partner shot it. Now your face is everywhere and you think—"

"He was not my partner!" Adam shouted, standing. "I didn't even know the crazy son of a bitch. I didn't know what was happening until he pulled the gun! Why don't you just tell *that* to the reporters. I mean, I was forced into it! I wouldn't even have been out with Rain if I wasn't afraid she'd turn me in. Besides, we already know the truth about Gwen. It's pretty obvious Rain was supposed to be—"

"We do?" The question lifted Horowitz's left eyebrow.

We didn't have this conversation, Max had said after telling Adam what he had learned about Gwen.

"Oh, shit," Adam muttered, turning to Max. His spacious forehead was cut with deep lines as he glared at Adam.

Horowitz turned to her investigator. "Max?"

Max nodded his head slowly. "Yeah, I asked him a few questions about it before I came to you. I shouldn't have, I know. But I wanted to make sure I had something solid before I brought it to you. There were some questions only Adam could answer."

"We will discuss it later," she said, then turned back to Adam. "You were saying?"

Adam blinked. "What? Oh. Um…what was I saying?"

"That you think something is obvious. What is obvious?"

"Oh, yeah. I think it's obvious Rain was supposed to be working with her mom. Rain was supposed to seduce me, then talk me into killing my dad. Gwen tells me Dad's beating her, shows up with a black eye, which is supposed to make it easier for me to go along with it. But Rain wanted me to help her kill *both* of them. Gwen didn't know it, but Rain was going to kill her, too."

Horowitz and Max stared at Adam. Looked at each other. Then at Adam again.

"I'm sorry," Adam said, "didn't that make any sense?"

"Yes, it made sense. If the judge will allow it."

"Allow it? But that's what happened. How can he not allow it?"

"*She* can do almost anything she likes. She is the judge."

"What do you know about her?" Adam asked.

Horowitz said, "Judge Vera Lester is an odd duck. She has reached the age at which each trial could be her last. A registered Republican, but politically moderate. Some judges typically lean in favor of the prosecution, some in favor of the defense. But Lester is unpredictable. A wild card."

"And that means…what?"

"It means we cannot rely on her to behave in any specific way during this trial." She turned to Max and Adam was surprised to see a smirk on her face. "But I think we might be able to exploit one of her weaknesses."

"What weakness?" Adam asked.

Horowitz said, "Lamont, would you please go into the kitchen and make some coffee."

"Coffee?" Adam asked. "Why do you need coffee?"

"We will all need coffee." She took off her jacket, hung it on the coat hook in the entryway. "The many hours we have spent going over our story have been hours wasted, Adam. Now we have a whole new story, and not much time left. We will be sleeping less and drinking more coffee in the coming weeks. And it would be extremely unwise of you to voice any complaints about it."

Adam asked hesitantly, "You're, uh…still going to represent me?"

Horowitz tossed her cigarette, smoked down to the filter, into the fireplace. Turned to Adam and burned his retinas with a long, silent stare. "Right now, I am so angry with you, Adam, I would love nothing more than to walk away from this case in spite of all the time and energy I have invested in it. But that would be unprofessional and could harm my reputation beyond repair. So I will see this case through, and I will win this trial for you. But when it is all over, Adam, I will do something to you that might be even worse than what the prosecution has in mind."

His eyes widened slightly. "What's that?"

"I will give you back your life."

A dam and Alyssa spent Christmas Eve having sex on every piece of furniture in the living room to the songs of *Dr. Demento Presents the Greatest Christmas Novelty CD of All Time.* At two in the morning, they exchanged gifts, then spent a long time simply kissing on the floor in front of the Christmas tree.

Alyssa's parents were visiting relatives up north in Humboldt County. "By tomorrow," Alyssa had said, "they'll be so stoned, they'll probably think it's Easter. They won't know if Jesus is coming or going."

Shortly before noon on Christmas morning, they were awakened by a call from the doorman, who helped Mrs. Yu carry two cardboard boxes to Adam's door. The boxes were warm and smelled of childhood and loss. In the kitchen, Adam and Alyssa helped Mrs. Yu remove from the boxes a twelve-pound roast turkey covered with warm aluminum foil, along with all the traditional trimmings. Their afternoon breakfast consisted of tender turkey, mashed potatoes and gravy, candied yams, dressing with diced almonds and apples, and Mrs. Yu joined them. She explained that her employers were out of the country until February, and she had no one to cook for but Adam.

Horowitz dropped by that afternoon and offered to take them all out for an early Christmas dinner at Patina. But when she smelled the aromas coming from the kitchen, she needed no convincing to eat there instead. She brought Adam a gift, *Rudolph the Red-Nosed Reindeer* on DVD. "Because you never got to finish watching it on television," she said.

Adam was surprised by how much Horowitz's gift touched him. "That was very thoughtful, Rona. I have something for you, too."

Surprise moved across Horowitz's normally calm, neutral face. She gave him a disarming smile. "You do?"

He led her over to the Christmas tree, took a small, festively wrapped cube-shaped gift from beneath it. But he hesitated before handing it to her.

"What's wrong?" Horowitz asked.

"Well, it's not, um…it's not as thoughtful as your gift. I mean, it's not exactly…well, actually, it's kind of a—"

She snatched the gift from his hand and tore off the foil wrap, opened the small cardboard box. Removed a white coffee mug from the box and frowned slightly as she looked it over. On one side of the mug was a shot of actor Alec Baldwin from the 1993 thriller, *Malice*, sitting at a conference table. He was speaking and looked rigid with controlled rage. On the other side of the mug were the lines Baldwin was delivering:

"You ask if I have a God complex?
I *am* God."

Adam took a deep breath. "It's…kind of a smartass gift."

She surprised him by smiling again. "But a charming smartass gift. Thank you, Adam. I will drink from it proudly."

A few minutes after Horowitz began to eat, Max called on her cellphone and she told him to come over for a bite if he was hungry. He joined them half an hour later. Adam loaded a CD cartridge with Christmas jazz. Brett arrived shortly after Max, having spent the minimum required amount of time with her visiting relatives. Horowitz's cellphone chirped again when Lamont called to check in. She invited him to come over, too, and to bring his boyfriend. They arrived fifteen minutes later with wine and a batch of Christmas sugar cookies Lamont had made. He introduced his boyfriend, a shy, blonde-haired young man named Ken.

As dusk dimmed the light of late afternoon outside, the Christmas music blended nicely with the comfortable chatter and relaxed laughter. Adam had to remind himself that these were the people who had created so much tension in his life—his attorney, her assistant and investigator. Adam's jailers and inquisitors since July. But they were all at ease with one another. Even Adam.

The doorbell rang and Adam was surprised to find Mr. Brandis and Devin in the hall. He stared at them a moment, suddenly ready to choke on his emotions. He had not seen them since the funeral. They looked older now. Both hugged him and came close to tears, but kept smiling. Devin brought a tin of homemade fudge and divinity, and Adam put the candy on the coffee table.

There was plenty of food and wine to go around. Mr. Brandis and Devin were the first to leave, but the others trickled out after them.

"Normally, I dine out with friends at Christmas," Horowitz said to Adam on her way out. "But this has been a delight. Thank you for asking me to stay."

"Um, actually, I...I didn't ask you to stay."

"But you would have had I given you a chance," she said with a quick smile. She was a little sleepy-eyed from the wine. "Whatever bad things you might have done in your life, Adam, and no matter how hard you try to convince people otherwise, you really are a nice young man. I do not expect that to be the case by the end of this trial, so I am glad I had the chance to enjoy some of it today."

By nine o'clock, everyone but Alyssa was gone. A holiday that Adam had hoped to avoid had been a pleasure after all. It held none of the magic or excitement of childhood, but it was not the miserable experience he had anticipated. Under the circumstances, Adam thought that was good enough.

✝

After months of vilification on television and in newspapers, months of counseling that had failed to end his nightmares, lessen his aching guilt, or stop the hate mail and death threats, Officer Stanley Pembroke went out to the garage while his wife and two young daughters slept in the dark early-morning hours of December 26. He put his service revolver in his mouth, and sent a bullet through his brain.

Before I begin, I would like to thank you, the members of the jury, for your patience during this process, and for giving it your serious and undivided attention." Raymond Lazar smiled warmly at the jury. "As you have seen, it can be slow and tedious, but you have been exemplary in your behavior and participation. Due to the celebrity of those involved, this trial has been the focus of a lot of attention in the media. For this reason, you have been sequestered. This is an added hardship that most juries do not need to undergo. You will be kept from your homes and families for the duration of this trial. This is necessary in order to retain the integrity of the trial, and once again, I would like to thank you for your understanding and patience. Now." He turned briefly to Judge Vera Lester. "Your Honor…ladies and gentlemen of the jury…as representatives of the people of California, I and my colleagues, David Piner and Barbara Cho, will prove that Adam Julian hired Nathaniel Cunningham to kill Michael and Gwen Julian and sixteen-year-old Rain Cardell. You might ask, why would he do that? For money? Yes, that is one part of his motive. Michael Julian was a very successful screenwriter. No doubt you have seen some of his movies. In recent years, he produced as well as wrote his films. His success in the film industry made him a very wealthy man."

Adam watched the tall deputy district attorney walk slowly along the rail. He never looked away from the jury. The four men and eight women followed him with their eyes.

Beside Adam at the defense table, Horowitz looked over notes written on a yellow legal pad, seemingly unaware of Lazar.

"But there is another factor in this case besides simple greed. We will show you that, since childhood, Adam Julian has immersed himself in an imaginary and desensitizing world of horror and violence and bloodshed. He has spent his life wallowing in blood-drenched horror movies and novels, and has even written his own stories of brutality and death. You will meet people who claim Adam was filled with hatred, and that he directed that hatred at his father. And you will come to see that Adam Julian is not the innocent victim his attorney would have you believe him to be. We will prove to you that he arranged and paid for the murder of his own father, his stepmother, and her sixteen-year-old daughter, a mere child. Blown to bits on the ocean, along with three crew members who happened to be on the wrong yacht at the wrong time. All because Adam Julian hated his father and wanted him dead. Wanted his fortune all to himself. And because, after years of living in a world of imaginary wholesale slaughter, after years of fantasizing about it, Adam Julian wanted to see for himself what it was like to kill someone."

Peripherally, Adam saw Horowitz turn to him. He knew she was just checking to see how he was taking it. He stared at the tabletop and tried not to listen to Lazar, but it was impossible. So he tried to pretend the deputy D.A. was not talking about him, or about anything real, just telling a story. But with each mention of his name, Adam's throat tightened. As Lazar continued, the reality of Adam's situation began to settle over him for the first time in seven months. He had been afraid before, worried, paranoid. But Lazar's words were like steel shackles clacking onto Adam's wrists and ankles. The courtroom itself, brightly lit with light wood paneling, suddenly took on a hyper-reality that made Adam sick. *This is happening to me,* he thought.

"Are you all right?" Horowitz whispered, leaning close to his ear.

Adam nodded. Swallowed the lump in his throat created by his sudden nausea.

"You look sick."

He nodded again.

"Do you need to step out?"

Adam took slow, deep breaths, then shook his head.

Horowitz sat up in her chair, but continued to watch him.

" — and doctors who can explain to you how this young man has become so desensitized and numbed that human life holds no value for him. When you have all the information our witnesses will provide, you will see that Adam Julian put a great deal of thought and planning into these six deaths. He went to Nathaniel Cunningham and paid him to plant explosives on *Money Shot*, Michael Julian's yacht, and then…and *then*…he went out on the town with his friends. He *celebrated*, knowing that his family would soon be dismembered and scattered over the ocean by those explosives. You will see that fifty-six-year-old Michael Julian, forty-three-year-old Gwen Julian, sixteen-year-old Rain Cardell, thirty-three-year-old Jack Craney, twenty-seven-year-old Charles Riley, and forty-nine-year-old Joseph McCullers all lost their lives on the cold, emotionless, desensitized whim of Adam Julian. Now, you have been instructed — "

"Feeling better?" Horowitz whispered.

She was so calm, so relaxed, Adam wondered if they were in the same room together. Could she hear what that man was saying about him? What those twelve people were hearing?

"No, but don't worry, I won't embarrass you by throwing up."

"I would rather you throw up during his opening statement than mine."

" — that this trial is *only* about the murder of these six people and nothing else. Don't let anything shift your focus from that," Lazar said. He went to the center of the rail, put his hands on it, arms spread. "Your duty as jurors is to push aside anything that obstructs your view of the truth. The truth is what you are here to find. And we will show you that the truth is this." Lazar pointed in Adam's direction. "The truth is that Adam Julian is a murderer." He added quietly, "Thank you." His shoes clocked on the floor as he returned to the prosecution table.

"Ms. Horowitz?" Judge Lester said. "Your opening statement?"

Judge Vera Lester's shoulders seemed to grow from the sides of her large head, just above her ears. Her steel-colored hair was short and wavy, and the thick glasses she wore made her eyes look twice their size. Horowitz had said she was old, but the wrinkles on her face made her look much older than Adam had expected. Her hands were large and liver-spotted, with knobby knuckles. She looked like an aged Muppet being operated by someone behind the bench.

Horowitz glanced at Adam. One corner of her mouth turned up as she stood. She walked to the jury box unhurried, smiled at the jury. Spoke in a level, friendly voice. "I would like to echo Mr. Lazar's appreciation of your dedication to this process. I know this is a hardship for you, and for your families. I wish there were some way we could speed up the trial, or avoid keeping you all sequestered. It is an unwieldy process at times, but it is still the best in the world. I have great faith in all of you." She smiled again, then became serious. "Your Honor, members of the jury. During the course of this trial, I am going to reveal facts that are in direct opposition to everything you have just heard from Mr. Lazar. It is the duty of the prosecution to prove Adam Julian's guilt beyond a shadow of a doubt. As the attorney for the defense, I need only to point out the weaknesses in the prosecution's case. But I will be doing more than that. I will prove a great deal in this case. Much more than the prosecution. I will prove to you that the six people whose lives ended tragically on that yacht were not the only victims in this situation. And I will prove that two of those people were not who they claimed to be. Gwen Julian had at least four other separate identities. Under those aliases, she is wanted in four states for killing four men, right now, as I speak to you. Each man murdered was Gwen Julian's husband at the time of his death. And each man, like Michael Julian, was very wealthy."

A ripple of voices moved through the courtroom, which was filled to capacity, and quickly grew louder. Adam turned his head just enough to see Lazar and the other attorneys at the prosecution table — David Piner, a rusty-haired man in his thirties, and Barbara Cho, an attractive, twenty-something Korean woman. They were huddled together, whispering frantically. *Didn't see that coming, did you?* Adam thought, trying not to smile. Suddenly, he felt a little better. But only a little.

The voices grew so loud, Horowitz had to raise her voice to continue. Judge Lester interrupted her with a single slam of the gavel. The voices fell silent immediately.

"Any more of that, and you can all go home and watch this on television like everybody else," she said in her loud, cigarette-gravelled voice. She scanned the crowd, gavel poised in her right hand to strike again should anyone make a sound. She lowered her hand slowly, turned to Horowitz. "Go on, Ms. Horowitz," she said. "The suspense is killing me."

"Thank you, Your Honor." Horowitz turned back to the jury. "I will prove that Adam Julian not only did *not* plan and pay for the murder of his father, or any of the other people on that yacht, but was in fear for his own life while living under the same roof with Gwen Julian and her daughter."

Another stir of whispers rose in the courtroom, not as loud as the first outburst. With a glare from Judge Lester, it quieted down, but heads turned and bowed in the crowd as spectators whispered to one another.

"I will prove also that Michael Julian was in far more danger from his wife and her daughter than from his son." A pause as Horowitz passed her eyes slowly over the jury. "I will prove as well that the explosion that killed those six people very well could have been an *accident*. By the end of this trial, ladies and gentlemen, I will have proven to you that Adam Julian is innocent of the crime of murder. And even though it is not my job to do so, I will have proven it beyond the shadow of a doubt. Thank you."

As Horowitz returned to the table, an explosion of voices came from the crowd. The sound of everyone trying to absorb the shocking information Horowitz had seemingly plucked from thin air. It had not been discussed on any of the talk shows or reported in newspapers or on the Internet. Horowitz had dropped a bomb, and it had landed squarely on the prosecution.

Several thunderous blows from Judge Lester's gavel quieted the voices, but did not quite silence them. She waved the gavel at the spectators as she said, "This is the last time I will warn you! It's a little early to be trying my patience like this. I will close this trial for the duration if it happens again. I've already told you I will tolerate no disruptions of any kind. If you can turn off your cellphones and beepers, you can turn off your mouths, too."

As the judge reprimanded the room, Lazar was still exchanging sibilant whispers with his colleagues. They seemed to have heard nothing since Horowitz's completely unanticipated claims about Gwen.

"Is the prosecution ready to call its first witness?" Judge Lester asked.

Lazar pulled away from the others and stood. "If I could have just a moment, Your Honor, to —"

"You've had months, Mr. Lazar. Are you ready to call your first witness, or not?" The noisy spectators had darkened Judge Lester's mood.

Lazar quickly whispered something to his two colleagues, then stood again. "Yes, Your Honor. I would like to call as my first witness Mrs. Dorothy Boam."

Adam closed his eyes and sighed. Lazar was calling one of the witnesses Adam dreaded most. His eighth grade English teacher.

✝

The past month had been the most boring and tiresome of Adam's life. Perry Mason and Matlock never had to attend the interminable preliminary hearings and jury selection. Those things received little more than casual mention on *Law and Order* and *The Practice*. None of the classic big-screen courtroom dramas had covered the days of monotonous perusal of evidence or prospective jurors being interviewed by the judge, the prosecution, and the defense. Adam was sure that after a few minutes of that, television remotes would start clicking, movie theaters would be vacated. Like most of reality, it was simply too tedious for television and the movies.

Horowitz had stepped up her coaching of Adam after the holidays. She and her staff put Adam through every conceivable attack that might come from the prosecution. They would continue to do so in their spare hours until it was time for Adam to testify. By then, he would be ready for anything.

"You do not seem to be enjoying the legal process, Adam," Horowitz had said one evening in the car on their way to dinner after a long day of interviewing prospective jurors. They rode in a black Lincoln rather than a limousine, which Horowitz had said would look too extravagant.

"Enjoying it?" Adam asked. "There's not a lot of action. Does the plot pick up soon?"

"I am disappointed. Being an aspiring writer, I thought you would be fascinated by the *voir dire.*"

"*Gezundheit*. What do you mean, fascinated?"

"Each prospective juror is a mystery that must be solved. Is this person likely to side with the prosecution or the defense? Does this person have something against young people? Rich people? White people? Will I be able to persuade this person to think the way I want her to? It requires an ability to read people, to spot their signals. I expected you to find that interesting."

"You don't need me to find that interesting," Adam said. "You've got that blonde to be interested for you."

"That *blonde* happens to be the very best jury and trial consultant in the country," Horowitz said, defensive for a moment.

"Sorry. I guess I'd be more interested in the whole thing if the people you were choosing were going to decide somebody else's future. This is too boring to bear. And too scary."

✝

Lazar asked, "How did you become acquainted with Adam Julian, Mrs. Boam?" He faced the witness stand from a lectern on which he had placed his notes.

"He was a student in my eighth grade English class," Mrs. Boam said.

Her face was just as Adam had remembered it—still frozen in a disgusted grimace of disapproval. Mrs. Boam looked no older than when he had last seen her, but she had always looked old, whatever her age. In yearbook photos from decades ago, she had not looked a day younger than she'd looked during Adam's eighth grade year. She looked no different on the witness stand.

"Do you remember what kind of student he was?" Lazar asked.

"He was a very intelligent boy with a great deal of potential. But he was terribly misguided."

"Misguided? Could you explain, Mrs. Boam?"

"He had a natural grasp of the English language and showed talent as a writer. But his use of that talent was…unsatisfactory." She wrinkled her nose and her already sour face shriveled a bit more.

Lazar asked, "What do you mean by—"

"No, unsatisfactory is not the proper word," Mrs. Boam interruped, frowning as she held up an index finger. "I suppose his work would have been satisfactory to someone who *liked* that sort of thing. I did not and do not, and it was inappropriate for an eighth grade English class."

"What sort of thing was that, Mrs. Boam?"

"Oh, they were awful stories about people killing and…torturing each other. He described the violence in such explicit detail. I came to dread those papers."

"Were these assignments?"

"They were all assignments. But no matter how benign the assignment, he would turn it into some kind of bloody horror story. I remember the first assignment I gave his class. I asked them for an essay on how their summer ended." She turned to Adam at the defense table. Her eyes narrowed and she shook her head disaprovingly, lips pressed together, mouth turned down. "Adam wrote that he and his friend Carter Brandis went on a killing spree across the country. They killed people at random, assigning points to people of different ages and with various physical attributes. And he wrote that they managed to escape the police so they could get back home in time for school to start."

Supressed chuckles came from the spectators.

Mrs. Boam's face made her disapproval clear as she looked over the crowd. "Well, *I* did not find it funny." She looked at Lazar again. "But *he* found it funny. And so did his friend."

"What friend?"

"Carter Brandis. A portly boy who shared Adam's fascination with violence."

"Do you remember any other details, Mrs. Boam? Details like that paper Adam wrote?"

"One particular story stands out in my memory. It was the last straw for me."

"Could you tell us about the story?"

"It was about a boy whose mother is regularly beaten by his father. The boy loves his mother very much and wants to make a better life for her, so he plans to kill his father."

A mild gasp fluttered through the courtroom.

"He decides to make it look like a robbery," Mrs. Boam said. "As if a crazed junkie came into the house desperate for money and killed his father. He waits until his mother is at work and brutally kills his father with a large knife from the kitchen. It was horribly bloody and gory and…awful, it was just awful. The boy plans the murder too well. The police do not suspect him for a moment, but they are suspicious of his mother. She is arrested and charged with murder. The boy tries to tell them the truth, but no one believes him. They think he is simply covering for his mother. She is convicted and sentenced to death. The story was made up mostly of graphic descriptions of the father's murder and the mother's death in the electric chair. It was dreadful."

"How did you handle the problem, Mrs. Boam?"

"Well, after that, I stopped assigning him papers and stories. I gave him assignments separate from the rest of the class. And Carter, too, because his papers were just as odious, but not as well written. The subject of the papers was not as important as the mechanics, you see. It was an English class, after all. It's my job to teach my students the proper use of the language, whether written or spoken. Assigning papers or stories aren't the only ways to do that. So I assigned Adam and Carter book reports."

Lazar said, "What went through your mind when you read those gory papers of Adam's?"

"I'm not finished, Mr. Lazar."

Even Judge Lester laughed.

"I'm sorry, Mrs. Boam. Please go on."

"The book reports were no different. At first, I gave him his choice of books. And what did he choose?" Her back stiffened. "Horror novels. True crime books about the most disgusting murders imaginable. Books about serial killers and rapists and c-cannibals. Can you believe that? A thirteen-old-boy reading such things? So I picked the books for him myself. At first, that didn't work, either. He would find a single violent passage in the book, or something even more disgusting than violence if it was there, and focus his entire report on that." Another put-upon shake of her head.

"What did you do after that?"

"I learned Adam had lost his mother a year or so before that. I thought perhaps I had been too hard on him. I spoke to Principal Neuman and told him I thought Adam needed some…help. It was arranged for Adam to see one of the school's counselors three times a week."

"Did that help?"

Mrs. Boam closed her eyes and sighed. "Only for awhile. Then he was at it again. I spoke to his father on the telephone, but Mr. Julian did not share my concern. He said, 'Imagination runs in my family.'"

Adam was surprised. He had no idea Mrs. Boam had spoken to his dad. Michael had said nothing about it. He held back a smile at his dad's response to Mrs. Boam.

"What bothered you most about Adam's writings, Mrs. Boam?"

"Well, as I said, they were terribly explicit. Adam wrote at length about people being stabbed or dismembered or tortured. He seemed to *enjoy* it so much. As if he had no natural aversion to violence or death. It was *fun* for him."

"Do you disapprove of violence in literature?" Lazar asked, turning a page on the lectern.

"Of course not," Mrs. Boam said with some indignance. "Some of the greatest literature ever written has involved violence, sometimes a great deal of it. Including the Bible, I might add. But the violence is there for a reason, and it is unpleasant, painful. More often than not, it is there to protest violence. It's not funny, it's not there to be *enjoyed*. Violence in literature must be accompanied by compassion, by a recognition of the priceless value of human life. Otherwise, it's nothing more than a kind of pornography. And that was how Adam wrote it. Like pornographic sex. And I found that very disturbing."

Adam thought, *You wouldn't recognize pornographic sex if Larry Flynt beat you over the head with a copy of* Hustler.

"Thank you, Mrs. Boam." Lazar looked at the judge as he gathered up his notes and said, "No further questions, Your Honor."

As Lazar returned to his table, Judge Lester said, "Ms. Horowitz?"

Horowitz was already on her way to the lectern, on which she placed her yellow legal pad. She stood in front of the lectern rather than behind it. Smiled with warmth at the woman on the stand. "Tell me, Mrs. Boam, how long have you been a teacher?"

Mrs. Boam returned the smile as she said, "Next year will be my forty-ninth."

"Forty-nine years! Congratulations, Mrs. Boam. It is an honorable profession and you should be very proud of those years."

Still smiling, she said, "I am. I may not be rich or famous, but my students mean far more to me than wealth or notoriety ever could."

"For just a moment, let's forget about the papers Adam wrote for you in class. Other than that, what kind of student was he?"

Mrs. Boam frowned, tilted her head slightly. "I'm not sure I understand your question."

"Well, was he…polite?"

"Oh, yes. He was always polite and well-spoken. Quite eloquent for his age."

"Did he have problems with the other students?"

"Not that I was aware of. You mean…did he get into fights?"

"Fights, arguments, any kind of trouble at all?"

"No."

"Was he popular among the other students?"

"He spent most of his time with Carter, and they kept to themselves."

"You mean they never interacted with the others?"

Mrs. Boam shook her head. "Not very much."

"Do you have any idea why they kept to themselves?"

"I suppose a few of the other students…well, you know how children are. They can be terribly cruel. Adam was a very skinny boy. And of course, Carter was quite rotund. Things like that…well, you know the kind of attention they get among youngsters."

"*Attention*, Mrs. Boam? Do you mean Adam was picked on by the other students?"

"Not by all of them, of course. But by some, yes."

"Did you ever intervene when you saw that happen?"

Mrs. Boam chuckled without smiling. "One can only do so much. That sort of thing is part of school life, a part of growing up. If teachers were expected to step in every time there was some name-calling or bickering, we'd never get anything done."

"I see." Horowitz looked down at her notes.

"Of course, if it gets out of hand, that's different," Mrs. Boam explained quickly. "The safety of our students comes first, and I would never stand by if someone were being hurt."

"Of course not." Horowitz looked up and smiled again. "Forty-nine years is a long time. During that time, do you think you have become good at reading your students?"

"I'm not sure I know what you mean."

"Well, let me put it this way. Do you think you are a good judge of character, Mrs. Boam?"

"Oh, I see. Yes, I think I am. People are people the world over, after all. The same can be said of children."

"When he was your student, what did *you* think of Adam Julian? What did you think of him personally?"

"What did I think of him? I believe I made that clear."

"Actually, you only told us what you thought of the things he wrote. What was your opinion of Adam himself?"

Mrs. Boam hesitated. A look crossed her face that Adam had seen before, whenever she suspected someone was up to something. "Well, naturally, I thought he was…troubled. Disturbed. Normal boys simply do not write such things."

"So, you thought he was abnormal?"

"Yes, you could say that. I'm not a psychiatrist, but I believe his fascination with violence was a symptom of a deeper problem, something the school counselor was unable to deal with or even reach. And if I may say so—" She looked at Adam with a slight smile of satisfaction, " —I think Adam has proven me right."

"Are you able to read all your students so well, Mrs. Boam?"

"I think so."

"Do you stay in touch with many of your students?"

"I see some of them at reunions now and then, but outside of that, no, I'm afraid not."

"You had a student in 1982 named Timothy Simon. Do you remember him?"

"Objection, Your Honor," Lazar said as he stood. "Mrs. Boam's other students, past or present, are irrelavent to this case."

"Your Honor," Horowitz said, "this line of questioning addresses Mrs. Boam's credibility."

After a moment, Judge Lester nodded. "I'll allow it."

"Thank you, Your Honor."

Lazar sat down again.

"You may answer the question, Mrs. Boam," Judge Lester said.

"Yes, I remember Tim well. He was an exceptional student."

"Exceptional in what way?" Horowitz asked.

"In every way. He was a straight-A student with outstanding athletic abilities. He was involved in school politics, edited the school paper. He was very popular with the other students. Everyone loved Tim. At the time, he said he wanted to be a journalist. And he always said it with such determination, I wouldn't be a bit surprised if that's exactly what he's doing today."

"How would you compare Timothy Simon to Adam Julian?"

Mrs. Boam frowned, looked suspicious again. "I…I'm not sure."

"You described Adam Julian as abnormal, correct?"

"Yes, that's correct."

"Would you use that word to describe Timothy Simon?"

"Oh, my, no. Tim was not abnormal. Not in that way. He was very…wholesome. He was above average in every way, but not at all abnormal."

"Would it be accurate to say, then, that in your opinion as a veteran teacher who has learned to read her students well over the years, Timothy Simon was *normal*?"

"Yes, I would say so."

"Do you know what Timothy Simon is doing today?"

Standing again, Lazar nearly shouted, "Objection!"

"Overruled," Judge Lester said. "Answer the question, Mrs. Boam."

"No, I'm afraid I don't," Mrs. Boam said with a shake of her head.

"On May fourteen, nineteen ninety-one, Timothy Simon murdered his twenty-two year-old girlfriend, Penelope Graham, and her nineteen-year-old sister, Abigail Graham. He dismembered them and barbecued them in his backyard. He told the—"

"*Objection*, Your Honor!" Lazar shouted, shooting to his feet. "Adam Julian is on trial here, not—"

"Overruled, Mr. Lazar."

Horowitz went on. "He told the police he was planning to eat them, but before he could, his neighbor dropped by to see what was on the grill and became rather suspicious when he saw Timothy flipping what were unmistakably human female breasts on the grill with a fork. Timothy Simon is currently serving a life sentence."

Mrs. Boam's small mouth hung open behind closed lips and her face lost what little color it had.

Horowitz asked, "Do you think, Mrs. Boam, that your assessment of Timothy Simon was correct?"

She did not move, just continued staring straight ahead.

"Mrs. Boam?" Horowitz said.

Her mouth closed and opened a couple times, but no sound came out.

Judge Lester said, "Answer the question, Mrs. Boam."

"I…I…suppose it wasn't," Mrs. Boam said, her voice suddenly brittle.

"In that case," Horowitz said, "do you think your assessment of Adam Julian could have been equally incorrect?"

"I...well...that doesn't change the fact that—"

"Could you give me a simple yes or no answer, Mrs. Boam? Do you think your assessment of Adam Julian could have been equally incorrect?"

Mrs. Boam's head slowly bowed. She muttered something.

"I'm sorry," Horowitz said. "Could you speak up, please?"

"I...I suppose it could have been."

"Thank you." Horowitz smiled at the judge. "No further questions, Your Honor."

Adam turned and lowered his head to hide his smile from the jury, thinking, *Take* that, *you tight-assed church lady!*

One evening in the third week of the trial, Adam got home and slumped on the sofa. He turned on the television and stared wearily from beneath low-hanging eyelids as he surfed the channels. He had no idea sitting in a chair could be so exhausting.

Horowitz's car had dropped him off in his building's parking garage. She had to go meet Max, and then appear on ABC's *Politically Incorrect*. She had been very preoccupied with one, or both, of her appointments and had said little in the car.

Adam stopped channel-surfing in the middle of *Rosemary's Baby*, which Raymond Lazar would no doubt claim was further proof Adam was a murderer.

But I am a murderer, he thought. He allowed his heavy eyelids to drop. Between Lazar and Horowitz, things were getting a little confusing. It was easy to forget the truth. Maybe that was best. He leaned his head back and dozed off on the sofa.

The doorbell woke him. He did not know how long he had slept, but *Rosemary's Baby* had been replaced by *The Goodbye Girl*. He opened the door to find Max standing in the hall in jeans, a plaid shirt, denim vest, and reptilian-skinned cowboy boots.

"How's it goin', trialboy?" Max asked as he came in.

Adam shrugged silently and returned to the sofa. Max sat in the recliner.

415

"I thought Rona was supposed to meet with you," Adam said.

"She did. I mean, we did. Now she's taping that television show." He nodded at the television. "You watchin' this?"

"No." Adam picked up the remote. "Something you want to see?"

"Turn on CNN."

"Oh, Jesus help us." He changed the channel.

Max smiled. "Wish I had time to sit in on the trial. I love watchin' her work."

A clip of the trial was running. Melonie Sands was on the stand and Rona stood in front of the lectern, facing her.

"I've apologized for what I did to him," Melonie said, her voice tense. "I'll keep apologizing if necessary, but at the time, I was having a substance abuse problem that severely clouded my judgment."

"Sounds rehearsed to me," Max muttered.

Adam shrugged. "Her whole story sounds made up to me. I don't remember ever seeing her at the house."

Melonie Sands claimed she had dated Michael Julian briefly, which was very possible. She also claimed to have been witness to an argument between Michael and Adam at their house during which Adam had threatened to kill his dad. Although Adam had thought often of killing his dad, he had never voiced it, except when talking to Carter.

"What substances were those, Miss Sands?" Horowitz asked.

The actress fidgeted. "Alcohol. Heroin. And, um…pills."

"You were under the influence of alcohol, heroin, and pills when you attacked Adam Julian in *Chinois?*"

"Yes. A couple of them, anyway."

"How long did this problem last?"

"It was over a period of…I don't know, four years. Maybe a little more."

"So, you would like us to dismiss that violent incident in the restaurant because of your addictions?"

"Like I said, I wasn't myself."

"Were you under the influence of any of those substances when you dated Michael Julian?"

"I might have been."

"Were you under the influence of any of those substances when you claim you heard Adam threaten to kill his father?"

Lazar stood. "Objection, Your Honor. Miss Sands' personal problems are—"

"Overruled," Judge Lester said.

"Were you, Miss Sands?"

"I…I could've been. I mean…it's not like I was stoned *all* the time."

"But this incident you've described, in which you say Adam threatened to kill his father — that took place during the four years you were addicted to alcohol, heroin, and pills, correct?"

Melonie Sands continued to fidget, avoided Horowitz's eyes. "Yuh…um, yes."

"Tell me, Miss Sands. If we dismiss the fact that you attacked Adam Julian with a knife in a restaurant while under the influence of alcohol, heroin, and pills, shouldn't we dismiss *everything* you did while under that influence?"

"Well…um, well…"

"If we dismiss that, shouldn't we also dismiss what you *think* you heard at the Julian residence on —"

"Objection!" Lazar said, on his feet again. "There was no uncertainty in Miss Sands' testimony."

"Sustained," Judge Lester said.

Horowitz nodded once and said, "Withdrawn. If we dismiss your attack on Adam Julian with a knife, shouldn't we dismiss your entire testimony here today considering the fact that these events all took place during your period of substance abuse?"

Lazar stood again. "Objection, argumentative!"

"Sustained," Judge Lester said.

"I have no further questions."

As Horowitz returned to her seat, Judge Lester turned to the jury, gave them a stern look. "You will disregard Ms. Horowitz's remarks."

Adam asked, "How can they disregard something they just heard?"

Max's body shook with laughter. "They can't. And Rona knows it. You hungry?"

Adam had been trying to ignore his stomach's growls. "I'm starving."

"Wanna grab a burger with me? I missed breakfast this morning and I could eat the cow right now, hair and all."

"Tommy's?"

"Fine by me."

✝

Max drove them to the Tommy's on the corner of Beverly and Rampart Boulevards in his black Cadillac Escalade SUV. The red-roofed shack stood on the original location of the first Tommy's, opened in 1946, and served as the company's logo. Tommy's hamburger, stacked with everything and sloppy with chili, was Adam's favorite food. It had been Carter's, too. As kids, they'd virtually lived on them during the summer, and had been on a first-name basis with the employees who came and went at the Beverly and Rampart shack.

The night air carried a chill, as well as the smells of fried foods and car exhaust. Rap music pounded from passing cars and the laughter and chatter of the people in line gave the hamburger stand a festive atmosphere. Instead of tables or chairs, customers ate their burgers standing at long counters that stretched along the outside walls of the building.

The smells and sounds were achingly familiar, and Adam began to wonder if it had been such a good idea to eat there. As he stood in line, the figure beside him, seen from the corner of his eye, felt more like Carter than Max. It always had been Carter before.

"You okay?"

Adam started. "Yeah. Fine."

"You look like you just had a bad thought."

Shrugging, Adam said, "Carter and I used to come here a lot when we were kids. The last time I was here was with Carter. And Alyssa and Brett. It just…made me miss him."

"Wanna go somewheres else?"

"No, this is good. It's crowded and noisy and there aren't any reporters."

"You said your friend Carter knew Billy Rivers better than you did," Max said.

Adam nodded.

"Did he ever say anything that might give a clue as to where Billy and Nathaniel would go while they're on the run?"

Adam turned Max with a frown. "You're looking for them? I thought the police—"

"Let me ask the questions, okay?" he said with a smirk.

Adam did not want to think about Carter. It hurt too much, made it harder to keep a distance from his whole situation. Thinking about

Carter made him want to scream. To break something. Hurt some-one.

When he heard of Stanley Pembroke's suicide, Adam had waited for a feeling of rightness, a sense of satisfaction. He remembered what Horowitz had said during their first meeting. *If we play our cards right, they might even do it to themselves.* It had been an appealing thought at the time, but he had not taken her seriously. It had been inconceivable to him then that a single person—the tiny woman who had stood before him—could do such a thing. Of course, that had been before she'd begun repeating the officers' names on television, day after day, reminding them, and the world, of what they had done.

He had seen footage of the funeral on television a few days later. Warren Buchwald had stood beside his partner's casket at the cemetery, about thirty pounds heavier than he had been at Carter's house last summer, face puffy and red. According to news reports, Buchwald had taken a leave of absence and was in counseling. It was unclear whether or not he would return to the police force. When Pembroke's widow had appeared onscreen, crying and holding a wailing toddler, Adam had hit the remote quickly, changed the channel.

Rona did that, Adam had thought. *For me.*

Adam wondered how much difference there was between hiring someone to kill his dad and paying Horowitz to, among other things, drive Stanley Pembroke to suicide. Not much, it seemed. Except that for Horowitz, there would be no trial or punishment.

"You sure you're feelin' okay, pardner?" Max asked.

Adam blinked several times. "Yeah. Just thinking." He shook his head. "I don't remember anything Carter said that would help."

"What about Nathaniel?"

"What do you mean?"

They reached the counter and ordered their burgers. When Adam reached into his pocket, Max opened his wallet and said it was on him. They took their burgers, fries, Pepsis, and paper towels—Tommy's provided paper towels rather than napkins—to an empty spot at the end of one of the stand-up counters.

Max said, "When you were talkin' with him at his house, did he say anything about...I don't know, maybe about plans he had?"

"You mean, plans like blowing up his parents?"

"Maybe," Max said with a shrug. "Just think about your conversation, things you said, things he said. Maybe he mentioned something in passing. A casual remark. Anything at all that might give a clue to where he and Billy ran off to."

"You *are* trying to find him. What are you going to do, hand him over to the police? What good will that do us?"

"I plead the Fifth," Max said. "On the grounds that I could piss off my boss."

Adam bit into his hamburger, chewed slowly and savored the flavor. Thought about Max's question, about his conversations with Diz.

"This's a damned fine burger," Max said with his mouth full.

"A religious experience," Adam said before taking another bite. He washed it down with a couple swallows of Pepsi. "I don't remember Diz saying anything."

"Well, let's see. You said you talked about, what…movies? Television?"

"Yeah, but that was it. I wasn't there long."

"Okay, okay." He stuffed a few fries into his mouth. "But give it some thought, willya? Somethin' might come to you."

They ate in silence for awhile. After only a few bites, Adam felt full. Thoughts of Carter and Pembroke had taken the edge off his hunger, but the idea of Max looking for Diz finished it off completely. Nothing Diz could say would match the statement Adam had given to the police. If Diz turned up, on his own or with help, and started talking, he would only ruin everything.

Did Horowitz expect Diz to help their case? Of course she did. She believed Adam's story, therefore she thought Diz would be able to back it up. What if they found him? If anyone could, it would be Max and Horowitz. What would Diz tell them?

The truth, Adam thought with a shiver.

"Diz and Billy are both wanted by the police, right?" Adam asked, turning to Max.

"Yep. And the feds." He chewed noisily, drank some cola. His lips curled with distaste. He was loyal to his Barq's diet root beer.

"So if you find them, you're going to have to turn them in, right?"

"Damn, this is a good burger, Adam. Glad you suggested it."

"If the police and the FBI want them, what are *you* gonna do with them?"

Max turned to face Adam, leaned an elbow on the counter. "Ain't you learned nothin' yet, Adam? You don't have to worry 'bout none of that stuff. Leave it to Rona."

"Okay, so I won't worry about it. But since I'm the one who's on trial, can't I at least *know* about it?"

Max took another bite of his burger, chewed leisurely. "Look, son. You gotta be more like me. Rona tells me to do something, I don't ask questions, I don't try to figger out how it fits into the scheme of things. I just do it. In the end, it always turns out to be the right thing to do."

"But I don't work for her. She's working for me, remember?"

Max sighed, sucked his teeth. "Rona Horowitz don't work for nobody. Maybe you're payin' her, but that don't mean she works for you. She just decided to save your sorry ass, that's all. If she does things you don't understand, you don't question it. You just wait for it all to finish up. Then everything'll make sense. And if not...well, then it won't matter 'cause it'll all be finished up."

It was clear he would get no answers from Max. Adam quietly finished his drink.

"Damned good burger," Max said before putting the last bite into his mouth.

"I'm just afraid something will go wrong," Adam said. "I don't want any surprises."

"Not gonna happen. Trust me, Rona's always in control of whatever situation she's in. Even if it don't look like it, she's pullin' the strings. She don't leave room for accidents. 'Bout the only thing she doesn't control is the weather. But I think she's workin' on it."

Adam chuckled. "Don't you think that's an exaggeration?"

Max's eyebrows rose above his glasses. "Nope." He ate the last of his fries, licked salt from his fingertips.

"Nobody is that good. I mean, there are always surprises, unpredictable things that—"

Laughing, Max shook his head. "Lamont told me you was hard-headed."

"What about the stuff I didn't tell you at first? The liquor store robbery and—"

"That was *your* fault. You didn't tell us. I said she's always in control of whatever situation she's in, I didn't say she was the Amazing Kreskin. She can't read minds. That's why she was so pissed off. She wanted to rip your head off when that liquor store tape showed up."

"It's still something she wasn't able to control until the tape was—"

"Do you think it's an accident that the public's on your side?" Max interrupted. "You think they like you 'cause you got nice teeth, or somethin'?"

"No. They like me because Rona's been all over television telling them what a wonderful guy I am."

"Nah. That don't make that much difference. She could talk till she's blue in the face, and if they don't like you, they just don't *like* you, that's all there is to it." He wiped his mouth and hands with the paper towel. Wadded up all the paper, stuffed it in the bag, then did the same with Adam's leftovers. Tossed the bag into a nearby garbage can. "Let's head back."

They walked away from the shack toward the Escalade.

"All the jawin' Rona's been doin' on television has helped, no doubt about that. But on its own, it wouldn't be enough. People out there like you 'cause they feel sorry for you. First, you lost your mama, then your daddy. Your stepmama and stepsister. Far as they're concerned, you got along with them just fine. A nice happy family."

They got into the Escalade and Max started the engine, drove into the traffic.

"So, you lost your family *and* your best friend, you're all alone," he continued. "And you're accused of murder. On top of that, with all the fuss and preparation for the trial, you have to go out on the internet to have any contact with your girlfriend. People love a love story, Adam. Always have. That whole Nick and Nora thing, they ate it up. They're still eatin' it up. Then some loony woman attacks you in a restaurant with a knife. 'This poor bastard,' they say. 'Nobody with that kind of luck is a killer. He's just a poor guy can't get a break,' they say. Everybody loves an underdog, and that's you. They like you even more 'cause they can get on the internet and chat with you. With everything else you got goin' for you, they find out you're not just a celebrity they been seein' on television and readin' about in the papers. You're a friendly, polite fella, intelligent, with things to say. You're just like their kids, their friends. You're one of them. They like that even more. Put all that together, they love you."

Adam waited for him to continue, but realized he was finished. "What's that got to do with Rona?"

Max smirked. "You think she didn't know there was a computer in that satchel?"

"She knew? But...she didn't want me to have any contact with anyone. That's why she didn't bring my laptop from Carter's house. Why would she leave the computer in the satchel if she didn't want me to..." He stopped talking, but his mind moved ahead, working on the puzzle. Finally, he turned to Max and said, "It doesn't make sense. Why didn't she just *say* it was okay for me to get on the internet and chat with Alyssa?"

"She wanted you to think it was your idea," Max said. "People're better at things if they think it's their idea. So she says you can't see your girlfriend no more. She gave you that story about Alyssa's parents, but that was just window dressing, a cover. Alyssa's parents really do use and grow grass, but they only share it with close friends. They're pretty safe. Just in case, though, Rona did have a little talk with 'em. But none of that mattered. The important thing was for you two to be separated. For you to be told you couldn't see your girlfriend no more. Then all she had to do was stand back and wait for you to do what you were told you couldn't. Which is exactly what you did, exactly the way she wanted you to."

"She planned all along...to get me on the internet? So people could come chat with me?"

"That was the plan. But you didn't hear it from me, y'understand? Think you can keep your mouth shut this time?"

Adam stared out at the oncoming headlights that swept by. It was very clever. More than that, it was devious. He was not sure how he felt about it yet.

"It wasn't an accident that Melonie Sands was at *Chinois* the night you went there, either," Max said.

"Oh, come on. She couldn't have planned that."

Max laughed. "We knew she had a problem with drugs and booze. Knew what her testimony was gonna be. Potentially damaging stuff, whether it's true or not. If she got on the stand and the jury bought her testimony, that could hurt. She was pretty sweet on your dad, y'know. Really fell for him. Rona knew she was gonna be at *Chinois* that night. There was no way to know exactly how she'd react to seeing you, 'course, but she had a pretty consistent record for making scenes and behaving violently. Rona hoped for the best."

"*The best?*"

"Sure enough, she went for the bait."

"Jesus Christ! What if she'd had a real knife? That crazy bitch could've killed me!"

Another laugh from Max. "Her security boys were there. They weren't gonna let nothin' serious happen to you. Just enough to make Melonie Sands look crazier'n a wet sack of ferrets. And it made everybody feel bad for you. Worked out nice and fine, don'tcha think?"

Adam did not know whether to feel angry about being so manipulated, or grateful. "How did she know Melonie was going to be there?"

"Wolfgang happened to mention it."

Adam nodded. "Does she plan to do any more of that during the trial?"

"Hell, I don't know. Have to wait and see. But don't worry about it. If she does, it'll be for the best. We're all just Rona's puppets, Adam. Get used to it."

The trial moved along with the speed of an extraordinarily complicated dental procedure. Sometimes, when it became especially dull, it made Adam's teeth ache. By the fourth week, he had a splitting headache at the end of each day.

Raymond Lazar called Wally Kirk to the stand. Wally looked uncomfortable, almost as if he were in pain. Lazar asked what kind of merchandise he sold in the Creature Features Book and Video Emporium in Hollywood. Asked if he knew Adam, how long he had been a customer. What kind of things he purchased, what kind of books and movies he favored.

Adam wondered what was going through the heads of the jurors as Wally answered the questions. Wondered what they thought of his fondness for horror movies and novels, of the titles Wally named. Herschell Gordon Lewis movies like *Two Thousand Maniacs*, *Blood Feast*, *The Wizard of Gore*, *A Taste of Blood*, *The Gore-Gore Girls*. Low-budget drive-in classics like *The Microwave Massacre*, *Blood Bath*, *The Corpse Grinders*, *Maniac*, *The Toolbox Murders*, and others. Movies Adam and Carter had watched repeatedly. They laughed at them, made fun of the garage-sale effects and atrocious acting. There was nothing funny about them now. The titles made Adam wince. They sounded much worse than they were, all of them. But how could the jurors possibly know that?

Once he had extracted from Wally a long list of damning movie and novel titles and a few plot summaries, Lazar returned to his seat. Horowitz went to the lectern.

"Mr. Kirk, if Adam wanted to purchase the comedies of the Marx Brothers, would he find them in your store?"

"No. I don't carry any Marx Brothers movies."

"What if he wanted to purchase a drama, or a musical? Would he be able to find either of those in your store?"

"No. I don't carry any of those, either."

"Why did Adam purchase only horror films and novels from your store?"

"They're the only kind of films and novels I carry. Horror and science fiction."

"Then it's not at all unusual that Adam purchased only horror films and novels from you?"

"Not at all."

"Tell me, Mr. Kirk, how many customers come through your store each week?"

"Oh, jeez. I couldn't tell you exactly."

"It doesn't have to be an exact number, just a ballpark figure."

Wally Kirk tilted his head back, pursed his lips. "I'd say between two and three hundred. More if an author comes in for a signing or a reading."

"Are all of your customers in their early twenties, like Adam Julian?"

"Oh, no, not at all. Most of my customers are middle-aged or older.

"What kind of people are they?"

"How do you mean?"

"Do they come from different backgrounds? Different professions? Incomes?"

"Oh, yes. They make up a pretty broad cross section. Everything from the unemployed to doctors and lawyers." He chuckled. "One of my regular customers is a judge."

There were a few quiet, cautious titters from the spectators.

"Don't look at me," Judge Lester said with a smirk. "I don't like the scary stuff."

Horowitz asked, "Do you have customers who regularly make bigger purchases in your store than Adam Julian?"

"Quite a few. They'll drop a couple thousand dollars or more a visit. I got some big spenders, but I've never considered Adam to be one of them."

"As far as you know, Mr. Kirk, are any of your customers murderers?"

His eyes widened. "What?"

"Have any of your customers committed murder?"

"Well…*no*. Not that I know of."

"Are they antisocial? Violent? Psychotic?"

"Objection!" Lazar stood. "Mr. Kirk is not a psychiatrist."

"Sustained."

"I will rephrase my question. Are your customers *normal* people, so to speak? Average people?"

"Oh, yes."

"They are productive citizens?"

"Yes."

"They have families?"

"Many of them, yes."

"Children?"

"Yes. Some of them shop for their kids in my store. Sometimes they bring them along."

"What attracts them to the books and films you sell?"

Wally shrugged. "They like their entertainment to be a little more imaginative and exotic than the mainstream. That's all."

"What about you, Mr. Kirk? What interest do you have in the things you sell?"

"Me? Oh, I've been a fan of horror and science fiction since I was — well, as far back as I can remember."

"Even as a child?"

"Oh, yeah. I never missed a monster movie at the Cascade Theater in the town where I grew up. Watched them on TV. Learned to read on horror and science fiction stories."

"Are you a violent man, Mr. Kirk?"

Lazar stood. "Objection, relevance."

"Overruled," Judge Lester said.

Wally shook his head. "No, can't say that I am."

"Have you ever physically harmed anyone?"

He paused a moment, shrugged. "Only when Uncle Sam told me to."

"You are a veteran?"

"Yep. Vietnam. Left my legs there."

"Outside of your time spent in Vietnam, have you ever physically harmed anyone?"

"No."

"Have you ever been arrested?"

"Once."

"What was that for?"

"Protesting the war after I got home from it."

"Did you enjoy the war, Mr. Kirk?"

Lazar stood. "Again, Your Honor, what is the relevance of this line of questioning?"

Horowitz turned to the judge. "Your Honor, I am trying to determine the effect horror films and literature have had on Mr. Kirk's life."

"Mr. Kirk is not on trial," Lazar said.

To Lazar, Horowitz said, "No, but you are suggesting the person who *is* on trial was influenced to commit murder by horror films and literature, and I am simply following up on that."

"Objection overruled," Judge Lester said.

Looking at Wally, Horowitz asked again, "Did you enjoy the war, Mr. Kirk?"

The usual twinkle left Wally's eyes. "No. I did not."

"Did you see a lot of violence and bloodshed in Vietnam?"

"Oh, yeah. A lot."

"Aren't violence and bloodshed staples of the horror genre?"

"Yes. Well, not always. But usually."

"And you love the horror genre, correct?"

"Yes."

"You love the horror genre, which is, by its very nature, bloody, gory, filled with killing. But when given the opportunity to *do* those things you so love to watch in movies and read about in novels…you did not enjoy it?"

"No, I did not."

"Why is that?"

He took a deep breath, exhaled slowly. "Those books and movies…they're fantasy. I read those books and watch those movies for entertainment, because I like a good scare, I like the weird stuff, that's just how I am. They're like…I don't know, an imagination massage.

Vietnam was real. It was bloody and scary, but there was nothing entertaining about it. I killed people there because I had to. But I didn't enjoy it. No more than I enjoyed watching people die all around me."

"So you recognize a distinct difference between the fantasy of horror movies and the reality of war, of life."

He chuckled coldly. "Of course I do."

"What about your customers? Do they recognize that difference?"

"Of course they do."

"Including Adam Julian?"

"Objection," Lazar said, standing. "Mr. Kirk is not a psychiatric—"

"I'll allow it," Judge Lester said.

"Yes, including Adam," Wally said, turning to Adam at the defense table. "He's a smart kid. So was Carter. Both good guys. One of the things Adam likes so much is the special effects in the movies, so he *has* to know the difference. Otherwise, he wouldn't know they were special effects."

"So, to the best of your knowledge, Mr. Kirk, neither you nor your customers have been adversely affected by regular exposure to the merchandise you sell?"

"No, of course not."

"No further questions."

✝

Lazar brought in his first expert witness next. Dr. Barton Goodman, a psychiatrist who specialized in the effect of the media on children. According to Dr. Goodman, constant exposure to the kind of movies and books Adam loved so much could conceivably blur the line between fantasy and reality, as well as the one between right and wrong.

When Horowitz took her turn at the doctor, she made sure the jury knew he had never spoken with Adam, nor did he know Adam personally. She asked if he had ever treated anyone who had been so transformed by violence in movies and television. He said he had not. She asked if he had ever met anyone who had been so transformed by violence in movies and television. He said he had not. She asked if there was any fact—any hard, cold, solid fact—in the things he had told Mr. Lazar. Dr. Goodman stammered and stuttered and glanced a few times at the deputy district attorney. Finally, he admitted there was no fact in it, no. Horowitz asked what it was, if not fact. With the same reluctance he had exhibited in answering the previous question, he said it was theory.

"Nothing more than theory," Horowitz said quietly before returning to her seat.

✝

The next witness, Albert Haas, was an explosives expert. A burly, balding man in his fifties, Haas was quite proud of his work in movies and television. He beamed as he told Lazar he had supervised the pyrotechnics on twenty-three features and over a dozen television series.

Haas had examined — "With great care," he assured the jury — photographs of *Money Shot* taken by Michael Julian and photographs of the remains of *Money Shot* taken by a Coast Guard photographer at the scene of the explosion. He used what he had learned to create a computer animation approximating the explosion. The animation had been transferred to videotape. A television was wheeled in on a cart, and the animated explosion was played for the jury.

"The red dots indicate the placement of the explosives," Haas said as it was played again.

"Drawing from your thirty-eight years of experience with and study of explosives, Mr. Haas," Lazar said, "what kind of explosive do you believe was used to blow up *Money Shot?*"

"My educated guess would be C-4," Haas said.

"And why is that?"

"Any other kind of explosive," Haas said, "in the amount that would be needed to do this kind of damage, would be difficult to hide. It probably would have been plainly visible to someone — probably everyone — on board. On the other hand, C-4 is easy to conceal and you don't need as much."

Horowitz took her notes to the lectern when Lazar was finished.

"Mr. Haas, are the red dots in your computer animation the exact — the *precise* — locations of the explosives on the yacht?"

"Well, they aren't precise, no," Haas said. "But the reconstruction of the explosion and placement of the explosives is as precise as I could make it using the material we have."

"So you are not one hundred percent certain that the explosives were in those exact places, correct?"

"Not a hundred percent, no. But I can say that—"

"They could have been, say…in the front of the yacht?"

"Well, they *could* have been, but it's not—"

"Yes or no will do, Mr. Haas. So they could have been anywhere on the boat, correct?"

"Well, not if they—er, um…yes."

"But you *are* one hundred precent certain that explosives were planted on the yacht and were the cause of the explosion?"

Haas tilted his head to one side as slices of concern slowly cut across his forehead. "That is the assumption I was working under, yes."

Horowitz's back straightened and surprise widened her eyes. "What? I'm sorry, did you say…*assumption?*"

An expression crossed Haas's face. It was the kind of expression that might cross a man's face just before he checks the soles of his shoes to see if that unpleasant odor was coming from something he had stepped in. He looked at Lazar uncertainly for a moment.

"Mr. Haas?" Horowitz prodded. "Is that what you said? That you were working under the *assumption* that there were explosives on *Money Shot?*"

"Well…yes."

"So you do not know for sure if the explosives were even *there*, correct?"

"Yachts don't just explode for no reason, there had to be—"

"Answer my question, Mr. Haas, yes or no."

He closed his eyes a moment, sighed. "Yes. But there's more to it than—"

"Mr. Haas, is it possible that the explosion that killed the six people on that yacht was not intentional at all? That it was an accident?"

Lazar again: "Objection, Your Honor, Mr. Haas is an explosives expert, he is *not* a psychic."

"I'd like to hear his answer. Go ahead, Mr. Haas."

He licked his lips. "Look, anything is possible, okay? But based on the evidence, it's my opinion that—"

"You are not answering my question, Mr. Haas. You have told us your opinion. I would like to know if it is *possible* that the explosion was accidental. Yes or no."

"Yes. It's possible."

"I have no further—"

"But not *likely!*" Haas said. "Given the trajectory of the—"

"That's *all*, Mr. Haas," Judge Lester said firmly.

Horowitz smiled. "Thank you, Your Honor." Then returned to the table.

✝

As the days turned into weeks and the first month gave way to the second, Adam began to worry again. It all seemed too easy. Watching Horowitz work in the courtroom was like watching someone engaged in a leisurely round of skeet shooting. Raymond Lazar saying, "No further questions," was the equivalent of shouting, "*Pull!*" as Horowitz stepped in front of the lectern, quickly lifted her rifle, and blew the clay pigeon into scattering pieces.

Adam wondered if it was killing the suspense for the television viewers. Most of all, he wondered when it would turn. Things seemed to be going too well not to turn around and head in the opposite direction. He shared his concern with Horowitz one evening in the car.

"It looks that way to you," she said, "because you know the truth. All of this happened to you, not to the judge or the jury or anyone else. Right now, it looks to you like everything is working in your favor. But your perception is distorted. The biggest mistake you could possibly make now would be to get overly confident. Do not think things are going well. Anything can happen. At any time. And when it is all over, there is still the jury to consider."

"I thought you and the blonde had the jury stacked with people on our side," Adam said.

"We did the best we could with what we had, which is all anyone can do. I guarantee you the prosecution felt the same way when jury selection was over. But ultimately, a jury is unreadable. Unpredictable. In the end, they could put you away for life. There is no way to know for certain one way or the other until the trial is over."

"Then...why did you bother with the blonde?"

"I think it would be irresponsible of me to fail to take advantage of every resource at my disposal on your behalf. Agreed? And that *blonde*—"

"Yeah, I know, I know. She's the best in the country."

"That blonde, as you call her, has been watching the jury from day one, and her read is that they like you."

"You just said juries are unreadable."

"They are. All of them. But her record is very good."

"Very good compared to what?"

"Compared to everyone else in the field of jury consultation, of course."

"Which is a pretty useless field if juries are unreadable."

"As I have told you so many times before, Adam, do not concern yourself with it. Everything is in hand."

"Yeah. That's what George Michael said to the cop just before he got arrested in the men's room."

As exhausting as the trial was, Adam tried to stay up as late as he could at night to spend time with Alyssa. His building had an indoor pool, and when Adam's muscles felt achy from sitting for long periods in the courtroom, they went swimming in the middle of the night. But usually, they watched TV or a movie and had a lot of sex.

Since the first day in court, sex had been hit or miss. Adam could not get the trial out of his head, either replaying the day's events in his mind, or worrying about what might happen tomorrow. As usual, Alyssa sensed this without having to be told. On those nights, she told him to lie back and let her do everything. Sometimes they simply held one another and kissed.

What they did with their time was incidental to Adam. The important thing was being together, and out of the courtroom. Without Horowitz breathing down his neck, without any objections or sidebars or long, mind-numbing testimonies by experts who appeared to be bored by their own field of endeavor.

"I wish I could come to the courtroom," Alyssa said one night as they cuddled naked beneath a blanket on the floor. They sat up against a stack of pillows. "Watching it on television just makes me miss you more."

"Sitting in the courtroom would just make you hate me," Adam replied. "It's like sitting in church all day. But instead of talking about Jesus, they talk about me."

The flat-screen television was tuned to a late-night rerun of *The Jerry Springer Show*. The theme was women telling their husbands and boyfriends they had been working secretly as prostitutes. So far, two women had introduced their boyfriends to their pimps, resulting in fistfights that made the feverish studio audience erupt.

"Think about it," Alyssa said with a sly smile. "I could sit right behind you and write you dirty notes while everybody else paid attention to the trial."

Adam chuckled and said quietly, "That would be nice."

"I could even whisper dirty things into your ear."

"Even nicer," he said with a laugh. "But you can't sit in on the trial because Rona's going to call you to the stand."

"Shit," Alyssa grumbled. "I don't get it. I mean, I'm watching it on TV. What's the difference?"

"I don't know," Adam said with a shrug. "How are your parents?"

"Still alive, Goddammit. They've cut back on the pot, though. Mom even cleaned up the house and got rid of all the joints and paraphernalia. I don't think I've seen them toking up for over a month. They probably do it in their bedroom."

"That's better than you're dad's dick in your eye."

She laughed. "No, they still let it all hang out."

Adam wondered what Horowitz had said to Sunny and Mitch that had worked so well.

"Turns out they're just as obnoxious straight as they are when they're high," she said. "Maybe even worse. Dad's been really quiet and brooding, and Mom always acts like she's starting her period. I used to think things would be better if they'd stop smoking pot all the time. But I still hate their fucking guts."

"Oh, well, the trial will be over sooner or later. Then I can kill them, too." He laughed at his joke. But his laughter was smothered by Alyssa's open mouth over his. She drew his tongue into her mouth, sucked on it.

She closed her hand around his erection and squeezed hard. "Tell me how you'll do it," she whispered against his lips.

"What?"

She squeezed a little harder. "How you'll kill them, tell me."

"Oh. Um...well, I could poison their pot."

Alyssa giggled as she straddled Adam's thigh and began to grind herself against him. She slowly eased her fist up and down his erection. "C'mon, no jokes."

Adam took a moment to respond. *Does she talk about this every time she gets horny,* he wondered, *or does she get horny every time she talks about this? How serious is she about it, anyway?* He wondered if he should ask her. Alyssa was wet against his thigh and already making small sounds of delight in her throat. The motion of her hand did not make Adam feel very talkative. He would ask her later.

Adam never answered Alyssa's question, and they did not see the rest of Springer.

FIFTY

Melonie Sands was not the only person to testify that Adam had threatened his dad's life. Adam remembered seeing Luci Therridge at the house a couple times. She had been Michael's second date after Adam's mom died. She'd been much too young for Michael, nineteen or twenty at the time. Luci was a lowly script girl who had never worked with Michael Julian before, otherwise Adam was sure she never would have dated him. Lowly perhaps, but drop-dead gorgeous, with an intellect stereotypical of her looks and blonde hair. Adam had overheard a conversation between her and his dad at the house. Michael had made a reference to *Birth of a Nation*, and Luci had asked, "Is that a Spielberg movie?"

On the stand, Luci told of an afternoon she had spent at Michael Julian's house before going out with him that evening. Michael had gotten into an argument with Adam. There had been a lot of shouting, enough to make Luci want to leave. At one point, she said, Adam had shouted at Michael, "How would you like it if I got rid of you? Huh? Just made you disappear? How would you like *that?*"

Adam remembered the exchange well. He had, indeed, said that, or something very close to it. But she was taking it out of context. He and his dad had been talking about some student protesters in China who had been in the news. They had simply disappeared. Michael had been of the opinion that they deserved whatever they got. "If

437

you live in China, you don't protest anything. You protest if you live in America. If you protest in China, you're an idiot, because they don't *allow* any protesting, they don't even allow messages in the fucking fortune cookies in China. Now, if they're so Goddamned dumb that they don't know that, then they *should* disappear. They're useless." Adam had spoken words similar to those quoted by Luci Therridge at some point during the brief but heated debate, but with an entirely different meaning. The shouting Luci Therridge claimed had frightened her so was commonplace in the Julian household. At home, Michael Julian had shouted most of the time, and more often than not, people shouted back at him, including Adam. The only one who had not was Mrs. Yu.

Adam wanted to shoot to his feet the way Raymond Lazar did about a thousand times a day and shout, "Objection, Your Honor, the witness is dumber than a box of rocks!" But Horowitz had warned him about reacting to anything during the trial.

"There will be times," she'd said, "when you want to rush the witness stand and give the person sitting there a sound beating about the face and neck with the heel of your shoe. Needless to say, that would be unwise. Remember, you will have your chance to say everything you think should be said. Uninterrupted. Just sit at the table calmly. You can react with a quiet sigh of disgust now and then. A roll of the eyes. But do not overdo it. That can become irritating very fast and the jury *will* notice. Think subtlety."

Thinking subtlety, Adam silently rolled his eyes and shook his head.

"What was the gist of this alleged dispute, Miss Therridge?" Horowitz asked, standing beside the lectern.

Luci's eyebrows rose slowly. "Huh?"

"You said Adam Julian had an argument with his father. What was it about?"

"Oh." She shrugged. "I don't know."

"Well, what else was said?"

"It had something to do with traveling."

"Traveling? What makes you say that, Miss Therridge?"

"Well, I'm guessing. They said something about China, so I figured it had something to do with traveling."

"Let's backtrack a little," Horowitz said thoughtfully. "You say you were sitting at the dining room table with Michael Julian?"

"Yeah."

"You were chatting about movies?"

"Yeah."

"And Adam walked in?"

"Yeah."

"And then they had an argument."

"Yeah."

"And?"

"They started yelling at each other. I hate it when people yell. So I told myself if they didn't stop in the next minute, I'd leave. I'd call a cab, or something." She leaned forward slightly. "I just told all this to that other guy, weren't you listening?"

Horowitz ignored the question. "Can you remember *anything* that was said?"

Luci Therridge sighed impatiently, irritated that she had to repeat herself. "Adam said, 'How would you like it if I got rid of you? Huh? Just made you disappear? How would you like *that?*' That part got my attention."

"But you remember nothing else they said?"

"Well, that was, like, awhile ago, you know? I probably heard what they were saying then, but it wasn't important, so I didn't think anything of it. But that one line, about making Michael disappear? That part really stuck with me."

"Was there anyone else in the room?"

"Um…the housekeeper, I think. Or maid, or whatever."

"Was she involved in the argument in any way?"

"I don't know."

"You don't know?"

Luci shrugged again. "I don't remember."

Horowitz nodded. "You don't remember."

Luci squinted. "Why are you doing that?"

"Pardon me?"

"Repeating what I say. Why are you doing that?"

"I am sorry, Miss Therridge. I guess I was thinking out loud. I am trying to understand how it is that you remember, word for word, a few sentences spoken by Adam Julian during an argument—you even remember what you were talking about with Michael Julian—and yet you cannot remember anything else that was said, what the argument was about, or who else was in the room, if anyone."

"I *said* the maid or whatever was there," Luci snapped.

"You said you *thought* she was there. You were not definite."

"Okay, then, I'm, like, pretty sure she was there."

"Pretty sure? That is not very definite, either. Were you distracted? Did you have something on your mind?"

"I don't know, Jesus, it was, what? *Years* ago."

"Which makes it even more surprising that you remember those three specific lines word for word."

"Are you, like, saying I'm lying, or something?" Luci's face turned pink as she became more upset.

She ignored the question. "Are you positive that Adam said those exact words?"

Luci nodded emphatically. "Yes, those exact words. Because it scared me. I didn't know him, okay? I mean, for all I knew, he was like this crazy person, and I didn't know what he was going to do next. And they were shouting, and that always scares me. If it wasn't for the shouting and what he said, I probably wouldn't remember anything about it at all."

"But you do not remember anything else that was said, or what they were arguing about?"

Luci hesitated. Sighed. "No, I don't."

"And you are not sure if the maid, or anyone else, was in the room?"

Another sigh. "No."

"You *do* understand what it means to be under oath, correct?"

"Yes."

"You approached the District Attorney's office with your story, is that right?"

"Yes."

"Why did you do that?"

"Because I thought they should know."

"Did you know that this trial was going to be covered extensively by the press?"

"Well, yeah. It's, like, a huge story."

"So you knew that, by involving yourself in this case, you would most likely garner the attention of reporters and be on television, is that right?"

"Yeah."

"Is it true that recently you have tried to launch an acting career?"

Luci's eyes widened slightly. She looked embarassed. "Well, I've been trying, yeah. Is...is there something wrong with that?"

"There is nothing wrong with wanting to be an actress, Miss Therridge. Unless you planned to use your involvement in this case as a means to get publicity and further your aspirations as —"

"Objection!" Lazar shouted.

Judge Lester said, "Sustained."

Horowitz took a moment to look over her notes, then said, "No further questions."

✝

On the stand in the uniform of the Los Angeles County Jail, Waldo Cunningham looked exactly like what he was: a dealer of drugs and illegal arms, a manufacturer of child pornography. The best casting agent in town could not have done a better job. Casting agents most likely would avoid Waldo Cunningham for the role because he was *too* perfect, a living stereotype. Everything about him was crooked. His dentures, his dirty glasses, even his toupee.

It was the day the press had been waiting for. Before leaving his apartment that morning, Adam had turned on the television to see them salivating like the hungry scavengers they were.

"Today, Assistant District Attorney Raymond Lazar plans to call to the stand Waldo Cunningham," a female reporter said breathlessly while standing before the Los Angeles Courthouse. "Known as the child pornographer to the stars, Cunningham is the man who told the police that Adam Julian hired Cunningham's son, Nathaniel, to kill his father, popular Hollywood screenwriter Michael Julian. All eyes will be on the courtroom today as Waldo Cunningham takes the stand."

As she went on, Adam had smiled. Amused by the fact that the heavily made-up blonde reporter bounced back and forth between stories, unable to keep straight which one she was reporting — the story of Adam's trial, or the story of Waldo Cunningham's famous clientele. It was a reporter's wet dream.

Before Lazar called Cunningham to the stand, he had questioned Special Agent Gregory Leary, the FBI agent who had arrested Cunningham. Leary established for the jury why Cunningham had been arrested, what he had been doing out there in the desert. He recited a list of material that had been found in and around Cunningham's house, with particular emphasis on the bountiful supply of the explosive C-4. Horowitz asked only a few questions of the agent, emphasizing the drugs, guns, and child pornography with which Cunningham had made his living.

As he waited for Lazar to begin questioning him, Cunningham stared at Adam. His lips squirmed into a half-smile as his small eyes found Adam's. *I may be in jail,* Mr. C.'s eyes said. *But they wanna* kill *you.*

"How did you meet Adam Julian, Mr. Cunningham?" Lazar asked.

"He came to my house in the desert. With his fat friend."

"What brought them all the way out to the Mojave desert?"

"Came to see my son."

"Who is your son, Mr. Cunningham?"

"Diz. Well, Nathaniel. Everybody calls him Diz. For Dizzy. On accounta he's got a little problem that makes him kinda dizzy alla time."

"Had you ever seen Adam Julian before that day?"

"Never. Didn't know who the hell he was. I was working, he and his fat friend come in like they own the place."

"How long were they there?"

"I don't know. They were in the house talking with Diz for awhile. Then they went outside. I don't know when they left."

"Did you know why he came to see your son?"

"Yeah, Diz told me." He smirked at Adam. "He wanted Diz to blow up his dad's yacht."

"Your son told you that?"

"Yep. Said that Adam kid, there—" He nodded toward Adam. " —wanted him to rig his dad's yacht so it'd blow up."

"Why would Adam Julian ask your son to do that?"

"Because that's what my son does," Cunningham said in a tone that suggested Lazar was an idiot for asking.

"Your son sells explosives?"

"No, he uses them to blow things up."

Lazar nodded. "So Adam Julian paid him to do this?"

"Yeah, he paid him. I don't know anybody does that kinda thing for free."

"The explosives found in a building on your property—they belonged to your son?"

"Yeah, mostly. He worked at home, just like me. Kept the explosives in a shed with special air conditioning outside. I used to do that kinda work, but retired for computer work. Less stress. Better for my pump."

"What kind of explosives did he keep there?"

"Oh, different kinds. A lotta C-4."

"A lot of C-4," Lazar said, looking significantly at the jury.

Lazar introduced the security camera videotape of Adam and Carter at Cunningham's house. The courtroom was silent as the tape played.

Adam thought he looked fifteen or twenty pounds heavier. He remembered his dad saying that video could put as much as twenty pounds on the most devoted anorexic. He looked like a different person. The video had been recorded before Horowitz had started dressing him. Instead of an expensive Armani suit, he wore shorts and a T-shirt. Not so long ago, that was standard dress for him. Now he thought he looked like a bum.

Horowitz approached the lectern. "Mr. Cunningham, did you talk to Adam Julian while he was at your house?" she asked.

"Yeah, a little bit."

"What did you talk about?"

"Hell, I dunno. Hollywood. The bidness."

"What business would that be?"

"The movie bidness. He said his dad was a screenwriter."

"Did Adam Julian tell you he wanted to kill his father?"

"No, he didn't tell *me*. He told —"

"While he was in your presence, did he do or say anything that led you to believe he wanted to kill his father?"

Cunningham thought about it, shook his head. "No."

"So this information came from your son only, is that right?"

"Yep. He told me."

"Why did he tell you?"

"Huh?"

"Was there a reason for him to tell you? Were the two of you having a conversation about blowing up yachts and killing people?"

Cunningham chuckled through a sneer. "That's funny. No, we *weren't* having a conversation about blowing up yachts and killing people."

"Then what were you talking about?"

"What difference does it make?"

"The fact that *you* are on the witness stand means that *I* ask the questions, Mr. Cunningham. What were you talking about?"

"I dunno. I don't remember."

"You mean he just brought this up out of the blue?"

"Maybe. I guess so."

"You and your son must be close, then. Are you close?"

"We get along okay."

"Really? Then why do you suppose he would plant explosives all over your house and try to kill you?"

"Objection," Lazar said, standing. "Nathaniel Cunningham's other activities are not relevent to this case."

Horowitz argued, "If so much weight is going to be put on what Nathaniel Cunningham said to his father, I think they *are* relevant."

"Overruled," Judge Lester said. "Answer the question, Mr. Cunningham."

"Hell, I dunno why he did that. Who knows why kids do the things they do?"

"Kids? Nathaniel is twenty-nine years old."

"Yeah, well, he's still a kid to me."

"You are telling us that your son just dropped this information into a conversation? For no reason at all? Is that what you are saying, Mr. Cunningham?"

"Yep."

"That doesn't strike you as odd?"

"Nope."

"You passed this information on to the FBI after you were arrested, correct?"

"That's right."

"And they made a deal with you in exchange for that information, correct?"

"Yeah, we managed to work somethin' out. Took awhile, though. Probably wouldn't've gotten anything if that dead screenwriter hadn't been on every TV set in the country."

"What was the deal you made?"

"I don't have to tell you that."

"I am afraid you do, Mr. Cunningham."

"What's it got to do with this case?" he asked. "I ain't the one on trial."

"But you will be soon, Mr. Cunningham," Judge Lester said. "And you might even end up in my court. Answer the question."

He sighed, rolled his head in a put-out way. "What was the question again?"

Quiet laughter rose in the courtroom like dustclouds, disappeared as quickly.

"What was the deal you made with the FBI and the police, Mr. Cunningham?" Horowitz asked again.

"I tell them what I knew about the screenwriter, they'd drop the sex offender charges."

"Sex offender charges?"

"Yeah."

"What were those charges, exactly?"

"Hey, I got no law degree. You'll have to ask my attorney."

"They were child molestation charges. Correct, Mr. Cunningham?"

"They weren't children, I can tell you that."

"Yes or no, they were child molestation charges."

After a moment, he muttered, "Sex with a minor charges."

"And your attorney managed to get these charges dropped? The child molestation charges?"

"Yeah. That's his job. And it's *sex with a minor*, dammit! There's a difference."

"Is there? I thought you had no law degree. Holding out on us?" Another puff of laughter from the spectators. "In that case, should you move to another town, you would not be obligated by law to inform anyone of your history as a child mol—pardon me, your history of having sex with minors. Correct?"

"Yeah, that's right," he said, irritated.

"Is there a chance, Mr. Cunningham, that the deal made by your attorney to have those charges dropped might color your testimony here today?"

He pulled his head back and his face screwed into a befuddled frown. "Huh?"

"You are a career criminal. You sell drugs, guns, you make child pornography, and you have sex with children, also known as *minors*. Considering the fact that some of your charges were dropped in exchange for the information you offered, why should anyone *believe* that information?"

Cunningham shrugged and smiled. "I don't care if you believe it."

At the prosecution table, Lazar held his pursed lips between thumb and index finger. His head dipped forward and moved back and forth almost imperceptibly.

Horowitz gathered her notes. "Your Honor, I will not dignify this child molester with any further questions."

Lazar shouted his objection before Horowitz finished her sentence. As Judge Lester sustained the objection, Cunningham shouted, "Hey, I'm not a child molester! I'm a child *pornographer!*"

"You know better than that, Ms. Horowitz," Judge Lester growled. She turned to the jury. "You will disregard the defense counsel's inappropriate parting shot and—"

As the judge spoke, Cunningham stood, put his hands on the front edge of the witness stand and leaned forward. "And you call that fucking hack a *screenwriter?*" he shouted at Horowitz, then turned to Adam. "You know how many scripts I've written? Huh? Over two hundred! Not two hundred, *over* two hundred! *All* produced!"

Judge Lester pounded her gavel in an apparent attempt to bludgeon the bench to death. To be heard over him, she shouted, "Mr. Cunningham, you will stop this—"

Two bailiffs rushed to the witness stand, clutched Cunningham's arms and pulled him stumblingly toward the door.

"I write movies for adults about teenage boys havin' sex!" Cunningham shouted. "That Hollywood bastard writes gory movies with people shootin' and slashin' each other and their fuckin' heads're explodin', and he writes 'em for *kids!* He's a screenwriter, and what'm I? A fuckin' child molester! *I'm* the devil here? I ask you!" His voice faded behind the closed door.

The last bang of Judge Lester's gavel lingered a moment.

The silence in the courtroom crackled with tension.

Judge Lester turned her stern owl-like eyes up to one of the small remote-controlled television cameras mounted on the wall. "That oughtta boost the ratings," she said with contempt.

During the trial, Adam lived for the weekend as he never had before, not even when he was in school. It was a welcome but all too short break from the endless hours spent in the courtroom. Although it gave him some free time, it was difficult to do much with it. In front of his apartment building, reporters continued to wait should he make an appearance. Sneaking out of the building became more and more difficult. They had grown wise to his tricks and were learning fast. Adam and Alyssa had tried to go to a movie one weekend afternoon. Somehow, the reporters had arrived at the theater ahead of them. Adam had told Leo to keep driving.

On Saturdays, they listened to reruns of *The Don and Mike Show* on the radio. With the trial taking up all of Adam's weekday afternoons, he had to settle for the weekend "Best of" shows. He found it at once funny and depressing that Don and Mike were the only ones who did not buy the image Horowitz had created for Adam.

"I saw that ball-busting midget lawyer bitch talking to the frog the other night, Larry King," Don said. "She keeps telling us this guy, this killer, what's his name?"

"Adam Julian: daddy-killer," Mike said in a Jack Webb monotone.

"Yeah, damned right. She keeps telling us he's such a fine boy, he's so traumatized by all of this, he's innocent. Gimme a break! I mean, Jesus *Christ*, isn't it obvious this kid's a friggin' killer? Are we the only ones who see this? Is everybody in the Goddamned world brain-dead?"

Mike broke into a dead-on impersonation of Horowitz: "He's such a *fine* boy, he's a *good* boy, he's a *kind* boy, he's a—"

Don shouted, "He's a *killer* boy, you effing C-word!"

"You know, those lawyers," Mike said, "you can't trust 'em as far as you can throw 'em. But the *midget* lawyers—"

"Oh, they're the *worst*, 'cause you can never look the little bastards in the eyes! And speaking of throwing, I could throw her pretty far, you know. I'd like to throw her off a cliff. You hear that, you effing dwarf shyster? Eat me raw with a flavor straw!"

As he laughed with Alyssa, Adam thought, *They're right! It's a comedy show, but they're the only ones who don't believe the story, and they're* right!

The sixth Friday of the trial, Horowitz invited Adam and Alyssa to dinner. Leo picked them up at Adam's building and took them to Annie's, a small Chinese restaurant in a Sherman Oaks strip mall. Max's Escalade was in the parking lot. He and Horowitz already had a table.

"What's the occasion?" Adam said as he and Alyssa joined them.

"No particular occasion," Horowitz said. "We had a good week. I thought you might like to have dinner in a place not filled with celebrities and photographers."

"No celebrities?"

"Not a single one. So keep it under your hat. If they start showing up, the prices will skyrocket. Did Leo lose the reporters?"

"Like a pro," Adam said.

Horowitz ordered for all of them.

"If *you* think the week went well," Alyssa said, "then it must have been great."

Horowitz said, "I only meant that we had five good days in a row. It means nothing, really, just a pleasant rarity. Anything can happen, though."

"Do you say things like that just to make me a nervous wreck?" Adam said.

"No, I say it because it is the truth. A trial is like making a movie. You have no idea how it will turn out until it's all finished."

"How much longer, do you think?" Adam asked.

"Ah, the big question," Max said with a chuckle.

"Another month, maybe six weeks," Horowitz said. "How are you holding up, Adam? I have been too busy to chat lately. Are you sleeping well?"

"Counting the hours I sleep in court?"

"Very funny." Her voice was chiding, but her eyes smiled.

"Yeah, I'm sleeping fine. I prefer it to being awake these days. I'm developing callouses on my butt from sitting in the courtroom."

She turned to Alyssa. "I suspect I will be calling my first witness early next week. Are you ready to take the stand when your turn comes?"

"I'll take the stand and recite Portia's quality of mercy speech from *The Merchant of Venice* in Esperanto while standing on my head if it'll help get this thing over with."

"Justice cannot be rushed," Horowitz said.

Max nodded. "It can be obstructed, miscarried, withheld, and bought. But not rushed."

Alyssa marveled aloud at Horowitz's ability to eat so gracefully with chopsticks and actually get food into her mouth. Horowitz spent a few minutes trying to teach her, but without success.

"Tastes just as good on a fork," Max said. "This walnut shrimp is makin' my mouth awful happy. How come you never brought me here before, Rona?"

"It has been my little secret until now."

A cellphone chirped, and Max and Horowitz reached for their pockets.

"It's mine," Max said. He opened the phone, put it to his ear. "Vantana."

They continued eating as Max listened, frowned, sucked his teeth. "Okay, be right there," he said. Scooted his chair back as he returned the cellphone to his pocket. Leaned toward Horowitz, said, "We got 'em," and stood.

Horowitz pushed away from the table and stood with him. Food still in her mouth, she said, "We have to go. You two finish your dinner, take your time. The bill is taken care of. I am going with Max. Leo will drive you home."

They rushed out of the restaurant.

"What was that all about?" Alyssa asked.

"Who cares?" Adam said, grinning. "Can you believe it? We're in a restaurant together, and we're alone!"

For the rest of their meal, Adam almost felt like a normal person.

✝

Lazar was to call his final three witnesses on Monday of the trial's seventh week. He called to the stand first Detective Wyndham of the Marina del Rey Police Department. He had headed the investigation into the murder of Michael Julian and had helped search Adam's house after his arrest. One of the items found was Adam's story "Father's Day." Lazar introduced it as evidence and instructed Detective Wyndham to read it aloud.

Adam was mortified. It was the story he had written in Mrs. Boam's class. It was terrible, one of the worst things he had ever written. He was surprised it still existed, regretted not burning it years ago. On top of being such a bad story, it simply did not look good for him.

When Detective Wyndham was finished reading the story, Lazar questioned him about the contents of Adam's bedroom.

As the detective answered Lazar's questions, Judge Lester became increasingly restless on the bench. Normally, the old woman hardly moved, and sometimes her magnified eyes closed behind her thick glasses. Horowitz had assured him that Judge Lester was always quite alert, but Adam wondered if she sometimes slept in court. She would rest her chin on her knobby knuckles and her large round eyes would stare at nothing in particular. The already sagging lids would lower gradually, almost imperceptibly, until they were closed. There she would sit, motionless, eyes shut, until someone said, "No further questions," or objected. Then she would sit up, eyes attentive, as if that had been her posture all along.

But during Detective Wyndham's testimony, she fidgeted and sniffed, shot repeated glances to the back of the courtroom. Her behavior led Adam to the conclusion that she had to go to the bathroom.

Horowitz looked casually over her shoulder. Only for an instant. When she faced forward again, she appeared quite satisfied. Lazar said he had no further questions, and Horowitz stood, went to the lectern.

As Wyndham droned in response to her questions, Adam looked to the back of the courtroom, disguising the movement as a restless shift of position. Jack Nicholson was ducking into a seat, trying not to draw attention to himself.

While Horowitz questioned Wyndham, Judge Lester continued to squirm and fidget. Adam decided either her bladder was about to burst or she had crabs.

The instant Horowitz said, "No further questions," Judge Lester's gavel cracked as she stood and said, "Court will adjourn for a fifteen-minute recess." Leaned forward and said something quietly to the bailiff, then left the bench and disappeared.

"Go ahead and stretch your legs," Horowitz said as she sat down at the table. "I think you have a visitor."

Adam nodded, left the table and met Nicholson. "Hi, Jack. What are you doing here?"

"Just thought I'd come over and see how your gig's going," he said with a grin. "Got a call from your attorney a few days ago. She said you were feeling a little down and I oughtta drop in on you. Cheer you up."

Feeling down? Adam thought. *What the hell is she up to?*

"Thanks, Jack, I appreciate it."

"Hey, no problem. I expected to see you before this. You should bring your girl over some night. We could catch a ballgame. Take your mind off all this happy crap."

The bailiff approached them somewhat reluctantly, an embarassed smile on his ruddy face. "Uh, 'scuse me, Mr. Nicholson?"

"Yeah."

"Judge Lester would like to see you in her chambers."

Nicholson's devilishly arched eyebrows rose. "She would, huh?" He turned to Adam and smirked. "What do you suppose I did?"

Adam shrugged, wondering himself.

"I'll be right back. You won't be goin' anywhere, will you?" Nicholson laughed as he patted Adam on the back. Followed the bailiff to the front of the courtroom and through the door through which Judge Lester had disappeared so quickly a minute earlier.

Adam went to the table, where Horowitz was scribbling on a legal pad. Sat down beside her and whispered, "Why did you ask him to come here?"

"Sorry," she said. "I thought you two were friends."

"We are, but I'm not feeling *down*. Why'd you tell him that?"

"I thought he might take your mind off things."

"Yeah. And what the hell does the judge want with him?"

"Oh, Judge Lester is a fan."

"A fan. What'd she do, ask him back there for an autograph?"

"Most likely. And she will probably want to have her picture taken with him. She will frame it and put it on her office wall. If I am not mistaken, Jack Nicholson is one of her favorites. She has a *Chinatown* poster on the wall behind her desk. Right next to her *M*A*S*H* poster."

"*M*A*S*H?*"

"The Altman movie. She loves it."

He remembered something Horowitz had said about Judge Lester before the trial began. "You said she had a weakness. Is that it? Movie stars? Is *that* why you asked him here?"

She turned to him with an irritated tightness to her lips and said, "Adam, I am busy. Take a walk. Get a drink. Go to the restroom. Something."

He knew better than to leave the courtroom. Reporters and photographers would be on him in a heartbeat. Instead, he waited at the table.

Fifteen minutes became twenty. The chatter in the courtroom grew louder, more restless. Twenty-six minutes into the fifteen-minute recess, Nicholson came out of the corner door grinning and went to the defense table.

"I'm really sorry about that, Jack," Adam said, standing.

"Hey, no problem at all." He leaned close and whispered, "Goofy old bat, huh? But harmless. Just wanted a couple autographs and a picture taken, is all."

"You don't have to stick around for this. It's boring beyond belief."

"Oh, I don't think so. I've been watching at home. It's a good show."

"All rise," the bailiff called.

Nicholson squeezed Adam's shoulder. "You watch your ass," he said with a smile before returning to his seat.

When Judge Lester returned to the bench, her cheeks were rosy and she wore lipstick. She smiled at the back of the courtroom as she took her seat.

Adam thought, *Unfuckingbelievable,* as he dropped into his chair to sit through Raymond Lazar's last two witnesses.

✝

Adam awoke to kisses on Tuesday morning. He opened his eyes to see Alyssa smiling at him, her face just a couple inches from his. Her naked body was warm against him.

"I've been watching you sleep," she whispered. "It was nice. But I thought you'd want to get up."

He looked at the clock and gasped. "Holy shit, it's late! I set the alarm, why didn't—"

"I turned it off. You've still got time."

Sitting up, he pushed the covers away and yawned.

Alyssa asked, "How about some quick hot monkey lovin' before another hard day in court?"

He put his arms around her. "I'd love to. But I don't even want to think about what Rona would do if I was half a minute late. She calls her first witness today. The trial's half over."

Alyssa swung a leg over his lap and straddled him, wrapped her arms and legs around him. "And then we can start our life. Together."

"Maybe. That's up to the jury."

She kissed him. "I'm gonna be optimistic."

"And I'm gonna be late." He returned her kiss, slid her off him and went into the bathroom. Turned on the radio on a shelf beside a stack of towels. Opened the shower and reached in to turn it on.

" —currently being held on charges of murder for hire, while Rivers is being questioned."

Adam pulled out of the shower, turned toward the radio. "Rivers?" he muttered. The news broke for a commercial and he rushed naked to the living room. Grabbed the remote, turned on the television and flipped to CNN. His mouth dropped open.

On the screen were two mug shots. One of Diz, the other of Billy Rivers. A male voice was speaking over the pictures, but it was babble to Adam. The ringing in his ears competed with the pounding of his heart. He dropped onto the sofa as Alyssa came into the room.

"What happened?" she asked. "What's the matter?"

He barely heard her as he stared at the television. The news reporter droned on. Adam made out only a handful of words: " —turned themselves in late Monday night."

Even after the story ended and the anchor had moved on to the next, Adam continued to stare slack-jawed at the television.

"What is it, Adam, tell me." She went to his side. "You're scaring me."

"It's, um…well, I guess it's…" He launched from the sofa, went to the telephone and dialed Horowitz's office number. When she came on the line, he asked, "Have you seen the news?"

"Yes."

"So you know?"

"Know what?"

"That Diz and—I mean *Nathaniel* and Billy have turned themselves in. They're in jail."

"Yes, I know that."

"Well?"

"Well what?"

"Did you know about this?"

"I just told you. Yes, I know."

"No, I-I mean…well, what does this *mean?*"

"It means we can put Nathaniel on the stand."

The thought of Diz on the stand telling the truth, the whole truth, and nothing but the truth terrified Adam. "Are you sure that's a good idea? I mean, who knows *what* he'll say?"

"I would never question a witness on the stand without knowing exactly what he is going to say, Adam. Relax. Everything is under control. I will see you in court."

"What's *wrong?*" Alyssa asked, putting a hand on Adam's shoulder.

He put down the phone, turned to her, and tried to smile. "Diz and Billy turned themselves in last night." He nodded toward the television.

"Is that bad? You look worried."

"No, it's not bad. I…I don't think it's bad. It's…good, probably. Yeah. It's good." He smiled again, but with great effort. Diz knew the truth that Adam had kept from his attorney and everyone else. If he revealed it in court, even Rona Horowitz would not be able to save him.

FIFTY-TWO

I will not get Nathaniel on the stand until this afternoon at the earliest," Horowitz said to Adam. They stood by the drinking fountain outside the courtroom before the trial began for the day. "Why are you fidgeting like that?"

Adam could not hold still. His nerves threatened to spring free of his body and shatter like icicles on the tile floor of the corridor. But he stuffed his hands in his pockets and stood straight when Horowitz chided him. "Sorry. I'm nervous."

"There is no need for you to be nervous, Adam. I am the one who has to do all the work." She winked at him.

"Are you going to put Billy on the stand, too?"

"No. Billy does not seem very…communicative."

"That's because he's brain-dead."

"I think Nathaniel will be more than enough."

Yeah, Adam thought. *But more than enough of* what? "Why this afternoon?"

"I beg your pardon?" Horowitz asked.

"You just said you won't get Nathaniel on the stand until this afternoon. I thought you'd get him on the stand first thing."

"First I have to tell Lester and Lazar. Lazar will object and claim it an unfair surprise, and I will have to remind the court that Nathaniel Cunningham turned himself in just last night. Lester will allow it,

455

but first, an investigator will be brought in to get a statement from Nathaniel. They will check his background, make sure he is who he says he is. He has no identification on him. None of his own, anyway. Lester will want me to call my next witness and continue the trial while this is going on, but I will argue that Nathaniel *is* my next witness because I want him to testify while Waldo Cunningham's testimony is still fresh in the minds of the jury before I muddy the waters with other witnesses. Factoring in bureaucracy, incompetence, and the usual unforseen hold ups, I will be *lucky* to get him on the stand this afternoon."

"You mean, there's a chance you *won't* get Diz on the stand?"

"Of course I will, and everyone knows it. But this is the way it works."

"Jeez," Adam said with a sigh. "If they did it this way on *The Practice*, I bet Camryn Manheim would be a lot thinner."

"Once things get underway this morning, you will be here for no more than an hour, maybe ninety minutes." Horowitz flashed a smile. "Then you can go home and watch *Lost in Space* reruns until we are ready."

✝

The day was hot and muggy.

"It's not just muggy," Adam said to Lamont with a whine hidden in his voice, "it's soup- *thick* with mug."

They were in Lamont's silver Porsche 911 Turbo. Lamont had just picked up Adam at his apartment and was driving him back to the courthouse. The air conditioner blasted icy air in their faces and Nine Inch Nails made the black, diamond-shaped speakers in the doors quiver. Lamont lit a cigarette with a silver Zippo, clanked it shut. Inhaled a long drag as if it were the fragrance of angels.

"You don't look so good, Lamont," Adam said as he took in Lamont's drawn face and mussed hair. His jaw was dark with stubble, but Adam decided not to mention it while Lamont was driving. The way he ran in a panic to shave every time Adam pointed out his five o'clock shadow, he was afraid Lamont would shoot across traffic and onto the sidewalk. End up killing a few pedestrians and sticking out of a Fotomat.

"Oh, yeah? I don't look so good?" Lamont glanced at him. Took a quick Bette Davis puff on the cigarette. "Well, everybody's lucky I'm conscious, that's all I can say. I've been in nonsmoking places all day, haven't had a cigarette since about five-thirty this morning. I think my fucking lungs have actually had time to reconstitute. I practically *begged* that dictatorial diva *bitch* to let me pick you up so I could have a couple smokes. I haven't gotten more than three hours of sleep since Thursday night. Nothing but running back and forth and waiting and making calls since Friday. All of it *my* responsibility, of course. Gerald is in the hospital with some kind of flu that was apparently brought to earth by an alien spore from another galaxy. I talked to his mother on the phone and I could hear him in the background, throwing up. He sounded like Mr. Creosote in *Monty Python's The Meaning of Life*. I could actually hear it hitting the wall. I was waiting for him to talk backwards, I was going to call a priest. It's nice to know someone's been *slightly* more miserable than I this past weekend."

"What were you doing over the weekend that kept you up all night?" Adam asked.

"*Working!* Carrying out the whims of that fucking tyrant. Doing her dirty work. On Sunday, I was so tired, I started hallucinating Egyptian pyramids and Roman columns. At one point, I thought I was Randolph Scott and Rona was Helen Gahagan, and we were in *She*. Rona threw a Dixie cup of water in my face and told me to have some coffee with plenty of sugar. Can you believe that fucking soulless bitch?" Traffic backed up and Lamont rolled to a stop.

Adam became more curious. "What were you guys working on all weekend?"

Lamont rolled his eyes, as if that were a stupid question. "What do you *think* we were working on? We were—" He stopped mid-sentence and stared silently out the windshield for a long uncomfortable moment, mouth open. Traffic began to move again as Lamont closed his mouth and let out a long, noisy, raspberry sigh through his lips. "We were working for *you*, Mr. I-Don't-Wanna-Spend-My-Life-In-Prison, Mr. I-Don't-Wanna-Be-Executed. We knew Lazar would wrap up his little show by Wednesday at the very latest. Rona prepares for trials the way James Bond villains prepare for world domination. I wouldn't be surprised if the tyrannical cunt has an underground fortress and a fucking shark tank tucked away someplace."

"Does she know you talk about her in such glowing terms?"

The Porsche slowed suddenly. A car beeped behind them. Lamont shot fearful bird-like glances at Adam. "You wouldn't. I mean, really, you *wouldn't*, right? Haven't I been good to you through this whole thing? Haven't I tried to make it easier on you?"

He had, there was no doubt about that. Especially when Adam was locked up in the Peninsula for what seemed a lifetime. But Adam said nothing, just looked at him.

"You little *shit*," Lamont hissed.

"Look, I'll make a deal with you. I won't tell Rona how you talk about her behind her back if you promise not to drive off the road and take out a family of four when I tell you that…you *really* need a shave."

Lamont's fists tightened on the steering wheel. His Anthony Perkins shoulders rose as he took in a deep breath. Shouted, "So I'm growing a fucking beard! Somebody just go ahead and shoot me, for Christ's sakes!"

✝

A problem with the courthouse air conditioning had caused the heat rather than the air conditioner to turn on and off all morning. It was fixed minutes before Adam arrived, but the courthouse still felt nearly as hot and humid inside as it was out. As he walked up the aisle, spectators on both sides fanned themselves with envelopes and folders and pamphlets taken from purses and briefcases. *All we're missing*, he thought, *are a couple ceiling fans and Gregory Peck as Atticus Finch.*

He sat beside Horowitz at the defense table. She was writing on her legal pad. Adam watched her a moment, then decided to interrupt. Lamont's remarks had bugged him all the way up in the elevator and he wanted an answer. "What did you do over the weekend that kept Lamont from sleeping since Friday?" he asked.

Horowitz scribbled for a few seconds more without acknowledging him. Stopped, reread what she had written. Turned to Adam and said, "I beg your pardon?"

Adam repeated his question.

Horowitz said, "Lamont is having personal problems and has been exhibiting signs of delirium. Claims to be growing a beard. And Sunday, he called me Miss Gahagan. As soon as this trial is over, Lamont will be going on a desperately needed vacation. As will I."

"All rise," the bailiff said. There was a low rumble when everyone stood.

"Okay, can we get back to it?" Judge Lester said. "At my age, I could go any second, and I'd kinda like to see how this thing turns out."

After the jury had been called back in, Horowitz stood. "I call Nathaniel Cunningham to the stand."

Adam cringed.

As Diz entered the courtroom and went to the witness stand, Adam tried to make eye contact with him. Diz did not even look in his direction. But Adam could tell Diz knew he was there, because he made such a concerted effort to avoid looking at him. It chilled his blood. Adam was certain it could mean only one thing. Diz was about to tell everything he knew.

No, no, he argued with himself. *Rona would never let him up there if she thought he would damage our case. But what else* can *he say?*

There was a ripple of reaction to Diz's appearance. His burned scalp and face, the hole in his cheek. Plain black patch over his eye, gnarled flesh where his fingers used to be. He was dressed like his father, but stood up straight and walked with dignity in spite of his shackles.

I bet Rona told him to walk like that, Adam thought.

After Diz was sworn in, Horowitz stood beside the lectern, propped her left elbow on it.

"Nathaniel, how long—may I call you Nathaniel?" she asked.

"Nathaniel, Diz. Whatever." His voice was full and clear. He smiled, and as sincere as it was, Adam saw some faces grimacing among the spectators in resposne.

"Nathaniel, how well do you know Adam Julian?"

"Not real well. I only met him once. That wasn't for long."

"Enough to recognize him if you saw him?"

"Sure. He's right there." Diz pointed at Adam with a thumb and forefinger on a stump. He looked at Adam, but did not make eye contact.

"Very good," Horowitz said. "So, you only met him once. How did you meet?"

"He came to my house. My parents' house, really."

"You had never met him before?"

"No."

"Then why did he come to your house?"

"He gave my friend Billy a ride."

"Who is Billy?" Horowitz asked.

Diz shrugged, and the gesture was all his. But it was just a glimpse of the strange young man Adam had met in the desert. Something about him was not quite right. It took awhile, but he finally realized Diz was not talking like Diz. He used no profanity, there were no verbal pauses. No words running together lazily. He was talking like Horowitz. Like one of her clients.

"A friend. I've known Billy five, six years," Diz said. "Billy Rivers."

"Why was Adam giving Billy a ride?"

"Billy makes stuff, like movie special effects stuff. Y'know, masks and bloody wounds. That kinda stuff. We got a lot of chemicals and stuff around the house. Billy uses some of 'em to make those things he makes. He needed some that day, but didn't have a way to get there, so Adam took him. Adam brought along his friend Carter. Billy and Carter was good friends, too."

Adam clenched his teeth to keep his jaw from dropping. He could not believe what he was hearing. *My God,* he thought, *he's sticking to the statement I gave the police, to the story I told Horowitz so many times. He's lying…with my lies.*

"That was the only reason Adam came out to your house?" Horowitz asked.

"Yeah, far as I know. Just a ride."

"When you met him, did you talk?"

"A little."

"What did you talk about?"

"Movies. TV, maybe. Nothin' much."

"And that was all?"

"Yeah."

"How long were you together?"

"I don't know, twenty minutes, maybe."

"Did you agree to meet again later?"

"No."

"You've had no contact with one another since that day?"

"No."

460

"At any time during your one brief meeting, did Adam offer you money to blow up his father's yacht?"

Diz rolled his eye. "No, he didn't."

"At any time did he mention wanting to kill his father?"

"No," Diz said with a firm shake of his head.

"Perhaps he just joked about it, Nathaniel. Did he make any funny remarks about, say, inheriting all his father's money?"

Diz chuckled. "No, he didn't."

"Did he mention his father at all?"

"Yeah, he said his dad wrote movies."

"Do you think he might have been proud of that fact? That his father wrote movies?"

"Probably. I would be. I'd be proud if my dad did *anything* I could tell people about."

"Did you tell your father, Waldo Cunningham, that you were hired by Adam to blow up Michael Julian's yacht?" Horowitz asked.

He chuckled again. "No, I never said that."

"Did you say something *like* that?"

"Something like it, yeah. It's stupid."

"Why don't you explain, Nathaniel."

Diz sighed. "Okay, look, my dad don't listen to me. Never has. My mom's the same way. They haven't heard a thing I've said since the doctor smacked my ass and I cried for the first time. And over the years…I kinda made a game of it, y'know?"

"Made a game of what?"

"When I was a kid, I used to see how far I could go before they'd pay attention to what I was sayin', you know? Once, when I was, I don't know, eight or nine years old, I was goin' out and my dad asks me, 'Where you goin'?' And off the top of my head, I said, 'Toby and me're gonna steel a car and drive to Mexico.' That kinda thing. I been doin' it ever since. And that's what happened. One day, I was goin' out, and my dad asks me, 'Where the hell you goin'?' and I said, 'I'm gonna go blow up a yacht.'"

"Those were your exact words?"

"Closest I can remember. It was just something that popped into my head."

"Did your father respond?"

"No. He never responds. He never hears me. I mean, asking me is just, like, a habit. That time…I guess he heard me."

"Tell me, Nathaniel, why did you and Billy turn yourselves in last night?" Horowitz asked.

"A few reasons."

"Could you tell us what they were?"

"Well, for one thing, it ain't easy hidin' from the law. I mean, Billy and me've had our pitchers on TV almost as much as he has," Diz said with a wave in Adam's direction. "I just didn't wanna keep doin' that. Neither did Billy."

"Were there other reasons?"

"Oh, yeah. *Mostly* because everybody's been sayin' I did somethin' I didn't do. It's all over TV and on the radio, people sayin' I blew up this yacht and killed those people and I *didn't*." Another wave at Adam as he said, "And *he* didn't try to hire me to do it. I've done some things. And I'll have to...y'know, deal with that. But I didn't *kill* nobody."

✝

By the time Horowitz finished questioning Diz, the day was over.

Raymond Lazar was quick and aggressive as he questioned Diz on the stand the next day. But he got nothing helpful. Diz remained calm and relaxed as he answered each question without hesitation. When asked where he was the day and night before Michael Julian's yacht blew up, he said he was at home. Was his father home at the time? Both his parents were there. Whether or not they had noticed him, Diz did not know.

Horowitz brought Waldo Cunningham back to the stand and confronted him with his son's story. Cunningham blustered and backpedaled, but maintained that his son had told him he had been hired to blow up Michael Julian's yacht. His story had been deflated, though, and even Lazar could not pump any air back into it.

Diz's testimony was the lead story of every news report and the focus of all the talk shows. It was generally agreed by all the talking heads on television that Rona Horowitz had been doing an excellent job of casting doubt on the prosecution's case. But they also agreed that Nathaniel Cunningham was a godsend for the defense. Diz added pathos to the already colorful story of California vs. Adam Julian. The public liked him, pitied him. And everyone loathed his father.

Adam decided not to ask Horowitz how she had managed it. She did not bring it up, of course. Neither did Max nor Lamont. Adam was afraid to jinx the maneuver by bringing it out into the light of day. It was the first time he felt with certainty that he would be found not guilty. A feeling he tried to shake because Horowitz had told him so many times that it was dangerous. After all, she'd only just started presenting her case to the jury. And juries were unpredictable.

But Adam could not help feeling that, after Diz's testimony, the trial was over.

Over the following weeks, Horowitz called to the stand a long line of extensively coached witnesses. She started with long-time friends of the Julian family — including Mrs. Yu — who, one at a time, claimed they had never seen any evidence of trouble between Adam and his father, certainly nothing more than the typical father-son tensions and the occasional testing of the boundaries of authority. If anything, they said, Adam had always been a little too quiet, polite but never very talkative.

Lazar questioned them vigorously, but his attempts to discredit or even confuse them met with little success.

Horowitz called to the stand several expert witnesses of her own. Dr. Locket and Dr. Remini, a couple other psychiatric experts, an expert in explosives, and even the designer of the yacht. The designer had very little to contribute and she could have done without him, but that sort of thing seemed to impress juries. Her explosives expert was puzzled by the question of whether or not there had been explosives on the yacht.

"If there were no explosives on the yacht, it wouldn't have exploded," he said. "Of *course* there were explosives on the yacht. The one we know about is fuel. There's evidence that it *was* a boat, and it *did* blow up. But beyond that, I see nothing that could lead to anything resembling a conclusion one way or the other. Not without the involvement of the paranormal."

"Could it have been accidental?" Horowitz asked.

"Yes, it could have been accidental. But it could have been hit by a meteorite, too. It could have been *anything*."

Her next witness was actor Donald Sutherland. He recounted the incident in which Michael Julian had nearly burned down his own house while trying to cook trout almondine.

"Michael was…well, he was not very well-coordinated," Sutherland said.

When Horowitz and Lazar were finished questioning the actor, Judge Lester adjourned for a thirty-two-minute-long fifteen-minute recess, which she spent in her chambers visiting with the star of *M*A*S*H*.

Alyssa took the stand and told of her relationship with Adam. She was an excellent character witness, and provided vivid descriptions of Adam's behavior around the time of the explosion, which she thought perfectly normal. But most of all, Horowitz allowed Alyssa to be herself in front of the jury. To show them she was an intelligent, sensitive, lovely young woman. Not the kind of person who would hang around with a murderer.

Adam and Alyssa had been coached separately. Less time had been spent on Alyssa, but when Lazar questioned her, it did not show. She handled herself beautifully as he asked her how she possibly could know that Adam's behavior was normal when she had known him for such a short time. Did she think the people closest to a killer were objective enough to realize he was a killer? Did she actually think Adam would have *confessed* his guilt to her? And what about her goth fetish? Wasn't she a regular at a dance club called Jugular? Didn't she hang out with people who drank each other's blood? She answered the questions thoughtfully, sincerely, and truthfully, and remained unrattled by the hostility that crept into the deputy district attorney's voice.

Horowitz called witnesses—two of Michael's ex-girlfriends, a former personal assistant, a producer, and a fellow screenwriter—who had known Michael Julian and testified that he was a clumsy man. It was not an obvious clumsiness, they said, but the kind you noticed after you had known him awhile. Then you came to realize he could not get through a room without bumping into something.

But it was Horowitz's next and final string of witnesses for which the press and the public had been waiting with such anticipation.

✝

From the moment Horowitz claimed in her opening statement that Gwen Julian was wanted in four different states under four different identities, the news media had chewed on it like an entire neighborhood of dogs on a dinosaur bone. The District Attorney's office reacted with outer calm while a frenzied investigation was conducted away from the press. The story began to unfold on television, in newspapers and magazines, and on the internet. Starting with the evidence Max Vantana gave them, the FBI launched an investigation.

Photographs of earlier Gwen Julians began to surface in the media. She had undergone excellent cosmetic surgery at various times in her past, altering her features slightly. Along with changes in hair color and style, it was enough to make her look remarkably different in each picture, under each identity. Each face represented a dead rich man. A stockbroker in New York, the founder of a nationwide chain of electronics stores in Seattle, a rancher in Montana, and a retired architect in Maine. No one famous enough to make things too difficult for her. All four had died in accidents that were so clean, they almost did not look suspicious. But they raised just enough eyebrows to be investigated. By the time suspicions became certainties, she had disappeared as if she had never existed.

Horowitz questioned the detective in charge of each investigation in each state. The detectives identified the women they were looking for among the pictures of the surgically altered Gwen Julian. The agent heading up the FBI investigation took the stand and confirmed that all the women in the photographs were indeed Gwen Julian. He also revealed that no records existed of Gwen's daughter Rain, nor was there any record of Gwen ever having a child. Technically, he said, Rain had never existed.

Lazar objected repeatedly on relevance, but was overruled each time.

Horowitz skillfully painted a picture for the jury, in bold, colorful strokes, of a beautiful, brilliant, soulless black widow who so pathologically craved the money she made from killing her husbands, she was willing to undergo painful operations to change her appearance so she could continue killing husbands without getting caught.

Somewhere, Adam thought as he sat in the courtroom, *Aaron Spelling is watching this and jerking off.*

✝

Meanwhile, the usual attention given the trial continued. Twice a week, a television screen lowered over Conan O'Brien's desk showing only the very top of a black-haired head identified as Rona Horowitz. Off camera, a man spoke in a falsetto voice, mocking Horowitz's clipped, abrupt speech pattern as he subjected Conan to a comic, hostile cross-examination.

On *Saturday Night Live,* guest host Alec Baldwin portrayed a bumbling, tripping, blithering Deputy District Attorney Raymond Lazar in a courtroom sketch that broke into a musical number a third of the way through.

Each night for a month, David Letterman introduced Rona Horowitz, and out walked a male dwarf in a replica of one of Horowitz's suits with a fat cigar clamped between his teeth. And each night, he delivered a different absurd line in falsetto, many of which concerned the high-profile attorney's plot to rule the world.

Everywhere, the gurgling of water coolers mixed with conversations about the trial, some loud with dissent. Many people believed Adam Julian to be a spoiled, amoral rich punk who possessed no values or conscience, and that he probably *was* responsible for the deaths of the six people on *Money Shot,* but they suspected he would never be convicted because of his wealth and Hollywood connections. The great majority, however, believed the prosecution's case to be unforgivably weak, and thought if Adam was convicted, it would be due to his wealth and Hollywood connections, which the jury might resent. Groups on both sides of the discussion demonstrated outside the courthouse with signs and banners. Sidewalk vendors sold T-shirts and caps and buttons and coffee mugs and flags, all souvenirs of the *Money Shot* trial.

An "unofficial" version of the story would be the subject of a Fox made-for-television movie to air right after the trial. In it, a young, relatively unknown soap opera actor who had golden hair, a deep tan, pouty lips, and piercing blue eyes portrayed Adam, and Heather Locklear made a special appearance as Gwen Julian.

A small northern California toy company called RawSpot Toys — the manufacturer of dolls in the likeness of real-life serial killers like John Wayne Gacy and Jeffrey Dahmer, and celebrity death scenes in the form of model kits — found itself at the eye of a storm of controversy when it added to its catalog an exploding model of *Money Shot*. The replica of Michael Julian's yacht was eighteen inches long and flew into pieces with the *ka-ching* of a ringing cash register. Each *Money Shot* came with six tiny figures made to stand on the deck and fly in all directions when the yacht "exploded." Once reassembled, it could be set to fly apart again. Newspaper columns and editorials expressed outrage at the company for making such an obscene toy. Call-in talk shows and internet chatrooms boiled with the angry words of indignant people horrified by the depths to which some would go to make money these days. The owner of the small toy company received several death threats. But he was able to afford excellent security with the money he was making in bundles from *Money Shot* alone, which was so popular it was difficult to keep in stock. Not to mention the tremendous increase in overall sales resulting from all the publicity. Suddenly, his toys — aimed at rebellious teenagers and adult collectors of the macabre — were so popular, he had to get a new server for his website, which was mobbed daily.

✝

As if the melodramatic story of Gwen Julian were not enough, Horowitz gave her audience one last surprise. She called Adam to the stand.

With no way of knowing exactly what might happen during cross examination, it is very rare for a defense attorney to put a defendant on the stand. An inarticulate, flustered, angry, or seemingly dense defendant is not typically a winning defendant. A flash of arrogance, an angry epithet exclaimed when cornered, and it could be all over, no matter how strong the case. Less than five percent of all defendants testify in their own defense. In most cases, attorneys will not let them, even if they want to.

Adam had known all along that Horowitz was going to put him on the stand. The very thought of it had paralyzed him with fear at first. Since then, he had been trained for it as a soldier is trained for combat. But it still paralyzed him with fear.

Lazar had tried to bring the liquor store security videotape into the trial during the pretrial procedures, but Judge Lester would not allow it because it was unrelated to the murder charge. But as she led Adam through the entire story he had told her, Horowitz herself showed the videotape to the jury. She used it to show what Rain had put him through, to establish that Adam was afraid for his life because of what Rain had threatened to do, and because of what he had overheard in her bedroom. There was a dramatic gasp in the courtroom when Adam said Gwen Julian and her daughter Rain had planned to kill his dad as well as Adam himself once he had outlived his usefulness.

"You knew your father's life was in danger, Adam," Horowitz said. "Why didn't you warn him? Why didn't you tell him what his wife and her daughter were up to?"

"I did," Adam replied. "I told him everything. He came into my bedroom one day and I just…I laid the whole thing out to him. In detail. From top to bottom."

"How did he react?"

"He thought I was pitching a script."

"What does that mean, Adam?"

"He thought I was telling him an idea I had for a screenplay. He…he really liked it, too."

Horowitz frowned, as if puzzled by Adam's response. She asked, "How could he think such a thing? After you had told him everything?"

Adam looked down at his lap. Waited a few beats, just as rehearsed. Quietly, sadly, he said, "Dad and I, we…we never communicated very well."

On the stand, Adam was able to address each and every point made against him throughout the trial. He and Carter, Adam claimed, had written bloody stories for Mrs. Boam in the eighth grade because they upset her so and made her screw up her face until she looked like the Grinch from the Dr. Seuss book, and it had made them laugh. He described the conversation he and his dad had been having when he made the remark Luci Therridge had interpreted as a threat on Michael Julian's life. It gave Adam a feeling a satisfaction to answer all the questions the trial had raised.

By the time Lazar took over, Adam and Horowitz had established that Adam's relationship with his dad, while not hostile, had been very shallow. Most of their conversations, Adam said, had consisted of Adam talking about one thing and Michael another. Lazar was brutal in his attack. How could Adam expect anyone to believe that such a story got no reaction from Michael Julian? Had he insisted to his father he was telling the truth? Adam said he had tried, but his father was too enthused about the script and how much it could make at the box office to listen. But why didn't he go to the police? Adam said he was too afraid—they probably would not believe him, either, and he was afraid of what Gwen and Rain would do if they found out. He was still trying to figure the whole thing out when *Money Shot* blew up on the water.

Lazar went on, grilling Adam like an all-beef patty. He asked about the influence of movies, television, and horror novels on Adam's life, about Adam's story, "Father's Day," about everything. He changed subjects suddenly, threw dates and times into the air like confetti to confuse Adam, to catch him off-guard. But having been through Rona Horowitz's witness stand boot camp, Adam stood up well to the attack. He remained calm, sometimes paused to think, even when he knew exactly what he was going to say. Secretly, he was afraid of making a mistake, of using the wrong word at the wrong time. But he kept thinking about Alyssa watching him on television at home, and when he did, his performance went smoothly.

Adam was surprised by the startling similarity between Lazar's questions and the questions with which Horowitz and her staff had prepared him in the months before the trial. It was almost like following a script.

✝

In his closing statement, Raymond Lazar appealed to the intelligence of the jury. He asked that they not be fooled by the nonrelated elements that had been brought into the trial by the defense to misdirect and confuse.

"A woman who assumes one identity after another as she murders rich husbands?" he asked. "What has that got to do with this case? A liquor store robbery? What has *that* got to do with this case? Think about it, ladies and gentlemen. If you are guilty and you have no defense, what is your best course of action? Your *only* course of action, short of confessing? It would be to confuse *you*, the jury. To muddy the waters enough so that *you* might not be able to see that tiny gold nugget of truth on the bottom of the stream. It's up to *you*, ladies and gentlemen, to make sure the defense does not succeed in doing that. You are the only twelve people in the world who can clear that water and find that precious nugget of truth."

Lazar stood before the jury, his face taut, intense. He paused a moment. Took a deep breath.

"This is a murder trial," he continued. "The defendant is accused of arranging the murder of his father, which ended up killing six people. Gwen Julian is not on trial here. She is a *victim!*" he shouted. "One of *six* who are not here today to tell their stories because Adam Julian hired Nathaniel Cunningham to blow up Michael Julian's yacht. And if you doubt that, consider this." He pointed at the empty witness stand. "The oath taken by those who sit in that chair is *not* a guarantee that they will tell the truth. They give their word of honor to tell the truth. But you must carefully consider their honor before deciding to believe them. Nathaniel Cunningham, who just happened to show up the night before the defense presented its case, was a last-minute surprise witness because he was a *fugitive!* He was running from the law! And he was put on the stand to muddy the waters more. And to *defend* Adam Julian. *That* should tell you something right there!"

After the trial, media wags would ridicule Lazar's closing statement for giving the jurors all the reason they needed to dismiss the testimony of Waldo Cunningham, his key witness.

✝

"Ladies and gentlemen," Horowitz said, "this case never should have come to trial. The charges were based entirely on the claims of a child molester. A child pornographer. A drug dealer. A seller of illegal weapons. The prosecution's case has only one leg to stand on—Waldo Cunningham. And that is a bum leg."

She stood with her hands on the rail of the jury box, no notes on the lectern, her attention focused completely on the faces of the jurors, as if no one else were in the room. "At the beginning of this trial," she went on, "I said I would prove that the explosion that killed those six people *could* have been an accident. Only you know if I have succeeded in doing that. But I remind you again that the defense is not obligated to prove *anything*. The burden of proof is on the prosecution. It is the duty of the prosecution to prove — beyond all doubt, beyond all question, beyond all further discussion whatsoever — that the defendant is guilty. Once again, only you know if the prosecution has succeeded in doing that."

Her voice was soothing as she went over the case again, speaking with them, not just to them. Discussing something they had just gone through together, solidifying a shared experience.

Adam was as mesmerized as the jurors and spectators, could not take his eyes off her. He listened to her words as if she were telling a riveting story he had never heard before. But it did not last. His eyelids lowered slowly and he turned away as he realized with disgust, *Jeez, she sounds just like Oprah!*

What Horowitz had taught Adam over a period of months came naturally to her. Everything she did, everything about her, was meticulously calculated. From her posture to the modulation of her voice, to her hairstyle. She knew how to talk to them as if they were all friends, had known one another well for months, years. She knew exactly what they wanted and gave it to them. And no matter how far from the truth, they lapped it up like thirsty dogs.

Adam thought again, *Just like Oprah.*

"If you think the prosecution has met its obligation," Horowitz said, "then you must turn in a verdict of guilty. But before you do that, I must ask you…are you *sure?* Do you have it all worked out in your head? Have you considered motive? Why would he do it for money? Adam has never been needy. His parents were very successful and wealthy. They worked hard to provide a life for their son in which money would never be a concern. Can you imagine that? Not living from paycheck to paycheck? Having the kind of life in which you never had to worry about juggling the bills, or getting the rent in on time, or going broke at the holidays? It would be wonderful, wouldn't it?"

Adam had no doubt that, for that moment, those jurors thought Horowitz was one of them, that she too had to worry about money and keeping groceries in the refrigerator. He suspected Rona Horowitz had forgotten long ago what dollar bills looked like.

"That's the kind of life Adam Julian has always had," she continued. "If you really believe that, with that kind of life, he would need money so badly he would kill his father and stepmother and four other people for it...well, I'd be interested to hear the reasoning behind *that*. Or perhaps you believe he hated his father. Was there any evidence to support that? I saw none. This is a young man who had the kind of relationship with his father that millions of other Americans have had, and continue to have, with their fathers. Maybe they didn't always get along, but what father and son do? Or father and daughter, for that matter? Maybe communication between them wasn't crystal clear. I remember trying to talk to my parents, even as an adult. I sometimes wished they had subtitles so I could figure out what they were talking about. Am I the only one? Is that such a rare thing? I don't think so."

It went on for a long time, but did not feel long at all. Adam was astonished once again by the transformation in Horowitz as she faced the jury. She was softer, gentler. She was warm and feminine and human for the jury. He had thought television softened her, but she did it herself, at will. Adam liked to think it was the real Rona Horowitz shining through. But he knew better.

"What about Gwen Julian?" Horowitz asked the jury. "Mr. Lazar would like you to believe I brought her up simply to confuse you. The truth is, had the police and the FBI been doing their jobs, I would not have *had* to bring her up. *They* would have investigated the possibility that the explosion of *Money Shot* was a botched murder attempt by *her*, not by Adam Julian. I am not saying that is what happened, but it is a very real possibility. There are many possibilities in this case. Too many to point the finger of guilt at my client without further investigation. As I said, this trial never should have taken place."

Adam became restless. Glanced at the clock.

"And there's the other question," she said. "What if it was just an accident? Until that question is answered, until that doubt is ruled out completely, my client is not guilty. The prosecution did not even *approach* the possibility that it was an accident. I had to bring it up. As defense counsel, that is not my job. But *that* is the kind of trial this is, ladies and gentlemen. A quick rush to judgment. Let's turn a vague, unsubstantiated possibility into a case of murder. Of course, the prosecution doesn't have to worry about money or paying the tab, either, because *you* get the bill for this. *This* is one of the reasons your taxes are so high. *This* is one of the reasons the courts are so backed up. So we can have trials that get the attorneys on television, and set them up with fat paychecks for lecture tours and books they don't even write themselves, they have someone *ghost*write them. Riding around in a limousine from talk show to talk show, staying in all the best hotels. I know what it's like because I do those things. But I am a private attorney. I work for myself, and all those things are part of my profession. I do not represent the people of the state of California. I do not decide how to spend their tax dollars. Whether Mr. Lazar gets the verdict he wants or not, he will get all those things, because he has been involved in a very high-profile trial. He is now a celebrity. He's not just an attorney anymore. He is now and always will be the attorney who prosecuted the *Money Shot* Trial. If he wanted to, he could quit his job the day after this trial ends and be assured of a very comfortable life. For that, all he had to do was show up. He did not even have to do a good job! And as far as I'm concerned, ladies and gentlemen, he did *not* do a good job. I have provided you with far more doubt than he has provided you with evidence that my client, Adam Julian, paid for murder. He could not even prove a murder had taken place, never mind who did it. The prosecution has given you something, however. He has given you no choice but to find my client not guilty. I have faith in you, in your reason, in your wisdom. And I feel in my heart that is the verdict you will deliver. Thank you."

There was not a sound in the courtroom except Horowitz's heels against the tile floor. They sounded like firecrackers going off in the silence. She took her seat, put a comforting hand on Adam's shoulder and whispered into his ear: "It's all over but the verdict."

That morning, dark clouds rolled in over Los Angeles. By the time Adam left the courthouse, a cool rain was falling. As Horowitz had instructed, they offered no comment to the reporters as they got into the car.

The backseat of the Lincoln seemed to shrink as Leo drove them away. The ceiling seemed to lower on Adam, the door to shove him up against Horowitz.

She asked, "Are you going to be sick?"

Adam took a few deep breaths. Shook his head. "I don't think so."

"Is that a no?"

"Jesus, I'm off the stand, gimme a break," Adam said. His lungs began to shrink and he started panting. He sucked in a breath every couple of words as he said, "I-I'm getting dizzy. I think I may be having a stroke."

"You are hyperventilating, Adam," Horowitz said, holding her left hand, palm up, out to Lamont, who sat on the other side of her.

Lamont fished around in the inside pocket of his suitcoat, removed three small pill bottles. He squinted at the labels from beneath a head of shaggy, mussed hair. His beard, which had to be trimmed two or three times a day, had grown in around splotches of hairless skin. "I've got one for depression, one for anxiety, and...and I can't read this third one. Fuck it." He stuffed the third one back into his pocket.

"Anxiety," Horowitz said.

Adam pressed a hand to his frantic chest, tried to calm himself. None of the relaxation exercises Dr. Remini had taught him worked. His lungs only got smaller.

Horowitz pressed a pill into his hand and said, "This is the anti-anxiety drug Dr. Locket prescribed for you. There is a bottle of water attached to the door by your leg." As Adam took the pill, Horowitz poked and prodded in her purse. Removed a small paper bag with the Tiffany's logo on it and handed it to Adam. "After you take the pill, put this over your nose and mouth and breathe regularly. I am sure you have seen it done on *I Love Lucy*."

Adam breathed into the bag as he replaced the bottle of water on its hook.

"Does everybody who uses the car drink out of the same bottle?" he huffed into the bag.

Lamont rolled his weary eyes. "I can't believe you could be getting the death penalty today and you're worried about germs!"

"That will be enough, Lamont," Horowitz said impatiently. "No one is going to get the death penalty today."

"I'm not?" Adam asked, pulling his face out of the bag.

"If that happened, we would appeal and you would probably do no more than life."

"No more than that? Y'think?" He put his face back in the bag.

"You will feel better after you eat," Horowitz said. "Wolfgang is sending food to the office. This would not be a good day to attempt a restaurant. I am famished."

Lamont said, "I could eat my own feet."

None of them had eaten at lunch because none of them had been hungry.

"We should have shared a vegetable plate in the cafeteria," Horowitz said, "even though we had no appetites."

Adam dropped his hands and the bag into his lap and slouched in the seat. "I can't believe I might get the death penalty and all you're thinking about is eating."

"You will only feel worse if you do not eat," Horowitz said.

Adam made a nauseated sound and said, "I feel...I feel like..."

Like Don Knotts in Caligula! he could hear Carter saying.

The food from Wolfgang Puck was waiting for them when they arrived at Horowitz's office. Adam smelled seafood. It sickened him.

Horowitz lifted sterling silver lids, sniffed rising tendrils of steam. "Oh, this is marvelous. Sit down, Adam. Eat."

"I can't eat," he said angrily, as if that fact should be obvious.

"You have had nothing since breakfast, if you ate that," Horowitz said as if she had not noticed his anger. "I will not let you get sick, you have to eat something. Here, have some of this French bread. Still warm."

"If I eat, I'll throw up in the car."

"If you do not eat, you will pass out at the verdict."

Adam's eyes grew round. "What? You...you think it's gonna be bad?"

She popped a scallop into her mouth, closed her eyes. "Mmm, Delicious. Sit down, Adam."

He went to the corner to get the chair he always sat in, but it was not there. Panic exploded in his chest. He closed his eyes, told himself to calm down, it was only a chair. "My chair's gone," he said quietly through tight lips.

"Oh, I needed it in the conference room," Horowitz said as she spooned food onto a plate. "Lamont, go get Adam's chair."

"Sure," Lamont said, muttering on his way out, "I'll get his blanky while I'm up."

Horowitz said, "Pay no attention to Lamont. He is just feeling cranky."

"Boyfriend problems?"

"No. He cannot decide whether or not he wants to have electrolosis performed on his face."

"Are you serious? He's upset about his beard? *That's* his personal problem?"

"You know Lamont. He obsesses about his facial hair. It grows like a Chia Pet on crystal meth. It is there even when it is *not* there. And yet, even when it is allowed to grow in, he has bald spots on each side the size of quarters. Rather odd, yes?"

"Why don't you just let him wear the beard?"

"I am, until the end of his vacation. Then he has to make a decision."

"What decision?"

"Whether to have the electrosis or find employment elsewhere."

"Are you serious? You're gonna fire him over his beard?"

"Not exactly. I am going to fire him because the people who like beards do not dislike men who do not wear them. People who do *not* like beards, however, tend to dislike people who wear them. Often quite intensely. It is an unnecessary obstacle and against the policy of this firm."

Adam frowned, cocked his head. "You work so well together. I thought you liked him."

"Oh, Lamont is the best assistant I have ever had. But this firm operates the way it does because it works. I will not change that over a beard." She walked over to Adam and offered him the plate. "Here."

"I told you, I can't eat." He stepped around her, lips curling at the smell of the food.

Lamont walked in carrying the chair. "Okay, you can stop talking about my beard now," he said, dropping the chair in front of Adam.

Adam looked at it as if he did not recognize it. Turned to Horowitz. "How long do you think this will take? Can I go see Alyssa?"

"The verdict probably will not come in today. It is almost four o'clock now, which does not leave much time for deliberation. That is as it should be, because typically, a quick verdict is a bad sign. But no, you may not go see Alyssa. If you like, she can come here or to your apartment. But between now and the verdict, I do not want you wandering around the city like some Dickensian urchin."

Adam took his cellphone from inside his suitcoat. Opened it, punched in Alyssa's number. Sunny answered and immediately began to cry. "Oh, Adam, we've been watching," she said. "I know how worried you must be, honey, but I've got really good vibes about this, I really do."

"Yeah, the vibes are, um...vibrating over here, too," he said. "Is Alyssa there?"

"She's here, Adam, but she's in the bathroom and can't come to the phone at the moment. She's having a pretty painful flow this month. Can I have her call you back?"

The Huffmans. Such open, honest people. "Yes, tell her to call my cellphone."

Chewing on a bite of bread from Adam's plate, Horowitz opened the cabinet that held her television and turned it on, clicked the remote. Adam sat in the chair after putting the cellphone back in his pocket and Horowitz stepped before him, offered him the plate. "I am very serious, Adam," she said. "You need to eat. You *will* pass out at the verdict."

"My God, you keep *saying* that!" Adam said, his voice higher than usual. He felt ready to pull out his own hair with clenched fists. "Why the hell do you think I'm gonna pass out? Are you *expecting* a guilty verdict?"

Horowitz leaned close and raised her voice slightly. "From malnourishment! If you passed out after receiving a guilty verdict, it would be appropriate. But after a not guilty verdict, it would only ruin a perfectly good exit. Now take this plate before I drop it in your lap and bill you for the carpet stains."

Adam took the plate.

Lamont gnawed on an oversized bite of French bread as he filled his plate. Horowitz made a plate for herself and took it to her desk. Put on her headset, punched a couple buttons.

"It's Horowitz," she said. "Do you have any numbers for me?" As she listened, she wrapped a scallop in strands of pasta on her fork and put it in her mouth.

Adam's cellphone warbled. He sat in the chair and answered. It was Alyssa, and she was terribly embarassed.

"I can't believe she said that to you," she said. "And she actually *told* me she said that to you, as if it was nothing. 'I just told him you were having a bad period,' she says, like it's no different than saying, 'She can't come to the phone right now.' I mean, do you see what I have to live with here? Death is too fucking good for them. I'd torture them for a few weeks if I had a place to keep 'em so they wouldn't be found."

Adam laughed. "Don't be embarassed. Shucks, ma'am, I know all about that stuff."

"Oh, no you don't. Just because you read *Carrie* and watch reruns of *Maude* on TV Land doesn't mean you know squat. Have some of these cramps, then we'll talk."

"You're funny when you're on the rag," he said.

Alyssa laughed. "Well, it just started this afternoon, so that means I'll be the life of the party for the next few days." Her words fumbled as she made the reference to the future. They said nothing for awhile. Then she whispered, "It's gonna be fine. I feel it in my gut, Adam."

There was another pause. Adam did not want to talk about what was coming, what might happen. Instead, he remembered something he had intended to bring up earlier, but had forgotten. He said with a chuckle, "Hey, I didn't know you were a party girl."

Horowitz's phone trilled again and she put her call on hold.

"Oh my *God*, I can't believe he said that!" Alyssa said. "A regular at the Jugular? I was there *twice!* Maybe three times. I never had a goth *fetish*, I just hung out with goths. I wanted so *bad* to tell him to kiss my ass!"

"Yeah, yeah. Your past comes back to haunt you." He laughed.

"What do you mean? You…you *believe* me, don't you?" Her voice dropped and she sounded genuinely hurt.

"Of course I believe you. How could I not believe you, Alyssa?" He whispered, "I love you. And if I get out of this, when I get out of this, whatever…I want to be with you." Clenched his teeth. "I *have* to be with you. I…I have a surprise for you. If things…turn out."

"A surprise?" Alyssa sniffled. "Can I see you? Now?"

"You wanna meet me at the apartment?"

"Adam," Horowitz said.

He turned to her and saw what looked like surprise on her face. Four fingertips lightly touched the curved black tube of plastic that ended near her lips.

"The jury has reached a verdict," she said.

"When do you want me there?" Alyssa said. "Right away? Please say right away."

Adam's jaw hung open as he stared at Horowitz.

"Adam?" Alyssa said. "Are you there?"

"I just sat down to eat!" Lamont said.

Horowitz stood and removed the headseat. Talked as she walked around the desk. Moved here and there. Adam wondered if he really *was* having a stroke, because he could not speak, and Horowitz sounded like the teacher's honking voice in the *Peanuts* cartoons.

Alyssa sounded worried as she said, "Is something wrong? What's the matter? *Adam?"*

"I-I have to—" He had trouble with the "g." "Go. The verd-ver-dict—"

"Oh, God, is it in?" Her voice was a breath.

"Yes."

Two sobs blurted up from her chest. "It's gonna be fine, I know it, I can feel it. I love you, Adam."

"I'll, uh…talk to you later." Adam's voice was drying up, becoming coarse. "One way or the other, I guess." He turned off the phone, dropped it in his pocket.

Adam walked between Horowitz and Lamont to the elevator but did not feel his legs. Horowitz's words blatted from a muted trumpet and made no sense. A few numbers got through. Percentages, statistics. And a few words now and then, just barely. Something about "overwhelming support in the polls." Horowitz and Lamont looked blurry in his peripheral vision.

In the elevator, Horowitz stepped in front of him, squeezed his elbows and jarred him. "Adam? Adam!"

Annoyed, Adam asked, "What?"

"Do you remember everything about the delivery of the verdict?" she asked. "Stand straight? Do not let the—"

"Yeah, I remember."

"All right, then. Are you ready?"

He shook his head slowly. "No. I'm not."

"Good," she said with satisfaction. "I would not want you to get overconfident."

It took great effort to understand a word she said. The malady continued all the way to the courtroom. Once inside, the babble in the room sounded like a pond full of ducks. Jack was there, patted Adam on the shoulder and said something to him as they passed. Nicholson's words were senseless quacks. Adam wondered if he should tell Horowitz to call an ambulance.

They stood when Judge Lester entered, sat when she sat. Then a lot of talking, blapping and honking back and forth. They stood again. Something tugged on Adam's arm and he looked down to see that Horowitz had taken his hand. He watched her squeeze it, but could not feel it.

Adam turned to stone again. Stone, all the way through. To the center.

The foreman of the jury handed the bailiff a rectangular sheet of white paper. The bailiff handed it to Judge Lester. She looked it over, honked a few words. Gave it to the bailiff, who handed it to the court clerk. The blurry, gelatinous courtroom fell silent and everyone listened as the clerk erupted into a series of honks and blats. Something cut through it all like the glowing blade of a light sabre. Two words.

"Not guilty."

Adam passed out.

FIFTY-
FIVE

On the day the verdict was read, the entire country experienced a remarkable drop in productivity. People called in sick, left work early, or went to work and did nothing but watch or listen to the trial coverage all day. Every television network covered it, and there were countless webcasts on the internet, which bulged with congestion. Even Comedy Central provided live coverage of the verdict, with legal commentary by Harry Hamlin, who played an attorney on *L.A. Law* back in the eighties, *Ally McBeal* attorney Peter MacNicol, and Dr. Ruth Westheimer.

For weeks, *Entertainment Tonight* and Liz Smith had been making a lot of noise about the bags of mail Adam received. They claimed a good percentage of the mail was made up of marriage proposals from total strangers. Talk shows and chatrooms echoed the question: How long would Nick and Nora last if he was found not guilty, with all those women falling at his feet? Just three days before the verdict was read, Horowitz had let Adam answer the question himself outside her office building. With her words, of course.

"I have not read a single proposal of marriage," Adam said into the microphones.

"Do you read your mail?" a reporter asked.

"Some of it. I can't read all of it. But I've read quite a bit, and if there are as many marriage proposals in my mail as some people

485

have been saying, I think I would've seen one by now. Besides, it wouldn't matter if there *were* any, because I'm not interested. Alyssa and I are too happy." He had smiled.

In the car afterward, Adam had asked, "Was that necessary? I didn't even want to acknowledge that stupid story."

"You and your girlfriend are a very popular couple," Horowitz said. "People like you and want you to be happy. They must not think your eyes might wander. Bad numbers that way lie."

Adam regained consciousness to the sounds of applause and cheering and the rapid-fire cracking of Judge Lester giving another savage beating to the bench. She adjourned the court, and Adam and Horowitz were escorted out of the hectic, excited courtroom by three of Horowitz's large, somber security men in charcoal suits. Through the building quickly, outside into the cool, rainy afternoon, and to the front steps and courtyard outside. A restless swarm of reporters, most with umbrellas, shouted questions as Adam and Horowitz approached the transparent plexiglass lectern mounted with several microphones.

Horwitz held up a hand and said, "We are not here to answer questions, not right now. Adam would like to make a brief statement." She backed away from the microphones and Adam stepped forward.

He cleared his throat and with real emotion in his voice said, "First of all, I'd like to thank God for what just happened in there. And for the American justice system that made it possible." Back in November, when Horowitz had first told him to start memorizing the not-guilty verdict statement to the press, he had complained about the opening line. Adam did not believe in God. Horowitz had said, "On that day, you will." That had not happened. Adam still did not believe in God. But he believed in Rona Horowitz.

His throat thickening, he continued. "I'd like to thank Rona Horowitz, who has not only been an amazing attorney, but a great source of support. And…and, um…"

Adam looked out over the reporters crowded together. Their faces watched him from beneath overlapping umbrellas, anticipating his next sentence, his next word. Rain tap-danced noisily on all the umbrellas. A siren sounded nearby, a joyous whoop accompanying the ovation.

There was more, but for a moment, Adam's mind went blank. Then: "I would like to thank you for all the support you've given me."

"Why would I thank the reporters for their support?" Adam had asked Horowitz back in November. "The reporters are weasels and egotistical airheads."

"You are not thanking the reporters for anything," Horowitz had said. "When you talk to a reporter, Adam, you are talking to the world. That is why most reporters are so unpleasant. No one ever talks to them, only to their cameras. It is rather sad, really. You thank the world, I will thank the reporters."

Feeling light-headed, Adam took a deep breath and went on. "The letters and cards and gifts have given me a lot of encouragement over the months, and I'm grateful. But now, I would like to quietly put my life back together. I have a...a lot to adjust to. Thank you."

Adam and Horowitz traded places again at the microphones as questions erupted from the crowd of reporters.

"No, no, I am sorry, but we are answering no questions right now," Horowitz said, managing to sound firm and apologetic at the same time. "I will be making a statement at my office building in about an hour, and I will be glad to answer your questions then. For now, I just want to say that I hope you will all respect Adam's wishes. The trial is over and he has a life to rebuild. Please give him the space and privacy he needs to do so. You have all been wonderful, thank you very much."

The questions did not stop as the three large men escorted them to the car. Nothing short of a direct hit by a Chinese missile with a nuclear warhead would make them stop asking questions. They did not know when to stop. They did not know how to stop. They asked even though none of them expected an answer. Their goal was not to gather the most facts, but to ask the most questions.

In the car, Adam asked, "Was that your thank-you to the press?"

"I wish," she said with a huff of breath. "My thank-you to the press is the big fat holiday party I throw for them every December." She looked through the tinted glass at the people standing on the sidewalk, waving and cheering as they drove away. "Wolfgang whips something up for me. Always enough booze to float the Titanic. Last year's entertainment was Tony Bennett. This year, we have Billy Joel."

"Sounds great," Adam said. "Can I come?"

"Are you a journalist who has made an effort to treat my clients with a fair measure of respect and dignity in your chosen medium?" Horowitz asked.

Adam rolled his eyes. "No."

"Then you may not come. The Christmas party is for them."

"But I'm your client," he said.

Horowitz laughed. "Not as of this afternoon." She turned to him and gave him the gift of a dazzling smile. It stayed in place longer than any other smile Adam had seen on her face. "You are a free man, Adam. No longer accused, and no longer locked in the dungeon of clientude."

Adam knew she meant well. The smile was genuine. She was proud of what she had done for him and happy for his freedom. But something about her words twisted Adam's heart.

"We will stop by my office and you may collect your things," Horowitz said.

"Collect my things? Sounds like we're getting a divorce."

She laughed. "You have some clothes and a few books at the office. Some videotapes. You may pick those up, then Leo will take you to your apartment."

Adam frowned at her. "You're really kicking me out, aren't you?"

Horowitz's smile melted away and she looked at him with mild concern. "There is no point in leaving your things in my office, Adam. You will no longer be *coming* to my office. Your time is your own now."

Still frowning, he turned away from her. Looked out the window.

"You might be interested to know," she said, "that the vast majority of my clients are unable to get away from my office and me fast enough. Typically, they are so eager to get on with their lives, they do not have a spare moment to spend with me. Are you an anomaly?"

"A lot of them *still* won't get near her," Lamont said.

"I take that as a compliment," she said. "Is something wrong, Adam?"

Adam said nothing. Looked at the waving people on the street. Watched the wobbly shadow of the helicopter that followed them overhead.

Rona Horowitz and her employees were all that stood between Adam and those stupidly grinning, waving strangers. They were his only protection from the helicopter, and from all the cameras and microphones. From the tabloid reporters who would go through his garbage and possibly break into his apartment to learn his secrets. And the "legitimate" reporters, who might hire someone to do their dirty work, or just report whatever the tabloids came up with. Anything to keep alive a story the world did not want to stop watching or reading. How long before he would be able to step outside his apartment building without being photographed or videotaped? How long would the mail continue coming in, and who would handle it for him?

Adam turned his thoughts to Alyssa. Told himself he should be on his way to her place by now. He did not want to think about the future. He had the present on his mind. Things to do, people to fool. A disguise to don, miles to travel. But without Horowitz, his future would be an ominous alien landscape.

"What am I going to do?" Adam said.

Horowitz nodded. "I understand your concern, Adam. I have something for you."

A life? Adam wondered.

Back in Horowitz's office, Adam sat in his chair while Horowitz's staff poured champagne and toasted their shared victory. After fifteen minutes of uncharacteristic revelry, Horowitz went to her desk, took something from a drawer and approached Adam. She sat at the end of the sofa nearest him. Handed him a square, white, paperboard envelope.

Adam looked inside and found a DVD-ROM. "A computer game?" he said.

"You will be in need of some services," Horowitz said. "For awhile, anyway. On that disk, you will find all the companies and services you might need. Personal security agencies, private detective agencies, car services, financial services, delivery services, catering, and a few other things that will make your life a little easier. There's no avoiding it, I am afraid. Those are all companies I use myself and I endorse them with great enthusiasm, so you know they are trustworthy. And for being my client, you get a fifteen percent discount across the board."

"A commercial," Adam said. He let out a slow sigh. "Thank you. So much."

Horowitz tucked her hands between her knees and leaned forward. "I think I should explain something to you, Adam. This afternoon, in a court of law, you were found not guilty by a jury of your peers. *Not* guilty. That means you *won*. Were you perhaps awaiting the arrival of an envelope with Ed McMahon's picture on it?"

"I know, I know," he said, nodding. "We won. Thank you. I *meant* that thank you when I was out there jerking off for the reporters. Without you, I'd be in prison right now."

"At least."

"I'm very grateful for that. But I'm sorry if I can't show it because I...I can't seem to feel anything. Or maybe I feel things, but they're very distant. I mean, I've got *plans*, and I'm really excited about them, but...my excitement is a couple floors up dancing around in some other office. Does that make sense?"

"That is not uncommon," she said. "You must continue seeing Dr. Remini and Dr. Locket. Dr. Remini will probably put you in group therapy for awhile, to keep you from withdrawing. Right now, you are extremely vulnerable to depression. Do what they tell you. Even if you do not want to. That is *especially* important for the next six to eight months."

Adam nodded in agreement. He would need all the help he could get.

"What are your plans?"

He flinched. Had he mentioned having plans? He had. But it was not a problem. Horowitz knew nothing about his real plans. He smiled and said. "Oh, I plan to have some fun with Alyssa. Enjoy not having to be anywhere at a specific time. Sleep in. You know."

Horowitz nodded. "I know it was a long and exhausting trial, and your life will never be the same as it was before all this happened. But the public likes you, and that makes a big difference. It could have been worse. Can you imagine what it would be like to be Linda Tripp?"

Adam said, "Can you imagine what it would be like to *do* Linda Tripp?"

Horowitz sighed as she stood, smiled a little. "I am so disappointed to see I have failed to scrub the last of the vulgarity out of you."

Adam stood and towered over her. "Will I see you again?"

"Of course you will see me, Adam. I am everywhere. You will see me on television. We will meet at charity benefits and parties. You will ask me to dance at the premiere party for Mr. Nicholson's next movie. And maybe the man himself will cut in, and he and I will have a few laughs over Judge Lester's star-struck eccentricities. And I expect you to invite me to your first book party, so you will certainly see me there."

She sounded as if she had everything planned and arranged. Adam would not be too surprised if it all happened exactly as she had described it, in the very same order.

"You have a lot to write about, Adam. That might be the key to putting it behind you."

He knew she was right. The page had been his dumping ground for everything for as long as he could remember.

They shared a brief hug as Lamont came into the office chewing on a hotwing and holding a glass of champagne. Grease and dollops of barbecue sauce glistened in his mustache and beard.

Lamont said, "Everything is in the car, and it's—"

Horowitz averted her eyes. "Lamont, you have food in your beard," she said with disgust. "Remove it or leave the building immediately."

Lamont tossed the hotwing into a garbage can, removed a paper napkin from his pocket and wiped furiously at his beard. He took a breath before trying again. "Everything is in the car, and it's waiting downstairs."

Adam shook Lamont's hand. "Thank you for everything, Lamont. You've been great. I don't know if I could've done it without you."

"I don't know if *anyone* around here could do it without me." He shot Horowitz a look. "Without me, someone would've killed her by now."

Horowitz smiled. Tilted her head to the right, lifted her hand beckoningly. As Lamont stepped toward her she said, "Lamont, my faithful and trusty assistant…the French Riviera is calling you. Heed that call. Now. Maybe you can get an earlier flight?"

"I already did. If I don't leave here right now, I won't have time to shower before I catch the plane." He turned to Adam and lifted his glass. "To your not-guiltiness! And you're welcome." He smiled, drank.

"I am unavailable for the next two months, Adam," Horowitz said. "After that, feel free to call me if there is anything I can do for you."

And that was it. Adam left the offices of Horowitz and Associates and never returned.

Reporters surrounded Adam's apartment building. Leo drove past the crowd, through the gate of the private parking garage. Carried the garment bag and satchel up from the underground garage to Adam's apartment, in spite of Adam's protests.

When Adam reached into his pocket for his wallet, Leo smiled and shook his head. "You know better than that, Adam. It's been a pleasure working with you, and I'm sure glad things turned out this way. I always knew they would."

"I'm really sorry about throwing up in the limo," Adam said. "And in the Lincoln."

Leo laughed, boxed Adam's shoulder. "That was no trouble at all. My brother's got a nervous stomach like that. My advice'd be to stay away from anything with little seeds in it. They'll play hell with your belly."

As soon as Leo was gone, Adam called Alyssa again. He had tried from the car, but had gotten no answer. The Huffmans had an ancient answering machine, and Adam had been waiting for it to die. A few weeks ago, it had begun to drag the cassette tape, making voices sound like foghorns. Maybe that had been its dying gasp.

He took off his suit, tossed it onto the bed. Took a quick shower while Vince Guaraldi played "Mr. Lucky." Afterward, he called

Alyssa's number again. Still no answer. He wondered if they were at the bookstore.

Sunny had hired a young woman named Liz to help out during the Christmas rush in December. It turned out Liz knew books better than Sunny and Mitch combined. She was so adept in the store, they decided to keep her on. At least for awhile, to keep Alyssa freed up for the demands of the trial. They had wanted her to spend as much time as possible with Adam.

Maybe Liz was off for the day, or had gotten sick, and Alyssa and Sunny had gone to work at the store while Mitch did whatever it was that Mitch did. Adam decided to call the bookstore next. But later, in the car, once he was on his way.

He put on a pair of faded jeans, a black short-sleeve shirt, a sloppy old green-and-tan cotton camouflage jacket, a pair of old sneakers. A convincing ponytail that matched his hair color hung from the back of the black cap he put on, with *The X-Files* logo in front. At his dresser, he applied a few strokes of spirit gum just above his upper lip. Gently pressed on a stringy mustache, which also matched his hair color. Clamped a tiny ring onto the edge of one nostril to give the illusion that his nose was pierced. Grabbed the cordless phone and made a call as he pocketed his keys.

"Garage," a voice said.

"Donald! You got my car?"

"It's waiting for you."

"I've got the rest of your money right here. In cash."

"I trust you. It's not like I don't know you. Hell, *everybody* knows you."

"Well, that's what we *don't* want, Donald." Adam went into the kitchen and opened the refrigerator. Grabbed a carton of orange juice off a shelf and took a few gulps, put it back. "That's the most important thing, here. That's why I tip so big, okay?"

"You got no problem there. Nobody's getting anything outta me."

"I'll remember that in a big way come Christmas time, Donald."

"I'm Jewish."

"I'll get you a Faberge dreidel. What kind of car is it?"

"A green ninety-two Toyota Corolla. Needs a tune-up, but it runs good."

As long as it gets us to the airport, Adam thought. "I'm on my way down. Have it running and ready, okay?" He severed the connection. Punched in the doorman's number.

Adam had thought ahead, but barely. Only three days ago, he had realized that if he were found not guilty, he would be able to do anything he wanted. After months of following Horowitz's rules and doing nothing without her permission, it was difficult to conceive of such freedom. Being able to do anything he wanted meant being able to go anywhere he wanted. His only obstacle would be the reporters. But if he could get out before anyone could adjust to the fact that the trial was over, he might be able to avoid them. He had decided then to prepare for it, just in case. Now that he had been found not guilty, Adam had the nagging feeling he should get out of town before the jury changed its mind.

Donald, one of the building's garage attendants, had a brother who owned a small used car lot in the Valley. During his last visit to his former Beverly Hills home with Lamont, Adam had emptied the contents of his dad's office floor safe. He had no plans for the money at the time, but was glad he had taken it. Only three days ago, he had given Donald enough cash for a down payment and told him to bring back a car, any kind of car, as long as it ran well. He tipped well, hoping that would keep Donald quiet, if only for awhile. Just a few days, maybe. Sooner or later, a tabloid reporter would come along with a far bigger tip, wanting to know what Adam was up to, and Donald very likely would take the offer. He was a blue-collar man surrounded by wealth and luxury that would always remain out of his reach—Adam thought he would be an idiot if he did not take it. Just as long as Adam had time to pick up Alyssa and get out of town first.

"May I help you?" a voice on the phone said.

"Hi, this is Adam Julian."

"Hello, Mr. Julian. Congratulations!"

"Thank you, Charles. Could you do me a favor?"

"Certainly."

"Well, Charles, I've decided to speak to the press."

"Yes, I see. Well, they certainly are eager to hear from you."

"Could you tell them I'm going to take some questions in the lobby in five minutes?"

"Here in the lobby?"

"Would that be okay?"

"I don't see any problem with that. You want me to tell them now?"

"Right now, please."

"No problem, Mr. Julian. See you in a few minutes."

Adam put the cordless back on its base, grabbed his cellphone and dropped it into his jacket pocket. Took the Guaraldi CD from the player and slipped it into his jacket pocket. In his bedroom, he went to the closet and removed the oldest, most unattractive piece of luggage he owned — an old, badly wounded medium-sized Louis Vitton suitcase, already packed. Snatched a pair of large black sunglasses from his dresser and put them on. Looked into the mirror and examined his appearance. Not bad. He even had captured a touch of Tom Cruise in *Born on the Fourth of July*. He hunkered down and opened the bottom drawer of his dresser. Removed a folded-over manila envelope that was thick in the bottom half. Tucked it under his arm and closed the drawer with his foot as he stood. Adam left his apartment for the last time and hurried to the elevator, which he took down to the garage.

Donald, a smiling, bullet-shaped fellow in his forties, waited for him, a ring of three keys dangling from his pudgy, oil-stained thumb and forefinger. A pinging green Toyota idled just a few steps beyond him, driver's door open.

"Good luck," Donald said.

Adam smiled as he handed over the envelope, snatched up the keys. "Thanks a lot, Donald, I appreciate it. I'll see you tomorrow," he lied. He tossed the suitcase into the backseat, slid behind the wheel. Gave Donald a final smile before pulling the door closed.

The spirit gum held up beautifully. A little itchy, but it was sticking. Adam followed the painted arrows out of the garage, the Toyota a pinball winding its way around the obstacles of its machine.

He turned on the windshield wipers as he drove out the main exit and up into the gray, rainy daylight. Past the clot of reporters piling into the front entrance of his building as if the sidewalk were on fire.

Adam knew that distraction would not last long. The reporters would stand around gossiping and fighting and flirting with each other indefinitely. They were accustomed to waiting. But Charles the Anal-Retentive Doorman would not tolerate a long wait. He would call up to Adam's apartment. When he got the machine and no one picked up, he might assume Adam had lost track of time and was in the shower, and under the circumstances—he'd been acquitted of murder only an hour ago, after all—Charles might give him a few more minutes. Then he would call Adam's apartment again, and when no one picked up the second time, he would send someone up. Then it would be minutes before the reporters discovered they had been tricked.

"You can fool the press only once," Horowitz had said early in their relationship. "It infuriates them, and they hold grudges. Once they figure out that you successfully pulled the wool over their eyes, they get embarassed and go to great pains to see that it never happens again. They will turn on you for awhile, make your life miserable. But they come back around once they think you have learned your lesson and know better than to poke the eye of the world with a stick. That is what happens if they get embarassed. If they get *humiliated*, you might as well go live in a cave, because they will never forget it. They will dine on your carcass until the last drop of marrow has been sucked from your smallest bone. Rather than fooling them, I have found it much more productive to simply provide them with what they need. That keeps them happy."

Adam was pretty sure this would be considered no more than a little embarassment. They might even get a charge out of it. America's favorite Internet couple, Nick and Nora, eloping and then disappearing for awhile to honeymoon away from the cameras. It was an ending right out of an American Movie Classics late show and could provide them with some lucrative headlines. Maybe they would let him get away with it this one time.

Adam had not told Alyssa, or anyone else, about his plans. Donald had helped him sneak out of the building, but had no idea where he was going and thought he would return by tomorrow. Otherwise, no one knew anything. Not even Horowitz, who would have advised against it for fear of alienating the press.

Along with the mustache, Adam had a goatee for himself, and eyebrows for Alyssa in the suitcase. He had made them with supplies from his Halloween box in the closet. If they worked at all, he had Carter to thank, because whatever Adam knew about making facial hair he had learned from him. And maybe a little from Lamont. Although the eyebrows and mustaches provided enough of an alteration to change the whole face, the real trick would be to keep people from looking that closely. *That* he had learned from Diz, whose own disguise fooled at first glance. No one had any reason to look closely at Diz, because that first glance told them everything they cared to know about him. Then they went about ignoring him.

Adam had decided the clothes of the masses and a relaxed attitude were the best disguise. Without microphones, designer suits, and a car and driver waiting, he would no longer be the Adam Julian the media and public had come to know. As long as he did not present the image everyone knew, he probably would be able to avoid attention for awhile.

Sunny and Mitch would approve, of course, because they wanted Alyssa to do her own thing, whatever her thing might be. Adam had decided to tell Alyssa where they were going once they were on the road. They had no time to spend on talk at her place. He assumed it would take her no more than five minutes to get an overnight bag together. Her parents would agree, he was sure, to tell the press, "Alyssa is in seclusion with relatives, and she is *not* with Adam."

Adam opened his cellphone and called the bookstore. Liz answered.

She squealed, "Oh, congratulations! I'm so happy for you!"

"Thanks, Liz. Is she there?"

"No, they all stayed home today to watch you on television."

"They're not home now," Adam said. "At least, they weren't a few minutes ago."

"Well, I know they were having problems with their answering machine."

"Yeah, I think the crank finally broke off. I'll try again, maybe they just didn't answer."

"I can't imagine them not answering the phone today, of all days," Liz said.

For the first time, it occurred to Adam that something could be wrong at Alyssa's house. "Thanks, Liz," he said before cutting her off.

He told himself not to worry. The Huffmans had their own way of doing things, and sometimes not doing things. But he was concerned. He called again, still got no answer. Let it ring until he turned down Alyssa's street, then turned it off, popped it closed and dropped it into his pocket.

It was a relief to see there were no reporters waiting outside Alyssa's house. Or, for that matter, no police cars or ambulances. The reporters would show up soon, though. The second they realized they had been tricked, they probably would call in some backup and start searching for him. And the first place they would look would be Alyssa's house.

Mitch's car was parked in the driveway, Sunny's was probably in the garage. Adam parked at the curb, got out of the car. Crossed the lawn and went up the steps, let himself in.

A suitcase stood in the foyer with something—it looked like bar-becue sauce—spilled on the handle. Adam stared at the suitcase for a few seconds, confused.

How could she know? he wondered. Surely Alyssa had not packed to leave with him, because there was no way she could know he planned to take her anywhere. Had someone died? Had they gotten one of those phone calls that meant everyone had to pack some black clothes for an unexpected trip?

He kept walking. The television played in the living room, but no one was there. He was about to call out her name when he heard her. At first, he thought Alyssa was stifling laughter. It came from the kitchen.

Oh, God, Adam thought, *not a surprise party, please.*

He stepped into the kitchen and Alyssa jumped with a shriek. All the lights were off except for the fluorescent over the sink. Hot water was running and steam sworled up from the basin, where Alyssa had been washing her hands and arms. She wore a red T-shirt and jeans. She took her hands from the steaming sink and held her forearms up like a surgeon scrubbing down for an operation. Soap bubbles sparkled on them. Her face was wet, too, but with tears. She stood facing him, hunched slightly. Her body shook with silent machine-gun sobs as she recovered from the shock of Adam walking in on her. She seemed to collapse in the middle and the top half of her body fell forward, as if in pain. She leaned an elbow on the lip of the sink to keep from falling, then slowly stood again, until she was almost standing straight. Crying so hard.

For a moment, Adam could not move. A million horrible things flew through his mind, but none of them lit.

"Please don't be mad at me Adam please don't be mad," she said, pressing her wet, trembling hands together between her breasts. Her nose was running, eyelashes clumped by tears.

Hot water continued to hiss from the faucet. Steam billowed furiously into the air.

Adam said urgently, "I'm not mad! Why would I be mad?" He moved toward her slowly, arms outstretched. His hands trembled, too, from fear. The hair on the back of his neck was rigid. Gooseflesh sprang up all over his body. Something was wrong with the kitchen. It looked, even felt, darker than the rest of the house. As if even the waning, steel-colored day outside would look darker than it was through that room's windows. "What's wrong, Alyssa?"

"I know we were gonna do it together but I just got fed up and couldn't take it I couldn't take it Adam I couldn't take it and I snapped." She stopped only because she ran out of breath. A couple more sobs, a deep breath, and then: "I'm so sorry Adam I wanted it to be perfect and wonderful but I spoiled it and I'm so sorry I'm—"

"Stop," he said, "stop it, you're gonna rupture something." He wrapped his arms around her and held her close. Reached down and turned off the faucet. He had hoped for a smirk, maybe a snort of laughter. But her body was stiff and quaking, as if she were feverish. Her shirt was wet, clung to her skin. Adam panicked and put an arm around her. Held her tight as he tried to lead her out of the kitchen, saying, "God, Alyssa, you're soaked, come lie down, we've gotta call an ambulance, you've got a bad fever, where are your *parents?*"

She resisted, rolled away from him, out of his grasp. Adam glimpsed his right hand. Did a double take. Held up his left hand. Both were splotched and smeared with what could be only one thing. He smelled its sticky old-penny odor, forever connected in his mind to the bicycle spills and skateboard crashes of his childhood. He looked at her shirt again, closely this time, and recognized it as her white Bugs Bunny T-shirt. The wascally wabbit gazed blearily at Adam through all the blood, between the tiny red peaks of Alyssa's erect nipples.

"I wanted it to be just the way we *said* it would be," she said with such deep and painful disappointment. "But I snapped and I'm sorry and I don't know what else to say except that we should probably go right away, y'know? We should get out of here right now." Brightening a little, she added, "I packed a bag!"

Adam saw it everywhere then. Spattered and streaked on the watercolor-yellow and -blue tiles. Dripping slowly from the brass handles of cupboards. He moved toward her again, slower this time.

"Alyss-lyssa, a-are you bleeding?" His voice took a low dip, then shot upward a couple times as he spoke.

She shook her head erratically. "No, I'm fine, I'm not hurt, really." Looked down at herself, shook her head angrily. "I've got clothes in the suitcase." She peeled the bloody shirt over her head. Wadded it up and tossed it into the sink. "I'll put something else on, but I think we should go now, Adam, if...if you'll just tell me you aren't mad that I snapped. I'm *so* sorry." Alyssa was calming down, pulling herself together. "But I'll have to make it up to you later because I think we should...don't *you* think we should go?"

He stared at her breasts, lightly smeared with blood. Even there in the dark, bloody kitchen with something very, very wrong, Adam was gripped by the urge to touch them. Squeeze them in his hands. Brush his lips over her hardened nipples. "Go...where?" he asked.

Her eyes widened slightly and she rubbed a wet, soapy hand over her face nervously. A lump of bubbles clung to the tip of her nose.

"C'mon, Adam, I...I mean, I thought we decided to go north. Up the coast. Together."

Adam could not speak for several seconds. Her words sounded as familiar as they did insane. "Alyssa, you...are you talking about that...you can't be serious, Alyssa, you can't—"

"What do you mean, I can't be *serious?*" She screamed, "It was your fucking idea, Adam, don't you fucking *do* this to me, you were the one—"

"—tell me you took any of that *seriously!*" Adam shouted. "That was fantasy, that was bullshit, you *knew* that, Alyssa, Jesus Christ, I didn't mean any of that and neither did *you!* I came to pick you up so we could get married, and you're telling me you thought we were going to—we were just bullshitting, we were *fantasizing,* what've you, what've you done, what've you—"

"—who wanted to go to around killing parents, Goddammit, that was *your* idea, don't tell me it was fantasy, don't you fucking *do* this to me, Adam, you told me—"

"—done to your parents, Alyssa, where are they, what have you—"

A wet sound from the dark side of the kitchen was just loud enough to bring an end to their panicky shouting. Then it happened again. A quick, wet *glorp* sound, followed by a long, gurgling gasp. A cough, then whimpering that gargled in something thick: "A...A...lytha?"

Alyssa shouted, "Oh, shit, will you look at *this*, now?" She paced back and forth rapidly a few times, feet stomping on the hardwood floor. Stopped and glared down at something on the floor on the other side of the island. "What does it take? Goddammit, what does it *take!*"

A moist rustle of movement beyond the island was what finally made Adam move. Someone was alive over there on the floor. Someone was hurt, something had to be done. But he could think of nothing specific to do or say. Without realizing he was doing it, he quietly repeated Alyssa's name over and over as he moved forward. Clutched her upper arms and pushed her back away from the island. "Alyssa. Alyssa. Alyssa."

She started to cry again as she jerked her arms away from him. "Don't touch me, Goddammit!"

Adam watched the movements of her breasts. In spite of everything, his penis began to harden.

"How could you say that to me, Adam?" Alyssa's words faded to a whimpering sob. She took a deep breath. "After everything we talked about, everything we planned! I mean, I fucked up and I'm sorry, but we can still *do* this! We just have to leave now!" Her lips peeled back over her teeth as she turned away from Adam, and glared at something on the floor. Leaned forward and buried her fists between her thighs as she screamed, "Except this fucking cunt is still *aliiive!*" Alyssa's cry was filled with hatred and anger, but ultimately it sounded pathetic and crippled. She pushed Adam's arm and shoulder, knocking him back a step. Pressed a hand to each side of her head, as if to hold together her fracturing skull. "Where is it?" she shouted. Her head jerked this way and that as she scanned the kitchen. Walked to the counter, searching. Erratic and speedy, like a video being fast-forwarded then stopped, fast-forwarded then stopped. Talking to herself frantically. "Where'd I put it, Goddammit, where is it, where'd it go?"

Adam turned to see what was on the other side of the island. He knew that was a mistake when he saw the blood. Everywhere. On everything. Cupboards, floor, stove, dishwasher, cat bowls. Dribbling down surfaces, dripping from edges.

In the instant before he fell, Adam saw them, naked in the kitchen for the last time. Sunny slumped against a cupboard door, arms limp at her sides. Heavy, stretch-marked breasts hung to each side. Her right breast had been severely gashed at the top and was barely attached. Looked ready to peel the rest of the way off and tumble drearily over the two rolls of fat bunched together around her waist. Legs splayed before her. Mitch lay facedown across her knees. Right arm stretched out as if to pull himself forward, left arm down at his side. Everything was dark red, covered with it. Smeared with handprints, lumpy with tissue. Caked in Sunny's thick hair. As if they had been playing in spaghetti sauce. Erotic foodplay gone terribly wrong. Both of them were covered with ugly wounds. Deep gashes, flesh sliced back like thick coldcuts. Sunny's mouth cut open like a melon, almost back to her ears. Blood poured from it and her jaw did not hang correctly. And yet she was alive. Part of her tongue still moved and slapped around in the blood as she tried to speak again.

At first, Adam thought Mitch's left hand was clutching Sunny's foot. No, only a momentary illusion created by the fact that the hand had no fingers. Those were scattered over the floor in front of Adam's feet along with something else. Tiny gray lumps in the blood on the floor. Teeth.

When Adam realized he was standing in the spreading pool of blood, he moved too quickly to back away. Feet slipped in opposite directions. All the way down, he heard Alyssa's rising and falling voice.

"Where did I, Goddammit, where is that fuckin', Jeeesus *Christ*, you can't find *anything* in this fucking kitchen!" On and on.

Found it! a mad, cackling voice in Adam's head declared when he landed next to Mitch and saw the hefty wooden handle of a meat cleaver protruding from the back of his skull. Adam rolled onto his back. Sunny's floppy face tipped forward and grinned down at him. He tried to crawl face up, crab-like, away from the bodies, but froze when Alyssa leaned into his field of vision from above, upside-down. Her face floated in the dangling tunnel created by her hair.

"You son of a bitch," she grumbled as she leaned down, reached for Adam's face with both hands. His hands and shoes lost traction on the bloody hardwood floor as he tried to avoid her grasp, then he realized she was not reaching for him. Alyssa's hands wrapped around the handle of the cleaver, pulled on it a couple times. Her father's forehead clunked against the floor with each jerk. The heavy blade came out with a deep, soft, sad sound, with bits of what used to make Mitch who he was clinging to its broad side in bloody clots.

In a high, quavering voice—almost a yodel—Alyssa cried, "Haven't you said enough, Goddammit, I think you've said enough, you've said *enough*, you fucking bitch!" as she swung the cleaver repeatedly. It swept by inches above Adam's face. Short, quick arcs that ended in the general area of her mother's throat.

Adam flailed his limbs, struggled away from the cleaver. Once he had wiggled his way out from under the blade's arc, he rolled away. Blood drenched him, turned his phony ponytail into a soggy rope, clung to the mustache on his face. Its odor oozed into his lungs. Its harsh taste dribbled over his lips and speckled his tongue as he retched. His empty stomach convulsed as he dry heaved. Again and again his shoulders hitched and his upper body jerked as Alyssa continued hacking with the cleaver. Bile burned his throat, made him cough. He gripped the slippery edge of the tile on top of the island. Got to his feet and found some balance, stability.

The hacking stopped. Alyssa stood up straight, made that odd sound that seemed a mixture of quick sobs and nervous, rapid-fire laughter. Adam turned to her.

Alyssa's right hand held the cleaver. Her shoulders and head shook as more tears coursed down her blood-streaked face. She turned her head to look at her mother's, held by the hair in her left hand. In a shrill, mocking voice, she said, "'We want you to do your own thing, Alyssa. Do your own thing, do your own thing.' Well how 'bout if *this* is my fucking thing, huh?" When she said the word "this," Alyssa threw her mother's head into the darkness at the back of the kitchen. A pane in one of the windows shattered. Alyssa shouted at the silent darkness, "Want me to make you some herb tea for that fucking *headache*, huh, Mom?"

"Alyssa. Alyssa. Alyssa." He could not stop saying it as he reached for her. Tried to sound soothing, friendly. Tried to smother the razored banshee's shriek that wanted to rip out of him. He grabbed her right arm just above the elbow.

Alyssa joined her hands on the handle of the cleaver. Ground her teeth together as she growled. Swung the meat cleaver up.

Adam lost his grip on the edge of the tile countertop and went down again. The blade landed two inches in front of his face. Smacked wetly into Mitch's bare back. She lifted it, brought it down again as Adam scrambled away from the spot, grabbed her arm and wrestled with her as he said, "No. Stop. Alyssa. Stop. Alyssa. They're dead.

They're dead, Alyssa." His voice became gradually louder, but he did not lose control, did not scream at her like he wanted to. He was afraid if he started screaming, he would never stop.

Alyssa slipped and fell on her side. Adam snaked an arm around her shoulders, held her close. Twisted the slippery meat cleaver out of her hands and hugged her to him. Felt the soft cushion of her breasts against him.

"Alyssa, we have to, we've got to, um…we need to…" Adam did not have a clue what needed to be done. He wondered if there was any point in doing anything.

"Yeah, I know, we need to go," she said. "Jesus, look at this mess. We've gotta wash off somehow. We'll leave a trail."

Adam let the words leave his mouth at their own speed. If he rushed them, he would stumble over them, stammer. "Let's…just…get outta this first, okay?"

Every attempt to get to their feet ended in a slip and a fall.

"Don't move so fast, be more careful," Adam said.

A slip and a fall.

"Goddammit, let go of me!

A slip and a fall.

It became ludicrous and Alyssa started laughing. In a few seconds, Adam laughed with her, not meaning to, still wanting to scream instead, at the top of his lungs, but laughter came out of him on its own, without any help from him, because there was nothing else to do. They laughed as they slipped and fell in Sunny's and Mitch's blood, onto their dead bodies.

During one fall, Adam grabbed desperately for something to hold onto, something to break his fall. Clutched Sunny's large bloody right breast. He was unaware of it at first, tried to get a hold, keep from falling. Then Alyssa's laughter shrieked as she pointed at Adam's hand.

Adam could not stop laughing.

Alyssa gagged on her laughter, coughed harshly.

Adam could not stop laughing.

Alyssa rolled on top of Adam and swallowed his laughter with a deep kiss. That made Alyssa laugh harder. She closed her hand over the erection in his jeans, pawed at the buttons, released it. Reached inside and found his cock, tugged it out, and stroked it with her bloody fist.

Every movement created moist smacking sounds. Every slap of any surface created a small splash.

Alyssa straddled Adam and ground against him. When she saw that her mother's breast had come off in Adam's hand, and that he still held it tightly in a fist, she started laughing again.

"You horndog!" she squealed, rocking back and forth on him.

The realization that he held a meat cleaver in one hand and a torn-off breast in the other set Adam off again. As he laughed hysterically, he thought, *Carter should be here to see this! Shit, he would* love *this!*

They should be doing something, he knew that. Going, they should be going somewhere. But where? What was the point? They were young and insane, and loved rubbing their bodies together, and they could not stop laughing.

They did not hear the footsteps storming through the house until they were just outside in the hall. A woman screamed and the kitchen filled with male and female voices. Bright lights, a rumble of footsteps on the wood floor. Voices speaking over voices.

"Oh, Jesus Christ, a *ritual* killing?"

"Looks ritualistic to me."

"Somebody better call the police."

"In a minute, in a minute."

Another scream, this time from a man, who turned and ran out.

"This is a slaughterhouse."

"Yeah, it'll keep that fuckin' Geraldo on the air another two or three years."

"You got a problem with that?" Geraldo said.

"Oh, hey, uh, sorry, Geraldo, I didn't know you were here."

The press had arrived sooner than Adam had anticipated.

Over his shoulder, Geraldo shouted again, "Would you bring that fucking light in here!"

"Well, this should push a whole boxful of envelopes."

"Bring that camera right over here."

"Do you think he lied about everything? Through the whole trial?"

"Anybody got any breath mints?"

And Adam, meat cleaver in one hand and severed breast in the other, suddenly could not stop screaming.